THE LIFE AND DEATH OF SYLVIA

ALSO BY EDGAR MITTELHOLZER

Creole Chips
Corentyne Thunder
A Morning at the Office
Shadows Move Among Them
Children of Kaywana
The Weather in Middenshot
The Adding Machine
The Harrowing of Hubertus
My Bones and My Flute
Of Trees and the Sea
A Tale of Three Places
With a Carib Eye (nf)
Kaywana Blood
The Weather Family
A Tinkling in the Twilight
The Mad MacMullochs (as H. Austin Woodsley)
Eltonsbrody
Latticed Echoes
The Piling of Clouds
Thunder Returning
The Wounded and the Worried
A Swarthy Boy (nf)
Uncle Paul
The Aloneness of Mrs Chatham
The Jilkington Drama

THE LIFE AND DEATH OF SYLVIA

EDGAR MITTELHOLZER

INTRODUCTION BY JUANITA COX

PEEPAL TREE

First published in Great Britain in 1953
by Secker and Warburg
First published in the USA in 1954 by The John Day Co.
This new edition published in 2010
Peepal Tree Press Ltd
17 King's Avenue
Leeds LS6 1QS
England

ISBN13 Print: 978 1 84523 120 0

Printed in the United Kingdom
by Severn, Gloucester,
on responsibly sourced paper

CARBON NEUTRAL

MIX
Paper from
responsible sources
FSC® C022174
FSC www.fsc.org

Supported by
ARTS COUNCIL
ENGLAND

JUANITA COX

INTRODUCTION

> "[A] man should always be judged by what he himself is – not by what his ancestors were. But I'm telling you what is – not what ought to be. I'm being a realist. I'm telling you what sort of world you're growing up in and suggesting how you should tackle it if you want to be tolerably happy in it—"[1]

Edgar Mittelholzer (1909-1965) finished writing *The Life and Death of Sylvia*, during his residence in Trinidad, sometime around September 1945[2]. He was, though, unable to secure publication for another eight years. As there was still paper rationing in the UK and the USA, it was too risky to invest in a long novel by a relative unknown whose manuscript contained material considered "too intimate" or "obscene", and which he refused to amend:

> ...one day Sylvia will be published, ... and there won't be any expurgations. In the meantime ... I have to live, so I shall turn out one or two horror-thrillers to get myself established.[3]

When the British firm, Secker and Warburg brought out *The Life and Death of Sylvia* in 1953, it was Mittelholzer's sixth published novel and a reversion to the social realism, poetics of landscape and early twentieth century British Guianese setting of his first novel, *Corentyne Thunder* (1941). As such it developed Mittelholzer's early objectives of capturing the spirit and richness of the Guianese locale whilst offering an honest, albeit subjective, evaluation of its "flaws and foibles"; of presenting the Caribbean as a valid setting for literary inspiration and exploring the relevance and application of Western literary traditions and ideologies to the Caribbean; and challenging representations of "race", and in particular, in *Sylvia*[4], that of the "Tragic Mulatto".

The Author: Background

Mittelholzer was very familiar with the novel's primary setting. During the 1930s, he made regular trips from his New Amsterdam home to the library in Georgetown, where he would spend hours, on the advice of potential publishers, reading the classics and studying the style of successful authors. He moved to Georgetown in March 1941 and remained there until departing for Trinidad in December of that year. It was during these nine-months that Mittelholzer made a close friendship with a young woman called Sylvia he had first met in New Amsterdam, and upon whom the novel is partially based. Though Mittelholzer secured a variety of odd jobs – including one as a typist for The Elmhurst Contracting Company (the builders of US Army bases on the Demerara River) – it is clear that he lived off a small income, supplementing his often meagre diet with a cocktail of vitamins, whilst living in "a cubicle, triangular in shape, the mere screened-off section of a room for which [he] paid three dollars a week"[5]. By the time he received notification in mid-1941 that *Corentyne Thunder* had been published (after around fifteen previous novel rejections) Mittelholzer was too mentally and physically drained to wallow in his success: "I did not celebrate ... The daily struggle merely to eat and keep alive was too exigent."[6] Mittelholzer fraternised, early on in his writing career, with people across class divides and developed an interest in, and empathy for, the lower classes[7]. According to one anecdote, when teased by his middle-class counterparts for not having a girlfriend, Mittelholzer announced he would be taking his girlfriend to the cinema if anyone cared to meet her. Those who took him up were scandalised to discover that his companion was a well-known prostitute from the area[8]. This inclination to challenge and reject the snobbish conventions of his class and appreciate the broad complexity of life is fully represented in *Sylvia*.

There is, for instance, an extraordinary cast of characters who, whilst only playing passing roles, are brought vividly to life, such as Clothilde Pumba, a Portuguese prostitute with a husky voice; Eustace Frank, a Syrian who smells of lavender water; Boodhoo, the Russell family's East Indian gardener with a kind face; Bam, a lanky coloured fellow; or Cora Barclay, a sophisticated dark-complexioned girl with artificially straightened-hair. The naming of these characters, alongside brief physical descriptions creates a sense of a complex, racially-diverse, vibrant society and offers, in contrast to the sociological descriptions of Guianese society (made by Grantley Russell with a hint of the absurdity of these categorisations) an affirmation of the individual humanity of its members:

> Positively astounding how life goes on at all. There are the whites in an exclusive little corner ... Then the high-coloured coloured in various little compartments, according to good, better and best families [...] the East Indians in another cluster, with a hierarchy of their own ranging from rice-miller to barrister-at-law and doctor then down to bus-driver, chauffeur, provision-shop-keeper and sugar-estate coolie. [...] the Chinese, either shopkeeper or business man. [...] the Portuguese, split up into rum-shop-pawn-shop class and professional-man class and big-business man class... [Whilst black men range from] Shovel-man-scavenger. Schoolteacher. Policeman, fireman. Newspaper-reporter-lawyer's-clerk-bank-messenger-office-boy ambitious type who hopes to become an editor or lawyer or get into the Government service (p.71-72; all references to this edition).

Mittelholzer includes amongst his cameo figures, the names of real people – A J Seymour (described as the "one poet of any substance") and Jocelyn Hubbard[9] (a prominent trade unionist) – who are both, by virtue of their presence, paid homage for their contributions to the development of Guiana.

The stuffy artificiality of the middle class is contrasted to the working class who are portrayed as energetic, natural and full of character. Consider, for example, the scene at Mrs Gournal's wake. Bottles of rum, salt-fish, green-plantain and black pudding set the background, whilst the women sprinkle cologne on the corpse and the men play Suck-the-well and Biskra (instead of Bridge and poker), whilst arguing over who can handle their drink:

> "Who say I had too much to drink? Which man here can drink wid me? If you t'ink so bring de rum, Basil! Bring de rum!

> I can put ten like you under de table and walk a chalk line! ..."
> "We not talking about rum. We discussing de ess o' clubs – "
> "Ssh! Ssh! Not so much noise!" [...] "You-all don't know a dead in de house? (p.54)".

Thus whilst the middle class are portrayed as educationally and culturally accomplished – Beryl's fifteen-year old sister plays pieces by Beethoven and Mozart – Sylvia's appreciation of the working classes is clear.

> ...she was more inclined to sympathize with Naomi and her crowd than with these artificial people. ... somehow, they seemed sounder at heart (p.171).

Spirit of the Place

This careful recording of the diverse population is mirrored by the representations of place: from the Seawall, where lovers rendezvous; the Botanical Gardens of Kissing Bridge and manatee fame; the bustling Stabroek Market; Bishop's High School; the sleepy town of New Amsterdam; to Village 63 on the Corentyne Coast where newly-weds honeymoon and the ill go to recuperate.

Climate and topography add to the rich atmosphere of *Sylvia*, as they did, very differently, in *Corentyne Thunder.* Take for instance this vivid description of a new day dawning:

> The cabbage palms stood out stern, jet-black, against the clouds, but the shorter trees seemed to absorb some of the colour of the dawn; their leaves glistened; they acquired a misty-mauve aura along the ragged outline of their foliage. The house-tops, too, glistened, the galvanised iron cool-looking and wet in the drizzly air. The rain was visible as flimsy threads. [...] Everything grew pinker and more singingly resplendent as the seconds passed. The clouds split and spawned deeper reds and new yellows that shot up fanwise so that even the cabbage palms exchanged their jet-black for a soft greenness (p.160).

Here the scene, viewed by Sylvia from a window in the middle-class environs of the High Street, captures – in contrast to the vast open landscapes depicted in *Corentyne Thunder* – the more restricted access to nature in the city. The experience is no less enriching, though, for the subtly changing colours of the sky, the clouds and trees create a moving image in the reader's mind as they, like Sylvia, partake in the experience.

Appeals to the senses play an important role in the depiction of place – in the smells and sounds encountered in the crowded vitality of a poor slum area of Georgetown:

> Ill-clad black people moved about between buckets and barrels of water, and tubs that rested on old soap boxes. The ground was muddy. Chickens pecked here and there, and smoke rose in thin puffs from a detached kitchen-shed out of which, also, came the smell of cooking rice and something frying – something oily and oniony. Now and then a raucous laugh would curl up through the damp air. Rain had fallen heavily not two hours ago, and you could smell the wet earth and grass (p.109).

Sylvia, from the perspective of a romanticizing middle-class child, sees nothing repellent in the "dirt or shoddiness" of the scene and instead experiences "a deep peace". She is so moved by the Guianese landscape that she believes it "ought not to be taken for granted or simply appreciated and forgotten (p.161)". Mittelholzer is inviting West Indian readers to see their world afresh, challenging the middle-class distaste for scenes of working class life, and proclaiming that his Guianese milieu is worthy of the most serious literary investment.

Though an idealising Romantic, Sylvia's personality is, like everything else in the novel, framed in a distinctly West Indian way. When troubled by conflicting emotions she is taunted by self-imagined brown Jumbies who live in the fronds of palm trees and swoop down around her. Her recourse to folk culture has been learnt through the tales she hears. Aunt Clarice tells her the tooting of an owl means someone must be in the family way, whilst Rachel, the cook, tells her of "Sick-mamma", a supernatural being that can "ketch de groaning" of a sick person and, when heard, is a sure sign of death. Grantley Russell's interracial marriage draws the widespread gossip that his wife must, with the help of her godmother, have worked obeah by putting a "stay-at-home" in his food. *Sylvia* captures with great skill the nuances of race, colour, class, and culture – the spirit of the 1930s and early 1940s Guianese locale.

The novel was, however, never intended to be merely a pleasurable read. As Gilkes[10] and Seymour[11] have concluded, it functions as an indictment of Georgetown society; most importantly, on the theme of sexual/gender relations. It is no accident that the opening scene takes place in a hotel which a Guianese readership would have recognised as a well-known brothel. The fictional *Viceroy* is unmistakably based on the now defunct *Regent's Hotel* which Mittelholzer describes in *With A Carib Eye*:

> "The Regent swarmed with some of the most attractive specimens who did a brisk business among the seamen off ships in port as well as among the middle-class bloods of the city".[12]

Whilst in the "Overture", *Sylvia's* readers are made aware of the lascivious drunken behaviour of the middle-class men and the laughter of prostitutes who accompany them, the atmosphere is so jovial that initially it distracts attention away from the degrading reality of the women involved. However, as the novel unfolds, so too does the ugly reality of their lives. These prostitutes, several of whom are friends of Sylvia's mother, are impoverished, vulnerable to disease – syphilis, pneumonia and tuberculosis – and living in despair. Janie Pollard talks of "breaking up"; and though her laughter is brave, Sylvia hears behind "the ring of despair" a "grim, reaching shadow behind her tissue gaiety" (p.159).

So when Sylvia is forced to contemplate the life of a sex-worker, she is fully aware of its sordidness:

> *Rooms to let*. Two shillings – short time. Five shillings – all night. From odd bits overheard at various times from her mother's friends, she could picture the whole business ...Perhaps the bed had been used by a couple only a few minutes before. The sheet was disarranged, the pillows dented – and there were grey, wet patches here and there. A frowsy smell permeated the room. ... And there she stood undressing... (p.301).

The vulnerability of working-class women is repeatedly highlighted. Bertie Dowden, a Customs Officer from a well-known family, forces himself on Naomi Herreira, a 16-year old girl and, with the mother's approval, marries her against her will. Sylvia is under threat of similar exploitation by the crooked businessman, Frank Knight, whose occupational achievements so closely resemble a real-life person[13] one can only assume Mittelholzer's intention was to surreptitiously name and shame. Knight, aside from eating Grantley Russell's promissory note, hopes that Sylvia's impoverishment will eventually force her to become his mistress. When she attempts to better her situation by getting a job, her boss's brother, Mr Dikran, sexually assaults her. But Sylvia is trapped between two poles of middle-class colonial sexual mores – between the male readiness to exploit the vulnerable, and their corresponding hypocrisy in demanding virginity from their wives to be. Sylvia desires her boyfriend, Benson, and wants an equal sexual relationship with him, but he repulses her with prudish awkwardness. In focusing on the interconnected issues of female impoverishment and sexual vulnerability; and addressing taboo subjects such as incest, sado-masochism, prostitution, adultery, and sexual harassment, Mittelholzer was being shocking, progressive and radical. Most importantly, he was giving voice to the marginalised and oppressed women of 1930's Georgetown.

Radical Bildungsroman

Sylvia is in some key respects a Bildungsroman. As the eponymous heroine passes from childhood into adulthood, she discovers much about herself and the world around her. When her father is murdered, she has to face, whilst dealing with the pain of his loss, an unforeseen change in circumstance which threatens her status. This is followed by a long and difficult phase involving a conflict between her idealism and the harsh realities of the society. In the kind of bildungsroman that is content to accept the world as it is, these conflicts tend to be resolved by the end of the novel with the protagonist's assimilation of, or acquiescence to, the norms of the society and a re-evaluation of her or his role within it. Sylvia, on the contrary, continues on her downward spiral and refuses to fight for her life when ill with pneumonia, because she refuses, despite being destitute, to live as a prostitute or the mistress of Frank Knight. While Sylvia suffers the loss of her physical life as a consequence of her nonconformity, she nevertheless achieves a kind of immortality and victory over society. This achieved through the nine page letter she writes for Milton Copps – and, of course through the novel's publication. Whilst it is clear that what she writes (in "swiftly scrawled words") has no pretensions to art – and we never see what she writes – the letter and the novel itself are clearly metaphors for each other.

The connection between the two is conveyed in Sylvia's relationship with Milton Copps – a thinly disguised self-portrait of the author – whose request to Sylvia hints at how the novel came into existence: "You've told me about your childhood, but you haven't yet given me a picture of the past few years (p.288)." In a friendship developed primarily through letters, Milton advises her to fight the forces that conspire against her, only to realise that this is beyond Sylvia's capacity. Anticipating death, Sylvia feels ashamed about the futility of her life and the thwarting of her inner desires. When even the goal of giving herself in love to Benson is denied, she is consoled only by the thought that "She must write and tell Milton of this night. Describe it to him in detail. ... The sublimation of the written word (p.352)." It is in this attempt to define and explain herself through writing that Sylvia's life is given meaning, preventing her death from being pointless.

But her presumed story is not the whole story, for as the metanarrative emphasises, whilst Milton is writing about Sylvia, he brings his own imagination to the story. Their symbiotic identity *and* their difference is suggested in this scene:

> He listened with grunts and nods, and frowned often. ... He looked like a gaunt cloud settled there in a chair, ... his deep-set eyes alert yet tinged with troublous dreaminess so that *she knew he was absorbing everything she said but at the same time weaving his own colours and incense around it* (p.292). [my italics]

Their shared identity is in the first place social:

> The instability of both their lives created a sympathy of desperateness between them which [...] precluded any yielding to sentiment. The feeling of being hunted down, of being cornered, was too strong in them. It shut out soft passages (p.318).

But they also share an inner romanticised affinity with the landscape that is echoed in their names. When Grantley Russell suggests that his daughter be called Cynthia Anne, her mother mistakenly hears "Sylvia Anne" and the name sticks. When conflated it becomes "sylvan", whilst her surname alludes to the onomatopoeic "rustle" of leaves. This idyllic metaphor connoting Sylvia also connects to Mittelholzer's self-perception, as he was to write in his autobiography, *A Swarthy Boy* (1963):

> Two elements have always lived within me, side by side and in restless harmony... The Idyll Element dreamed of a peaceful, *sylvan* situation... with rain, thunder and lightning, sunshine and the *rustling of trees*... The Warrior Element listened always to the sound of the Conflict... perpetually ready to resist, to repulse, to do battle to the death with any foe that might appear. [my italics][14]

Milton Copps's name embodies this duality: "Milton" arguably being an allusion to the "masculine", the warrior, to the harsh urban image of the mill town[15], and Copps to the idyll, as "copse", a thicket of small trees. Their names signify their similarities, and their differences: whilst Sylvia has a non-aggressive, peaceful personality, Milton has a steely willpower and fighting spirit that (like his poetic namesake) is determined to overcome any obstacles: "The bourgeoisie are close on my heels, Sylvia. They'd like to see me rolling defeated in the dust. But they'll never get me" (p.316).

The duality is further embedded in the metaphorical, punning association of the sylvan **id**yll with Sylvia's unconscious creative potential, or in Freudian terms with the id and its two components: Eros (sex/life-instinct/procreation) and Thanatos (death/death-wish) that constitute the novel's basic terms.

The metanarrative also highlights a duality in the way that Milton views Sylvia, not just as a young woman whose story needs to be told, but also as a specimen through whom he thinks it is possible to explore, with his "scientific specimen look", the role of environment and heredity:

> "Let's revert to our specimen under examination, Sylvia Anne Russell – may the Lord, if not ourselves, have mercy on her sensitive feelings!" (p.321).

But if Milton's language (and we need to remember that Milton for all the autobiographical elements is no less an imaginatively constructed character than Sylvia) suggests scientific rigour, the naming of the episodes that mark Sylvia's biological creation and her extinction ("Overture with Loud Trumpets" and "Finale with Cymbals and Low Drums") suggests quite another kind of framing – the metaphor of symphonic composition that is discussed later in this introduction. Milton is both the would-be Godwinian rationalist of the *Enquiry Concerning Political Justice*, and the romantic novelist of tragic feelings revealed in *Caleb Williams*.[16]

Subverting the Tragic Mulatto

Some earlier criticism has placed *Sylvia* in the literary tradition of the tragic mulatto; it is better seen as a sophisticated response to and subversion of that tradition. The tradition appears to have originated in two short stories written by the American abolitionist, Lydia Maria Child: *The Quadroons* (1842) and *Slavery's Pleasant Home* (1843)[17]. The beautiful, well-mannered protagonist is, in both stories, the progeny of a white slavemaster and black female slave. In the former, she grows up believing she is white until, following the death of her father, her true identity is revealed. After her white lover forsakes her, she is remanded into slavery, and soon dies from the hardships she faces. Over the next one-hundred years literary portrayals of the tragic mulatto placed great emphasis on her pathologies: "self-hatred, depression, alcoholism, sexual perversion, and suicide attempts being the most common"[18]. Sterling Brown was, in the 1930s, the first to argue that these literary portrayals had been influenced by the racist pronouncements of early nineteenth century abolitionists:

> The mulatto is a victim of a divided inheritance; from his white blood comes his intellectual strivings, his unwillingness to be a slave; from his Negro blood comes his baser emotional urges, his indolence, his savagery.[19]

The tragic mulatto's pathology was believed to arise out of the "warring blood" that coursed through her veins. Her fate was deemed so inescapable that she was destined to "go down, accompanied by slow music, to a tragic end."[20] Brown criticised this theme in the 1930s and '40s for its clichéd, unrealistic portrayals, lack of psychological depth and its failure to recognise the more serious social facts that impacted on the lives of mulattos.

Whilst there is as yet no concrete evidence that Mittelholzer was aware of Brown's critical evaluations, it is known that he read – around the time of writing *Sylvia*[21] – Lillian Smith's *Strange Fruit* (1945). Set in the segregationist south of the USA in the early twentieth century, the story centres round the doomed love affair that takes place between Nonnie Anderson, a young "negro" woman of "egg-shell white" complexion and Tracey Deen, a young white man. When Nonnie's brother finds out that Deen has made her pregnant and paid his black servant, Henry McIntosh, to marry her, he kills Deen. The white community revenges Deen's death by falsely accusing and lynching McIntosh. Blacks have to be kept in their place, as a white preacher reminds:

> "...you have to keep pushing them back across that nigger line... Kind of like it is with a dog. You have a dog, seems right human... And you a lot rather be around that dog than anybody you ever knew. But he's still a dog. You don't forget that."[22]

Strange Fruit evidently inspired Mittelholzer to explore the racial stratification of Guianese society; and to tease out the similarities as well as the differences with the American South. The different Guianese racial dynamic is conveyed in the gusto with which the father of a coloured girl at the Telephone Exchange refers to Grantley Russell as a "damned English rat" and a "cheap, dragged-up Cockney" (p.45), whilst threatening to disinherit his daughter if she marries him.

Nevertheless, Guiana was a society imbued with colour prejudice, of which Mittelholzer was himself a victim. As he records in his autobiography, *A Swarthy Boy*, his fair-skinned Negrophobe father seemingly believed that his "dark skin" was an index of doubtful "intelligence" and was unable to conceal his lifelong "resentment" towards him: "I was the Dark One at whom he was always frowning and barking"[23]. These personal attacks, cushioned by the equally absurd redemptive assurances that his German blood made him different from everyone else, led Mittelholzer to express an acute interest in, and sensitivity toward, prevailing representations of race, whether literary or otherwise[24]. He was almost certainly aware of the so-called pathologies attributed to the tragic mulatto. In dramatising the different ways that Sylvia and Milton confront their mulatto identity, Mittelholzer finds a means of examining his own biographical issues with "race" and heredity. It is an imaginative strategy very much within the Romantic tradition of doubles as a means of understanding the conflict/ dynamics between the inner and the social self.

Racial Constructions of the Social Self

One of the achievements of *Sylvia* is the skilful representation of Sylvia's shifting attitudes towards race, colour and class in the colonial world "into which, without asking, she had been thrown..." (p.305). The complexity of that world is built up as the novel progresses. Although Sylvia doesn't come from a "good" family, she is eventually accepted into the coloured middle class because her father is an "English man of means" and she is light enough in complexion. As a child she attends the private school in Camp Street, run by a liberal Trinidadian lady for white and coloured children, yet Sylvia is the only one of her peers not invited to Myra Bertrand's birthday party on account of her "dubious" family background. Her childhood friend – who later rejects her "inferior" company – goes on to attend a Catholic convent school from which Sylvia is barred: her complexion "just a trifle on the wrong side".

From the beginning Sylvia's family situation and class background leads her to a fatal ambivalence. Her most disturbing perceptions, directed towards her black/Amerindian mother, are initially informed by the views her white father expresses: "DaDDy says its because Mother is too Inferioour thats why she behaves like that and hes right, Im learning plenty things from Daddy..." (p.91). These feelings are certainly not helped by the class prejudices she has internalised or by the fact that Charlotte (her mother) has brutally punished her during early childhood:

> Her mother was, she felt, in some way inferior to her father. Mother was no lady. ... Jeanne's mother and Miss Jenkins did not shout and wave their hands and suck their teeth, and say words like "Jesus God!" and "shit" and "move you' ass" She did not respect her mother. For her she had only fear and dread (p.78).

By the time Sylvia is a teenager, her negative view of her mother is expressed in racial terms: "Her dark negro-Indian face looked really stupid. [...] Stupid and weak. No character at all" (p.179). Instead of attributing Charlotte's behaviour to a lack of education or the cultural differences that exist between her and Grantley Russell, Sylvia unconsciously views her mother's manners and behaviour as being biologically determined and thus worries about becoming like her: "She must remain noble – not degenerate into a poor specimen like Mother." Shortly afterwards, however, she discovers "how very little more capable than her mother she was" (p.194). Indeed, Sylvia's tragic flaw relates directly to this self-conception of her genetic weakness, to her capitulation to her social self and the idea that she lacks the will to fight for the type of life her "deeper" self wants to lead.

Sylvia's view of "race" – inextricably embedded in the middle-class preoccupations with phenotype, hair texture and complexion – changes along with her situation. Her observation of a gathering of the coloured middle-class denotes both a sense of the absurdity of such distinctions and her inability to place herself outside them:

> In the Town Hall, she felt as good as any of the coloured people present. Beryl did not seem any better (besides, Beryl's hair had small waves: it was not as good as her own). Nor did the Dowdens or the Baynes who sat in the row behind; the Dowdens were dark-complexioned, and the Baynes, though sallow-complexioned, had definitely bad hair; the two Bayne girls had had to use a hot comb to straighten theirs (p.144).

The pernicious nature of these preoccupations is further highlighted by Sylvia's shifting view of Jack Sampson, the young black radical, whom she initially find appealing:

> Jack Sampson was a pure-blooded negro, slim and strong, with large teeth widely spaced so that when he laughed you could see the darkness at the back of his mouth. It was an attractive laugh. Sylvia liked him (p.113).

Later in the novel, at a point where she feels unable to ignore the asset of her skin, she reassesses her relationship with Jack through the prism of race:

> She danced with him, but all the while she was aware of his shining dark-brown face and his close-cropped woolly head.

...Jack Sampson was black and kinky haired, of no family; she liked him as a human being true, but she knew in years ahead she would have to exclude him from her society. It would be impossible for her to be a success with the coloured middle-class if she kept the company of black people like Jack (p.154).

It is important to see that Mittelholzer challenges Sylvia's views on race. Whilst her mother is black and weak; it is not because she is black that she is weak. Her character is countered by the presence of dignified, strong and intelligent black characters who, like Mrs Gournal, do not suffer from an inferiority complex. Indeed, if there is a hero in the novel it is the very person that Sylvia's upbringing has taught her to keep at a distance. Jack Sampson's meteoric rise in status (he becomes a Town Councillor) ironically matches Sylvia's decline and fall and mirrors the political side-lining of the coloured group.[25] In coming out with comments such as "Rule Britannia me backside!" Jack is portrayed as a disciple of the subversive trade unionist, Jocelyn Hubbard. He is anti-British, anti-monarchy, anti-capitalist, and communist. When he hears that Sylvia is being paid only $15 a month, he advises her to join the Clerk's Union and is disgusted that she is satisfied with this poor level of pay:

"You see dat! Same old story! Passivity! Indifference! Look, Sylvie, you know why we in dis colony can't develop all de jungle-country we got? ... It's because we mesmerized. It's because we walking about in a dream. And dat's why we'll always be kicked around and exploited by dose imperious sons of bitches in de Colonial Office in London" (p.215).

Jack Sampson represents the emerging grass root politics of the period and burgeoning trade union activities, whose communist rhetoric even pervades the language of the unpolitical Milton Copps[26], when he proclaims that he detests "bourgeois society".

But whilst Sylvia's mixed origins, angst-ridden psyche and premature death has drawn some critics to read her in the literary tradition of the tragic mulatto, her predicament cannot be related, in any simplistic way, to the "warring bloods" motif. The conversations between Milton and Gregory offer a much broader analysis: one that takes into account not just heredity, but environment, past experience and upbringing, as well as the defects of will that are particular to Sylvia's psychological make-up. Even here Sylvia's response to their discussion reminds that she isn't just a specimen to be talked about in such a dispassionate way, but a very particular individual engaged in a concrete struggle for survival:

> ...Milton and Gregory seemed futile, absurd pedants... The human will, heredity, sum of past experiences... Words... What concerned her ... was what she was going to tell Mr. Ralph in a few days from now [she is seeking financial assistance] (p.322).

As Kenneth Ramchand recognised, Sylvia's destiny is rooted in the "spirit of her time" and "not in the fact of her mixed blood"[27]. She, indeed, expresses weariness with the terms of the debate:

> It will be so peaceful knowing that all my miseries will be disappearing behind me. All the plaguing problems we've talked about. The purpose in my being alive and if it's heredity or environment that has made me what I am – all that will be going behind me into blankness (p.357).

Ultimately, Mittelholzer subverts the literary tradition of the tragic mulatto through the contrast he creates between Sylvia and Milton, in particular the latter's fighting spirit, willpower and creative skill as the fictive composer of *Sylvia*.

The Theme of Sex: A Freudian Metaphor

Even with respect to the connection the novel makes between Sylvia's angst and her fears that her sexuality is perverted – which might appear to place it at the heart of the tragic mulatto tradition – Mittelholzer's position is altogether more complex. Sylvia is, for instance, disturbed by the intensity of her attachment to her father, but he offers sensible Freudian reassurance:

> ...it's quite the accepted thing for children to be strongly attached to the parent of the opposite sex during the early years. With you I daresay it's gone on longer than it should, but the circumstances of your upbringing have been unusual (p.141).

Here, Mittelholzer uses one field of Western thinking (psychology) to invalidate another (pseudo-scientific racism). Since Freud's

Oedipus complex theory had the *male*-child sexually desiring his mother, and resentfully viewing his father as a competitor, Mittelholzer's gender transformation of Freud's theory suggests other purposes. Here, Sylvia is a metonym for Guiana's coloured middle class that had, since its origins as the progeny of black and white under slavery, tended to assimilate to European culture and continued in the early years of the twentieth century to believe in the superiority of the whites (as long as they had the right class credentials) and the inferiority of the blacks. In this context, the portrayal of Sylvia as having an Oedipal complex becomes a social metaphor rather than an index of sexual pathology.

Whilst Sylvia's open-minded father has enabled her to learn "many ways of speaking and of looking at the world", it is not a good thing, as Naomi points out, that: "Everything you say you have to quote him. That isn't wise" (p.204). This viewpoint is reinforced when Jack Sampson tells Sylvia that the coloured middle class are pawns of their British colonisers:

> "Look at you and your upper middle-class! All you-all strive to do is to be cultured and polished – cultured and polished ...like de English. I don't say culture and refinement isn't a good thing. But de English people clever. They encourage you-all coloured people to be cultured and refined – to be cultured and refined ... like *dem!* Because de more English culture you imbibe de more loyal you will be to de British throne! Yes! Dat's where they got you by de balls!"(p.215).

For Sylvia to reach her full creative potential, she must overcome her oedipal attachment to her "white father" (the white coloniser). Though Grantley Russell has some positive qualities, he is still, as he admits, an expatriate whose role stands in the way of Guianese independence and nationhood. As he tells Teresa, he is an engineer recruited to build a bridge: "Your local engineers could have built it on their own, but they're coloured, and your damned silly government felt that it was the proper thing to send out to England and get an Englishman to be in charge" (p.39). And, reinforcing the image of the latter-day colonial conquistador, Russell is portrayed as a conscienceless sexual predator whose adulterous philandering (with Delly Simpson, Jessie and Mrs Teller) spreads misery and results in his own violent death.

But if Sylvia has been in thrall to her English father, she can derive no positive model from her Guianese mother. As Grantley notes of his attempts to "cultivate" Charlotte and her contemptuous treatment of his cultural gifts of books and records: "I can't *make* you into a somebody if you won't try to be somebody" (p.57). Whilst Charlotte has some redeeming features – she is generous with her friends and a skilled dressmaker – she is basically a caricature: literally and symbolically underdeveloped. She is generally represented as languishing at home, gossiping with friends, moaning about the ingratitude of others and feeling sorry for herself. Her feelings, when she expresses them, are presented as inauthentic and melodramatically self-serving:

> As soon as Uncle had announced the death Charlotte had exclaimed as though not even aware that Godmother had been ill. Then she had shrieked. Clapped her hands together. Tore at her hair. Collapsed on the floor with a whimper that, without warning, rose to another penetrating shriek (p.53).

When during a bout of malaria, Charlotte breaks into a song of double-entendres, Mittelholzer highlights how crude and limited her creativity is:

> "Oh, madam, I hear that cocks do crow-w-w-w! Do *crow-w-w-w*!
>
> "Oh, madam, I hear that cocks do crow-w-w-w! Around your cunt . . . ree-ee-ee garden!" (p.220).[28]

It is a criticism of the fact that Charlotte (in contrast to Naomi) never seizes the opportunity presented by her educationally superior husband to expand her knowledge.

Without any positive relationship to Charlotte, and following Grantley's death, Sylvia is portrayed as thinking she has incestuous feelings for her light-skinned brother, a further suggestion that she is still inordinately entranced by all things white. This time her affliction is attributed to her overactive romantic imagination, as her friend Naomi tells her:

> "Sylvie, it's only your imagination, child. Look, take it from me, you're as normal as anybody can be normal. ... you're the last person anybody could accuse of being a pervert" (p.204).

The opportunity for Sylvia's sexual development and creative potential to be normalised and realised is represented by Benson. When she reflects on her first close encounter with Benson (she cannot dispel the memory of his voice, handsome face or muscular shoulders) it stimulates her imagination in unsettling ways that connect her to the imagery of the Guianese landscapes of her "deeper" self:

> "It made her stare from her bedroom window into the fronds of the cabbage palms ... *weave into being* the Brown Jumbie-men. Small, cynical fellows who dwelled amid the dense shadows of the fronds ... At first, she heard them chortling, but without warning they swooped down to argue with her, lurking invisibly about her" (p.142). [my italics]

It isn't long, however, before Sylvia discovers that Benson "has no poetry in him" and cannot relate to the romantic/imaginative side of her personality. When she describes an old plantation house as "sad and tragic", he looks at her as though she might have said it was an "alligator", and she has to reflect that "He did not understand her language very well so she must repeat whatever she said and try to explain her meaning" (p.270). The immense sense of loneliness she feels signals that the relationship is destined to fail.

The Sea-sex Leitmotif

The centrality of the connection between sexuality and creativity is reinforced through the romantic leitmotif of the sea. In scenes where sexual activity takes place, reference is nearly always made to the sea (or words associated with the sea). In making the link, Mittelholzer offers a particularly Guianese metaphor: the Seawall being where couples in Georgetown go for "a little bit of sex". In terms of visual connotation, waves rhythmically simulate the sexual act – whilst playing on the auditory senses (i.e., crashing surf) as an orgasmic image. Sylvia's sexual tension is symbolised in just this way:

> ...she trembled in her frustration.
> She listened to the roar of the waves, and tried to let the sound – it had a dramatic grandeur – distract her senses from the physical (p.282)."

When Benson asks Sylvia to join him by the *canal* in Plantation Ruimveldt, instead of spending time by the sea, he signals his dull, shallow sexuality. Her quick exit from the canal – she is a timid swimmer – signals her inability to seduce him, and it is no coincidence that her final failed attempt to give herself to Benson takes place at the aptly named Brickdam. By contrast, in the "nigger-yard" (in Sussex Street) where none of the residents suffer from sexual inhibitions,[29] the sea-sex leitmotif is present, albeit implicitly, in jazz songs such as *Red Sails in the Sunset* or *Moon over Miami*, played over the wireless, hinting at off-screen passions. The lyrics for these songs, though not quoted in the novel, further highlight the link between love, sex and the sea: "Red sails in the sunset, way out on the sea / Oh, carry my loved one home safely to me" and "Moon over Miami / Shine on my love and me / So we can stroll beside the roll / Of the rolling sea" . Mittelholzer uses this leitmotif as a way of emphasising how normal and ever-present sex is without expressly needing to say so. He selects highly popular songs from the 1930s, which many of his readers would have known.

Music & Death: Sylvia's Georgetown Symphony

Sylvia is a work of more extensive artistic ambitions than this discussion of its acute treatment of race, class, gender and the individual psyche in colonial Guiana has so far suggested. That ambition is expressed in Mittelholzer's imaginative attempt – a richly achieved one – to create a Georgetown symphony. This goes far beyond Sterling Brown's phrase about the clichés of the tragic mulatto destined to "go down, accompanied by slow music". Mittelholzer creates a pattern of sound imagery that both articulates Sylvia's inner creative self and provides an organic integration for the novel as a whole: "She listened to Georgetown. All the sounds that had impregnated her deep, deep self" (p.336).

Throughout the novel, the reader's auditory imagination is stimulated by references to contemporary songs that would have been popular in Guiana during the 1930s and 40s: "Lullaby of the Leaves", "Stormy Weather", "Red Sails in the Sunset", "Moon over Miami", "The Music goes Round and Round", "Love is the Sweetest Thing", "Thanks a Million", "A Pretty Girl is like a

Melody", "Thanks for the Memories", "Oh Daddy", "When I Grow too Old to Dream"[30] as well as old music hall pieces, hymns and calypsos, such as, respectively, "Daisy! Daisy! Give me your answer true!", "Oh Happy Band of Pilgrims" and "Advantage will never done, Mussolini, you know you wrong" which are "heard" being played on the gramophones or wirelesses of local residents. With its generally upbeat tempo, this soundtrack works as a counterpoint to the novel's focus on the negativity of social oppression and the tragic trajectory towards Sylvia's death.

In addition to the songs, Mittelholzer makes virtually every object that appears in the narrative into an acoustic instrument with its own unique tone and sound-details. For instance: "The tin sauce-pan went clink-clink as Janie lifted the lid to see how the rice was getting on" (p.304). When brought together, these "instruments" become an orchestra, collectively making chords and rhythmic accompaniments to the unfolding drama:[31]

> Poultry sounds came up from the back-yard. Duck-quacking and the squawk of a hen, the throaty gurgle of a rooster. Far off a dog was barking, the jerky gruffness of the sound blending with the low rumble of symphonic music being played next door on the Hammonds' gramophone (p.77).

These musical chords are repeated with sufficient variation and at large enough intervals to prevent the reader from consciously registering any repetitiveness, whilst becoming aware of a pattern of inherent musicality in Georgetown:

> She heard dogs barking, pigeons moaning, roosters sending yearning coils of sound through the half-gloom of a back-yard. From a large white house came piano music. Frail and tinselly Chopin music (p.102).

Three distinct types of instrument are recorded: those with a "voice" (the people and animals); those which only make sounds when other forces come into play (e.g., the rustling of leaves); and those, like stars, which, in maintaining their distance from earth, appear forever silent, though these silent musical instruments are as important in the narrative as the acoustic ones:

> She watched the stars again. They looked so passive. Cool-blue

and aloof. ... Like cabbage palms and breadfruit trees, the star-apple trees. Like long purple clouds at sunset. Silently intelligent. Always *silently* (p.332).

This passage marks the end of chapter 8 in the last part (5) of the novel as circumstances close in on Sylvia. The repeated use of the word "silently", and alliterative use of "s"-words (which create a shushing sound) almost compel readers to lower their voices.

Music as metaphor

Music is more than just an atmospheric accompaniment to the narrative. As highlighted in the episode of the crude song that Charlotte sings, it is used to add depth to the information we have already been given about the novel's characters: it represents their level of education, their differences in taste, personality, as well as class. It helps to reveal how characters are feeling, without the need of further explanation. When Grantley Russell tells Sylvia about Knight's "widow-fleecing" habits, the cacophonous soundtrack indicates just how unsettled Sylvia feels about this information:

> Now it was *Stormy weather*. And Mrs France was playing *Oh, happy band of pilgrims* – and a car in High Street streaked it all out with a long blare of its horn. Two kiskadees were fighting in the star-apple tree – or it might be a little sex they were after. (p.93)

The reference to the fighting birds and sex reminds that discord is intrinsic to the laws of nature, and vital to our creativity. It is in his capacity to deal with the discordant that is the most crucial difference between Sylvia and Milton. He tells her:

> The louder and more thunderous [the music], the weirder and more *dissonant*, the better I like it (p.288)." [my italics]

And while Sylvia is attracted to the sound of soothing music, Milton is not: "...Music for me, Sylvia, must be *strong and passionate – flaming*" ([my italics] p.288), a remark that can be read as a statement of authorial defiance, locating creativity in resistance to a reactionary society. In his early poem, *In the Beginning – Now – and Then*, Mittelholzer makes just this point:

> ...and the Spirit urged
> subordination of Matter
> and sounded the first drone of strife:
> *sad, but needed, friction,*
> *for without strife, without friction,*
> *ice would have remained ice,*
> *rock rock, silence silence.* [my italics]

It ought to be clear in all this that the notion of duality in the novel is not specific to the "tragic mulatto" but part of the human condition. Sylvia never reaches Milton's state of self-awareness, but she does see the absurdity of rigidly divided dualities:

> In such moments she saw herself as two beings – one ugly and deformed, the other lovely and striving to be good and clean. Then invariably she would remember Frederic March in *Doctor Jekyll and Mr. Hyde*, and laughter would spread like a gold cloud over her, and she would see herself as an absurd romantic trying to make herself into an ogress (p.218).

In the novel as a whole, duality is dialectical – a unity of opposites: e.g., black and white, social realism and romanticism, rural and urban, heredity and environment, Eros and Thanatos, individual and society, good and bad. It is life and the new that is created out of these tensions. Thus whilst Sylvia does die to the sound of music ("A lovely piece, that. Can you hear it? The Militia Band is playing it... On the Sea Wall... I can hear a kiskadee..." She was quiet after that" (p.359)), music becomes a signifier of the complexity of life – its harmonies and discords. Above all, in the particularity and vividness of the novel's soundtrack, Mittelholzer returns an abstract cliché to being live metaphor. And it is in this metaphorical thread that Mittelholzer again points to Milton as the "assumed" composer of *Sylvia* (with its *Overture with Loud Trumpets* and *Finale with Cymbals and Low Drum*), when Milton says: "The drums and cymbals are my favourite instruments. And I rave about trumpets" (p.288).

Music as a Structuring Device

But this thread of musical imagery is not the only use that Mittelholzer makes of music in *Sylvia*. The naming of the novel's beginning and ending, as "overture" and "finale", points to the shaping of the novel in terms of musical structure. There is room here only for an account of how musical structure works in Part One, but it reveals the method of the whole.

In keeping with symphonic form, the first part of *Sylvia* has analogies to the sonata in being made up of components – exposition, development, recapitulation and optional coda – that perform different functions in what is termed the musical argument.

In section 1.1 three key events take place: Mrs Gournal talks to her god-daughter, Charlotte, about Grantley's extramarital indiscretions; Mrs Gournal dies from jaundice and Sylvia's brother, David, is born. The two themes that were central to the overture (death and sex) are thus reintroduced and set the tone of the novel. This expositional section, taking into account David's birth, is also intended to introduce a sub-theme on the cycle of life.

In the development section of a sonata, the harmonic possibilities of the exposition are explored, elaborated and contrasted. This stage of the argument is represented in sections 1.2 through to 1.5 as the occasions in life when problems are positively or negatively resolved, and when the unexpected happens. Section 1.2 for example opens with Charlotte's violent treatment of Sylvia and ends with her being persuaded to treat her more kindly. Section 1.3, in contrast, opens with Naomi tearfully telling Charlotte she doesn't love Bertie Dowden and ends unhappily with her marriage to him. In Section 1.4 another negative situation occurs when Sylvia discovers that her request for a birthday party has been turned down. The unexpected moments in life are meanwhile represented when, in Section 1.5, Sylvia receives a surprise present, gets taken on a trip to the Botanical Gardens, and is invited to a picnic on the East Coast. The various emotions created by these events are in effect extended metaphors for the consonance (harmony) and dissonance (discord) that is found in music.

Sections 1.6 to 1.8 represent the recapitulation component of the sonata; they offer a completion of the "musical" argument and issues (or keys) that remain to be raised (or sounded), are brought to the surface. There is also, in keeping with the patterns of recapitulation, a return to the "sex-death" theme, although this time the sex theme is seemingly more insistent (louder) with references to Teresa's contraction of syphilis; Grantley's and Sylvia's conversation about sex; Grantley's growing promiscuity and, in the final sentence (or cadence) of section 1.6 to "Two people, a man and a lady, on their way to Dixie. For a little sex" (p.90). Sections 1.7 and 1.8 prepare the ground for two events to occur later on in the novel: firstly, Grantley alludes to Mr Knight's habit of fleecing widows, and secondly Sylvia becomes aware of her father's reputation as a "bloody rake". The death theme resurfaces, taking centre stage, with the suicide of Bertie Dowden and Sylvia's prophetic dream of her father's death. The final sentence of Section 1.8 picks up the life-cycle theme of the novel by concluding (with a reference to a popular jazz song): "The wireless was playing *The Music goes Round...*" (p.115).

Section 1.9 acts as the sonata's coda, a conclusion that goes beyond the recapitulation segment played out in Section 1.8. During a visit to New Amsterdam, Sylvia comes across three photographs in the pocket of her father's suit: all are of women, one of whom is naked. The shock of this discovery – a growing awareness of her own sexuality and Oedipal feelings for her father – concludes with Sylvia crying herself to sleep. This coda – and there is a similar passage in all the closing sections of each movement (or Part) in the novel – is used to highlight a new stage in Sylvia's troubled sexual development. In the final section of Part 2, Sylvia, newly distressed over her father's death, is shocked to find her best friend's partner in bed with another woman. Part 3 ends when her brother, for whom she thinks she has developed incestuous feelings, reveals his plan to travel overseas. Again, though increasingly inured to the adversities of life, Sylvia expresses dismay when at the end of Part 4 she hears that her boyfriend, Benson, has secured passage on a Canadian cargo ship and, at the end of Part 5, she fails to make love to him as she has intended. Each of these codas feeds into the novel's "Finale with Cymbals and Low Drums", which offers "death" as the resolution to her life's futile struggles.

By virtue of being the opening word of the overture and the closing theme of the finale, death represents the tonic (or dominant) key of the composition and acts, whilst threading its way melodically through the novel in its various forms, as a constant reminder of the fate that awaits us all:

> Age sidled in slyly upon you all the time. It pulled down your breasts, made gutters in your cheeks, sucked the brown and the black from your hair, dimmed the gleam in your eyes. Death was always on the way (p.302).

Sylvia's death is only one of many. Besides her father's murder, several other characters die – from jaundice, tuberculosis, pneumonia, from having a stroke, drowning and, in the case of Bertie Dowden, committing suicide. In conjunction with sex (the secondary key), the novel draws attention to sex and death as twin actualities in an impoverished colonial society where early and unnecessary death still stalks the land, but where, at least among the working-class, sex is a force of life.[32]

Beyond this realism, the sex-death melody is intended to represent the Freudian[33] battle that takes place within the Id: between Eros (sex / the life-instinct / creativity) and Thanatos (death / the death-instinct). The "real-life" Sylvia (on whom the fictional character was partially based) in fact married, so the novel's "negative" rather than a "positive" conclusion must be read as indicative of Mittelholzer's well publicised view that to remain in colonial Guiana was to become creatively dead. As Michael Gilkes observed: "The stifling of the creative urge was, to Mittelholzer, the most pernicious of the evils of the colonial condition."[34]

Mittelholzer may well have thought that when a society's libido becomes stifled, the death-wish instinct is activated and given the opportunity to dominate, and that if allowed to take over, the death-instinct culminates in the annihilation of the individual and the society, or at least its creativity. That is not the final position that *Sylvia* reaches, for whilst the novel is an indictment of colonial society, it maintains a positive centre by highlighting (e.g., through the sex-sea leitmotiv and the "Georgetown symphony") the creative potential of Guiana. Indeed without Guiana, *Sylvia* would never have been created.

A Philosophy of Death

How, though, are we to read the treatment of death, particularly Sylvia's death, in the novel? It is probable that it would have been considered by Nietzsche, a philosopher favoured by Mittelholzer, as a *good* death. In the chapter, "On Voluntary Death", in *Thus Spake Zarathustra*, the concepts of both a "consummating" and "voluntary death" are celebrated.

> "I commend to you my sort of death", Zarathustra announced, "voluntary death that comes to me because I wish it. *And when shall I wish it?* He who has a goal and heir wants death at the time most favourable to his goal and heir. And out of reverence for his goal and his heir he will hang up no more withered wreaths in the sanctuary of life."[35] [my italics]

Sylvia's death is certainly voluntary: had she wanted to survive she could have relinquished her ideals and become the materially comfortable mistress of Frank Knight. Timing, as suggested by the statement "when shall I wish it?" becomes all important. In Sylvia's case, death has to correspond to the moment when her financial independence and therefore autonomy draws to an end. It can also be seen as a consummating death in that the story of her life and death bring together her life's lessons. We are all destined to die. What matters is how we live. Sylvia, in contradistinction to Grantley Russell, for instance, tries her best to be true to herself and remain noble to the end. Her principles are echoed by another female heroine in the novel Mittelholzer published just before he died, *The Aloneness of Mrs Chatham* (1965):

> I'm determined to be myself. I'm determined to know myself, realise myself, feel that I'm alive in a living, positive way.[36]

And lest Sylvia's attitude to death be seen merely as a defeat, or an instance of the mulatto's so-called tragic pathology, we see that the robust Milton also embraces the idea of death:

> We should all look forward to death, my dear girl. It's the one dream that once having come true – and it always comes true – will cause none of us any disillusionment. The final emptiness. The final cessation of all pain and striving and back-biting and anxiety. What greater heaven could one desire! *I live for death* (p.295). [my italics]

Nevertheless, for Milton Copps the contemplation of death creates not the consummation of Sylvia's quiet repose, whatever its integrity, but a recognition of the urgency of life, an impulse for energy: the importance of using our time wisely, of living life to the full:

> "My creed is simple: I believe in Destiny – and myself. *Work like the deuce* on my own schemes, and leave the rest to Destiny" (p.290). [my italics]

Mittelholzer's presumed view that death was something to look forward to (after a full and successful life) was in keeping with his belief in "oriental occultism" – a broad and eclectic interpretation of Hindu and Buddhist sacred texts found in the works of writers such as Yogi Ramacharaka, though he didn't feel able to give full expression to these views until some six years after the publication of *Sylvia*:

> [*A Tinkling in the Twilight* (1959)] is the first time that I've cared to bring out so clearly into the open my strong attachment to Oriental occultism and Yoga. I've held these beliefs since I was 19, but in my writings have never liked to reveal them because I knew perfectly well I can prove nothing I say on the basis of plain logic (and unfortunately, the Western World can only be convinced by "rational" arguments).[37]

Mittelholzer's critics have accused him of "furious preaching"[38] and "undisguised sermons"[39] in his later fiction. Whether that is so is not discussed here, but in *Sylvia*, at least, there is no such ideological closure. It is true that, like Sylvia, Mittelholzer is known to have suffered from bouts of depression and was, prior to the publication of *Corentyne Thunder*, plagued by the idea that his efforts would amount to nothing. Sylvia's wish no doubt expresses something within Mittelholzer himself:

> "She would have given anything to have been clairvoyant, to have been able to view the panorama of the future *now* so that she could know whether it would be worth putting up a struggle in its cause. She would hate to struggle and not win, to go through the welter of agony and then fade out like the tints in a sunset sky" (p.223).

But in the dynamics of the relationship between Sylvia Russell and Milton Copps, two sides no doubt of Mittelholzer's promptings, there is no preaching, only the dramatisation of the most lively and engaging fiction.

Mittelholzer went on to forge a career that for a long time fulfilled his need for self-expression and resulted in the publication of over twenty novels, an autobiography and a travel journal. By 1961, however, Mittelholzer's popularity was beginning to fade. The novel, *The Aloneness of Mrs Chatham* (1965), was rejected fourteen times before eventually being published by a small, little known firm. With a large family to support, Mittelholzer was once again financially stretched. On 5th May 1965, he was found in the devotional posture of a Yogi having committed suicide by self-immolation. It seems very likely, as Joyce Sparer observed, "that the answer to why he ended his own life so terribly lies in *Sylvia*."[40] If that is so, then the argument he was having with himself probably also accounts for the extraordinary aliveness of a novel written more than sixty years ago.

Endnotes

1. Mittelholzer, E. *The Life and Death of Sylvia* (John Day: New York, 1954) p. 63. Hereafter page references are given following the quotation in the text and relate to this edition. This is based on the earlier Secker edition of 1953, supplemented by several expurgated passages that appear only in the 1954 John Day American edition.
2. It is clear, based on the letters held in the Frank Collymore Collection in The Department of Archives, Barbados, that *Sylvia* was completed before the end of September 1945. See, for example, Mittelholzer's letter dated 3rd December 1945 which points out that Harper's have had his manuscript for over eight weeks. However, a letter that Mittelholzer sent to his US publishers, on 2nd June 1952, states that he had only just "completed Sylvia". It would seem, on reading all of the Mittelholzer letters in the John Day Collection that he was trying to create the impression that he was a prodigious talent, more than capable of producing on average one novel a year. In reality, most of his Caribbean-set novels were conceived/written before 1950. See Cox, J. "Edgar Mittelholzer: A Caribbean Voice – Part One" in *Stabroek News* [Online] Available at:

http://www. stabroeknews.com/2008/guyana-review/05/28/literature/ (Posted: 28 May 2008).

3. See letter dated 29th January 1946 from Mittelholzer to Collymore held in the Frank Collymore Collection.
4. Later editions of the novel were simply entitled *Sylvia*.
5. Mittelholzer, E. "A Pleasant Career" in Ives, J. *The Idyll and the Warrior: Recollections of Edgar Mittelholzer* (unpublished and in the possession of Mrs J. Ives) p. 82. [Published version appears as "Edgar Mittelholzer – A Wife's Memoir" in *Contemporary Review* (Sept 1996) and also as Mittelholzer, J. "The Idyll and the Warrior: Recollections of Edgar Mittelholzer" in *BIM* (June 1983: Vol. 17, Nos. 66 and 67)].
6. Mittelholzer, E. "A Pleasant Career", Ives, op. cit., p. 80.
7. See Mittelholzer's poem "For Me – The Back-Yard" from which the following excerpt is taken: "Assuredly for me – the naive back-yard / Where bajak ants, without hypocrisy, troop by / And no gentlemen politely smile and lie." (See: *Kyk-Over-Al* (Vol. 3, December 1946).
8. My thanks to Mark Adamson, ex-Queens College, for this anecdote.
9. H J M Hubbard is recorded as being the Assistant Secretary of the Clerk's Association in 1939, becoming Field Secretary in 1940/41 and later President. The records of this organisation were destroyed in the great fire of 1945. He was an early associate of Cheddi Jagan and in 1969 published a short book, *Race and Guyana*. For further information see: Chase, A. *A History of Trade Unionism: 1901-1961* (New Guyana Company Ltd: Ruimveldt, 1964), pp 92-93.
10. Gilkes, M. *Racial Identity and Individual Consciousness in the Caribbean Novel* (The Edgar Mittelholzer Memorial Lectures – Fifth Series: Georgetown, 1974).
11. A.J. Seymour, *Edgar Mittelholzer: The Man and His Work*. 1967 Edgar Mittelholzer Memorial Series, 1st Series, Georgetown, 1968.
12. *With a Carib Eye* (Secker and Warburg, 1958), p.177.
13. Since Frank Knight is represented as a successful business man and said to have been mayor of Georgetown twice, he is most likely based upon the real-life personage, Percy C. Wight. Information courtesy of Mark Adamson and corroborated by Ian Wishart, both of whom are members of the QC alumni and recall hearing stories about Percy C Wight allegedly eating promissory notes.
14. Mittelholzer, E., *A Swarthy Boy* (Putnam: London, 1963) p. 126.
15. Perhaps associated in the author's mind with the steel-producing mill town in Lancashire where his maternal grandmother's family were from.
16. There is no evidence that Mittelholzer ever read William Godwin (see *Enquiry Concerning Political Justice*, first published 1793, and

Caleb Williams, first published 1794, and in Oxford World Classics, 2009) but so frequently in his fiction does Mittelholzer encompass both the voices of the radical utilitarians and the poets of imagination and feeling of the Romantic period in warring dialogue, that further investigation would seem worthwhile.

17. See Thorp, J "The Tragic Mulatto Myth" in Pilgrim, D (ed) *Jim Crow Museum of Racist Memorabilia* [On-line] (Ferris State University: November 2000). Available at: http://www.ferris.edu/htmls/news/jimcrow/menu.htm.
18. Cited in Sollors, W., *Neither Black nor White Yet Both: Thematic Exploration of Interracial Literature* (Harvard University Press: London, 1999), p. 224.
19. Sollors, W., *op. cit.*, p. 224.
20. Ibid.
21. See letter dated 29th January 1946 from Mittelholzer to Collymore held in the Frank Collymore Collection.
22. Smith, L. *Strange Fruit* (The Cresset Press: London, 1945) p. 72.
23. Mittelholzer, E., *A Swarthy Boy*, p. 28.
24. Mittelholzer's views on "race" were complex and cannot be fully explained in a short footnote. He refers in *A Swarthy Boy* to "one drop of German blood" being all that is needed to succeed. This was said in backlash to the "one-drop of Black blood" rule used in the Southern States of America, which conferred inferiority upon anyone who wasn't pure "white". Whilst believing strongly in the idea of genetic inheritance, Mittelholzer also argued: "we are each one of us a mass of inherited contradictions and inconsistencies. There is no set "behaviour pattern". See Mittelholzer, E., *A Swarthy Boy*, p. 30.
25. Writing in 1961, C.L.R. James made the following observation: "[The Caribbean middle classes] have no trace of political tradition. Until twenty years ago they had no experience of political parties or government. Their last foray in that sphere was a hundred and thirty years ago when they threatened the planters with rebellion of themselves and the slaves if they were not permitted to exercise the rights of citizens. Since then they have been quiet as mice." James, C. L. R., "The West Indian Middle Classes" in *Spheres of Existence* (Allison and Busby: London, 1980) pp. 132-133.
26. Mittelholzer referred to himself a communist/Marxist during the 1940s. Later on in his life, he developed an anti-communist stance in response to the atrocities that had and were taking place in Russia, as well as to the restrictions they placed on art and creative writing: "all the talk of equality and brotherhood of man could not win me over to Communism so long as I know that I would have to live under a state of things where a Party is going to try to dictate to me what I

should think and say, and put me under arrest when I deviate." Mittelholzer, E., "At Forty-Three: A Personal View of the World" (unpublished: 1953) p. 11. Document courtesy of Lucille Mittelholzer.

27. Ramchand, K. *The West Indian Novel and Its Background* (Ian Randle Publishers: Kingston, 2004) p. 27.
28. This passage was censored by Secker and Warburg and doesn't appear in any previous UK editions of *Sylvia.*
29. In *With a Carib Eye* (Secker and Warburg, 1958), Mittelholzer notes: "South of the Stabroek Market is Lombard Street [a road which intersects with Sussex Street] ... It was the one district of Victorian Georgetown where nobody, not even the best families, could doubt the existence of Sex." p. 179.
30. The lyrics of these popular jazz songs can be "Googled" or listened to on "You Tube".
31. As an avid cinema-goer, Mittelholzer may well have been influenced by Rouben Mamoulian's film, *Love Me Tonight* (1932), starring Chevalier, where everyday items are represented as instruments which collectively sound and function as part of the film's soundtrack. Sylvia, notably, "always enjoyed Maurice Chevalier", *Sylvia*, p.105.
32. Despite the high death rate, rates of birth were also high and the population in fact increased from 301,000 in 1931 to 318,000 in 1941. See Brereton, B. (ed.) *General History of the Caribbean: Volume V – The Caribbean in the Twentieth Century* (Unesco Publishing: London, 2004) p. 48.
33. Grantley Russell notably makes direct reference to Freud on p. 103 of the 1954 edition of *Sylvia*.
34. Gilkes, M., *Racial Identity and Individual Consciousness in the Caribbean Novel* (The Edgar Mittelholzer Memorial Lectures – Fifth Series: Georgetown, 1974), p. 24.
35. Nietzsche, F., *Thus Spoke Zarathustra* (Penguin Books: London, 2003) p. 97.
36. Mittelholzer, E., *The Aloneness of Mrs. Chatham* (Library 33: London, 1965) p. 1.
37. See A J Seymour collection at the University of Guyana – Mittelholzer letter (circa 1959) addressed to A J Seymour.
38. Seymour, *Edgar Mittelholzer: The Man and His Work*, p. 38.
39. Gilkes, "Edgar Mittelholzer", in *West Indian Literature*, Ed. Bruce King, 1979, p. 108.
40. Sparer, J. "Attitudes to Race in Guyanese Literature", in *Caribbean Studies* (Vol. 8: No. 2, 1968) p. 25.

OVERTURE WITH LOUD TRUMPETS

"Death," Bertie Dowden was saying, "can be a joy – I mean, the contemplation of death in relation to the fullness, the crowded exigency of living." He hiccuped.

"I have no luck," Robby van Huisten told the man who was pestering them. "I don't want a ticket. Grantley, do you want a ticket in the Calcutta Sweepstake?"

"Have you never felt, Jack," Bertie persisted, "that you've reached a point in life where you feel glutted with experience? Hic! You halt and say to yourself: 'Life is good. Full. Overcharged with interest. Brimming with richness. I have lived. I am living. I have had enough. More will prove a burden. Now for death. Soothing death. When will death come and relieve me of this load of teeming interests, gushing riches?' Of course, you don't really want to die, but, nevertheless, you feel comforted at the thought of death a certainty in the future. It's the one accomplishment none of us need fear of never achieving. Think of the sweet, the blossom-cool, dark closing down upon all our activities and laughter and ambitions and conceits, transmuting into oblivion our garden schemes. Lovely. Softly creeping. And certain – dead certain – solution of all our fears and problems. Hic!"

"Buy a sweepstake ticket, Bertie."

"Don't want a sweepstake ticket. Death, Jack..."

"I'll take one," said Grantley Russell. "How much is it old chap?"

"Ten shillings, sir. Only ten shillings. And you might win tousands and tousands of dollars."

"Not even tens, my man, but I'll still take a ticket since it seems the only way to stop you from making yourself a bloody nuisance. Here's your ten shillings."

"Oh, good shot! Good shot!" Jack Ralph stamped his applause. It was the East Indian who had made the shot. His opponent, a Portuguese, thumped his cue on the floor to add to the shouting and stamping applause that exploded all round the bar. The whole room glittered and clattered with applause. There was applause even in the laughter of the prostitutes.

"Death is a glowing pinnacle in all our futures. We should cherish the wonderful image—"

"What's yours, Bertie?"

"Gin and lime-juice, Jack."

"Rum and ginger for me," said Robby.

"Same for you, Grantley?"

"Yes, Jack. Choose any number you like, my man. I simply don't care what number it is."

"Awright, sir. Tek dis one. Ah wish you luck, sir. You might win tousands and tousands..."

"Frank, what's yours?"

"I want a whore," said Frank Knight. "Time," he insisted, "to go and look for a whore, Jack. Tiger Bay whore." He put his hand to his mouth to muffle the belch.

"...like a treasure awaiting us. Caskets of emeralds and ear rings of lapis lazuli could not be more lavish a gift..."

"Come on, Frank. Behave yourself. What're you having, man?"

"Gin and kola tonic, Jack. And a whore. Nice, fat whore."

"Whole night before us, Frank," said Grantley. "I want a whore myself. Fat nigger girl."

"I want a coolie. Must have a coolie. Coolie sweet like hell, boy."

"Frank, I've got a sweepstake ticket. Have it, Frank." He held it out, but Frank waved it off. "Wipe your backside with it, Grantley."

"Jack, when I think – ponder," amended Bertie, "on the thousands – hundreds of thousands – of people all over the world who, on this Easter Eve in the year of our Lord, 1920, are unhappy in some way. Know what I mean by unhappy? Downcast. Sobbing. Crying softly. Or not crying at all but simply suffering silently. When I ponder on them I wish I could speak to them – every one of them. Jack, you listening to me? I'd say to them: 'Why are you unhappy? Why are you sobbing? Why are you downcast? Don't you know there's no need for despair? Don't you know of the cool blue night waiting at the end of your travail?' Hip!"

"Bertie, you're drunk."

"Death. A pale blue plumbago in the shade of the guava tree. Or a new moon in the west seen through the silhouette of a bread-fruit tree. Images of boyhood idylls. Won't we relive them when death is draping us with purple sleep? Hip! Death comes to all of us at all ages, Jack. Some of us go at seventy, some at sixty, some at fifty –"

"Some at forty," said Grantley.

"Some at thirty," agreed Jack.

"Twenty," said Robby. "Ten. Five."

"Some in the bloody womb," growled Frank. "I want a whore."

"Oh, good stroke Good stroke!"

"Yes, damned good stroke. That coolie can play, y'know!"

"Coming home with me tonight, sweetheart?" asked Clotilde.

Frank shook his head. "No, Clotilde. I want a coolie tonight. Must have a coolie." Clotilde sat in his lap, and he patted her cheek languidly. "Have a drink, Clotilde. Not a bad-looking Puttagee, y'know."

Teresa sat in Grantley's lap. "Teresa what?"

"Feria," she told him. She had a lot of gold-filled teeth. "You're not a creole, eh?"

"No. English."

Later, in bed, in Tiger Bay, he told her that he had come to British Guiana to build a bridge for the government. A bridge over a river in the interior. "Your local engineers could have built it on their own, but they're coloured, and your damned silly government felt that it was the in thing to send out to England and get an Englishman to be in charge. So I came." He had stayed on, he explained, after the bridge was built and was employed now as a road engineer with the Georgetown Town Council.

"I got the job through Robby van Huisten."

"Oh. Yes, Ah hear about 'im. 'E's a big man in business."

"Junior director of Roos & van Huisten's. Belongs to one of the oldest coloured families in the colony. Father and grandfather were Members of the Court of Policy and Mayors of Georgetown and all the bloody rest of it. Robby is a Town Councillor himself."

"Ah is see a lot of dese big-family men in de Viceroy Hotel," said Teresa. "You sleepy, na?"

Grantley did not answer. He was asleep.

At about seven o'clock the following morning there was a knock on the door. "Who is dat?" Teresa called out sleepily. And a timid voice replied: "Me, Charlotte! You wake up yet?"

"No, she's asleep!" called Russell. "Can't you hear?" He guffawed. Stale drunk and in an impish mood, he sprang up, got out of bed and opened the door. And Charlotte exclaimed: "Oh, Lawd!" But despite her shocked tone, she did not withdraw.

She smiled with coy amusement, evidently quite unmoved by his nakedness. He had no hair on his chest, and he was a man of medium build, five feet eight in height, fair-haired and with greenish blue eyes and a small trimmed moustache.

Charlotte said that she had come about the crochet thread Teresa had promised to give her to make the doyleys for Teresa's cousin Angie. She was a dark girl – dark of skin and dark of eyes and hair. But her features were not wholly negroid. Her eyes had a Mongolian slant, and Russell asked her what was her full name and whether there were Chinese blood in her. She told him with a snigger that her full name was Charlotte Timmers, and, no, she had no Chinese blood in her. Her mother was a Buck.

"Ah, a Buck," said Russell. "You mean a Guiana Indian?"

"Yes."

He patted her cheek and put on his clothes, and after a lot of trivial, friendly chatting between the three of them – about crochet thread, Easter and going to church, the cigarette-holders left by various men on Teresa's dressing-table, and why did Teresa have such a husky laugh? – he put a five-dollar note on Teresa's dressing-table and left.

Not three weeks later, at about sunset, he ran into Charlotte on the Sea Wall promenade. Like himself, she was taking a walk. He stopped and smiled. "I know you. You're Charlotte."

Charlotte smiled shyly.

"You don't remember me?" asked Russell.

"Yes. You was in Teresa' room Easter morning."

After some conversation he suggested seeing her home.

She lived in a narrow, rocky street called Fort Street, not far from the Sea Wall. He asked her to meet him on the Wall the following night. She met him, but when he tried to make love to her she withdrew from his touch and said that she was not that kind of girl. He persisted, and, after a while, she gave in and they went to a quiet spot near the site of the old Dutch fort.

They met again on three or four nights during the next week or so, then she failed to appear one night and he went to her home in Fort Street and was told by neighbours that with Mr. and Mrs. Gournal, her uncle and godmother, she had removed to another quarter of the city. The neighbours told him the name of the street – Broad Street – but he decided that this must be the end of the affair. He was sorry, because he rather liked the girl. However, she was supposed to be low-class; she did not come of a family that mattered, and her education was poor. His upper middle-class coloured friends would certainly have objected if they had discovered that he was getting too attached to her. Not that he cared a hoot about class, he assured himself, but there was no reason why he should upset the sensibilities of his friends if it could be helped.

About three months later he was having lunch – called breakfast in Guiana – at his boarding-house when the maid told him he was wanted on the telephone. It was Charlotte. She asked if she could see him that night on the Sea Wall. He replied in surprise that he thought she had forgotten all about him.

"What's the trouble? Your voice sounds as if you're just from your mother's funeral."

She reminded him that her parents had been dead for years.

"I'm only pulling your leg, Charlotte. Very well, I'll meet you. Near that circular sort of shed – what's it called? The Round House?"

"Yes, de Round House. We can walk from dere toward de fort."

He kept the appointment, and she told him that she was going to have a child by him. "Me?" he said. "What's this? Trying to make me a scapegoat for your sins?" He spoke jovially.

She insisted it was true. She wasn't fooling him. It was his child, and what was he going to do about it? Her godmother was a very strict person. "She stop me from going on de Sea Wall since we moved from Fort Street to Broad Street. She say I mustn' go out so far from home. She gone to prayer-meeting dis evening, dat's how Ah manage to get away and come here."

"And how do you know it's my child you're having?"

She said that she wouldn't deny that she had had to do with other men once or twice before she had met him. "But not once since we was friendly dat time a few months back. I didn't have anything to do wid a man about four or five months before dat."

She sounded tearful. It was his child. If he doubted it let him wait until it was born and he would see. Oh, Lord, she was so worried. What was she going to tell her godmother when she began to show? Her uncle was a Seven Days Adventist, and he was strict about things like this. He would want to beat her and put her out the house. She had tried to throw away the child. She had taken something to drink – boiled-bush medicine an old black lady had given her – but it had made her very sick and she had vomited the whole night, and it hadn't got rid of the child. If only she knew of something that would work! Did he know of any pills or medicine she could drink?

"But why try to polish off the little thing?" he protested. "Why not let it come?"

"Let it come!"

"Why not! Don't you want to have a child? Oh-oh! Look at the tears! Let me dry your eyes. There, that's better."

She smiled.

"Now, you simply don't worry," he told her. "You go ahead and have your child. If they threaten to put you out come and tell me. Come to my office at the Town Hall and I'll fix things up for you. Don't let them scare you with silly threats. There's nothing disgraceful in having a child – in or out of wedlock. Do you know how many dried-up spinsters would give their eyes to have a child, Charlotte? Dried-up, frustrated spinsters and widows who keep cats or dogs as child-substitutes. Oh, what a world! And we call it civilized! Look here, you promise me you won't go drinking any more nasty concoctions. Promise?"

"Yes."

When they parted she was in a much brighter mood – much less fearful of the wrath to come from Uncle and Godmother.

Months went by, and he saw nothing of her. Then one day, after lunch, he entered his office at the Town Hall and found a dark-skinned young woman awaiting him. She was seated on a chair near his desk, an infant in her lap. Behind her stood an elderly black lady in dark green and a broad-brimmed black hat with red berries. The young woman smiled, and he recognized her as Charlotte. She had got plumper and broader.

"Well!" he said. "I say!"

"Dis is de baby," she said.

"The baby?"

"Yes."

"Oh. Yes, of course. The baby. Good God! I'd almost forgotten."

He bent and looked at the child. It had blue eyes and was of a pinkish complexion. The features were European, though the cheekbones were high like Charlotte's.

"What's it? Boy or girl?"

"A girl." She spoke with some disappointment.

"Good! I like girls. Don't look so crestfallen."

He glanced up at the black lady who was smiling reluctantly and with some austerity, as though she wanted to show disapproval but, somehow, felt that the situation called for good humour and pleasantness.

"You're Godmother, I suppose? Mrs. Gournal?"

"I am," said the lady. The smile faded.

"Charlotte has spoken about you."

Silence.

"Well," said Russell. He touched his tie.

Charlotte kept smiling, eyes downcast.

The infant began to twist its body about. It made fretting sounds.

Russell snapped his fingers at it and whistled softly. "Well, just fancy!" he exclaimed. He glanced from Charlotte to Godmother.

Godmother, solemn-faced, her eyes fixed on a calendar on the southern wall, spoke. "Charlotte is a poor girl, Mr. Russell," she said. "Ah want you to realize dat. Her mudder and fadder both dead. And dis child means she has another mouth to feed beside her own."

Silence. Russell fingered his tie.

Godmother spoke again. "She had a hard pregnancy, Mr. Russell. And we got midwife and doctor bills to stand. And physic. She was sick all through de pregnancy."

There was nothing threatening in her manner. She was merely stating the case as it stood. She succeeded in achieving dignity.

Russell said yes, he had wondered why he hadn't seen anything of Charlotte for such a long time. It was really beastly of him not to have dropped in to inquire. No excuse at all. He frowned at his desk, drummed on the back of the swivel chair. Suddenly grinned and said: "I'll support the little thing. No need to get in a dither about it."

He gripped Charlotte's arm. "I'll do what I can to make you both comfortable. And I say! I was nearly forgetting. You brought me luck, you know, Charlotte. I won over seven thousand pounds in the Calcutta Sweepstake. I bought the ticket the very night before I met you – in the Viceroy Hotel. Remember Easter Sunday morning in Teresa Feria's room?"

"Ah glad," said Charlotte.

"Humph!" said Godmother, stiffening.

"I've bought two houses in Kingston – one in High Street and the other in Fort Street, not far from where you used to live. I've rented them both out. And Frank Knight has invested the rest for me. The solicitor chap. He was with me in the Viceroy that Saturday night. Oh, we had a terrific binge!" He snapped his fingers and whistled. "But look at the little devil, eh? I say, what are you going to call her? Have you thought about it?"

"No," said Charlotte, shaking her head. "We was waiting to see you first to hear if you want any special names."

"You were, were you? H'm. I'll have to think up a few good names. What about having a drink on it and discussing the question. Eh?" He glanced up at Godmother. "Couldn't we drop in somewhere and have a drink, Mrs. Gournal? I know of a little bar off Croal Street –"

"I don't take strong drink, Mr. Russell," Godmother interrupted. "I am a woman of God."

"Oh. Of course, of course. Just an idea, you know. Well, look here, let's see. What *can* we call her? Helen? I believe I had an aunt called Helen. She was a barmaid in Soho." He grinned. "I have no aristocratic blood to boast about. My father was a hall-porter, but quite a respectable old chap in his way, I can tell you. I was the only child, so they sent me to Grammar School, and I won a scholarship and studied engineering. Nothing for me to put on airs about. Oh, but I say, isn't she a lovely little thing! I believe she's got Mother's eyes. Look here, I tell you what. We won't call her Helen. We'll call her Cynthia Anne – after my mother. How's that?"

"Dat's nice," Charlotte smiled.

Godmother, overwhelmed, at last, by Russell's ebullient charm, was smiling, too. "They are very nice names," she concurred.

As they were preparing to go – after the exchange of further pleasantries – Russell fumbled about on his desk, put some bank notes into an envelope, and handed the envelope to Charlotte. Something for the child, he told her. He would come and see them the following day. Were they still in Broad Street? They were. Good. He would be round tomorrow evening.

Russell, who had been friendly for some months with an olive-skinned coloured girl at the Telephone Exchange, fell out with her. The girl's father had, from the outset, disapproved of the friendship. He had told his daughter that he would have nothing to do with her if she married Russell. No damned English rat for a son-in-law for him! Hadn't the man himself admitted to Robby van Huisten that his father was a hall-porter in London! "I may be coloured, but my father, grandfathers and great-grandfathers," said the telephone girl's father, "were gentlemen – every one of them. Not cheap, dragged-up Cockneys!"

Russell and the girl had not actually been engaged to be married, but when it leaked out that he had had a child by a low-class girl and was actually a visitor at her home, the telephone girl said that that was the limit, and put an end to the friendship forthwith.

Russell did not mind. He continued to visit Charlotte. He went every afternoon, and always took something. A bottle of calves' feet jelly, oranges or bananas, Bovril, a tin of biscuits. The child had been christened Sylvia Anne, for it appeared that his English accent had made "Cynthia" sound to the ears of Charlotte and Godmother "Sylvia".

Soon his visits increased to twice a day – at lunch time as well as in the afternoon after leaving the Town Hall. He became very attached to the child. When she was a year old he suggested marriage. He told Charlotte frankly that he did not love her but that he had an idea they should be able "to muddle along together, if you know what I mean." He was awkward and stammered. He was getting on for forty and it was high time, he said, he settled down. And – and – well, the fact was, he was devilishly fond of the little tot, and he thought it would be a beastly shame to have her grow up illegitimate.

The ceremony, though performed quietly at half past six in the morning, created much talk in the city. Some said that Charlotte and her godmother had worked *obeah* on him to catch him as a husband. They had put a "stay-at-home" in his food, people said. A concoction of musk and asafoetida and boiled bush.

The coloured middle-class sniffed and said: "I told you so. The man is only a cheap, low-class Englishman. Just what you could have expected of him!"

Many of his acquaintances were thoroughly disgusted. His own close friends, Frank Knight, Jack Ralph, Robby van Huisten, Bertie Dowden, did their best to dissuade him, but when they saw that he could not be shifted in his decision and that he only laughed at the comments that were circulating, they held a binge in his honour. A stag party at which they poked good-natured fun at him and made obscene jokes about copulation and childbirth. Toward the end of it, at three in the morning, they turned him upside-down, gave him a spanking on his behind, then lifted him on to their shoulders and sang "For He's a Jolly Good Fellow!"

PART ONE

1

The big two-storeyed house in High Street, Kingston, Russell's own property, had four large bedrooms, the windows of two of which looked out on the street. Sylvia liked to watch the trams rumbling past on their way to the Sea Wall or toward the central part of the city. They fascinated her, and she would howl when she could not find a stool or chair near one of the windows.

Pale olive in complexion, she had coppery-gold hair that eventually turned light-brown. Her eyes remained blue until she was seven when they became hazel-green, a tint they retained for the rest of her life.

She was a very spoiled child. Her mother, weak-willed and sentimental, let her have whatever she wanted, and her father, strong in many respects, could not bear to hear her cry, and gave in to her, too. He took her often for rides in the tram – sometimes to the Sea Wall, sometimes two miles out of town to Peter's Hall on the east bank of the Demerara River. He bought her innumerable toys.

The house could comfortably have accommodated Uncle and Godmother as well, but Russell would not have them. He told Charlotte that he meant to do his utmost to live in harmony with her, but that he saw no reason why he should go out of his way to try to adjust himself to the ways of Uncle and Godmother. He was no churchman, he said, and, fortunately, Charlotte herself was only a lukewarm churchwoman. But Uncle and his Seven Days Adventist habits and Godmother and her Gospel Tabernacle were no fit persons to have in his house. A Sabbath that began at sunset on Friday and no cooking on Saturday! And Godmother singing hymns all day and quoting from the Scriptures! No, it would never, said Russell, have done for him.

Charlotte agreed, but secretly she never forgave him for debarring her people as permanent guests.

When he was at work Godmother would come to see Charlotte to discuss topics that seemed to Godmother to demand discussion.

The favourite topic was Russell's ungodliness in bringing his friends to the house in the afternoons or evenings to drink and play bridge or poker. Godmother said: "He ain' got no consideration for you to be allowing his friends to come here. They are not friends of yours. Dese high-colour young men look 'pon you as dirt. But they should remember dat you is mistress in dis house. You're his wife. Eh-eh! But why you should keep in de background when they come here to drink and play cards All dat ungodliness! Gambling and drunkenness! Child, you must hold your own wid him. Don't let him get do better of you."

Charlotte would say: "Yes, Godma," but she would do nothing about it. She had no will to equal Russell's, and no sooner had Godmother left when she was the docile worm again. Russell did not force her to be a worm. The choice was her own. She was by nature a worm. Russell's pink complexion and English accent had, from the outset, awed her, and his money and this big house had bewildered her still more. A cook and a housemaid made her uncomfortable. She had been accustomed to doing menial tasks for Godmother and Uncle; she did not know how to give orders to servants. With her elementary education and her slum background, she spoke as brokenly as the servants. The servants did not respect her, and only addressed her as "ma'am" when Russell was present.

Sylvia roamed the house at will. She crept upstairs and downstairs and sometimes fell asleep on the rug in the sitting-room. Sometimes under a table in the pantry.

One morning when Godmother and Charlotte were in the gallery discussing Russell's ungodliness there was a crash and a shriek upstairs. They went up and found Sylvia in Russell's room bawling in frightened spasms. Around her on the floor lay her father's shaving-brush and shaving-bowl – this in fragments – hairbrush and comb and a pipe and tobacco pouch. Also the dressing-table cloth.

While Charlotte coaxed her into silence Godmother gathered up the scattered toilet things. Suddenly the older woman stiffened. She was holding a small tin bearing on its cover the two words THREE SAFES.

"Eh-eh!"

"What wrong, Godma?"

"But you never tell me about dis, Charlotte. Ent you say you going to have another child soon?"

"Yes, Godma, we just begin to send for it."

"You tell me dat more dan two months ago."

"Yes, Godma – about two months ago, but no signs yet. Ah had me sickness last week."

"Den why you' husband using dese t'ings?"

"What t'ings?"

"Dese t'ings."

Godmother thrust the tin up to her face, and Charlotte stared at it blankly. She shook her head and said no, he wasn't using them with her. He had never used them with her.

"Never?" said Godmother. "Oh!"

Charlotte went slightly grey with fear – fear of Godmother.

"He never use dem wid you," said Godmother. "Den why he have dem here! Why? You can tell me dat, Charlotte?"

Her goddaughter was silent. Sylvia began to wriggle and fret to indicate that she wanted to be put down. Charlotte put her down.

"You know what dis mean?" said Godmother. "It mean he has committed adultery. It mean he going out wid other women."

Charlotte hung her head. Moisture gathered in her eyes.

"You is a stupid girl," said Godmother – and cuffed her in her chest.

"Ow, Godma!" whispered Charlotte, recoiling.

"You too blind and stupid!"

Godmother advanced and cuffed her again, grasped her by the front of her dress and shook her. The dress tore.

"You don't know how to hold de man Right under you' eyes he going to other women. Why you so stupid, eh, girl?"

"But, Godma, how I going to stop 'im?"

"Don't talk back at me! Ah saying dis for you' own good! You too stupid and foolish! Why you so stupid and foolish?"

Bup! Godmother's fist landed in Charlotte's chest again.

"Ow, Godma!"

Sylvia had paused to watch them. Her face looked like a dirt-smeared mask. All morning she had been sucking a toffee.

"You ain' got two grains o' sense in you' head. You don't know you must try and keep de man home at night! Talk to him and tell him not to let his friends come here and tempt him to drink and go outside whoring about and calling down God's wrath!"

Charlotte wept.

"Make a noise when his friends come to de house, and shame him before dem, and he must stop his ungodliness!"

Godmother dashed the tin of THREE SAFES into a corner.

"It's some high-colour girl he going to – dat's what it is! Dat telephone girl. I bet you what you like he taking her in a car to Scandal Point. You got to talk to him and put a stop to it. You hear me?" Godmother cuffed her on her shoulder. "You listening to me good, child?"

"Yes, Godma."

"De next t'ing you know he will put you out de house and bring one of his high-colour lady friends to live wid him. And den you will punish. You going to talk to him about it? Tell me."

"Yes, Godma. Ah going talk to him."

Charlotte, however, did not have the courage to broach the subject with Russell. She was slightly cool toward him for the next day or two, but he took no notice of this, for it was not unusual for her to fall into a sulk over some trivial or imagined grievance.

When Godmother tackled her, Charlotte said: "Yes, Godma, Ah talk to him. Ah quarrel wid him, but he say it's not true. He say he not going to no other women. He say he had dose t'ings in de tin since long before we get married."

"Ah don't believe it. He lying. He trying to cover up his sinfulness wid lies."

Charlotte was silent, head bent.

Godmother wagged her finger. "All right. You wait good. Ah going to make inquiries and find out who de girl is he meeting. Ah believe you ain' talk to him loud enough and make him know you serious. But no fear! Ah going to work in secret and pray to de Lord to shame him. Because he white he t'ink he can do what he like? We going to see before long. He got to respeck de ring he put 'pon you' finger!"

Godmother, however, did not have much time in which to see about anything. Not a week after this visit to Charlotte she took ill with jaundice. It was a severe attack, but Uncle, who had faith in God but not in medical men, treated her himself, aided by God, and Godmother died ten days after the attack came on.

Uncle said it was God's will, and invited friends and relatives to the wake. He invited Charlotte and Russell. He came to the house himself to announce the death. It was the first time he had come for a long time, for he had been deeply offended at Russell's refusal to have him and Godmother live at the big house in High Street.

Russell was at work when Uncle came, but Uncle told Charlotte to tell Russell that they must let bygones be bygones and not bear malice in their hearts. He said she must ask Russell if he would be a pallbearer, that he did not expect a big turnout at the funeral, but that it would look well if Russell was one of the bearers, seeing that he was, in a manner of speaking, the deceased's son-in-law.

"I'm sure," he said, "the deceased would have wished it so."

He would be happy, too, if Charlotte and Russell could come to the wake tonight. Did she think Russell would want to come?

Charlotte had never seen him in so humble a mood. It made her shriek more often and louder. As soon as Uncle had announced the death, Charlotte had exclaimed as though not even aware that Godmother had been ill. Then she had shrieked. Clapped her hands together. Tore at her hair. Collapsed on the floor with a whimper that, without warning, rose to another penetrating shriek.

Uncle, unperturbed – from Uncle's manner it was obvious that he considered her behaviour perfectly correct and conventional – went on speaking in a grave voice.

Russell postponed a poker date and went to the wake. "I don't like funerals," he said, "much less wakes. But I suppose this is an exceptional instance."

They took Sylvia to the wake. She was put in Godmother's big four-poster with Henry Madhoo, Godmother's cousin's child. He was two years older than Sylvia and a *douglah,* which is to say half East Indian and half negro. Sylvia and Henry slept soundly throughout everything. The hymn-singing did not disturb them, nor the talking and uproarious laughter.

At about two o'clock Charlotte feared that they would have awakened, because a noisy argument developed between the men-folk, who had been drinking heavily and playing cards since eight o'clock. Uncle had provided six bottles of rum and Mrs. Charles Madhoo, Henry's mother, had seen about the salt-fish, green plantains and black pudding.

The argument was about the ace of clubs. Some were playing Suck-the-well and some Biskra, in Uncle's sight innocuous games. Uncle would not countenance bridge or poker; that would have been gambling and a sin in the Lord's sight, doubly so in view of the presence in the house of the deceased. It was the Biskra group that began the argument about the ace of clubs.

"Somebody palm dat ess of clubs," said Mr. Best. He was sure about it, because he had shuffled the cards himself and the ess had been there then. Nobody could fool him about that ess. After all, they weren't playing for money, so why anybody should want to cheat? Eh? He was ashamed.

"Oh, God, man, Ah shame!" he repeated.

Mr. Thomas called him to order. "Nobody cheat here," Mr. Thomas said. "No, Aubrey, you shouldn't use a word like dat. You must remember we is all friends here and respectable persons."

Mr. Raymond laughed and told Mr. Best that he could excuse him. "You had too much to drink, Aubrey. You let me down, man! Eh-eh! I did always thought you could hold your liquor!"

Mr. Best sprang up, nearly turning the table over. "Who say I had too much to drink? Which man here can drink wid me? If you t'ink so bring de rum, Basil! Bring de rum! I can put ten like you under de table and walk a chalk line! Bring de rum if you doubt me!"

"We not talking about rum. We discussing de ess o'clubs –"

"Ssh! Ssh! Not so much noise!" cautioned Mrs. Thomas, who was Uncle's niece's godchild. "You-all don't know a dead in de house?"

Uncle's aunt's cousin, Mrs. White, said that they had better strike up another hymn. The women were sitting round the coffin in the small dining-room. Henry's mother was sprinkling cologne on the corpse, already dressed and laid out in the dark-brown coffin with nickel-plated fittings. Godmother was dressed in her black silk dress – the dress she used to wear to church on Sundays.

"Come on! Quick!" urged Mrs. White. "They look as if they want to mek a fight. Only one t'ing to stop dem. We must sing 'pon dem. *T'rough de night of doubt and sorrow,*" sang Mrs. White, and the others joined in with "*Onward goes de pilgrim band…*"

In the one bedroom the cottage possessed Uncle produced a bottle of gin from the lowest drawer of the chest of drawers. He took a swig at it, then glanced round to make sure that no one had observed him. He returned the bottle to the drawer and went back into the sitting-room to watch the card-games, his face solemn as befitted the deceased's husband.

Russell, one of the Suck-the-well group, glanced up at him and smiled, and Uncle returned the smile and said that he hoped Mr. Russell was enjoying himself.

"Eh? Oh – rather!" Russell replied, fidgeting.

Uncle, who had spoken out of self-consciousness and an over-anxiety to be the perfect host to his white godson-in-law, did not fail to note the uncertainty of Russell's tone nor Russell's fidgetings and the flickering-glance he cast toward the dining-room. Uncle, realising that he had committed a *faux pas,* moved with a jaunty haste toward the Biskra group, where Mr. Best had been persuaded to sit down and resume the game. The ace of clubs had been found on the floor under the table. Uncle slapped Mr. Raymond gently on the back, the jauntiness abruptly gone from his manner. "Ay, Basil," he said, his voice a grave rumble, "you see what happen, young man! In the midst of life we're in death."

"Yes, sir. Oh, yes, sir," Mr. Raymond agreed, his expression one of deep sorrow as he played the king of hearts and collected the trick. He gave a low groan.

Uncle sighed. Uncle was a tall man. His bearing was dignified and demanded respect. His chin was firm, his jaw strong and jutting. Stubborn. His gaze steady and penetrating.

The funeral was a morning one. There were many carpenters

present, for Uncle was a carpenter-boss (a building contractor). But the crowd was not as big as Uncle had wished. Uncle told Russell that he was very sorry it had had to be a morning funeral. The turnout, he said, would have been much better in the afternoon. But there had been no help for it. Godmother had died at half-past seven the morning before, and the corpse would not have been able to keep until the afternoon of the present day. He could have had the funeral the previous afternoon but that would have meant having no wake – or not a proper one; the corpse must be present for a proper wake – and it would have been too short notice for friends and relatives, some of whom lived far up the East Coast.

Russell's presence at the wake, and at the funeral as a pallbearer, pleased Uncle very much. "We must forget all our grievances and misunderstandings, Mr. Russell," he said, holding out his hand. He could not bring himself to say "Grantley" or even "Russell"; the marked difference in race and class proved too much for him. "All that is past, and we must begin afresh." Russell told him he must come and see him whenever he liked. No formalities involved. "Just drop in whenever you like."

Uncle came on the following Sunday at about ten in the morning, and Russell set before him whisky, rum and gin and told him to make his choice. "You don't have to be modest," Russell grinned. "Anything and any quantity goes." Uncle guffawed self-consciously and helped himself to a finger of gin in a large tumbler. By midday, however, he was helping himself to over three fingers, and what was more, held it with the ease of an experienced toper. He stayed to lunch at Russell's invitation, and Russell told him to come again next Sunday.

Thereafter it was the accepted thing, this Sunday morning visit of his. Russell found that, despite his rigid religious precepts, Uncle was an intelligent man and always well-informed about both local as well as foreign affairs. He read his newspaper carefully. Municipal politics was his pet subject, and whenever he happened to be talking about the Town Council his voice would become sonorous and earnest and he would lean forward and tuck his feet under the chair.

Often Sylvia paused to gaze at him when he was in this

attitude. She would watch, fascinated, his steady, intense eyes staring at her father, as words thundered out of him, his long, heavy-browed face dark brown and shining faintly. One Sunday – she was four at this time – he tried to teach her the alphabet, and she never forgot the smell of gin in his breath as he bent toward her with the alphabet card, pointing at the letters and pronouncing them in a loud, deep monotone.

Sylvia was nearly three when David was born. David was a shade fairer in complexion, and with his blue eyes could have passed for pure white. His arrival, however, in no way decreased Sylvia's popularity with her father.

2

Russell, through sheer charm of personality, soon retrieved his former popularity with the coloured middle-class, but Charlotte and his children remained in the background. Charlotte grumbled, and once he told her in disgust: "You're hopeless. You were born negative. I do my best for you, but you respond like a log. I can't inject you with the qualities you lack. I can't *make* you into a somebody if you won't try to be somebody. I've bought you books, I've bought you a Victrola and records. You give the books to David to destroy. You let Sylvia smash up half a dozen records a week or two ago."

Uncle, when he came on Sundays, supported Russell. Uncle would bellow at Charlotte in a deep, threatening voice. "There it is. Mr. Russell is trying his best to shape you up into a respectable lady, and this is all the thanks you have to give him! Grumbles and curses behind his back! Shame upon you, Charlotte! The gentleman has given you a *Chambers's Dictionary* and a *Pear's Cyclopedia.* And look! Shakespeare's plays! And that big cabinet gramophone! Why you can't uplift yourself with these things, eh? God meant us to uplift ourselves – not to lower ourselves in men's sight. You're an ungrateful girl. You will bring down Jehovah's wrath on your shoulders if you continue to lead this neglectful life and not raise yourself!"

One Sunday Uncle left her in tears, and Russell put his arm around her and tried to coax her. "I admit he was pretty severe on you. Uncle doesn't mean half he says – and you know what he can be like after two or three gins."

Sylvia was growing to fear her mother, for when Russell was not at home Charlotte would wreak her hatred and frustration on the child.

One morning Sylvia would not take her egg-flip. She said it did not have enough essence (it was generally flavoured with essence of vanilla). Her mother told her to drink it at once. "You not getting one drop more essence in it. Jest understand dat!"

"I'm not drinking it if I don't get more essence," muttered Sylvia. She was a spoiled child, accustomed to having her own way.

Charlotte grunted and turned off.

Sylvia sulked.

David drank his egg-flip, and began to suck at the froth left in the tumbler. He made a hissing sound. Sylvia told him to stop it. "Daddy says we mustn't do that. It's ill-mannered."

David went on doing it.

"Dave, don't you hear me? It's bad manners. Daddy says it is."

"Go 'way!" said David belligerently.

Charlotte turned upon Sylvia. "So you ain' drink dat egg-flip yet! Look, Sylvie, don't try me patience dis good morning! I going flog you bad if you don't drink it!"

"I want more essence."

"Ah going buss you' tail bad if you don't drink it!"

"Not drinking it. I want more essence."

Charlotte reached out and snatched the glass from the child's hand. She dashed it out of a window, caught Sylvia by the arm and dragged her into the kitchen. Sylvia shrieked and fought.

The iron stove was still alight with the remains of the fire that had heated the water for coffee that morning. Charlotte snatched up the long iron spoon the cook used for scraping out the grate, pushed it among the live, glowing chunks of firewood, scooped up a chunk, swung the spoon round and clapped the glowing wood against Sylvia's bare leg.

"Dat will learn you! Dat will learn you, you stubborn little bitch!" Charlotte threw down the spoon as Sylvia reeled off in strangled gusts of shrieking. "Your fadder can spoil you, but you not bringing it to me!"

Later that morning, she dressed the child's leg with lint and vaseline, and warned her that if she told her father what had happened she would get more. They were upstairs in Charlotte's room, and Charlotte spoke in a low voice, for the cook and housemaid, who had been out shopping in the market, had now returned. "You jest tell you' fadder anything and see if I don't hamstring you' tail!" Charlotte threatened.

Russell thought that the time had come for Sylvia to go to school. She already knew the alphabet and could count up to sixteen. He arranged for her to attend a private school for small children, kept by a Miss Jenkins in Camp Street.

Sylvia was delighted – and glad to be out of the house away from her mother. What increased her pleasure, too, was that her father took her to school himself in the new car he had bought. It was great fun, and the other children talked about it. Only three other girls had fathers with cars... "It's a Buick, and Daddy can drive it himself, but we're going to get a chauffeur soon, Mother says. Mother told Daddy that we have enough money to have a chauffeur, and Mother says Daddy must get one, but Daddy told her to go to hell..."

Miss Jenkins, who had overheard, pursed her lips and stiffened. She made no comment, however – it was recess time – until Sylvia said: "Mother says she knows a coolie who might take the job."

"You must not say coolie, Sylvia. You must say East Indian. A coolie is a labourer. All East Indians are not coolies. Many of them are well-to-do and live in big houses like the one you're living in."

Miss Jenkins smiled a friendly, good-natured smile. She was a pleasant lady of fifty, cultured and of a liberal outlook. A widow who had resumed her maiden name. She was a Trinidadian and had been married to one Mr. Newton, a New Zealander and the owner-manager of a cocoa plantation he had bought when he first came to Trinidad. Eight months after he had married Miss Jenkins he was drowned when on a Whit Monday beach picnic.

Five months later, a lady and two children had arrived in the island from New Zealand with full proof – marriage and baptismal certificates – that she was Mr. Newton's wife and Mr. Newton the father of her children. So great had been Miss Jenkins' humiliation that she had reverted to her maiden name and come to live in British Guiana, leaving her own son – born after his father's death – in the care of her married sister. She was coloured but passed for white. She moved among the whites exclusively. She was obliged to admit coloured children into her private school. She had white pupils, but these were so few that they would not have proved an adequate means of livelihood. However, only coloured children of good family and light complexion she accepted. In Sylvia's case, Sylvia failed on the grounds of family, but she had the approved shade of complexion. Furthermore, her father was English and a man of means, so Miss Jenkins had seen it fit to waive the family question.

Miss Jenkins was intrinsically a person with a strong sense of fair play and decency. She treated all the children alike, without any thought to race or class.

Sylvia was an attractive child. Her light-brown curls moved shiftily about her neck and shoulders, and gleamed with streaks of gold and red. She had large blue eyes with a touch of green, and when she smiled dimples appeared in her cheeks. She had a neat, well-set-up body, square shoulders, and walked with a natural grace. Miss Jenkins more than once commented upon this grace of carriage. "But isn't she a dear!" she smiled at Russell one afternoon. "She's a born walker, Mr. Russell. You ought to be proud of her."

"I am," Russell nodded. Later, in the car, he smiled at Sylvia: "Did you hear what Miss Jenkins said? She said you can walk. You're a born walker."

"And she said today I have pretty eyes, Daddy."

"She did? She'll be getting you perfectly vain before long."

"She's always telling me nice things. Not like Mother. Mother only says nasty things. Daddy, tell me the story about how you killed the snake in the jungle when you were building the bridge."

One day she came home and said that all the children had admired her dress and that Miss Jenkins, too, had liked it and had said that Mother tasted good in dressing.

Russell laughed. "You mean, she said Mother has good taste in dressing you. Yes, I agree. It's about the one thing she can do well."

Charlotte was so pleased at Miss Jenkins' compliments that she began to take special interest in Sylvia's clothes. She certainly had good taste in clothes, and was adept with her needle. Russell had bought her a Singer machine, and she designed and made dresses for the child as well as for herself. She had learned dressmaking, she said, with Agnes Feria, the sister of Teresa Feria (the girl who lived in Tiger Bay), and Teresa's cousin, Angela.

Before Godmother Gournal had adopted her at the age of thirteen, Charlotte had lived with her Arawak mother in the slums of La Penitence and Albouystown (for a short time in Tiger Bay, too). Her father, a negro punt-man on the Berbice River, who had never supported her mother, had been drowned in a boating accident when Charlotte was a year old. Charlotte's mother had earned a living by cooking in a Chinese cook-shop in Lombard Street; she had died of tuberculosis.

Within a short while dressmaking had taken a strong hold of Charlotte. She used one of the unoccupied bedrooms as her sewing-room, and soon her old friends of La Penitence and Tiger Bay, and relatives of Godmother and Uncle, began to visit her to discuss styles and to plan dresses.

Clarice Madhoo, a second cousin of Godmother's, came, and so did Agnes, Angela and Teresa Feria – "de whole Feria tribe", as Teresa once jokingly put it. Naomi Herreira came, too; she was a Eurasian girl: Portuguese and East Indian. And Sarah Johnson, a niece of Uncle's, a negress.

Since her marriage to Russell, Charlotte had seen little of these old friends. Godmother's daytime visits, then Uncle's regular Sunday morning sessions with Russell, and a furtive call by Clarice Madhoo or Teresa or Agnes Feria – who came to ask Charlotte for money when they were hard up – comprised all her remaining contacts with her old life. Her cronies had seen her as a lady of society, idle and pampered in this big High Street house, attended by servants and entertaining Russell's highfalutin' coloured friends. It was no place for them, this house. They were poor low-class strugglers: black and East Indian, Chinese, poor Portuguese, poor coloured; small-fry people who did embroidery work for a living, worked in cook-shops, or in Lombard Street dry goods stores for five shillings a week, or hired out their bodies when there was no work to be had. But now that it had got around that Charlotte had a Singer machine and was doing dress making, one by one they began to find the courage to come up to the big house. They felt that dressmaking gave them an excuse to come. Dressmaking put Charlotte back on the old level of interest and camaraderie.

They always took pains, however, to come when they knew Russell was out. Charlotte, too, in her cringing inferiority, saw to it that Russell did not come home and find them in the house.

Naomi Herreira always came on Saturday mornings because she liked to meet Sylvia, and Saturday was the only day when she did not have to help her mother. Her mother was an illiterate Portuguese who kept a dry goods stall in the Stabroek Market, and Naomi had to help her to sell. But on Saturdays Miss Herreira closed her stall and went up the East Bank to spend the day with a "friend" (rumour had it that this friend was Mr. Seeparran, the East Indian magistrate). She left Naomi to fend for herself in the little two-roomed cottage in La Penitence.

Naomi, who was nearly sixteen, was perfectly capable of fending for herself. She was a bright girl and could cook and sew and take care of the home. She had left primary school at thirteen, but was eager to better herself, and read as much as she could of whatever literature came into her hands. This literature generally consisted of *True Story Magazine,* the daily papers, the local Christmas annuals, and dream-books advertising kidney pills. Occasionally she dropped in at the barber's shop run by her father in Lombard Street – he was an East Indian called Sooknanan – and secured a ragged copy of *Tit-bits* or *Answers* or *News of the World.*

She took a great liking to Sylvia, and always brought her something when she came. A mango or a banana or a custard-apple. Or a cheap toy filched from her mother's stall in the Stabroek Market.

Charlotte was glad of Naomi's visits on Saturday mornings,

for it gave her more time for her sewing and dressmaking conferences with her visitors. The housemaid kept an eye on David, and Naomi took charge of Sylvia. Charlotte had complete confidence in Naomi. She had known Naomi since Naomi had been a small child. Cousin Clarice Madhoo was Naomi's godmother, and Naomi's father, Sooknanan, was a cousin of Clarice's husband, Charles Madhoo. Charlotte looked upon Naomi as "family".

Charlotte knew the hard life her friends and foster relatives led, and she was quick to do what she could to help them out whenever possible. She never let any of her visitors depart without offering her a meal. She lent them money – with the silently mutual understanding that it would not be returned. They brought her dress materials, and she made them dresses; sometimes they paid her, sometimes not; she never pressed for payment. To put them at ease she told them that she enjoyed dressmaking; the labour meant nothing to her.

One Saturday morning Naomi could not come, because her mother happened to remain in the city. Sylvia kept running to the gallery windows, on the lookout for her. When ten o'clock came and there was still no sign of Naomi, Sylvia, desperate, decided that something had to be done. She must go to the Stabroek Market and find Naomi. Aware that she was doing something that was strictly forbidden, she left the house and made her way south along High Street until she came to the railway crossing. Here she paused, dismayed at her own intrepidity. Suppose the train came up and killed her.

She noticed, however, that the safety-gates were shut, and cars and trams and people were moving along the street without fear. She got close up behind a lady in a green dress and crossed the tracks. The lady glanced round at her, and smiled, and Sylvia saw that she was a Chinese. "Hallo, little girl!" said the Chinese lady.

Sylvia took the avenue in Main Street, walking in the shade of the saman trees. It was a bright morning, but though bright not hot. The trade wind kept blowing all the while in cool gusts, and birds twittered and chirped in the trees and in the flower-gardens in the grounds of the big private residences. The residences where all the best people lived. Listening to the conversation of

Russell and his friends, she had gathered that Main Street was a street exclusively for the well-to-do.

So much confidence did she feel in the people she saw in Main Street – all of whom she assumed must be well-to-do – that when she came to the War Memorial she was not afraid or uncertain. She turned west along Church Street and then south into Water Street, and, in the distance, saw the Stabroek Market. She was passing the Museum Building with its tall white tower when a car came to a stop by the kerb, and two gentlemen got out and approached her. One was in a cream drill suit and the other in a light grey serge. She recognized them both at once. The one in the drill suit was Mr. Knight and the other was Mr. Dowden. Frank and Bertie, she had heard her father calling them. Often of an evening they would call her to the bridge or poker table and pat her head and smile at her and ask her how she was getting along. Mr. Knight and Mr. Dowden and Mr. Ralph and Mr. van Huisten. Her father's good friends.

"My God, but Sylvia!" It was Mr. Knight who spoke. "What on earth are you doing here all by yourself?"

Mr. Dowden uttered a thin, whinnying sort of laugh. He was a tallish, slim man of about twenty-eight, deep olive in complexion with kinky hair cut close to his head. His features were more European than negroid, and his eyes grey-brown. His air was the air of a man of the world. There was an amused, ironical twinkle in his eyes as he regarded Sylvia. To Sylvia, however, he appeared a pleasant, kind man, a friend of her father's.

Mr. Knight was shorter and more heavily built, of a lighter olive in complexion, with European features entirely, and his hair was jet black and bristly but not kinky; it was also closely cut. He had a black mole at the side of his nose that had always fascinated Sylvia. And his jet-black eyes, mocking and worldly, appeared to her friendly and good-natured. He was one of Daddy's friends, therefore he must be friendly and good-natured.

Albert Dowden was a Customs Officer, and came of a well-known coloured family. His father was the Chief Accountant at Cartwroth's, the big hardware firm in Water Street – not two blocks from where they stood. His grandfather had been the Reverend Barton Dowden, a Presbyterian minister. He was educated at Queen's College, and on leaving school at the age of nineteen, had immediately been manoeuvred into the Civil Service.

Francis Knight was the illegitimate son of a tinsmith, but at the age of seven he had been adopted by a wealthy coloured widow as a companion for her own son, an only child. He was a solicitor and a successful speculator, and had interests in virtually every business concern of any standing in the city. He was a Town Councillor, and had been Mayor of Georgetown on two occasions within the past seven years. At thirty-two he was unmarried, but an East Indian girl on the East Coast had borne him an illegitimate daughter. He was a charming man, though in many quarters he had such nick-names as Chicken Hawk and Widow-fleecer; it was rumoured that he had fleeced many a simple-minded, trusting widow, his own foster mother not excepted.

"Grantley would explode if we 'phoned him and told him," laughed Bertie. He bent down and fondled her under the chin.

"Where do you think you're off to, young lady?" asked Mr. Knight.

"Where's the young man you're eloping with?" Bertie uttered his whinnying laugh.

"I'm going to Naomi," said Sylvia.

"Naomi? Who is Naomi?"

"It's that Uncle fellow who goes to see Grantley on Sundays," said Bertie gravely. "It's he who's been telling her Bible stories. I hear he's a Seven Days Adventist or something equally blistering."

"Who is Naomi, Sylvia?" Frank Knight asked again.

"She's in the Stabroek Market. I'm going to the Stabroek Market."

"Oh, are you? So you think you're big enough to go out on your own, eh? Nothing of the sort, young lady. You're hopping into the car and going straight back home with Uncle Bertie and me."

"Who is Uncle Bertie?"

"Standing right before you," grinned Bertie.

"You're Mr. Dowden."

"There you are, Frank. She refuses to accept me as an uncle."

"Can I go to the Stabroek Market to Naomi, Mr. Knight?"

"No, you're going home. I don't know who you're talking about. What Naomi is this? Have you Jewish friends?"

Sylvia gazed blankly from one to the other of them. Her eyes grew watery, and her mouth began to twist preliminary to her bursting into sobs.

Bertie patted her head, and said: "There, there! Don't cry. Frank, let's take her to the Market. Just to humour her. We have an hour to spare before going aboard the *Chomedy*."

"All right, come along, you little monkey." Frank Knight lifted her into his arms and gave her a hug, then took her over to the car. "How did you know to find your way as far as here?"

"Daddy brings me early on Sunday mornings," she explained. "I always ask him to take me for a walk to the Stabroek Market on Sunday morning."

"But it's shut on Sundays."

"Yes, but I like to look at the clock and hear the clock strike. Daddy says it was built by Dutch people long ago."

Bertie whinnied. "Imagine Grantley getting out of bed early on a Sunday morning to take her for a walk! He's a bloody hero!"

"Guard your tongue, Bertie. She's only a kid, you know."

In the Market, they walked among the crowds from stall to stall. The crowds jostled them. The jabber and laughter and lisp of footsteps made her grip tightly the hands of her escorts. She walked between Frank and Bertie, each holding a hand. People stared at them, but she did not mind their stares. She wrinkled her nose at the smells. A thousand different smells. The butchers' stalls gave off the worst.

They passed furniture stalls, dry goods stalls, little chemists' shops, toddy booths, fruit-sellers, fisher-folk with trays of fish, a stall where old books were sold. She kept asking about Naomi. Where was Naomi? Did they know?

"Naomi who?" asked Frank. "What's her other name?"

"Naomi. Just Naomi."

"Afraid you have me beaten, child."

"Perhaps she's one of Grantley's indiscretions," mooted Bertie.

They bought her toddy and a bag of sweets. They were on their way out when Sylvia suddenly exclaimed: "Look! Look at Naomi!"

She pointed toward a dry goods stall far on their left, and they paused and looked. She tugged them forward and they allowed her to guide them to the stall where Naomi and her mother sat on stools before the step-like tiers on which bolts of cloth, lace, thread, bottles of perfume, cakes of soap and a miscellany of other articles were arrayed.

Naomi rose, a look of surprise on her face.

"Sylvie!"

Frank Knight looked at Bertie Dowden, and Bertie returned the look.

Naomi's mother had risen, too. She smiled at Frank and Bertie. "You bring her for a walk, na, Mr. Knight?" Her manner was simpering and ingratiating. "She's such a sweet lil' chile. Ow!"

"How did you know my name?" asked Frank.

Miss Herreira recoiled. "Ow, Mr. Knight! Ow! Who ain' know you! You wasn't Mayor of Georgetown year before last! Eh-eh I must know you!"

"Such is fame," murmured Bertie. He kept throwing furtive glances at Naomi, and Naomi, as though conscious of these glances, kept fidgeting on her feet and looking round her in an aimless fashion. She had large, dark eyes, and her complexion was pale olive. Two long plaits of dead-straight hair hung down behind her back. She was well developed in figure.

Her mother was over developed. In the print dress with dark-blue spots she wore her body looked like a pumpkin on the point of going bad. One prick, you felt, and she would come pulping out of her smooth, tight skin, though it would be firm, hard pulp that could be rapped with the knuckles. The knuckles would rebound. She was about forty, and her hair was cut in a bob, as was the fashion then. Her dark eyes kept goggling continually, as though she felt this would be fatal in its effect on every male who happened to be watching her.

"You like children, Mr. Knight?" she simpered.

"Sylvia got away from her home. I found her in Water Street – Mr. Dowden and I. She said she was looking for Naomi."

"Ow! Ow, Sylvie! Naughty chile! Get away all by you'self! Mudder must be worried. She was looking for Naomi, Mr.

Knight? Dis is Naomi. She my daughter. I sometimes goes to de East Bank on Saturdays wid a friend, but dis Saturday ah didn't go, so Naomi helping me. Ah generally shut up de stall on Saturdays."

"Well, look here, we'd better be moving along, Bertie."

"Naomi, you're coming with me?"

"No, Sylvie," smiled Naomi shyly. "I helping Mudder today."

"Can't you come home and play with me?"

"Ow! What a sweet lil' chile! Naomi busy dis morning, Sylvie. When annoder Saturday morning come she will come and see you."

"I want her to come now. Naomi, please come now."

"Couldn't you spare her?" asked Bertie, raising his eyes from Naomi's thighs. "We have a car outside. We could run her along to Mr. Russell's place with Sylvia."

Miss Herreira gave a melting wriggle. "Oh, you would like her to go! Awright, Mr. Dowdy. Certainly, Mr. Dowdy. If you want her to go wid Sylvie let her go. Ah will manage by meself for de morning."

Frank Knight drove, and he put Sylvia to sit beside him. Bertie sat in the back with Naomi, and once, as they moved north along Water Street, Sylvia heard Bertie utter his strange, horse-like laugh, and Sylvia glanced back to see Bertie's head bent close to Naomi. He seemed to be asking her something, but Naomi kept shrinking away from him and shaking her head.

Later, when Mr. Knight and Bertie were explaining to her mother what had happened, Sylvia stood in a corner of the room and watched her mother's face, a tension of fear slowly building up in her.

"Nothing at all to be upset about, Mrs. Russell," smiled Mr. Knight. "All children indulge in these pranks."

"I'm sure you were no better yourself at her age," laughed Bertie. He was casually stroking Naomi's plaits, one restraining hand on her shoulder. Please don't flog her. She won't do it again. Will you, Sylvia?"

Sylvia shook her head.

"Very well, Mr. Dowden and Mr. Knight. As you beg for her, Ah won't flog her. But she too hard-ears! She's a child who don't like to hear when you talk to her. Only blows she understand."

Mr. Knight laughed. "Weren't we all like that?"

Bertie whinnied. "Children can only be children. Trite but true."

Charlotte smiled through her scowls, overcome by their charm.

That day Frank and Bertie were heroes in Sylvia's sight. After they had gone, she said to Naomi: "I believe they are fairy-princes. Don't you think they're fairy-princes, Naomi?"

Naomi made no reply.

"Don't you think so, Naomi?"

Naomi smiled and grunted. "When you grow big you won't t'ink so."

"Why? Why won't I think so when I grow big?"

"Nothing," said Naomi. "Let's play doll's house. Come."

3

Events moved rapidly for Naomi, and one day, about three months after the Market incident, Naomi paid the High Street house a surprise visit. She came at five in the afternoon, on a Tuesday.

Sylvia was in the back-yard playing housekeeper to David and Henry. Henry Madhoo's mother – Aunt Clarice to Sylvia – often brought Henry to play with Sylvia and David.

Sylvia had just served David with his second cup of "tea" – the juice of hibiscus petals – when Naomi appeared. Sylvia dropped the teapot, ran up to her and hugged her. "Naomi! I didn't expect you!"

Naomi's response, however, was poor. Only a breathing sound came from her, and her eyes stared wide, and were red as though from much crying. What, thought Sylvia, could be the matter with Naomi?

"Where's you' mudder, Sylvie? She upstairs?"

"Yes. In the sewing-room. Do you want to see her?"

"She alone?"

"Yes, she's alone. But, Naomi, this isn't Saturday. Why have you come? Today is Tuesday."

"Oh, God," murmured Naomi. "Oh, Jesus." Her voice was distracted.

Sylvia followed her upstairs to the sewing-room. Charlotte exclaimed at sight of the girl, and for a long while she and Naomi sat talking while Sylvia stood by the Singer machine and listened. The conversation proved in no way intelligible, but she still listened.

She heard them discussing marriage and men and Naomi's mother – and Mr. Dowden. More than once Naomi cried: "But I doan' love him, Charlotte. I doan' love him. Ah tell Mudder dat over and over!"

"She ain' no mudder to you," said Charlotte, "to be forcing you to marry de man. Ow!"

"Mudder say he's a big-family man and he in a good Government job, and I is a fool not to see how lucky I am. But Ah still doan' want to marry him, Charlotte. Ah doan' like de man at all, and Ah tell him Ah don't like him. But he mad in love wid me, and he say he will kill himself if he doan' marry me."

"You' mudder ain' got no heart," said Charlotte. "I will tell she dat to she face. I know de young man. He is come here to Grantley to play bridge and poker. All dat ungodliness. And he got such a stupid laugh! Jest like a horse neighing!"

"Because Mudder whore out wid men she would like me to do de same. If I marry dis man it will be jest like if Ah turn a whore."

"And you only sixteen years old! God must punish her. Ow, Naomi! Ah hate dese high-colour people. Ah hate dem bad! Because they come from bigwig families and they got lil' education and good positions they think they can parade on poor people. It's nutting but advantage dat man taking of you. Ah bet you he wouldn'ta dare go to any good-class girl and force his attentions on her!"

"Since dat Saturday when Sylvie get away and go to de Market to look for me Ah ain' had no peace. Mr. Dowden always coming round to de Market and talking to Mudder about me – and Mudder encourage him. He wanted to take me for a drive to Scandal Point, but I refuse and Ah run away whenever he come to de house. Mudder beat me and say I is a foolish girl – if Ah doan' know de man is a Customs Officer and can give me anyt'ing Ah want! One night he come to de house, and he bring me a box of chocolates, and Ah tell him Ah doan' want dem, but Mudder mek me tek dem, and she mek me sit alone wid him in de house. He paw me all over wid his hands, but Ah couldn' do nutting because Mudder lock de doors, and she sit on de steps outside. And last night she tell me sudden dat he told her he want to marry me. He say I is de first girl he meet who he want to marry, and he ain' care how poor I is. And Mudder say I got to marry him. She say if Ah doan' marry him she will put me out de house and Ah will got to starve on de street." She broke into loud sobs.

Sylvia sobbed in sympathy.

Charlotte frowned, just growing aware of the child's presence in the room. "Sylvie! What you doing in here! Ent Ah tell you you mustn't listen when big people talking! Get outside! Fire you' tail out de room! Go back and play wid Henry and David!"

Not many days after Naomi's visit Sylvia overheard her father say: "Did Naomi tell you what's happened? Bertie Dowden wants to marry her." (Russell had come to hear of Naomi after the Market incident.)

"Yes, she told me," said Charlotte coldly.

"His people are in a fearful stew about it. They're threatening to disown him if he persists. Bertie was always an unpredictable chap."

Charlotte was silent. Sulky.

Sylvia sat on the floor making mud-cakes.

Russell laughed. "I've never seen a more complicated social set-up. Such a tangled mass of cliques and clans and sub-cliques and sub-clans!"

Charlotte uttered a long-suffering groan.

"Positively astounding how life goes on at all. There are the whites in an exclusive little corner of their own. Then the high-coloured coloured in various little compartments, according to good, better and best families, with money and quality of hair and shade of complexion playing no small part in the general scheme of grading. Take two steps aside and you're up against the East Indians in another cluster, with a hierarchy of their own, ranging from rice-miller to barrister-at-law and doctor and then down to bus-driver, chauffeur, provision-shopkeeper and sugar-estate coolie. Stumble around and you're face to face with the Chinese, either shopkeeper or business man. Stagger off a pace or two and you're sniffing at the Portuguese, split up into rum-shop-pawn-shop class and professional man class and big-businessman class. My God! If it isn't bewildering!"

"Hee-heep!" sniggered Charlotte. Her face as sour as a lime.

"What's the trouble?" said Russell.

"Ah notice," she said, "you ain' mek no mention of black man. Ah suppose black man ain' important enough."

"Ooops! A million pardons! By God, the black man! What a grave omission! Now, where does he come in?" He began to reckon with his fingers. "Shovel-man-scavenger. School-teacher. Policeman, fireman. Newspaper-reporter-lawyer's-clerk-bank-messenger-office-boy ambitious type who hopes to become an editor or a lawyer or get into the Government service. And, last of all, the imposing figures of the few who Have Got There. Doctors and barristers and solicitors whose one aim is to crash into coloured middle-class society!" He suddenly swept Sylvia up into his arms. Threw her up and caught her. "Goo-goo, my high-colour belle! Where do you come into the picture? What's your rating? Money but no family background. Good hair, light-olive complexion, European features. How will you end up, Goo-goo?"

A week later Naomi and Bertie Dowden were married in the Registrar's Office. Agnes and Teresa Feria and Clarice Madhoo came to discuss the sensation with Charlotte. They spent a whole half-day discussing it.

"Ah hear they going to live in a small cottage in Queenstown."

"De family raving mad. Ah hear his mudder say he must never cross de threshold of her door again as long as he live."

"Serve dem right! Ah ain' sorry. All dese big puff-up high-colour people – Ah never sorry when Ah hear they get tek down a peg or two."

"And his grandfather was de Reverend Barton Dowden, a Presbyterian parson. And he had a great-grandfadder who was a manager of Plantation Vyfuisheid on de West Coast – a pure white man.

"Ow! You see dis world, eh? Godmudder used to say: 'Tek heed he dat stand lest he falleth'. Ay, girl! Godmudder was a wise woman, yeh!"

"But, Charlotte, you realize dat but for Sylvie he wouldn'ta never meet Naomi! Is Sylvie who cause all dis!"

4

One afternoon, two weeks before her eighth birthday, Sylvia sat on the front steps and watched carrion-crows in the sky. Black and graceful against the blue, they circled, dived and soared. She thought it odd that they never collided. Suddenly she tired of looking at them. She watched, instead, the cars going past in High Street. The trams had stopped running. The tracks had been taken up. Buses and cars, her father had told her when she asked, had killed the trams.

She was waiting for her father to come home. Nowadays he worked at the Water Works. He had been promoted to this post about a year ago – through the influence of Robby van Huisten and Jack Ralph. Jack Ralph had been elected a Town Councillor, too.

Boodhoo, the East Indian gardener, was watering the plants in the garden. The late afternoon sunshine glittered in the jet of water that Boodhoo kept playing on the marigolds and zinnias. Abruptly he turned the nozzle of the hose round and sent the jet on to one of the tubbed rose plants. She could smell the fragrance of the flowers and the fresh water-smell and earthiness of everything. A kiskadee stood on the fence crying, "Kiskadee!" In the next yard, out of view, another one answered, "Key-y-y!" plaintively. Suddenly the one on the fence flapped its brown wings as the other one approached over a garage roof – the garage in which the Murdocks' car was kept – and cried, "Kisk-kisk-kiskadee!" in a kind of joyous challenge, its yellow breast bright in the sunshine, the feathers on its head lifting in a nervous crest. Both of them flew off into the star-apple tree across the street.

Here was her father. She ran down the steps and smiled and

waved, and he jerked his head and smiled back at her as the car flashed past and went under the house into the garage. The garage was built in between the tall brick pillars on which the house stood.

She sat at table with him while he had his tea (called lunch in Guiana), and when he had poured himself the second cup she said: "Daddy, I want to have a birthday party when my birthday comes week after next. Can I have it?"

He turned his head quickly and raised his brows in a quizzical way he had. "Birthday party? What's put that into your head now?"

"Myra Bertrand's birthday is today, and she's having a party."

"Oh, I see." He sipped his tea. He had no moustache nowadays. He had cut it off about a year ago. He was different in other ways, too. He fell frequently into thoughtful moods and was far less gay and boisterous. He had got stouter around the waist.

She watched his face. He seemed to be looking at the sideboard where the pink and blue glassware glimmered in the dying sunshine that came in through a western window – sunshine filtered through the foliage of a breadfruit tree in the next yard. She heard a kiskadee – perhaps the same one she had seen on the fence – kee-kee-ing mournfully. A car went past with a whoosh and a sharp blare of its horn. Boodhoo was still watering the plants; she could hear the hiss and rattling spatter of the drops on the fan palms near the gate.

"You weren't invited to the party, were you?"

"No, Daddy. Mrs. Bertrand asked the other children, but she didn't ask me."

He nodded, his face expressionless.

The Murdocks, next door, had a puppy – an Airedale. She could hear it yapping and snarling. It was always racing about in the back-yard with an old tennis shoe, shaking the shoe to pieces.

"Have you spoken to your mother about it?"

"No, Daddy."

"Well, tell her and see what she says, then we'll discuss it." She said nothing.

He stretched out and tweaked her chin. "You don't like the idea of telling Mother, I suppose?"

"She's not going to say yes."

He shrugged with an air of resignation. "I'll think it over."

There was something weary in his manner. When he was getting up he gave her arm a squeeze and asked her what she was going to do now. She told him that she was going across the street to the de Groots to see Jeanne de Groot and feed the rabbits. "Don't you want some more biscuits."

"No. But you can get my pipe."

She was off at once, and when she returned she filled it herself, for she was adept at it now. He had taught her how to shred the tobacco and roll it between her palms and how to pack it into the bowl of the pipe. She waited for him to light it, and when he smiled and nodded at her she knew that she had done a good job. She felt content and warm inside on her way across the street to the de Groots.

She always enjoyed herself at the de Groots. Besides rabbits, the de Groots had orchids. It was Mr. de Groot's hobby. He kept them in a shed roofed with dry palm leaves. A shady, mysterious shed. She and Jeanne went in there sometimes and pretended they were in the jungle, pretended that the hanging roots of some of the orchids were snakes.

Jeanne was nine, and had dead-straight black hair and a sallow-olive complexion. Her father passed for white, and her mother was light-brown, with hair wavy and heavy like the hair of a *douglah.* Both Mr. and Mrs. de Groot came of old coloured families. They had nothing whatever to do with Charlotte, but nodded and smiled at Russell. They welcomed Sylvia as though she were a sister of Jeanne's, gave her the run of the house, and let her go with Jeanne for walks to the Sea Wall or the Promenade Garden to hear the Militia Band on Monday afternoons. The year before they had invited her to a Christmas party held for Jeanne.

As the only daughter, Jeanne got everything she wanted. Her brother was eighteen and fair-complexioned like his father, and had secured employment on a sugar-estate as an overseer (the sugar-estates employed only white men as overseers); he was a ne'er-do-well who had left school at seventeen and had refused to be controlled by his parents. Jeanne had come unexpectedly into the world when her mother had long given up hope of having any more children. Her parents were extremely fond of her. She did not go to a private school, but attended the convent school in Camp Street, though her parents were Church of England. The Camp Street convent school admitted children of fair complexions only. Had Jeanne been a trifle darker she would not have passed muster.

Sylvia had asked her father to send her to the Camp Street convent school, but he had told her: "No, you couldn't go there. Your complexion is just a trifle on the wrong side – and, in any case, I don't want you to have anything to do with Roman Catholicism. The other Churches are bad enough with all the syrupy muck they serve up to bamboozle the masses – but the R.C. Church! Phew!"

After they had fed the rabbits, Jeanne suggested going up to her room to look through the *Children's Cyclopedia.* When they tired of that they shut the books and talked about themselves.

"Dad says I must start to learn music next term," said Jeanne.

"I'm going to begin soon, too," said Sylvia. "So Daddy says. Daddy says he wants me to be cultured."

"Beryl's sister played at the concert we gave for prize-giving."

"She's seventeen, eh?"

"No, only fifteen, but she can play pieces by Beethoven and Mozart."

"Miss Jenkins can play well, too. She likes Screwbert."

"Schubert."

"Oh. I thought it was Screwbert. She plays his 'Marche Militaire' for us some mornings, and we have to walk in time and take our places."

"Dad likes Schubert, too. He has his Unfinished Symphony downstairs in record albums. After dinner some nights he plays it on the Victrola. And once he asked Captain Fawcett to play it on the Militia Band in the Botanic Garden, and we all went on a Thursday afternoon to hear it. Mabel was there, too. She had on that dress with the different animals you like so much, remember?"

"Oh, yes. The blue elephants and pink giraffes."

Cars droned past in High Street, and the west grew red and orange. The room glowed softly with the tints of sunset. The air cooled and smelled of jasmines and leaves and earth. Poultry sounds came up from the back-yard. Duck-quacking and the squawk of a hen, the throaty gurgle of a rooster. Far off a dog was barking, the jerky gruffness of the sound blending with the low rumble of symphonic music being played next door on the Hammonds' gramophone. The room began to darken as a cloud like an anvil, slate-grey in hue, drifted across the reds and yellows in the west. The telephone rang downstairs, and footsteps came on the stairs. The negro maid came in and said: "Miss Sylvia, your mudder ring up to say you must go across home at once."

She found Boodhoo in the back-yard sharpening his cutlass under the star-apple tree. She reminded him about his promise to build her a rabbit-hutch, and he smiled and said: "Yes, missy. Me mek am for you soon. Soon as me get de box-wood. Next week time me go start on am."

She liked Boodhoo – his kind, dark, mild face and his slow way of moving about. One day Charlotte had shouted at him and called him a lazy good-for-nothing, and Sylvia had been so sorry for him that she had cried in the toilet. She had taken a sixpence from her savings-box and given it to him. "You must buy *ganja* with this, Boodhoo," she had told him.

The telephone rang as she entered the pantry. She went into the dining-room to answer it, but her father forestalled her. "I'm pretty certain it's for me, Goo-goo."

It must be the lady called Delly Simpson, Sylvia told herself. She had heard Charlotte referring to Delly Simpson. He went to Scandal Point with Delly in the car at night. Charlotte had told Agnes Feria one day: "Let him have his fling, me dear. What I care? So long as he doan' trouble me at night. I doan' want him no more. Let him carry on!" One day during a quarrel, he had told her: "But for Sylvia, I certainly would have left you a long time ago, I can assure you." Though she had not understood what the quarrel had been about, Sylvia had sided with her father. She always sided with him. Her mother was, she felt, in some way inferior to her father. Mother was no lady. She spoke and behaved differently from Miss Jenkins and Mrs. de Groot. Jeanne's mother and Miss Jenkins did not shout and wave their hands about and suck their teeth, and say words like "Jesus God!" and "shit" and "move you' ass". She did not respect her mother. For her she had only fear and dread.

Charlotte was calling her. She was in the sewing-room.

Sylvia went in and saw her sitting at the machine. Teresa Feria lolled on the couch near by smoking a cigarette, her long white legs sprawled out anyhow. Teresa, too, was no lady. Miss Jenkins or Mrs. de Groot would never have sat like that.

"Look, Sylvie, don't let me have cause to ring up to call you over in future. Ah can't understand why you got to haunt de people' house every day like dis. You mean you can't stay home *one* af'noon and play wid you' brudder or Henry?"

"Mother, David and Henry went to the Sea Wall, and you've told me I mustn't go there with them."

"Dat's a lie! Ah never tell you dat! Ah tell you not to go *after* dem alone. Ah never tell you you not to go *along* wid dem. You too pretensive. Ah suppose you feel Henry ain' good enough company for you, na? His skin too dark. Only dem high-colour children you want to talk to. But Ah suppose you can't help it. You' fadder always filling you' head up wid his ungodliness. You go and tek example from you' fadder! See where he going to end up before long! Gambling out his money at de club and taking Delly Simpson to Dixie in de car! Follow you' fadder example and you will prosper good!" Charlotte stamped. "Don't stand dere watching de floor as if you is a saint! Fire you' red ass out de room and go and do you' homework! Go on!"

Doing her homework in the next room, Sylvia overheard scraps of the conversation in the next room. Teresa was talking about Naomi's baby. "It just like de fadder, Ah hear, but it got good hair like Naomi's."

Charlotte grunted.

"God, Ah hear it's a shame," said Teresa, "de way he does beat her. He not too right in his head, Ah hear – and he is one o' de kind o' men who must beat a girl before he can get any fun. He beat her and bite her. One night, Ah hear, he beat her and put her out naked in de rain on de back-steps. De whole neighbourhood is talk about dem."

Grunting sounds from Charlotte.

"And he come from such a good family. It just show you!" Teresa sucked her teeth.

That night there was a quarrel between Russell and Charlotte, and the following afternoon Russell told Sylvia that the birthday party could not come off. "I warned you, didn't I?" he grinned, pinching her cheeks.

5

It was the custom, on her birthday, to lay her presents on her bed during the night so that she could see them first thing on opening her eyes. On the morning of her eighth birthday she awoke at a quarter to six. She could hear cocks crowing in the neighbourhood, and the Murdocks' pigeons were moaning softly. The air was cool and laden with water-vapour as though rain had fallen during the night.

There were four parcels. One was longish and shaped like a box. She knew what that one was. A pair of shoes. Charlotte always gave her shoes on her birthday. Last time, Russell had chuckled: "On your birthday it's shoes. At Christmas two yards of dress material. Christ!" Charlotte's presents never failed to be dull and uninteresting.

One parcel was from Aunt Clarice who had stood godmother for her at her christening, and, therefore, as a matter of duty, had to give her a present at Christmas and on her birthday. On her last birthday, Sylvia had overheard Henry saying to David: "Mother had to borrow money from your mother to buy a present for Sylvie!"

The second parcel was from David, who lay asleep on his back in the same bed with her. His present was a pink face-towel, exactly the same as Aunt Clarice's. He probably knew nothing about it. Charlotte generally bought something and wrapped it up with a slip of paper on which was written: "To dear Sylvia, from David, with many happy returns of the day."

She was sure the third parcel was Russell's, though it seemed flattish and soft, as though it contained cloth, and this seemed odd, for Russell's presents were always exciting – never simply a face towel or shoes or a handkerchief. She opened it and discovered that it was a small handkerchief with a lace border and her initials worked on it in pink thread. The card said: "With many happy returns of the day from Teresa!"

The light had brightened. The greyishness had gone, and the corners of the room were not so misty-dark now. She could see the sheen of the paint on the walls and the colour of the wardrobe. The Murdocks' Airedale puppy was yapping. It yapped whenever the newsboy threw in the paper at the front gate.

The box-like parcel contained shoes. The card said: "To dear Sylvie, with many happy returns of the day from Mother."

A car rushed past in High Street with a damp swish of tyres. The road must be wet. Rain must have fallen during the night. A smell of leaves and earth came up from the garden, and in the morning stillness she heard a donkey-cart rattling far off – perhaps down Barrack Street. The slow bong, bong, bong of the Angelus sounded blue and forlorn coming through the trees of Main Street and over the housetops. A lovely sound. Far more lovely than the greyness in this room.

The box with the shoes slipped off the edge of the bed and made a clip-clonk on the floor, but her eyes were so blurred with tears that she would not have seen it if she had leaned over to pick it up.

She heard a bed creak, and her father called: "Goo-goo, are you awake?" The sound of the box falling must have disturbed him. She called back: "Yes, Daddy!" in a croaking voice, and heard him grunt and mutter something about its being damned early to get up. He came in, nevertheless, wearing his purple-and-green dressing-gown over his pyjamas. He stifled a yawn and hiccuped. He seemed stale drunk. He sat on the bed and said: "Aren't you going to show me your presents?"

"This is from Aunt Clarice – a towel. And Dave has given me a towel, too. This is from Teresa – a handkerchief. And – and Mother gave me these shoes."

He scratched his head. "Four presents. But is there nothing from the old man?"

She was silent, her head bent.

He nudged her in the ribs. "You come downstairs with me. Have something to show you." He spoke in a tone of conspiracy.

She went downstairs with him. He led the way to the kitchen

and out through the back door down the back steps. The steps were wet.

A rooster in the Murdocks' yard crowed a hoarse, languishing crow, flapping its wings, and the ice-man's whistle shrilled thinly in Barrack Street. The star-apple tree dripped in solemn deliberation. Plep-plip! Plep-plip! Rain must have fallen very heavily, she thought.

He took her into the garage, and she exclaimed.

"But, Daddy, Mother said –"

He interrupted her with a guffaw – a reckless, rollicking guffaw. His old sort of laugh. The laugh he used to laugh when he had had his moustache. Not his dry laugh of nowadays that followed the twisted, weary smile. "Forget what Mother said. It's yours. I say you can have it, and there's an end to it. She could prevent you from having a birthday party by threatening to make herself objectionable to your guests, but I'll be damned if she can stop me from giving you what I want to give you!"

She touched the saddle to make sure that it was real. "Now I can go for rides with Jeanne to the Sea Wall and the Botanic Garden. Can't I, Daddy? If you say I can go I can go, can't I?"

"Certainly – and I do say you can go." He guffawed again and ruffled her hair. He hiccuped. "Let's go up. Chilly down here."

"You came in late last night, eh?"

"About two-thirty, I think. Got a head." He winked at her with an air of wickedness, and grinned as he urged her out of the garage.

"My word ain' got no count in here," snarled Charlotte. "I is jest dirt in dis house..."

Later to Agnes Feria: "Yes, child, he know very well Ah didn't want Sylvie to have a bicycle. All she going to do is ride about de city wid her high-colour friends and Ah won't know where to find her. Anyway, when a car knock her down they will take her to hospital. I wash my hands of her from dis day..."

There were pleasant moments, however, to compensate for her mother's gloomy truculence. Like the Sunday morning when Uncle did not turn up. He sent a boy with a message. "Mr.

Gournal send to say he down in bed wid bellyache, sah, and you must excuse 'im not coming dis morning."

"Too bad, too bad. What's the trouble?" asked Russell.

"'E eat pumpkin and shrimps last night, sah. At Cousin James' house. Shrimps is 'e *kinna,* sah."

"His what?"

"'E *kinna,* sah."

The housemaid gave a smothered laugh. "*Kinna* is somet'ing dat doan' agree wid you, sir," she explained.

"Ah! You mean he's allergic to shrimps. First time I've heard the term. African, I suppose. Must make a note of it. Anyway, tell him to buck up and get well. I'll look out for him next Sunday."

It was because of Uncle's not coming that Russell decided to take Sylvia and Jeanne to the Botanic Garden. They watched the manatees being fed, ugly and squat like solemn, whiskered old men poking up their dirty faces from out of the black water. Jeanne had brought her camera and took a picture.

They crossed over the arched bridge – the Kissing Bridge – to the islet in the artificial lake, and it was as though they had entered the jungle. The bamboos and palms and ferns and vines made a mysterious tangled wall around them. The sunshine came through in thin, shifty beams – and the air was heavy with the scent of dried leaves and fungus and strange blossoms. Sackies and coconut canaries made a lisp and twitter amid the fronds of a dense palm, and once they heard the squeak-squeak of bats, and Jeanne pointed up and said that there were bats asleep among the dead hanging branches of the palm. Yes, there were bats up there, Russell endorsed. He told them about vampires in the interior – the big bats that sucked your blood while you slept at night.

A hawk stood on the branch of a tall tree with spreading limbs whose trunk was hidden amidst the denseness of the bamboos. It gave screechy cries, and they could see other birds diving at it – a kiskadee and a grey coconut sackie. It ducked and opened its wings every time one of the other birds swooped close.

Jeanne was looking at the initials and hearts that lovers had carved on the trunk of a tree. The sun went under a cloud, and the shadows of the trees darkened and made the mystery of everything more uncertain. An insect clicked sharply amid the bamboos, and the blossom-scents thickened like an unseen swirling mist, sweet and choking and melting before they could breathe them in deeply.

There was the holiday Monday, too, when he took her with him to the picnic on the East Coast. They left in the car at seven, and stopped outside a big white house in Brickdam. Russell sounded the horn, and somebody in the house called out: "Rightee-ee-oh! Coming!" A lady's voice.

Shortly after, a fair-complexioned lady and a swarthy young man came down the steps. The lady was dressed in a short red skirt and a white stockinet shirt, and had a bathing-suit over her arm. She was bare-legged and wore tennis shoes. The young man – he was of a deep olive complexion – was in shorts, too, and sports shirt. The lady smiled and asked if this was the little film-star she had heard so much about.

"The apple of Grantley's eye," laughed the young man.

"She's a peach!" the lady exclaimed – and kissed Sylvia's cheek. She sat in front, Sylvia between Russell and herself. The young man got in behind. When they were moving off Russell said something to her, and he addressed her as Delly. This, thought Sylvia, must be the Delly Simpson who was the cause of all the talk at home. Later in the morning she discovered that the dark young man was Delly's brother.

They stopped in another street for some other people. A very dark – he could have been pure negro – gentleman of about Russell's age, with close-cropped kinky hair, and a sallow, stoutish lady who had a deep, chuckling laugh and showed a set of very white false teeth. The gentleman pinched Sylvia's cheek and remarked: "This your girl, eh, Grantley?" And the lady chuckled: "She has a sweet smile." This couple, Sylvia heard afterwards, was Mr. Grainger, the magistrate, and Mrs. Grainger.

When they had left the city and were on the country road, the grey Sea Wall on their left and the wide savannah lands on their right, Sylvia had a glimpse of the train. The train always fascinated her – its length of carriages and trucks and the smoke from the engine.

"Grantley, you should take her to Berbice one of these days."

"I mean to."

"There's Manny's car ahead of us!" exclaimed Delly's brother.

Sylvia was the only child on the picnic. Most of the time she kept looking round in awe at the grown-ups as they lolled about on the grass under a mango tree. A big lunch-basket stood near the base of the tree, and bathing-suits lay in pink and blue and green clumps on the grass.

The car with the gentleman called Manny – he was a Portuguese – had brought the lunch-basket. Another car had brought a portable gramophone. One or two couples danced; the grass did not seem to bother them; they got along as easily as though they were on a smooth floor. One young man who seemed to have had a lot to drink did a Charleston and kicked up tufts of earth and grass. Everybody called everybody else darling and sweetheart and sugarplum. Once, the Portuguese young man called Manny exclaimed: "What a sweet lil' girl Grantley got! Come to me, sugarplum!" He swept Sylvia into his arms and did a pirouette. Sylvia could smell the rum in his breath.

Russell very seldom noticed her. Most of the time he lay on his side talking to Delly. Everybody seemed to be split up into couples lying on their sides.

In the distance the heat trembled over the savannah where cows and sheep grazed, and far in the south trees could be seen – the beginnings of the jungle. In the west – Georgetown-way – stood a cluster of cottages amid coconut palms and one or two big trees with spreading branches. It was a village. They had passed through it on their way to this spot.

They were not far from a canal with muddy water, and now and then couples would disappear behind the cars, undress, get into their bathing-suits and plunge into the canal for a swim. Other couples wandered off in a northerly direction toward the Sea Wall. Her father and Delly took her on one of these jaunts, and when they got to the wall they stood in the blazing heat and looked out upon the ugly grey waste of sand and mud and grass.

In the distance the sea, grey, too, and drab, roared dully and with a low menace, as though wishing this wall did not exist so that it could come creeping over the grass and mud and sand and go rushing savagely into the village and savannah to drown and wash away cows and people, to crash its salty way through canefields and rice-fields and provision patches.

A steady wind – the trade wind – was blowing, and it smelt of fish and mud and grass. And the sea.

"The tide seems to be coming in," Russell said. He was holding Delly's hand. Delly nodded. Her head was tied with a bright-coloured silk scarf as protection against the sun. Her cheeks were slightly burnt. Russell's face was very red, his eyes weary-looking but alive and steady. Sylvia saw him glance at Delly, saw Delly look back at him and bite her lip. Her eyes narrowed. Russell gave a slight smile, and his shoulders moved just perceptibly in a shrug that could have meant anything.

Sylvia enjoyed the journey back to the city. The sun looked like a large round chunk of lipstick behind the blue-black clouds in the west, as though all the lips of the ladies in the picnic had come together to make it. She took a sidewise glance at Delly's lips. Both she and Russell seemed very quiet – and somehow at peace.

The air was cool and soft with the chill of night, and with the sweet, rankish smell of the Demerara East Coast; dry-weather grass and muddy canals and the iodine of the sea were contained in it, mingled with the sourness of rice-field water. Perhaps a whiff of coal-dust from a passing train was also part of the coolness and the soft chill that was not really a chill but simply a lessening of the day's heat.

The rice-fields, thought Sylvia, looked like a doll's jungle.

6

Shortly after her ninth birthday there was a disaster.

Jeanne's father, who was a civil servant, received orders that he had been transferred to Springlands, on the Corentyne Coast. Sylvia looked at the map of British Guiana at Miss Jenkins' and saw that Springlands was at the extreme eastern end of the coast – far away in Berbice. Over a hundred miles from Georgetown.

She felt breathless with misery as she stood on the platform at the station and watched the train move out. Jeanne and Mrs. de Groot kept waving – Jeanne a tiny green handkerchief and Mrs. de Groot a pinkish silk scarf. There were other friends to see them off. Fair and olive people. Several of Jeanne's other chums – Beryl Dell and Mary Pimento and Frances Harris and their parents. Once Sylvia overheard Mrs. Dell whisper to Mrs. Harris; "That's Russell's child. Remember that half-Buck girl from La Penitence he married?"... "Oh, is that the child?" whispered back Mrs. Harris.

Sylvia left in a hurry and without waiting for Beryl and Mary who had come with her to the station in the de Groots' taxi.

"You'll make other friends before long," Russell told her that afternoon. "Don't let it get you down." He gave one of her curls a playful tug. "Tomorrow we'll go to the Botanic Garden. How's that?"

That same afternoon, when Sylvia returned from music lessons at Miss McTaggart's, she heard Charlotte talking and laughing in the sewing-room with Janie Pollard, a girl who dressed and painted up like Teresa – except that Janie was black. Charlotte said: "De family across de street gone to Berbice. Ah want to see now who Sylvie going to tek up wid!"

Janie said: "Ow, Charlotte! But de poor chile must have friends!"

Charlotte sniggered. Laughed. In the sound was a mean, cruel pleasure. There could be no doubt, felt Sylvia, Mother was a low person.

Soon came awareness of the real and the ugly.

One afternoon she was in the dining-room when Teresa came in (all her mother's friends came in through the back). Teresa smiled in her usual way and said: "Hallo, Sylvie!" But when Sylvia approached her and proffered her face to be kissed Teresa waved her hand in a negative gesture and moved on. Sylvia, surprised, said: "Don't you want to kiss me?" Teresa gave a queer smile. "Na, man," she said. "Not today." She seemed embarrassed, and hurried upstairs, leaving Sylvia curious and a little hurt.

A few afternoons later Sylvia overheard Sarah Johnson say to her mother in the sewing-room: "So Ah hear Teresa pick up a dose." Charlotte mumbled something inaudible.

"You better see she don't kiss Sylvie when she come here, Charlotte."

"No, Teresa won't do dat. She know better."

This conversation puzzled Sylvia so much that she tackled her father about it when he was at tea the following afternoon. "Daddy, what does it mean to pick up a dose?"

He glanced at her sharply. "Where on earth did you hear that phrase?"

"Sarah Johnson told Mother yesterday afternoon that Teresa had picked up a dose and that she mustn't kiss me when she comes here."

"Oho." He sipped his tea.

"What did she mean? Why can't Teresa kiss me?"

"Because she's diseased," he said, staring at the sideboard.

"Diseased? You mean that little boil she has on her lip?"

He nodded, his eyes with a faraway look. He set down his cup and explained to her in detail what sort of disease syphilis was and how it was contracted. He spoke in an even, unemotional voice.

He sounded in no way alarmed or shocked or put out. She was profoundly impressed.

"But why," she asked, "did she have to be in bed with a man?"

"Ah," he said, and winked solemnly. "That's Chapter Two."

He rose. "Come into the gallery with me, and I'll tell you Chapter Two. Go and get me my pipe."

He settled down in the Berbice chair. She sat on one of the long projecting arms, and he told her about sex and babies.

Yes, she had heard about babies, she said, coming out of their mother's bellies. Jeanne had said that she had overheard Mabel Thomson's elder sister talking about it to another girl. But they had talked about it in whispers, and Jeanne had said that you mustn't let people hear you discussing such things. It was not nice.

"She was perfectly right. Children are not supposed to know anything about such matters, and I was going to warn you not to speak about it to any of the girls at Miss Jenkins'."

"You mean it's just a secret between you and me?"

"That's it. A secret between you and me. You see, Daddy ought not to have talked about it to you, but Daddy often does things that everybody doesn't approve of. That's why most people don't consider him a nice man."

"What! But that's not true. Of course you're nice!"

He gave her a gentle nudge, and smiled at the corner of his mouth. He kept puffing at his pipe all the while and staring up unconcernedly at the roof of the gallery. A mason-marabunta had built a mud nest near the porcelain rosette from which the drop-cord of the light hung. The smoke from his pipe drifted up and made a blue mist around the mud nest. She watched it and felt troubled.

"When you get older you'll see why people don't think me nice."

"But you have a lot of friends." She found herself wanting to cry.

"Oh, yes. I don't deny it. At least, I call them friends for lack of a more convenient term." He nudged her again, and broke into a slow smile – a smile full of affection and a quiet amusement. "I'm rotten at explaining things, Goo-goo."

She stroked his hair and noticed that one or two grey hairs streaked the yellowish-reddish fairness of his head. "Why didn't you and Mother have any more babies after David?"

"Because I was afraid another sweet little creature like you might have come along, and I couldn't stand seeing it suffer." He patted her knee. "How are you getting along with Miss McTaggart? Can you play the Moonlight Sonata yet?"

"Oh, heavens! I don't think I'll ever be able to play anything so difficult. I'm playing scales now, but I don't like it, Daddy. It's dull."

"Well, don't do it against your will. Chuck it up as soon as you get fed-up."

"But I'd like to play. I'd like to play dance pieces."

"Your taste lies that way, does it? Bloody Philistine! One of these days I'm going to teach you to dance. Would you like to learn to waltz and foxtrot and one-step and all the rest of it?"

"Of course! Beryl's sister can dance all the latest dances."

The telephone was ringing.

"That's for me," he said, and got up – but not in a hurry." Daddy, do you and Delly have sex together?"

"Eh?" He went red, then laughed and nodded. "Yes. Used to. Christ! What a question! Took me off my guard, hang it!" As he was going into the sitting-room he glanced back at her and grinned: "Nowadays it's Jessie, though – but mum's the word!"

She knew it was wrong to listen when anything private was being discussed – Miss Jenkins had scolded them at school about this – but she could not resist the temptation. She seated herself in the sitting-room just beyond the door that gave into the dining-room, so that she could eavesdrop. The conversation he was going to have with Jessie was sure to be about sex and babies.

"Well, that's left to you," he was saying… A long pause. "I should think so. Two, three of them if you wish…"

"Yes…"

"Was Knight with them? I didn't know that…"

"Yes…"

He whistled. "What!…"

"Yes, I've heard those tales about Knight before…"

"A promissory note for six thousand?…"

He laughed – the guffaw she liked so much.

"No, I don't believe that, Jessie…"

"Chewed it up and ate it – the promissory note!…"

"Sounds tall to me. I can't see Frank doing such a thing…"

She was suddenly bored and disappointed. The eagerness to listen left her. She looked round the sitting-room slowly, at a loss to know what to do. It had darkened. It must be after six. She glanced out of a window and saw the leaves of the star-apple tree purple-black against the bright yellow in the west. The wind had fallen to a soft hum around the building, cool and bringing into the house the scent of leaves and grass and flowers. It always reminded her of Jeanne when she smelt flowers and leaves.

She listened to the cars rushing past – one with a whooming swath, another droning and tooting, another soft and with a singing purr. People were going for drives to the Sea Wall and to the East Coast. White people and well-to-do coloured people. Rich Portuguese and East Indians. Some of the cars would park at Dixie – or Scandal Point, as some people called it. They would stay there until night came down so that the people inside them could have sex together in the dark, as they did every evening just as Daddy had just told her. He himself, he had said, went there some nights. Nowadays it was Jessie – but mum's the word!

Something occurred to her. It must be sex that her mother and Agnes and Teresa and the others talked about in the sewing-room in quiet voices! A pleasant, excited feeling moved in her. She felt as though she had just made a tremendous discovery about life and people. She began to feel afraid. She listened to the trees rustling in the low breeze – the big sandbox in the Frances' yard, the mahogany in the Murdocks' yard – and the sounds seemed to contain a future threat. A grey jumbie wreathed between them. The pigeons were moaning over at the Murdocks', and from the kitchen came the smell of cooking. Fried yellow plantain. She stirred uneasily. The fan-palm at the gateway had just made a muttering in the breeze.

A car went past in a blue streak... Two people, a man and a lady, on their way to Dixie. For a little sex.

7

Jeanne wrote her about once a fortnight at first, then once a month – then not at all.

In her first letter Jeanne said that she was not staying with her parents at Springlands but was "bording with the Brankers in New Amsterdam they have a nice black Dog called Jet and hes not cross only at night, I'm going to the convent in New Amsterdam the nuns are nice but its not the same as in George-Town some of the girls are black in this convent and even Chinese and east-Indians oh child our French nun is too sweet I like her best of all..."

Sylvia told her about the girls at Miss Jenkins' and the people who had "come to live in the house where youall lived, they're portugeese people and Mother says she knew them as a child in Lapinatense they had a saltfish shop and were common, common ordnary people mother says but now they have plenty money and they have got Proud and think themselves too good to speak to ordnary people like what they knew Before, Miss mc-TaGGart says she wants me to sit First grade in music but I dont know if I could pass it I want to play jazz and daddy bought a Poartable gramafhpone for me and some Records and he says I am a good dancer because he taught me to do some steps in waltzes and foXtrots and I did it nicely he says I have grayce he says I am a born dancer and child I had a big surprise when who came to see me Beryl and Mabel came and rapped Wensday afternoon and David went to the door and then he called me and said two girls to see me and when I went out it was Beryl and Mabel and they said they came to go riding with me their parents said it was all right Daddy was surpriZed when I told him you should have seen him open his eyes and say what happen their parents said it was all right, He said he thought the colour bisness and Family would have made their parents say no since then Beryl and Mabel come a lot of times to go riding with me and we're good friends now but Mother as usual is vexed because I go out with them, She says why I must be always looking for these HighColour girls to be friendly with but DaDDy says its because Mother is too Inferioour thats why she behaves like that and hes right, Im learning plenty things from Daddy He talks to me and tells me plenty things and we have Secrets I wish I could tell you some but its a secret between us and He says when I get older he will tell me more things when I can understand them, well child my hand is tyred from writing such a long letter don't take long to write next time and write Plenty like this Letter Tell your mother and father I send my love and thanks for sending me their Love, I remain yours loving friend Sylvia."

In September 1933 she began to attend Bishop's High School. She wore a green uniform and a straw hat with a band bearing the letters B.H.S. Murray Street became a magic street where she tinkled her bicycle bell for the sheer joy of hearing it tinkle in the bright sunshine of three o'clock, because school was over for the day, and in an hour or two she would be returning for Games.

Some days the boys from other schools waylaid the girls to tease them. They whistled and threw gravel or palm seeds and uttered queer calls and snarling sounds as though they were wild beasts. Among them was a tall, slim Portuguese boy who was very handsome. He had a hooting, gay, adventurous laugh.

Doing her homework in the evenings, she would think back on the days at Miss Jenkins' and remember the girls there and how nice Miss Jenkins was and how sorry she had been to leave, but, anyway she was getting old – she was in two figures now; one and a nought, and soon it would be two ones – and life had to move on, as Daddy had said one Sunday. You couldn't always remain a Miss Jenkins girl.

"Quite right! Quite right!" Uncle had agreed. "The world moves on, my child, day to day we keep travelling toward the Promised Land. Cast your eyes around and see what's happening in the world. Aeroplanes in the sky, and cars travelling at three hundred miles an hour – and soon we will be having war again. Ah, yes! It's coming. You see the new man in Germany what he's doing for the country! They made him Chancellor. Keep your eye on that man. You don't agree with me, Mr. Russell?"

"Who? Adolf Hitler? Oh, I believe he's just an upstart. Another of these political cranks like Mussolini. He won't cause a war."

"Ah! But read the Scriptures, Mr. Russell. Don't follow the course of events as recorded by men. I know you scoff at the Holy Word, sir, but I tell you, when I read my Bible and see the prophecies! Ha! It must come, Mr. Russell. God's word must be fulfilled. Jehovah's wrath must descend upon the wrongdoers that abound –"

"Have another drink, Uncle."

"You take that Book and see what it says!" – gug-gug-gug from the cut-glass decanter – "You read what the prophets say! Turn to Isaiah –"

"Or Jeremiah."

"Yes, or Jeremiah..." Gug-gug... Clink. "A-a-ah! Good gin, this, Mr. Russell. Excellent gin!..."

Upstairs sounded the whirring of the Singer sewing-machine. Over at the Frances' Mrs. France was playing hymns on the piano, and the Murdocks' gramophone competed with "Lullaby of the Leaves". Coconut sackies and blue sackies twittered in the star-apple tree in the backyard, and a dog was barking in the street. And the cars. Whoom and whoosh... To Dixie. To the Sea Wall... To Belfield Hotel... "Lullaby of the Leaves."...

The day before she had danced to the same piece with her father when she had put the record on her own portable gramophone. She glanced out of the window. The sun shone brightly, for this was the long dry season, and the days were hot and blazing. After lunch her father was going on a picnic on the East Coast, but she would not go. He did not take her to picnics nowadays.

"You're of an age," he had explained, "where the company of my sophisticated friends might be more harmful than beneficial for you." Every day his eyes grew more weary-looking. One day, a few weeks ago, he had told her: "This business of living can be a barren affair. Pleasure, Goo-goo, without an oriented outlook, affords no satisfaction. That may be above your head, but never mind. I like saying profound things to you."

"Daddy, why couldn't you and I go away somewhere together alone and not come back?'

"We've done that many times – in my imagination."

"But why couldn't we do it really?'

"Because life has complications – money and people. For instance, there's the Chicken Hawk. I've got to keep my eye on him."

"The Chicken Hawk?"

"There's a gentleman called the Chicken Hawk. I've got to watch him closely or I might be penniless."

"You mean Mr. Knight?"

He guffawed. "You know his nickname, eh?"

"Yes, I've heard people calling him that. And Widow-fleecer."

He put a finger to his lips and winked. "Mum's the word!"

Now it was "Stormy Weather". And Mrs. France was playing "Oh, Happy Band of Pilgrims" – and a car in High Street streaked it all out with a long blare of its horn. Two kiskadees were fighting in the star-apple tree – or it might be a little sex they were after. She heard Henry Madhoo and his friend shouting. They were in the backyard playing. Henry nowadays tolerated David only because Charlotte would have been offended had he stopped being friendly. Henry considered himself a big fellow and had other friends of his own age. David, five years younger than Henry, worshipped Henry and his friends, and followed them everywhere. He imitated them in everything. David, though nearly three years Sylvia's junior, was already as tall as she was. Teresa had remarked one day: "It look as if Sylvie going to be short. It must be the Buck blood. All Buck people short." And Janie had rebutted: "But she got good looks, though. Dat what matter most, chile."

One afternoon in October of the following year, 1934, she came home from school to find Teresa and Agnes and Janie in conference in the dining-room. Teresa had got over her syphilis – she had been privately treated at Charlotte's expense – but she seemed debilitated and dowdy these days; her skin looked cracked with powder and rouge. She was thinner, too. Agnes had got thinner, too, and had a cough that refused to go away. Janie, much younger than either of them, still retained her youthful, flashy appearance.

"You' mudder take ill," said Teresa. "De doctor upstairs wid her."

"What's the matter with her?"

"A bilious attack."

"It's jaundice," Janie said. "Her godmudder dead of de same t'ing."

"You shoulda see what she vomit up! Green and yellow stuff."

Later, the doctor told Russell that it was serious. She was in a low condition. Russell shrugged and said that he was not surprised. "She stuffs herself from morning to night with a lot of rich, indigestible food, and takes no exercise at all. Sits all day at that sewing-machine."

The doctor sent a nurse – a youngish negro woman with a pleasant manner and an intelligent face.

All night Charlotte moaned and called upon God and her heavenly Saviour. The whole house reeked of bay-rum. Sylvia could not sleep. About midnight she went into her father's room and found that he was awake, too. He sat by the window looking out at High Street.

"Not asleep yet, Goo-goo?"

"No, I couldn't sleep."

She seated herself on the arm of his chair. He was smoking a cigarette. The smoke curled out of the window like a shapeless jumbie.

"Daddy, you think she's going to die?"

He shrugged.

Tree-frogs were chirruping in the garden below. She could feel the dampish chill in the air; it seemed to come up from the plants in wisps of invisible water. The fragrance of flowers came up with it. Flowers and grass and tree-leaves. She watched the dark plumes of coconut and cabbage palms interspersed between the housetops. The stars glittered in millions; she could not see a cloud anywhere. For no reason at all she thought of the tall, handsome Portuguese boy. A girl had told her last week that his name was Benson Riego.

Charlotte was moaning again. They could hear the nurse murmur.

In the reflected light from the street lamps she could make out her father's face clearly. He seemed solid and real: something she could depend upon. Trust in utterly.

"I just saw a star pitch."

"A meteor," he corrected.

She could hear the clock on the dressing-table. Ticking.

Somewhere in Barrack Street an owl was tooting. She had heard Aunt Clarice say that when an owl tooted it was a sign that somebody in the neighbourhood was in the family way. She liked to hear an owl toot late at night – especially if the night was a moonlight one and she was smelling the fragrance of stephanotis from the arbour in the Hammonds' garden. It gave her a feeling of complete snugness and safety.

Footsteps on tiptoe sounded in the corridor. It must be the nurse.

The ticking of the clock beat like an intelligent pulse in the dark. They heard the flushing of the toilet.

The Stabroek Market clock struck a solemn bong!

Charlotte moaned.

Sylvia remembered something she had overheard Rachel the cook say one day to Milly the housemaid. It was about a Sick-mamma. Rachel had told how her aunt had been sick for a week and was groaning all the time. Then the Sick-mamma caught the groaning – "yes, it ketch de groaning," Rachel repeated – and they heard it under the bed, and sometimes outside just under the window. Rachel said it was a sign of death when the Sick-mamma made itself heard – a sure sign. And that same night her aunt died.

Sylvia's skin began to tingle. She looked round slowly into the corners of the room.

When the Stabroek Market clock struck two o'clock, Russell insisted that she should go back to bed. She obeyed, and, to her surprise, found that she was tired. She fell asleep at once.

Her head was throbbing when she awakened. It was ten to five by David's luminous watch which he had got on his ninth birthday. He always hung it up on a nail on the wall at the head of the bed. The room was still thick with darkness, and she closed her eyes tight and listened to see whether she would hear the Sick-mamma.

Charlotte seemed to be asleep. She was not moaning.

Sylvia turned over and tried to go back to sleep, but sleep would not come. The deep travelling boom of the cannon at the old Dutch fort rammed powerfully through the stillness, as it had been doing every morning at five and every evening at eight since the days of slavery. An alarm-clock tinkled somewhere in the neighbourhood, and a donkey brayed in Barrack Street. A network of cock-crowing began : thin, wistful ghost-wires of sound crossing and re-crossing each other. Past and between the trunks of coconut and cabbage palms and the foliage of breadfruit and mango trees. Star-apple trees and saman trees. Early-morning Georgetown sounds; they soothed her throbbing head somewhat and made her forget about the Sick-mamma.

The thought occurred to her that perhaps her mother was dead. That must be why she was not moaning. She opened her eyes and stared round the room, listening to the last leisurely notes of the bugle at the barracks at Eve Leary sounding the Reveille.

Charlotte, however, was not dead. Within a fortnight she could sit in the easy chair in her room, weak and hollow-cheeked but definitely alive. Irritable and abusive. She swore at the nurse in filthy language. One Saturday morning she dismissed the house-maid because she discovered a small fly in the glass of milk the girl brought up for her.

She was completely recovered when, on a Monday morning, the news of the sensation concerning Naomi broke on Georgetown. Sylvia heard it at school. One of the girls, Mavis Deeble, lived next door to the Dowdens, and Mavis said that the Dowdens had received a telephone message from New Amsterdam saying that Bertie Dowden was dead. He had shot himself in the bathroom.

Sylvia exclaimed: "I know him. He used to come to play bridge with Daddy years ago. Long before he was married and the Government transferred him to New Amsterdam. He used to live in a cottage in Queenstown in the city here when he first got married. I knew his wife, too. When she was single she used to come and see Mother every Saturday morning."

They crowded round her. "You knew his wife? And the man who shot himself? You knew him, too?"

"I hear he wasn't too right in his head," said Mavis. "He used to beat his wife and put her out naked in the rain." She added this in a lowered voice.

When Sylvia got home, she went to her mother's room and found Janie Pollard and Agnes Feria with Charlotte. She gave them the news, and there were loud, expressive exclamations and comments.

The next morning it was in the newspapers, but the papers played it down. They tucked it away into an inconspicuous corner on a middle page and gave it a one-column headline in small type: *Government Official Found Dead.* The text simply stated that, after hearing a loud report, Mrs. Dowden rushed upstairs to discover her husband in a bleeding condition. He died in hospital.

"See dat! Not a mention of no gun or revolver! If it was a low-class person you woulda hear all de details, but because he come of a big family they trying to hush it up." Charlotte spoke bitterly, and Agnes and Teresa and Janie and Sarah, who had all come to discuss the tragedy, agreed with her.

"Yes," said Teresa. "If it was a common Puttagee like me it woulda splash all over de paper."

"What to do, child?" said Janie. "Dis world ain' fair. So long as you got lil' position and money and a fair skin you can do no wrong."

Sarah brought up the instance of her brother, a bus-driver. He had knocked down an old man in Regent Street and killed him, and the newspapers had put it in headlines on the front page. "And day after day when they was trying Freddie for manslaughter de newspapers used to publish long reports on de case. Why? Jest because de old man was a coloured man of good family and his people got money!"

Sylvia, who overheard this, asked her father whether it was

true that the newspapers always tried to hush up sensations like the one about Bertie because of family influence.

"I suppose you heard that from your mother and her Tiger Bay friends. Yes, quite often that sort of thing happens. It's no untruth."

"But, Daddy, what is there in family and colour? Why does Mother talk so much about it? Aren't we a good family?"

He laughed. They were in the Botanic Garden and had paused by a canal to watch the round, wide, floating leaves of the *Victoria regia.* "I've been waiting for years to hear you ask me that." He looked up into the beard-like foliage of a huge tree. "Now, let's see. Are we a good family or are we not? It's a question I dread having to answer, but we must face it, mustn't we?" He gave her a grin. "Strictly speaking, we aren't a good family."

He went on to tell her how the society in the colony was graded. If he had married a white lady, yes, they would have been one of the very best families. But as he had married her mother, whose parents had been black and Arawak Indian and who did not come of an old and respected family, well, his family wasn't rated as much, if she saw what he meant.

"But don't let that scare you too much. If you can succeed in marrying a man of good family you'll be all right, because I'm white, an Englishman, and I'm no pauper. That will count heavily in your favour. Mother will be forgotten and overlooked in the general reckoning."

"But what are good families? Are there any good East Indian and Portuguese and Chinese families, or must I only choose from the good coloured families? And what about the black people? Have they no good families, too?"

He shifted his feet about and cleared his throat. "Well, I'll tell you what. If I were you I'd give the Portuguese, the Chinese, the East Indians and the blacks a wide berth where choosing a husband is concerned. It seems absurd that I should be talking to you about such things as choosing a husband at your age, but it's no harm – and, of course, all this is between us, eh? Our secret?"

"Our secret. Mum's the word!"

"Mum's the word! Excellent. Look, there's a plantain bird. Haven't seen one for a long time. Over there – near that clump."

"Oh, yes, I see it."

"Well, I was saying. You give the Portuguese and the coolies and the Chinese and the black people the go-by and stick to the coloured, and I'll tell you why. The Portuguese and the East Indians and the Chinese only came to this colony as immigrants – that's to say, they came as labourers and shopkeepers. The East Indians worked as indentured cane-cutters and shovel-men and so on on the sugar estates, and the Portuguese and Chinese set up in business as provision-shopkeepers. That happened within the past sixty or seventy years. The East Indians and the Chinese and the Portuguese, being good at saving their money, gradually became rich people. The East Indians left the estates and came to town and turned shopkeepers, too, and some planted rice in the country and piled up money that way. The black people came here over two hundred years ago – some later – and they were slaves –"

"You mean under the Dutch? Oh, yes, Miss Crandon told us in school how the Dutch used to treat the black slaves. Beat and torture them."

"The English, too. They saw old Harry under both Dutch and English. They were freed only a hundred years ago, and, poor beggars, they're only now really beginning to shake off the under-dog feeling. As you know, we have one or two black barristers and doctors and magistrates. But these are exceptions, and they lead a precarious social existence, anyway. Most of the black people are poor, half-fed, half-literate sons of guns struggling their way up to be postmen or policemen or lawyers' clerks and bank-messengers. That rules them out for you, naturally, because you don't want to live in poverty, do you?"

"Of course not. I'd like a car and a Victrola and radio and two big houses – one in town and one in the country."

"That's it! That's it, by George! Bloody lady of society, what!" He saluted her. "Poverty is no good, Goo-goo. No good at all. Now, the Portuguese and the Chinese and the East Indians are somebodies today in the world of money, but, socially, they're still considered inferior. The background of a genteel past is lacking. Their grandfathers and grandmothers were ordinary ignorant estate coolies or Jose-and-Maria saltfish vendors or

Hong Kong peasants. They have nothing to look back on and so are not respected. All bunkum, of course, because a man should always be judged by what he himself is – not by what his ancestors were. But I'm telling you what is – not what ought to be. I'm being a realist. I'm telling you what sort of world you're growing up in and suggesting how you should tackle it if you want to be tolerably happy in it –"

"I'm sure I must be happy. I'm going to live to seventy and be happy every day."

"I bow, and applaud your optimism." He lit a cigarette and went on to tell her about the social set-up. The Portuguese and East Indians and Chinese were clannish groups. A Portuguese for a Portuguese, an East Indian for an East Indian, and so on. And the Portuguese were Roman Catholics and inclined to be intolerant of people of other creeds. The East Indians were cunning, and had not yet lost their Oriental craving for intrigue and mystery. The educated ones, the doctors and barristers, were, of course, thoroughly westernized, though many of them were stupidly nationalistic and never failed to let you know how proud they were to be Indians descended from Indians of India. The Chinese group was the most tolerant of the three, but even the Chinese were nationalistic and exclusive in their policy. So, by a process of weeding out, she had the coloured middle-class remaining from which to choose a husband, for the whites were always far outside the pale. "Never to be considered for a moment," he said, shaking his head. He tapped his chest. "Me? Oh, I'm a freak. I deviated from the conventional pattern. That's how I came to marry your mother. Cases like mine are as rare as pink mourning. To continue, however. Now that you've wound me up I don't want to stop. The coloured middle-class have Background. In the far past, their ancestors were Dutch and English and Scottish planters – the de Groots, the van Huistens, the Dowdens, the McTaggarts. It's true, slave-blood made a most annoying mess of their hair and complexion, but that is overlooked in the face of Blood – genteel Blood. Respectability. They have a trail of refinement and good breeding behind them. They are snobs. They lack unity, too. They're split up into cliques, and complexion and quality of hair are given absurd importance. They live above their means in their efforts to keep up to a certain standard of dignity. They'd rather starve than be not properly dressed –"

"Yes, I heard Mr. de Groot saying that once to Mr. Malone."

"I can well believe it, because they are aware of their faults. It's only that their traditions are so firmly grounded in them that they find it difficult to change. That's why the Portuguese and the East Indians and the Chinese attained their prosperity and left the coloured middle-class behind. The Portuguese, Chinese and East Indians got their prosperity by niggardly habits and shabby living; they stinted themselves and piled up their gains. But the coloured gentlemen always had to live, or at least make an attempt to live, as well as their planter ancestors –"

"And even though they have these faults you still think I should marry a coloured man of family?"

"I still think so. With the kind of education and upbringing you're having you'd be most at ease with a coloured man of family. He would be able to sympathize with your desire to possess a car and radio and two big houses –"

"And a Victrola."

"And a Victrola. Pardon the omission. He wouldn't want to stint you the good things of life, and his manners wouldn't jar on you. My God! But look at the time. We must be getting back."

"So soon! I was just starting to enjoy being here."

"Five minutes more, then. I have a date." He gave her a solemn wink. "With Delly."

"Delly? You mean with Jessie."

"I mean Delly."

"You've made friends again, then?"

He nodded.

"You've fallen out with Jessie?"

"I'm friendly with both of them."

"You go for drives to Dixie with both of them?"

He inclined his head gravely. "But on different nights, each in her turn. Let's go and tap the travellers' palms for water. Just by way of diversion. We've talked enough on the subject of social relations."

"Let's look at the sundial first. I want to see if the shadow is lying over six." She caught his hand, and as they began to move off they heard a bubbling in the canal. Ripples circled, fragile and glimmering, among the large, round leaves afloat. The sun made the little blebs of water poised on the leaves glitter with a ruby light. Some of them looked like miniature fortune-telling crystals, some like squashed glass marbles.

She could smell the fragrance of a hundred blossoms. Sackies uttered a loud twittering in the upper branches of a mahogany tree. They seemed to be catching insects before settling down for the night. A thrush sang a lulling, secret-filled melody amid the thick gloom of a bamboo clump, and one or two tree-frogs had begun to cheep.

She felt all this seeping deep into her. Distilling an undying essence within her. If she lived to ninety she would never forget these sounds and these sights.

On the way home, the evening air billowed down in invisible cool-chilly swathes from the pink and orange sky, and tingled in her lungs. Creole voices and laughter spiralled through her hearing, and all the car-tooting and honking and the rustling of trees rioted through her senses. She swept her gaze around at Georgetown, and took note, as though for the first time, of the brown and olive and sallow faces, of the looming dignity of cabbage palms, the languid fragility of coconut palms, the mysterious shadows in the foliage of mango trees; breadfruit trees stamping the silhouette of their grotesque leaves, like devil-hands, against a patch of mauve sky, gave her a singing weakness inside.

She heard dogs barking, pigeons moaning, roosters sending yearning coils of sound through the half-gloom of a backyard. From a large white house came piano music. Frail and tinselly Chopin music.

8

It was from Charlotte's sewing-room-cum-bedroom that Sylvia generally obtained the most spicy bits of news. She had long ceased to feel guilty about eavesdropping. The walls were thin wooden walls, and conversation came through with ease; one simply could not help overhearing anything that was said in the next room.

One evening when Sylvia was doing her homework, news of Naomi trickled through from the sewing-room.

"...Ah hear she living wid a fellow in Charlestown."

"What sorta fellow?"

"A coloured fellow. Some motor mechanic, Ah hear."

"Eh-eh! She looking down instead of up nowadays?"

"De child living wid her. He's a sweet lil' boy. He got good hair like Naomi's, but his face is his daddy's own face. You can't mistake the Dowden looks."

One afternoon, shortly after this, Sylvia was having tea with her father when there was a knock on the front door. Sylvia sprang up, and, forestalling the maid, answered the door. She saw a tall, slim, well-shaped lady in dark green. She was bareheaded, and her smooth, Indian-looking hair was coiled up attractively on her head in an elaborate coiffure. Sylvia stared, wondering whether this could be one of her father's lady friends who had decided to be bold and come to the house in defiance of the proprieties. Then the lady smiled and exclaimed: "My goodness! But, Sylvie! Look what a big girl you've grown into!"

Sylvia realized who it was. "You're Naomi, aren't you?"

"Yes. You don't remember me, eh?" She spoke like a lady. In Sylvia's eyes she abruptly took on an exciting air. Naomi the girl who had been married against her will to Bertie Dowden. Naomi, who had been beaten and put out naked in the rain. Naomi who had seen a man lying dead in a bathroom with bullet wounds in his head. Naomi who was living now with a motor mechanic.

"No, I wouldn't have known you," Sylvia smiled. "I was very young when I last saw you. Won't you come in? Mother is upstairs."

Russell appeared from the dining-room, an inquiring look on his face. "Oh! Mrs. Dowden, isn't it? How are you, Mrs. Dowden?"

"How do you do?" said Naomi, inclining her head.

"Won't you sit down?"

After she had gone upstairs to Charlotte – for Charlotte would not come downstairs as a lady ought to have done, but sent down to tell Naomi to go up to her sewing-room – and after Sylvia and her father were settled again at table, Russell said: "Her marriage might have been an unhappy one, but have you noticed how much it's improved her manners? Do you remember her before she was married?"

"Only slightly."

"Well, I can tell you she was pretty raw – both in speech and in manners. No better than any of your mother's Tiger Bay cronies."

"What changed her? Just getting married?"

"Not just getting married, but the type of people she has been mixing with since she has been married. Bertie's friends didn't cut him – only his immediate relatives, so Naomi had the opportunity of first-hand contact with the cream of the middle-class. You can see the results today."

One afternoon when Sylvia was coming home from school she saw Naomi in the avenue in Main Street, lovely and elegant with the shadows of the saman trees playing upon her well-groomed person. Sylvia dismounted and called to her, and Naomi waved and came across the grass border.

"Child, I always marvel when I see you! You've grown so much!"

"You think so? I wish I were taller. I'm only four feet eleven."

"You'll grow a little more, don't worry. You have what men like. Don't bother about the height so much."

Sylvia felt her cheeks grow warm. She said quickly: "I want to come and see you one afternoon, but I don't know your number. You live in Sussex Street, don't you?"

Naomi told her the number and said: "I'd be glad to see you – if your mother wouldn't object to your coming."

"I can come this afternoon."

"No, I want to see a picture at the London this afternoon. How about tomorrow?"

"No, tomorrow is hockey, but the afternoon after, if you like."

"Yes, that will suit me. You're sure your mother won't mind?"

"I don't ask her permission about anything nowadays. I always ask Daddy, and he never prevents me from going anywhere."

"Well, come with me this afternoon to pictures."

"You want me to? Good, I'll come."

Sylvia found it a great thrill sitting beside Naomi in the gloom of the cinema. It made her feel grown-up and on a par with Naomi. They were two attractive women together. She kept remembering what Naomi had said in Main Street an hour or two earlier. "You have what men like." Naomi had been referring to her rapidly developing body. Boys often looked at her and whispered and giggled. Benson Riego and his friends of St. Stanislaus College. A pity Benson Riego was a Portuguese, because she liked him. He was just, she assured herself, the kind of man she would have wanted for a husband. If only he had been of the coloured middle-class!

She enjoyed the picture – she always enjoyed Maurice Chevalier – and was in high spirits when she and Naomi left the cinema and crossed Camp Street to the central avenue. The flamboyant trees that lined the avenue, on either side, were in bloom, and the avenue and the grass borders were scarlet with fallen petals.

Sylvia heard a voice among the crowd – a male voice – remark: "That's Russell's girl." A sneering laugh from a female, then the male voice said: "That bloody rake! One day he's going to get a shot in his backside!"

Naomi had heard, too, for Sylvia felt her hand suddenly pressed.

Naomi murmured: "Don't look round, Sylvie. Don't take any notice."

Sylvia felt a burning in her chest. The words kept circling in her imagination. Scarlet carrion-crows in a nightmare...

"Naomi, do you know who it was that said that about Daddy?"

"No, I don't know. Don't let it worry you, child. Forget it."

A car came to a stop by the grass border, and a voice called: "Naomi! Hi, you there!" And Naomi called back: "Jerry!" The next minute she was introducing Sylvia to the olive-brown young man in a rickety Chevrolet. "Jerry, this is my little friend – Sylvia Russell. This is Jerry Rathbone, Sylvia."

Jerry made them get into the car. He said he would see them home. Naomi told him she had seen him in Water Street today, and he smiled back with gold-filled teeth and said: "Yes, I was going to Ruimveldt to see after a lorry for a fellow." His manner and accent were on the crude side. He smelt of car-grease and wore only shirt and trousers – no coat. But he had a clean look.

Clean and strong and male. His hair was close-cut, stiffish, curly – not kinky but not what you would call Good Hair. Not soft and wavy as good hair should be. On the whole, Sylvia decided that she liked him. She had a trembling vision of himself and Naomi in bed, saw them kissing and heard them murmuring, watched their legs entwined. The mystery of Naomi moved in a scented wisp through her fancy. She went off into a reverie and watched the trees that lined the avenue in Main Street – they were in Main Street now – and listened to their rustling. She saw the lights of the Park Hotel as though they were miles off in a mirage. The soft-lit windows of the big residences seemed like the eyes of vague monsters far under the sea.

Naomi told her not to forget to come and see her. She would look out for her. Jerry gave her a gold-toothed smile and extended his hand which was hard and rough-palmed. Its grip was powerful and masculine. A shiver of delight went through her.

She found her father playing bridge with Mr. Knight and Mr. van Huisten and Mr. Ralph. He waved casually and smiled, and Mr. van Huisten called: "Not coming to tell me good night, Sylvia?" in an avuncular voice. She liked him. He was looking a trifle bald these days, and the close-cut slightly-wavy hair that receded from his forehead was greying. He had a kindly, distinguished face, and his voice every day seemed to grow more cultured and silky. At school she had heard it said that he was one of the best speakers in the Legislative Council.

She had been about to pass on hurriedly into the dining-room, for this evening she was extremely conscious of her body. She was aware of it curving under her clothes, and she felt a shyness in the presence of her father's friends, long-familiar as she was with them. She still approached the table, however. "Who's winning tonight?" she asked.

"Who would you guess?" said Mr. Knight, and smiled at her as he played the Queen of Hearts and casually collected the trick. She definitely did not like him, though he was as charming as ever. The hints her father had from time to time thrown out about his dishonesty had served to prejudice her against him.

For Mr. Ralph she had a quiet affection; he might have been really her uncle. He was a timid-looking man, very fair in complexion, with greyish-brown eyes, immaculately dressed. He had a soft, kind voice.

She said good night and went inside. She found David at dinner. "You went to pictures, Sylvia?"

"Yes."

"I'm going to see a cowboy picture tomorrow. Tom Keene. Plenty fighting, girl. You should go. It's on at the Olympic."

"I don't like fighting. Anybody upstairs with Mother?"

"Agnes, I think."

She watched him over her knife and fork, and felt a little envious. He was an inch or two taller than she, and every day he looked more and more like their father. He could easily have passed for pure white. He had light-brown hair, blue-green eyes, fair complexion and her father's type of features.

After dinner she went upstairs to do her homework, but found that she could not concentrate. She kept smelling car-grease and the perfume of Naomi. Hearing the voice amid the bustle in Camp Street. She looked up "rake" in the dictionary. Looked up "licentious" and "dissipated".

In the next room, Charlotte and Agnes Feria were engaged in quiet conversation, and now and then from downstairs would come the clink of decanter and glass as her father or one of his friends helped himself to whisky or rum. She forced herself to do a French exercise. She would have preferred to get into bed and read one of the stories in *True Story Magazine.* Beryl Dell had lent her a *True Story Magazine;* it was in her drawer hidden under her clothes. Beryl had said that there was a story in it about a woman who had been raped and that she must be careful not to let anyone know she was reading it. "Mother would rave, child," Beryl had said, "if she knew I read it. I have to go in the W.C. whenever I want to read a story."

That night she did not sleep well. She dreamt about old men turning somersaults along the avenue in Main Street. Naomi stood on the grass border and laughed and clapped her hands. Naomi opened her dress and revealed round breasts that Sylvia recognized as her own. A *True Story Magazine* fell out of Naomi's clothes, and the wind blew it toward the metalled roadway where the old men stopped somersaulting and pounced on it with old-men chortles. A car rushed past with a whoom and a whoosh, and the people in it shouted: "Rake! Rake!" A ship sailed after it. It sailed on the hard surface of the street as though it did not need water. Sylvia moved about the deck in a panic asking the other passengers if they had seen her father, but everyone shook his or her head. One girl laughed and asked her if she was Russell's girl. She kicked off her shoe and began to hop around and sob. "My name is Dixie, but I haven't seen Grantley. Really I haven't seen him, Jessie!" Her voice and sobs grew remote, and from the top of the ship's funnel Sylvia watched the sunset, saw the amber-white Demerara with ships at anchor, and the bush on the opposite bank. The sun made the water sparkle with a thousand eyes. Old men turned somersaults on it and sank out of sight... "Daddy, where are you? I want to pick up shells on the beach! Quick! Let's go off alone together somewhere and pick up shells on a beach!"... She wanted to cry. Something terrible was going to happen. She heard confused voices on deck, but could see nothing because a flock of *True Story Magazines* and a jostling crowd of round breasts kept weaving and interweaving before her eyes... More than ever she wanted to cry... "Russell is dead!" a voice wailed. "Oh, Russell is dead! Bertie Dowden shot him in his backside!" It rose to a scream. "Russell is dead!" The *True Story Magazines* rustled animatedly. Like gnashing teeth. She was being suffocated in a dense, pressing cloud of printed pages showing a woman being raped. Thousands of pages closing in around her, and the voice beyond them screaming: "Russell is dead! Dead! Do you hear me? Dead!"...

Somebody was shaking her shoulder. She awoke to find herself in tears. David was bending over her. It was daylight.

"Why are you crying, Sylvie? You're dreaming?"

The dream, coupled with a new shyness for which she could not account, prevented her from telling her father what she had over-heard after the cinema show. When she went to see Naomi, however, she told her about the dream, and that the incident in Camp Street had been on her mind. "Do you think it's because I had it on my mind that I had such a bad dream?"

Naomi smiled in her sophisticated way and said: "Of course.

Nothing unusual in that, child. Don't let it prey on your mind. You told your father you were coming to see me?"

"Yes."

This comforted her, gave her a more settled feeling, renewed her faith in her father – for, somehow, her faith in him had sagged, much as she had tried to assure herself that this was not so.

The cool of the afternoon entered her as she looked out of the window. Naomi lived over a tailor's shop. It was a shabby building in a shabby neighbourhood, but Naomi had repapered the three rooms of this upper flat she was occupying, and decorated them with taste. There were dark-blue curtains at the windows, and the tables and chairs were modern and low – of a dull grey-brown; not shiny and bright brown with varnish like the tables and chairs of Charlotte's choice.

In the backyard stood a tenement house of about five or six rooms – a dilapidated-looking place that must teem with vermin. A family of six or eight probably occupied each room. Ill-clad black people moved about between buckets and barrels of water, and tubs that rested on old soap-boxes. The ground was muddy. Chickens pecked here and there, and smoke rose in thin puffs from a detached kitchen-shed out of which, also, came the smell of cooking rice and something frying – something oily and oniony. Now and then a raucous laugh would curl up through the damp air. Rain had fallen heavily not two hours ago, and you could smell the wet earth and grass. The sounds of the city seeped muffled and as though filmy with grime past grey walls and rusty corrugated iron roofs-car-tooting, the crowing of cocks, the tinkle of bicycle bells.

She experienced a deep peace. At this moment the tenement scene with its dirt and shoddiness did not seem repellent at all.

"Sylvia, you're very romantic, you know."

Sylvia started. "Romantic? Why do you say so?"

"From the things you say sometimes – and from your face."

"Daddy has said that, too."

After a silence: "Naomi, were you very unhappy in New Amsterdam?"

Naomi's dark Eurasian eyes came alight with an elusive whimsicality. She was attired in a blue-and-green flowered kimono. She smoked a cigarette, and looked in every way like a lady of good family. She flicked ash off her cigarette into an amber glass ash-tray that stood poised on the arm of the Morris chair in which she reclined. In a slow, deliberate voice she said: “I could write a whole book about what happened to me since I got married – but I don’t want to talk about it. I want to forget it.”

After another silence: “How is life with you, Sylvie? Any boys in love with you yet?”

Sylvia fidgeted and said: “There’s a Portuguese boy I like a lot – but I’ve never spoken to him. He’s at school – St. Stanislaus. I’ve heard his name is Benson Riego.”

Naomi regarded her. There was affection on her face. She might have been a big sister.

“He’s tall and handsome,” said Sylvia, her gaze on the tenement. “Really nice. I like to hear him laugh. He has a great laugh.”

“I know of some Riegos in Bourda, but I don’t know if it’s the same family. They have a small provision shop.”

“No, I’ve heard Benson’s people own two rum-shops. They’re well off.” The topic made her self-conscious. “By the way, what of your mother, Naomi?” she asked, changing the subject. “Do you still see her?”

“No – and I don’t want to. I can support myself now. I get some pension money from the Government. Bertie was high up in the Service.”

“Oh, I see.”

“Child, this is a terrible world, but you mustn’t let it get you down. I’ve learnt that if you want to be happy you must please yourself. Don’t try to please anybody else or you must be unhappy.” She stretched herself with luxury and abandon. Her long black hair shifted in two slippery plaits over the back of the chair. Don’t you see how fresh I’m looking, Sylvie! It’s because I don’t let worries kill me. Hallo, Susie! Sit down, child. What are you doing with yourself these days?”

The girl who had come in was tall and slim, sallow like a Portuguese, but her features were negroid and her hair curly – fairly good hair. She gave a wide smile, and then you saw the holes in her teeth. She was well dressed and well groomed. Her manner was rather quiet, and, on the whole, she seemed to have a negative personality. She said in a soft voice: "How's it, Naomi?"

"Always smiling, Susie. This is Sylvia Russell. Sylvia, this is Susie Peters."

Naomi asked after Susie's baby. Susie seated herself, shrugged and replied: "She awright. Ah leff she wid Joyce. She had bad bowels."

After a while, Sylvia gathered that the baby was illegitimate. Susie talked about Cedric. She said that she had not seen Cedric since Saturday night, and that he had been drunk then. "'E cuss Joyce upside-down," said Susie casually. And Naomi remarked: "I'm sure his sister must have put him up to do that."

Susie shrugged. "Ah ain' know – and Ah ain' care. But Daphne better not make de mistake and come round to me, or she going hear me tongue, and I got a nasty tongue, as everybody know." She said this in a soft, easy voice like the fine drizzle that was falling outside and making a veil against the yellow, feathery clouds in the east.

"Have a fag, Susie child. Keep your sunny side up!"

"Naomi, where is Garvey, your little boy? Is he outside? It's raining."

"Jerry took him to the Sea Wall in his car."

"Oh."

The roof of the tenement house looked shiny with wetness, but the sun was slanting in mild shafts through a breadfruit tree in the next yard, and the gloom and mud of the yard had a glittery and even cheerful mien, especially with the chickens making their peep-peep sounds. A wireless set somewhere was playing "Red Sails in the Sunset". The tune came like a blue-and-red coil out of the drizzle, blending with the bluish smoke that rose from the grey-black kitchen-shed.

"Naomi, I'd better be going now," said Sylvia. She rose. "You'll see me again soon."

"Going through the rain?"

"Rain doesn't trouble me."

"Stay well, then. Drop in any time you like. No ceremony," Naomi smiled. She rearranged herself more luxuriously in the chair. The kimono parted and revealed a full, brown-nippled breast. "Keep your chin up, Susie child!"

A trail of male laughter rose up from the tailor's shop, trickled away, then appeared again with new heartiness. Sylvia, going down the dark, rickety stairway, heard a loud voice holding forth. It was talking about Hitler and Germany. When she was unlocking her bicycle to ride off she heard a dull thud-thud. Somebody pounding green plantains in a mortar. The drizzle had stopped.

After that visit, Naomi's place took on magic hues in Sylvia's imagination. Whenever she had a chance she dropped in to see Naomi. Most times she found Jerry there. Sometimes Susie Peters or Greta Soodeen, an East Indian girl who, Naomi said, was a cousin of hers. Greta was very pretty and had a lovely figure, and was engaged to be married to a black young man called Jack Sampson, an engineer on the Demerara ferry steamer.

Sometimes it would be Clothilde Pumba, a Portuguese girl with a husky laugh – like Teresa Feria's. And like Teresa, Clothilde was a Viceroy Hotel girl. Sometimes Teresa herself would be there, or Agnes or Janie Pollard, or Eustace Frank, a Syrian. Eustace was a fat, hook-nosed young man, and was in love with Greta. Despite Greta's being engaged to Jack Sampson, Eustace refused to give up hope. His people ran two dry goods stores in Lombard. Street, and Eustace never came to Naomi's without bringing a handbag or a pair of stockings or some such gift for Greta.

One afternoon a coloured young man, Aubrey Deleon, came in with Garvey, Naomi's son, whom Aubrey said he had found in Broad Street.

"Naomi, you ought to be ashamed of yourself to let dis child wander about de neighbourhood alone. He will turn into a street centipede."

Eustace, who was present, shook his head deprecatingly. "Uh, Gott, yes," he rumbled. "You let heem walk round too mush, Naomi. Car might knock heem down."

"We all have to die one day, Eustace," sighed Naomi.

Greta threw a cushion at Eustace, and Eustace uttered a deep grunting laugh, his beady black eyes alight. He gave off a faint scent of Lavender Water.

Aubrey pulled up a chair close to Sylvia and began to talk to her, his eyes all over her body in a searching male intensity that made her shy but flattered her. He was about twenty-two, fairly handsome, with kinky, close-cut hair, and, like herself, olive-complexioned. He came of no well-known family, and was a sales-assistant in a hardware store in Water Street. He was very cheery and gay, and sometimes talked politics with Jack Sampson, Greta's fiancé, who frequently brought Communist literature and could tell you anything you wanted to know about Russia and the Communist movement. Jack was always cursing the local government and the capitalists... "It's de people like us they sucking dry!" he would shout. "But no fear! It got to end one day! De revolution coming! You see what happening in Abyssinia! Dis Abyssinian war going to have resounding effects on world history!"...

Jack Sampson was a pure-blooded negro, slim and strong, with large teeth widely spaced, so that when he laughed you could see the darkness at the back of his mouth. It was an attractive laugh. Sylvia liked him. She liked all the people she met at Naomi's. They were so varied and interesting. So vital. So easy and informal. So exciting and full of unknown passions. She felt that at any instant one of them might pull out a revolver and say: "Stick 'em up!" as the gangsters did in the films. To her they were like people in a screen drama. They had an unrealness and a glamour. Their faces seemed to hint at mysterious, unusual events – strange, sophisticated happenings in bedrooms and dark alleyways, in hotels and bars, in places where she could never hope to venture. Whatever they said and did seemed somehow right, and she found herself imitating their easy, gay manner – trying to laugh huskily like Clothilde or stretch with luxury and abandon like Naomi, or snap her fingers and jerk her head and exclaim: "Ah, boy!" like Aubrey Deleon.

One day, at home, Janie Pollard warned her about Naomi's place. "For me it's awright, girl. I is a whore. But you is a decent girl, Sylvia. Dat ain' no place for you to go."

Sylvia, however, assured her that she could take care of herself. "I'm fourteen, going on for fifteen. I know all about sex and babies, Janie. Don't worry about me."

One Saturday afternoon, after lunch, when Sylvia and Russell were dancing to music coming over the wireless, Russell paused and said: "I don't remember teaching you that step."

Sylvia jerked her head and exclaimed : "Ah, boy! That's a new one. Somebody taught me. Never mind who!"

He said: "Oh," in an unconcerned tone and went on dancing, whistling the tune softly. It was "Moon over Miami". She whistled it, too, and moved her head in swaying time to the music. Then she began to sing the refrain.

Russell glanced at her and raised his brows mildly. "Somebody seems to be teaching you many things. Picking up new friends at Madame Dowden's?" He spoke without alarm – simply in a tone of inquiry.

"Yes, I meet a lot of interesting people at Naomi's. Aubrey taught me this new step. Naomi has a radio. Jerry got it for her, and sometimes we dance. Oh, we have good times!"

"Who and who are we?"

"Aubrey Deleon and I and Naomi and Jerry Rathbone, and sometimes Greta Soodeen and Jack Sampson. And Clothilde Pumba. Even some of Mother's friends turn up sometimes. Agnes and Teresa and Janie. Naomi's place is always bright."

"Not too dazzling for you, though, I trust?"

"Too dazzling? How do you mean?"

He did not reply. His eyes grew faraway and weary. He puzzled her. She could not guess whether he were pleased or displeased, whether he were disturbed or not. He seemed detached. Locked up within himself and isolated from everything and everyone around him. He danced automatically, as though it might have been a light duty he was performing – something that was necessary for her entertainment but not particularly his own. Within the past two or three months a slight gap seemed to have opened between him and her. Could it be since she had overheard that remark after the cinema show? She told herself that she was not sure.

A feeling of depression came upon her. A sadness. A sense of loss.

"Daddy, let's stop dancing and play two-hand bridge."

"As you like. Certainly." He glanced at his wristwatch.

"You have a date?"

He shook his head. Unfathomable. Like the cloud-mass she could see above the house across the street. You never knew whether rain would fall from it or whether it would pass over and dissolve in the west. Wind came in a cool drift from the north-east, and the palms at the gateway made their muffled, secretive sound. A low scraping. The ice-man's whistle trilled thinly in Barrack Street.

The wireless was playing "The Music goes Round..."

9

The twenty-ninth of December was Mabel Earle's birthday, and Mabel's parents held a Christmassy birthday party to which Sylvia, as one of Mabel's school chums, was invited. There was dancing to gramophone music, and the presents Mabel received were hung on the Christmas tree with its fairy lights and cotton-wool snow.

The party came to an end shortly after eight, and with the memory of it fresh in her fancy, Sylvia arrived home to find her father in the Berbice chair in the gallery reading the *Strand Magazine.* He glanced up and asked her whether she had had a good time.

"Oh, lovely," she told him. "Simply lovely. I don't know when I've ever had such a good time."

"How about a trip to Berbice tomorrow?"

"To where?"

"Berbice."

"Berbice?"

"Have you gone deaf?"

"But – you're joking, Daddy!"

He shook his head. "I've lost the art of banter. You'd better get busy at once and do some packing. We're leaving by the eight o'clock train."

"But I can hardly believe it. You've always promised to take me to New Amsterdam and you've never kept your word. How long are we staying?"

"A week. I'm going on business. There's been trouble at the

New Amsterdam waterworks and they want me to go into consultation with the engineer up there. Go and change at once. You're perspiring."

When David heard he said he wanted to go, too, so Russell told him to get packed. They travelled first class, and had a compartment to themselves. The smell of the black leather-lined seats, the two mirrors facing each other, the shrill shriek of the train and the whoof-whoof of the engine, the jerk forward and the gradual moving sensation seemed to Sylvia like a dream coming precisely true.

The weather, however, soon upset the perfection. Rain came down in a thin drizzle as they were approaching Kitty, the big village which had become welded on to Georgetown as a suburb. The sun could be seen through a grey-white wad of clouds banking overhead, and before they were halfway between Kitty and Plaisance, the next big village, the rains of December were hissing down in thick curtains from a sky grey all over.

The East Coast stretched flat and hazy to the north and south of the railway tracks. In the north they could barely make out the Sea Wall in the fog of rain. Sheep and cows sloshed miserably through the rising lakes of water, and where rice-fields had made yellow carpets in September and October only muddy water could be seen, with straggly tufts sticking up – the remnants of the reaped crop. Here and there intruder weeds, fresh and green, stood unbowed, resisting the pelting drops. On occasional islets she could discern long-legged grey gauldins or white ibises, perched like elegant hieroglyphics against the uncertain background of drab wetness.

"You think we'll see Jeanne de Groot in New Amsterdam, Daddy?"

He shrugged. "Have no idea." He was lighting his pipe which she had filled for him. "I believe her father was transferred to the Essequibo a year or two ago. I may be wrong."

David, restless and eager to explore, had left them and had walked along the corridor to the door that opened on to the narrow landing where the following carriage was coupled to theirs. He stood there gazing into the second-class carriage, the rain slashing at his face.

Sylvia kept putting her head through the door of the compartment to watch him. At length, she said anxiously: "Do you think I should call him, Daddy?"

"Why?"

"He might fall between the carriages. You know how reckless he is."

"Don't you believe in Fate?"

"Fate?"

He told her that there was an ancient theory that everything was predestined – that nothing could happen but what had long ago been planned.

"Do you believe in that – really?"

"I'm not discussing what *I* believe in. I'm simply telling you of the old theory. What *I* believe in myself is immaterial." He smiled his crooked smile. There was the suggestion of a sigh in his manner. "I wish I did believe in something, Goo-goo. But there is nothing to believe in. God, as I've often remarked to you, is only a poetic myth that men fool themselves with for their own sweet self-delusion, and unfortunately I'm not one who can delude himself; that's why I'm lonely and empty."

"Are you lonely and empty?"

He nodded, pulling gravely at his pipe.

"But you mix with so many people – and you play bridge and go to picnics and dances, and – and you go for drives with ladies to Dixie. How can you say you're lonely?"

"Ah. How." He gave her a solemn wink, but his manner was not facetious.

"But I don't understand."

He began to whistle "Stormy Weather", as though forgetful of her presence. She stared at him and felt a dull sadness hissing through her. It could have been the rain. The lines of his face, in this dim light, seemed deeper, and his hair looked more silvery than reddish-yellow. His shoulders, too, had a droop she had not noticed before. She bit her lower lip and wanted to cry. The tune seemed very mournful whistled as he was whistling it. It emphasized his loneliness. He jerked his chin toward the window and murmured: "There's another ibis. A pink one. *Curri-curri,* I think it's called locally."

"Yes."

"You look serious, Goo-goo. What's on your mind?" He patted her arm.

"Serious? No. I – I was just thinking a bit." In this instant she knew that the gap between them had closed. "I don't like to see you looking down-spirited. I always feel saddish."

"Oh, at the moment I'm feeling pretty good," he smiled. He tapped down the contents of his pipe with a finger. "The rain makes it snug in here – and there's you for company, eh?" He added in a mumble that he would soon be getting her bloody conceited.

The vampa-vampa of the train soothed her in its monotony. A sense of solidity came upon her. She looked about the compartment and felt its realness. A realness that tingled far down in her, so that it touched a depth of utter peace. Rain trickling down the glass of the closed windows. Her father smoking, his face non-committal. The chill in the air. It affected her as the tenement scene at Naomi's in the late afternoon sometimes did. It Existed. She felt powerfully alive. Alive and apart. Nothing could trouble her.

They were coming to a big station. The train shrieked. They began to slow down. White railings. And now the roar of voices and the bustle... "Mangoes! Pineapples!"... The face of a black woman above a tray laden with fruit appeared at the window... "Bananas! Pears!"... "Any donce? Cashews?"... David came in and asked for a sixpence to buy some Buxton spice mangoes. Two minutes later, the train's whistle sounded, and the train jolted forward once again.

It was midday before they reached the train terminus at Rosignol. They boarded the small ferry steamer, and from the upper deck looked across the wide estuary of the Berbice River, amber and rippled in the brilliant sunshine – the rain had stopped about an hour ago – and saw New Amsterdam.

From this distance the town looked like a slightly faded, trampled bouquet. Sylvia saw two white church steeples jutting up bravely against the pale blue of the horizon sky. Lilies that had survived the battering of Time. The analogy was Russell's. He added: "The glory of New Amsterdam lies in the past, I've been made to understand. All the best families lived in New Amsterdam forty or fifty years ago when the town was an active port. Now the harbour is mud-silted, and only the best families of crabs survive to enjoy any prestige."

He pointed out Crab Island in the north, a green mass of jungle blocking the mouth of the river.

When the steamer was about halfway across the two-and-a half-mile wide estuary, the town looked much better. It had a picture-post-card unrealness – the bright greens of the trees and the red splashes of roofs, the bluish-white of residences against a bright blue sky with small white clouds.

When they disembarked on to the long *stelling* – a quarter of a mile long – the wide brown mudflats depressed Sylvia, and, later, when they were on their way to the hotel in a car, she did not like the streets. They were not asphalted but built up with rocks and burnt earth. Clouds of dust followed the car.

The hotel was a large, square building in the main business thoroughfare, the Strand, with a slated roof and a balcony that overhung the street, and a long veranda on the northern side.

Their room had a good view. You could see the trees and housetops of New Amsterdam as well as the river. The town looked pretty with its two white church steeples and its red and grey roofs and trees, but compared with the vastness of Georgetown it seemed dull – lacking in the dense rumble and excitements, the feeling of wider events, of Georgetown. She did not feel as thrilled as she had expected she would have been.

At lunch, they found four other boarders in the small dining-room. An East Indian gentleman was laughing boisterously at something a white gentleman had just said – chewing and laughing, his broad chest heaving, his laughter zooming around the room and dominating everything and everybody. The other two at the table were coloured – an olive-complexioned gentleman and a sallow lady. The four of them were chatting like old friends.

The manager appeared, and slapped Russell on the back, for he and Russell were well acquainted. He was a coloured gentleman of medium height and build, genial and full of cheerful guffaws, handsome, with European features, a fair complexion and greying, kinky hair cut short. He spoke in a cultured voice, crisp and rather English.

He showed them to the table which had been prepared for them, and sat down to lunch with them. He asked Sylvia whether this was her first trip to Berbice, and when she nodded and told him it was he said he was certain it wouldn't be her last. He was a gentleman who swore by the Ancient County – so Russell told her afterwards. She liked him. He had a brittle humour that appealed to her.

When the meal was over, she and David decided to go out and explore the town. It did not take them more than two hours to see everywhere of note, for the town, they discovered, was hardly a mile in length by less than half a mile across – about the size of the Botanic Garden in Georgetown.

That night, long after David had fallen asleep in his bed, Sylvia lay awake in hers under the mosquito net. The unfamiliarity of her surroundings kept her imagination active. She was not accustomed to sleeping under a mosquito net; in Georgetown there were no mosquitoes. In the bluish light of the street lamp – an Osira lamp – the net had a ghostly look. She felt as though she might open her eyes and see it dissolve about her into the gloom.

After an hour of tossing, she got out of bed and went to a window. The sky was starry but not clear. It had a watery, December look, as though rainy mists were gathering but afraid to form into heavy clouds because of the vigilant eyes of the stars. The air was cool and filled with the smell of grass and leaves – far more so than Georgetown. It must be the nearness of the jungle, she supposed: Crab Island and all the dense bush on the Canje Creek over there to the east – bush which had once been flourishing plantations, Russell had told her that afternoon when he had taken her and David for a drive up the Canje Creek. She remembered how they had stood on the narrow road beside the car and watched the black, sluggish water of the Canje visible through the dense bamboo and *mucca-mucca* shrubs that grew along the banks.

"All jungle now," said Russell, his face reflective, faraway. "Hard to believe that in the eighteenth century it was all well laid out and cultivated, and that some Dutch plantation house stood on this very spot, perhaps."

She looked east now and smiled, told herself that the jumbies of the Dutchmen must be walking in the jungle at this very minute. Black jumbies, too – of all the slaves who had worked on the plantations.

She heard the clear, slow beat of a motorboat's engine. It was coming from the east – from the Canje. In her fancy she saw the boat cutting through the ominous black water.

With a laugh she turned away from the window and switched on the light. She looked at herself in the dressing-table mirror. She hugged herself as a gust of wind came in. She looked about the room slowly. With expectancy. Expecting she knew not what.

Her father's bed was empty; they were all three occupying the same room. He was downstairs in the hotel manager's room playing bridge. The manager was a keen player. It would probably be midnight before her father came up to bed. She looked at David's watch and saw that the time was half past ten.

She let her eyes explore the room. She saw her father's coat hanging on a peg on the door – the coat he had worn in the train. She crossed over and stroked it. A coat of pale yellow drill. It smelt of tobacco. She took it off the peg and put it on. It reached her nearly to the knees.

She went to the dressing-table and looked at herself in the mirror, giggled at what she saw. It made her look ridiculous but it felt snug and comfortable. She liked the feel of the slippery satiny lining against the thin stockinet of her nightgown.

She whistled "The Music goes Round" and began to dance with an imaginary partner. A thick batch of letters in one of the inner pockets chafed the sensitive tip of one of her breasts. She took out the lot and dumped them on the dressing-table, then resumed her solo dance. She did a slow-motion waltz, imagining herself in a film. Then she laughed and one-stepped across the room. Then she did a tango. A screech-owl flew past the window and cackled weirdly. It startled her. She was about to resume dancing when something on the dressing-table caught her eye. A photograph peeping out from amid the batch of letters and papers she had dumped.

Her sense of honour troubled her at once, but curiosity won. She pulled out the picture and saw the eyes of Delly gazing back at her – a smiling, attractive Delly retouched by the photographer; it was a studio picture. Furtively and with a feeling of guilt, she slipped the picture back between the letters and papers. But even as she did so she noticed the edge of another peeping out; this one seemed an ordinary amateur snapshot. She hesitated, told herself it was wrong, not playing the game, as Miss Jenkins would have said. But again curiosity triumphed. She pulled it out, looked at it and uttered a gasp. Delly again – but in this picture she reclined at ease on the beach – there was the Sea Wall in the background – and she was naked.

Sylvia fumbled the picture back among the papers and put them all back into the inner pocket of the coat. She took off the coat and returned it to the peg on the door. She switched off the light and got into bed. Her imagination thrust her back into the past, and she was walking with Naomi along the avenue in Camp Street... "That bloody rake! One day he's going to get a shot in his backside!"...

The rain-chilly air drifted in through the window upon her. She had not bothered with the blanket before, but now she unfolded it and snuggled under it. Her lips kept forming into an O and her breath came out in a silent whistle. She told herself it was her own fault. What right had she to be looking through his private papers! It was unfair. Suddenly she wanted to cry. Through the net she could see the room bright with the reflection of the bluish street lamps – a soft moonlight reflection.

She thought about sex. What was there in it that people should get so excited and worked up over it, talk about it in whispers, call each other names because of it? What did it matter that her father kept a picture of Delly naked in his pocket? Did that make him a dissipated man – a rake? What was wrong with a naked body that people should make such a fuss whether you were clothed or not?

She sprang out of bed and pulled off her nightgown, stared at herself in the mirror. She was about to switch on the light but changed her mind. Again changed her mind and switched on the light. She pushed her face nearer to the mirror to study the colour of her eyes. Brownish-green. Hazel-green, as her father had described them one day. Aubrey Deleon had told her she had glamour-girl eyes. But the big trouble was her height. She was not getting tall. Last week she had measured only five feet and a half-an-inch. Anyway, she was pretty, she assured herself. She tilted her head and smiled. Her teeth were white and even. Naomi had complimented her on her teeth one afternoon. And her breasts were upright and jutted far out – the way men liked them; so Greta Soodeen had remarked that afternoon when they were talking about good figures.

Of a sudden, however, fear attacked her. Fear of the unknownness of the future. Tomorrow was the last day of 1935. The years were going by. She was getting older, turning into a woman. Her father was getting to be an old man. Her mother got embittered and sulky more and more as age lined her face; she whined and snarled whenever she spoke. Uncle was already an old man; he had had a stroke two months ago but had recovered: the next one might kill him. Everything was changing. Moving on.

What of herself? Just an ordinary girl. She had no talents for anything in particular. Even in personality she was not striking. But, like everyone else, she would change with the years. How would her own life move on? What would the changes be like? And to where and where, what and what, would she move on?

She looked around the room slowly. The night seemed, without warning, to have become strange. Weighted with unseen presences, unseen passions, premonitions. She rubbed her hands idly down her body, listened to the faint lisp of skin on skin. What would he be like – the first man who would caress her and pin her down in the love-embrace? Where was he now – at this moment? Would it be against her will, or would she be in love with him?

Footsteps sounded remotely in the corridor. She tensed, her eyes on the door. A man was coming. He was going to open the door and come in and find her naked like this. A stranger. He would stand and look at her, and his eyes would get bright. Then he would rush at her. In less than a minute it would happen. Fine wires of heat probed through her belly, groped upward to the tips of her breasts. Her throat felt dryish with fear – fear and pleasurable anticipation.

The footsteps faded, but her gaze remained on the door. On her father's coat. In his sleep David sighed and turned over. She had the impulse to move across quickly and fumble out Delly's picture again – the naked one. Show it to David. Wake him and say: "Look! Look at her! Daddy must have taken this picture himself!" No, she couldn't do that. It would be unfair.

She thought of God. There was no God. Her father had told her so more than once... "Have faith in yourself," he had said. "For yourself, only you are God. Only you matter. Like myself. For myself, only I am God. Ignore the vapourings of people. People suffer from fear. People are ineffectual escapists. People strive always to sidestep reality, because reality baffles them, or is more often than not ugly or terrifying. Reality generally carries with it the threat of death – or discomfort. So people try to runaway from reality into the pretty bubble-lands of religion. Only you are real. Only you have significance. Believe that and you're saved. Be afraid and drug yourself with religion and you're lost."

He's right, she told herself now.

She looked at herself in the mirror again. She stroked her cheeks, tilted her head from side to side, cupped her breasts, rubbed her hands luxuriously, voluptuously, down her stomach and her hips.

Real. I can see and feel I'm real. Only I matter.

Her gaze went back to the coat.

He is real, too. For me, he's real. I like him a lot. Love him. She felt dizzy with revelation.

Whatever one loves is real – and matters.

A warm fuzz enveloped her.

I've just discovered something. A big thing. Nobody told me. I've learnt it all by myself in this room tonight – at this moment.

She felt huge. A woman of forty. And huge. A great living statue.

She moved across to the coat. The floor felt like a silken cloud under her feet. She took the coat off its peg, rubbed her cheek against it. David's bed creaked. David turned over again, sighed again, in his sleep. A feeling of absurdity swept her. The floor was hard as before. She was a girl again – fourteen years old. Sylvia Russell, a pupil of Bishop's High School.

Remnants of the revelation, however, lingered. She looked down at herself and felt a sense of consolidation. She mattered. She existed. Her blood tingled as though blebs of fire were in it. The coat dropped. She picked it up. She smelt it – the tobacco, male smell made her heart race, created an ache in her breasts. The blebs of fire in her blood coalesced, rushed to her head. A quiver went through her. Her teeth clicked together. Her skin burned. She plunged her hand into the inner pocket of the coat and withdrew the papers. She flung them to the floor, stooped and searched for the pictures of Delly. She discovered that there was another one; it was of a woman she did not know – a clothed woman, young and attractive.

She ground her teeth together and tore them into small bits – all three pictures – went to the window and scattered the pieces into the night. She gathered up the papers from the floor and returned them to the coat pocket, hung the coat up again on the peg. She trembled. Perspired.

She put on her nightgown, switched off the light and got into bed, began to sob. She slept and dreamt of the old men.

PART TWO

1

Life moved on. It moved on, felt Sylvia, like a wind – a loud wind – she could hear but could not feel. It never touched her. She was safe from it.

Mussolini gassed his way into Addis Ababa, and the Trinidadians composed a calypso about the Duce which Aubrey sang for them one afternoon – everybody was singing it – and Jack Sampson raved about the Fascist dogs. "Their day coming," he said. "Communism going to sweep dem off de earth!"

Greta Soodeen was going to have a baby by Jack, but no wedding had taken place yet. Eustace stopped visiting Naomi's. Hitler sent his troops into the Rhineland, and Uncle poured gin from the decanter and predicted that the Lord God of Hosts was preparing a great punishment for mankind. "Yes, Mr. Russell sir, you watch out! War is coming. Read de Scriptures. It's all prophesied in de Good Book. Mankind must pay for their sins..."

Mabel Earle fell from her bicycle and broke her arm. Teresa Feria died of pneumonia through a wetting she got one morning on her way home from the Viceroy Hotel, and only a few weeks previously her cousin, Angela, had died of tuberculosis... "I did know she got T.B.," said Janie Pollard. "Agnes, her sister, got it, too."

Charlotte fell ill again, this time with a nervous breakdown. The doctor said she was overworking at her sewing. She should take a holiday in the country for a few weeks. So Charlotte went to Berbice and spent a month at Number Sixty-three Village on the Corentyne Coast. She took Aunt Clarice Madhoo with her as a companion. On her return, she looked filled out in the face and was a deeper coffee-brown in complexion. She arrived in Georgetown at about the time when everybody was talking about the new war. General Franco had started trouble in Spain.

A civil war had broken out. Jack Sampson cursed the Fascists again.

Susie Peters had succeeded in getting a job in a dry goods store in Regent Street, and Jack advised her to join the Clerks' Union.

"Go and see Mr. Jocelyn Hubbard," Jack said. "He's de Secretary. Go and join up de Union and keep dese capitalist dogs from taking advantage of you." But Susie only laughed and never joined the Clerks' Union... "Dat's why we in dis colony can't progress!" Jack shouted. "We not politically conscious! We ain't wake up yet and realize what happening. De whole of dis colony got de complacent, bourgeois spirit. Politics don't concern dem. Only de working classes interested in politics – and why they interested? Because de capitalists on top squeezing dem!"...

There was a new visitor at Naomi's – Gregory Brandt, a good friend of Jerry's, though everybody knew that he was secretly in love with Naomi. He was coloured, was rumoured to be connected with a good family, and seemed well educated. He had a smutty wit, and once made them all laugh when he said that the marriage vows should be revised; the woman instead of saying that she promised to obey and serve should promise "to serve and be serviced". Another time when Naomi advised Susie that in future she should keep off men, Gregory said: "You mean men should keep off her."

One afternoon in August, Sylvia found herself alone with Naomi.

"Naomi, you know this is the first afternoon for the year I've had a chance to chat with you alone."

Naomi smiled. She seemed abstracted – not quite herself. Sylvia wondered whether something could be worrying her.

"I always wanted to ask you this, Naomi. Are you happy with this crowd that comes here, or would you have preferred the people you used to mix with when you and Bertie were together?"

Naomi laughed. "How old are you, child? Fifteen? You ask the questions a person of thirty would ask." She fell silent and looked out of the window. Clouds were piled up into huge domes in the south. Now and then thunder rumbled. The air was hot and taut. Naomi stirred and said: "Sometimes I wonder about that myself,

Sylvia. I'm happy as I am now – in *my* way. But I think I would have preferred to see more of Bertie's friends. I used to enjoy listening to them talk. I miss those days for that. I've always wanted to improve myself – to speak correct English and learn about the big world happenings – and about music and painting and books."

She shrugged. Her face suddenly looked empty and frivolous. "What's the use of crying for the moon, child! Those days are over. I can never go back to them. I must drift on as I'm doing now and make the best of it."

"Why doesn't Jerry marry you?"

Naomi made no reply. She was staring out of the window again. There was the suggestion of a sigh in her manner, thought Sylvia. Her eyes were steady, though, and filled with a calculating light, as if she were thinking out a problem quietly and without any fuss or emotion. She turned her head abruptly and said: "You tell me about yourself now, Sylvia. Of late I've noticed you seem more womanly and quiet. Grown-up."

Sylvia nodded. She was not in any way discomfited. She had been prepared for the remark. For a long time she had been expecting it. "I feel grown-up. Since the thirtieth of December last I became grown-up."

"What happened then?" Naomi sat forward and glanced toward the door; there was expectancy, even slight nervousness, in her manner. One of her long plaits of black hair swung past her shoulder into her lap. She pushed it back casually as she leaned backward again in the easy chair. She made a slight adjustment to the diaphanous pale green negligee she was wearing. The pink brassiere and pink panties she had on could be clearly seen through the thin material. She wore blue kid slippers lined with velvet inside; Sylvia had heard that they were a gift from Gregory Brandt.

"Nothing that would seem very important," Sylvia replied; she tried to make her voice sound sophisticated and impressive. "But it meant a lot to me." She told Naomi about the events of the night of the thirtieth of December in the Strand Hotel. "When I woke the next morning everything looked different. I felt calm and happy. I knew there was really no God. I knew that God is something people themselves invent – and I told myself that I'd invented my own gods. Myself and Daddy. I'll never worship any other gods but these two."

A look of interest and wonder appeared on Naomi's face. "I've always said you were a strange child, Sylvia."

"Strange? I thought I was very ordinary."

"I mean – you have something everybody hasn't got. I can't explain it exactly."

"It isn't that. I'm like everybody else – but I was brought up differently, and I've learnt things everybody doesn't learn at my age. I have a father who isn't like most fathers."

Naomi smiled. "I can see the worship on your face."

"If you had a father like that I'm sure you'd worship him." A silence came upon them. They heard the thunder.

Naomi cocked her head, stirred uneasily.

A woman in the tenement yard laughed.

"Did he discover it was you who tore up the pictures?"

"I don't know. He never asked me anything. I was a fool to do it. But I couldn't help it. I felt terribly jealous of his women that night."

"I understand."

"He said something a month or two ago that puzzled me. We were at dinner alone one evening, and it was raining. David was out with Henry and his friends at a scout meeting. He caught me looking at him, and he gave a grin and said: 'Ever heard about an Oedipus complex?' I asked him what he meant but he told me not to bother – it didn't matter. Do you know what's an Oedipus complex?"

Naomi shook her head. Her manner was still abstracted. "Gregory should know. I must ask him."

"Don't let him know it's I who asked you about it."

"Of course not."

Naomi sat forward. Her breath made a lisp.

Footsteps were ascending the stairs.

"I knew we wouldn't be left alone for long," said Sylvia. Naomi said nothing. Her manner was tense, but she tried to conceal the fact by toying with one of her plaits.

Sylvia watched her, puzzled.

Jerry came in, greasy, grimy, as though just from his workshop. His pale blue shirt had several brown smears and smudges. His hands and forearms were shiny and black with grease and dirt. The smell of him saturated the room at once. The smell of car-engines. A smile was on his face – a slight fixed smile. He uttered no greeting. He moved past them into the bedroom. Sylvia felt the danger.

"Naomi." He spoke very quietly. The thunder rolled at the same instant; it had a flat foreboding note – the same note that Jerry's voice contained. Naomi did not move.

Sylvia rose. "I think I'd better be running off now, Naomi."

"No, stay, Sylvia. Don't go. Please." It was an appeal. Sylvia kept standing.

"Sit down, Sylvia."

Sylvia sat down slowly. A slight gooseflesh tingled over her arms.

"Naomi."

"Yes, Jerry. What is it?"

"Come."

Naomi made no move. She toyed with the plait.

A bucket clattered in the tenement yard, and the sewing-machines whirred downstairs in the tailor's shop. It was very hot. The heat seemed to move in swathes through the room. Leisurely – and unsure to the vision. Like ghosts only partly materialized.

The bed creaked. Jerry appeared at the bedroom door. He leaned against the door post, and looked at Naomi. He was rubbing his elbow – slowly. He had large muscles. They had a gritty look under the light-brown, shiny-smooth skin. His smell went through the room again. A smell of car-engines – and of maleness. The strength and hardness of him sent invisible lightning all over the room, and Sylvia felt an ache in her stomach. She wanted to get up and move about.

Naomi's eyes were large. Round and black. With fear and with... Sylvia was not sure with what else. Naomi puzzled her. Naomi sat so still there might have been no breath in her.

Jerry moved toward her. Not hurriedly. His body seemed to glide through the thick, hot air. He might not have been touching the floor. He gripped the upper part of Naomi's left arm. Her flesh sank under the hard fingers, and Sylvia saw his wrist graze the shoulder of the negligee and leave a brown smudge.

"Jerry, you're hurting me," said Naomi, but her voice expressed no pain. She did not wince.

The smile appeared on Jerry's face again – a smile without mirth or any purpose, it seemed to Sylvia. "Tell me about last night," he said.

"I have nothing to tell you," said Naomi, her voice as low as Jerry's.

"You have plenty to tell me."

"I have a visitor, Jerry. I'd be glad if you'd behave yourself."

He laughed. A brief, deep sound far down in his stomach. He might have been entirely unaware of the presence of Sylvia.

"I'm waiting for you to talk," he said. He twisted her arm, and she gave a swift breath and bit her lip but uttered no sound of pain. No cry.

"Why you locked me out last night? Who was in here?"

"You've asked me that twice for the day already, and I've told you nobody. I was here alone. I wanted to be alone."

"You're still with that story?"

Naomi said nothing.

Jerry tugged at her arm. Naomi cried out softly in pain as her body was jerked upward out of the chair. Jerry pulled her toward him and then pushed. She went hurtling through the bedroom door. She collapsed on the floor at the foot of the bed.

Sylvia rose and followed Jerry to the bedroom door. Her mouth opened to cry out, but no sound came.

Jerry grasped Naomi by a shoulder and jerked her up from the floor; the negligee tore. He hurled her on to the bed, and she struck the bed with a swish and a tearing twang of the springs in the mattress. She gasped, and lay still, her face buried in the crook of her arm. The arm that was smeared dark-brown with the dirt and grease from Jerry's hand. A black plait lay coiled on the pale blue bedspread like a fuzzy snake; it was semi-unravelled. Naomi uttered not a sound.

Jerry, too, was silent. He stretched out and grasped the back of the negligee. Pulled. The thin cloth ripped, came off Naomi in long shreds. Jerry grasped Naomi by a shoulder, brought her up with a snap, pushed her down into a sitting posture. There was a strange rigidity about her body – almost a rigidity of anticipation. Her face was calm. She might have been experiencing a secret pleasure. Jerry ripped the rest of the negligee from her body, and she made no move to resist him, made no protest. He tore off the brassiere, slapped her face hard, smashed his fist into her chest. Grease smears streaked her cheeks and turned reddish-brown as the blood welled up under the skin. She blinked rapidly and bit her lip, but that was all.

A black woman's voice came up from the tenement yard singing a hymn. "Jerusalem my happy home," the black woman sang.

The window-curtains swayed gently in a faint, warm gust of wind.

Jerry was staring at Naomi, his eyes like shiny stones in his head. He breathed slowly. His hands were clenched. He swallowed.

Naomi stared before her, her eyes wide and bright. A fly buzzed and alighted on her thigh. It buzzed off and came back and alighted on the red mark between her full breasts – the mark left by Jerry's blow.

A slight dizziness attacked Sylvia. A dizziness of unreality. Sylvia thought: If it hadn't been for that woman's voice singing and the machines downstairs I wouldn't want to believe this was happening.

"You ready to talk now?" said Jerry.

Naomi was silent.

Jerry slapped her face again, rammed a fist into her chest. She fell back gasping, whimpering. Struggled to a sitting posture again, an arm held before her weakly in protection. She still said nothing.

Jerry kicked her shins. He wore brogue shoes which had once been brown but now were grey and greasy and dirt-clogged.

Naomi whimpered and Jerry grasped her by both shoulders and pulled her up at one heave. Sylvia could hear Naomi's breath coming in laboured rasps. Jerry flung her down upon the bed, pummelled her with his fists – in silent savagery. Sylvia cried out.

Neither Jerry nor Naomi heeded her. She might have been ten miles off. Naomi uttered low moans. Jerry continued to smash blows into her.

Sylvia, of a sudden, took note of the expression on Naomi's face. Naomi's lips were slightly parted, and the light in her eyes revealed pleasure. A deep, luxurious pleasure. Her body seemed to writhe and quake in spasm after spasm of delight at every blow Jerry struck.

"But..." The word came out before Sylvia could check it. Then her throat went dry. Trembling, she turned and hurried away.

On the stairs, she heard the mutter of the thunder. It seemed more remote now. The black woman was still singing.

2

About six weeks later, on an evening in September, a boy brought the message. They were having dinner – Sylvia, her father and David; Charlotte always ate upstairs in her sewing-room – when the maid came in and said: "Sir, a boy just come to say dat Mr. Gournal dead. He had a stroke and dead a hour ago."

"What! Uncle dead!" David's face looked blank.

Sylvia murmured: "Poor Uncle. He said the doctor warned him he might get another stroke. Only last Sunday he said so – remember, Daddy?"

Russell nodded, his face grave, sad. "Go up and tell the mistress, Priscilla."

The meal continued in silence. It was as though a segment of the warm September night had entered the room and settled upon them like a muffling cloak. Before Priscilla had brought in the message David had been talking about a trip up the Demerara River his school was planning.

Sylvia listened to the sounds outside the house. The fan palm at the gate rustled softly, for there was a slight breeze blowing. Two cars went past in High Street with swift, deep hums. The distant toot and blare of other cars was always present: a background curtain of sound enmeshed with the agitated chorus of muted voices that was humanity.

Uncle was dead. Mr. James Gournal, an elderly black gentleman – a building contractor. It made no difference to the traffic or the muted voices. The silence in this room did not respond to the fact that another human had ceased to breathe; it did not spread and encompass the whole city because life had left Mr. James Gournal. Somehow, felt Sylvia, it should have. Wasn't death a big thing? A terrible thing?

She looked across the table at her father's face. It was pensive. The forehead was wrinkled slightly in horizontal lines. The pale blue eyes held a remote light: a defeated light; years ago they used to be greenish-blue and filled with gaiety. There were sacks beneath them now – and a multitude of minute wrinkles. On some day unknown, in the future, there would be no light at all in these eyes. They would stare into emptiness before someone pulled down the lids…

The shudder that went through her felt like a thin, chilly scarf wrapping her round. But consolation came at once. She looked across at the sideboard mirror and saw her own eyes looking back at her. Some day, she thought, they, too, will stare into emptiness, so what does it matter? Every pair of eyes everywhere in the world…

"There was a night in the Viceroy," murmured her father.

"In the Viceroy?"

He started, as though surprised that he had spoken aloud. "Yes. The Viceroy Hotel," he said.

"What happened there?" asked Sylvia.

"Oh, nothing startling. It was before you were born. About a year before you were born. The Saturday before Easter. We were on a spree – the usual bunch. Robby, Jack, Frank and Bertie. Bertie was very drunk, and he started talking about death. 'Death can be a joy,' he said. 'The contemplation of death in relation to the fullness, the crowded exigency, of living.' I think those were his exact words. He always talked about death when he was drunk."

"Perhaps he foresaw his death."

"Perhaps he what? Foresaw –"

Their conversation was interrupted by a shriek. It came from upstairs.

David was the first to reach the stairs.

Priscilla was coming down. Russell asked her what was the matter, and the girl said: "It must be de grief got she, sir."

"The grief?"

"De grief at de news, sir."

"Oh, I see." Russell turned off and moved back into the dining-room.

Sylvia and David went upstairs. They found their mother on the floor of the sewing-room. She lay on her side. She was beating the floor with her fists. "Oh, Jesus God! Oh, Jesus!"

"Mother, what's the matter?"

Charlotte ignored the inquiry. Her breath came in laboured spasms. She writhed. She thumped the floor again with her fists. "Ow, God! Ow, Almighty! Uncle! Uncle! You really gone, Uncle? Never no more? Never no more?" She screamed. She sat up and rocked herself from side to side, her arms clasped around her drawn-up legs. She moaned.

Sylvia glanced at David. David returned the look.

Charlotte turned her face upward. "Godma! Godma, you call him Home? Ow, Godma! Ow! He was all Ah had leff on earth! All *All*!" She began to clap her hands distractedly, looking from side to side. "Oh, Christ! Charlotte girl, wha' going become of you now? Not a cricket leff! Not a cricket in de world to care for you! Oh, shit! Oh, cunt! Oh, Jesus *Christ!*" Charlotte stretched up her arms and shrieked.

Sylvia took David's elbow and urged him out. On the stairs David said: "But why is she behaving like that?"

Sylvia was silent.

"And only the day before yesterday I heard her cursing Uncle. She told Janie that Uncle is one of the biggest hypocrites in the world, that he only comes here on Sunday to drink Daddy's gin."

Sylvia laughed. "That's nothing. I've heard her say more than once that Uncle hated her, that he's always sided against her. She said she'd long ago stopped looking upon him as a relative."

They found their father in the sitting-room smoking his pipe.

"Daddy, aren't you going to finish your dinner?" David asked.

Russell shook his head.

"You're going to let Mother's bad behaviour stop you from eating! Not me. I'm finishing my dinner."

Sylvia watched him return to the dining-room, and smiled, sudden affection in her eyes. She remained with her father. She sat on the arm of an easy chair. Russell reclined on a Chesterfield not far from the Victrola.

"I myself can't eat anything more – after all that display."

"After? It's still going on. Is your hearing defective?" He scowled and rose, fumbling out the switch-key for the car.

"You're going out?"

He nodded.

"Let me come with you."

"What of your lessons?"

"I only have a French exercise and two algebra problems to do. I can get them done some time before morning."

"Very well. Come on."

Neither of them spoke again until they were on the Sea Wall road.

"Are you going to the funeral tomorrow?"

He shrugged. "I'll decide that tomorrow. I've told you before what I feel about funerals."

"I know. A lot of foolishness. Tolling of bells. Wearing black. A hearse with wreaths on it."

"Exactly. 'Oh, Death, where is thy sting?' Yet, to judge from the fuss they make, you'd imagine it was a stab."

She nodded. The concord between them was complete. It was like an unseen ribbon linking them together. She looked at the pale moonlight on the grey wall, on the open swards on their right. The shadows of trees seemed snug; she might be lying on them now – several ghosts of her, each on a shadow. An owl would toot in a croton clump if she shut her eyes and listened. The lights of the city dotted amid the silhouettes of the farther trees suggested a perfumed smile. She took deep breaths of the warmish September breeze. Uneasiness came, all the same, and the visions faded.

"I don't know, though, Daddy. If I were you I'd decide to let's all go. Don't you think Uncle would have liked us to attend his funeral?"

"What have we got to do with what he would have liked?" He gave her an impatient glance. "Do you think he'll see us at his funeral tomorrow and be pleased? Haven't I hammered it into you enough that when a man is dead he's dead? He can have no more likes and dislikes when his brain has stopped functioning."

"Yes, that's so." She felt as though he had struck her on the mouth, but she did not mind. A cringing delight moved within her. She stiffened, her lips parting in dismay. Naomi's face welled into her memory. Naomi's face that day some weeks ago when Jerry was pummelling her. Intuitively she knew that the way she felt now was the way Naomi had felt that day.

"Daddy, I've never told you about something that happened at Naomi's a few weeks ago." She narrated the incident, and he listened with interest. When she had finished his boredom and irritation had vanished. He grunted, and she saw him smiling in the dim light from the dashboard.

Far ahead, the red rear-lights of parked cars were visible. Dixie... In each car a couple.

"Why do you think she looked as if she was enjoying it?"

He told her about masochism. She listened, and did not even notice that he had brought the car to a stop about five yards behind another.

"Let's get out and sit on the wall," he said.

They sat on the wall and stared across the long stretch of beach toward the distant surf. Beach that was sand and mud and clumps of shrubs. The sea drummed softly about two or three hundred yards off. But for the moonlight it would have been a depressing spectacle.

"I dropped in the very next day, and they were friends again. You wouldn't have thought anything had happened the day before. Naomi had a black eye, and marks on her arms, but she was quite cheerful."

He nodded, and lit a cigarette.

"Are all women masochists?"

"Basically – yes." And after a brief silence, he added: "Frustrations and civilized inhibitions often cover it up, but it's always there."

"Don't men suffer from masochism, too?"

"Only the kind who have in their chemical make-up a strong infusion of the feminine."

"I don't think I could like that kind."

"I know you couldn't."

"Sometimes I tell myself I'll never get married."

"Why?"

"Because I don't..."

He waited.

"Because I don't think I could like any man except you."

"You're a little ass." He chuckled and gave her a nudge in the ribs. It reminded her of the old days when he was gay and frolicsome. A car rushed past behind them at about fifty.

"Daddy, what's an Oedipus complex?"

He told her, adding: "But you haven't got to imagine you're unique. In fact, the Freudians say it's quite the accepted thing for children to be strongly attached to the parent of the opposite sex during the early years. With you I daresay it's gone on longer than it should, but the circumstances of your upbringing have been unusual. Your mother has never really been a mother to you. You had more reasons than Freudian ones to hate her. She was cruel to you. Once she burnt you with live coals in the kitchen. You were about five. Four or five –"

"I remember. But how did you know? Weren't you at work?"

"I coaxed it out of you a few days after."

He returned to the Oedipus theme. He was certain, he said, that she would outgrow this attachment. He asked her about Benson Riego, but she said that she hardly thought of him nowadays, though she saw him often on her way to or from school. The girls teased her about him sometimes, because it was rumoured that he liked her. One afternoon in the cinema he and another boy had sat in the row behind Mabel Earle and herself and had tried to get friendly, but she and Mabel had not encouraged them. They were too shy, for one thing, and, for another, Mabel had whispered that the boy with him was not of good class.

He grunted and said: "Oh, well, never mind! You'll soon get interested in the young chaps. Wait until you're eighteen or nineteen and..." He said the rest in an undertone, and she knew it must be something obscene. She was too accustomed to his habits to feel shocked or curious. She gripped his wrist and held it tightly, and he made no attempt to repulse her. He sat very still staring out to sea. He looked at peace. One night when they were on a bench on the Sea Wall promenade, farther west, she had asked him: "Do you like me to hold your wrist like this?" and he had replied: "Of course I do. When you hold my hand or my wrist I get a sense of peace, purity and complete absolution."

"You really mean it?"

He had nodded gravely, and she realized that he was not being ironical. After a silence, he had said: "None of the bitches I take to Dixie can give me what you give me, Goo-goo."

3

It was a year-end – for Sylvia – of important events.

One Sunday morning when she and Beryl Dell were cycling along Vlissingen Road, Beryl's front tyre suffered a puncture – and with a whizzing hum Benson Riego and two of his friends appeared. They might have been summoned by magic. Benson took charge of the situation, and in less than fifteen minutes the tyre was mended and the five of them moving along Vlissingen Road toward the Sea Wall. Benson rode with Sylvia in the rear of Beryl and the two other boys, and it took Sylvia several days to dispel the memory of his voice and of his powerful shoulders and handsome profile, of his self-conscious grins and hooting laughter – laughter deep and male one instant, the next a wavering, boyish falsetto.

The encounter disturbed her because it threatened to upset the values she had been at such pains to build up during the past months. It made her stare from her bedroom window into the fronds of the cabbage palms that showed above the roof of the Hammonds' house across the street, and weave into being the Brown Jumbie-men. Small, cynical fellows who dwelled amid the dense shadows of the fronds of the cabbage palms. At first she heard them chortling, but without warning they swooped down to argue with her, lurking invisibly about her.

"Didn't you say you could never love any man but your father?"

"Of course – and I meant it."

"Well, what's this you're feeling about Benson Riego?"
"Who said I'm feeling anything about Benson Riego?"
"You can't fool us, you know. Hee, hee!"
"You're silly. I only like – I only admire Benson a little."

She would turn from the window with a click of her tongue, but some time would elapse before the sound of their chortles ceased to mock her.

There was roller skating, too. It was the craze with everybody this year-end. One afternoon she and Mabel and Beryl went as far as Plaisance Village – four miles out of town – on their skates. And, somehow – again it might have been magic – Benson Riego and his friends materialized and overtook them on the public road before they were well out of Kitty. Benson skated alongside of Sylvia, and once stretched out and held her hand to show her how to execute a new figure they had been discussing. It all proved such great fun that they arranged to meet again the following day for another "expedition" – the word was Dick's; Dick was one of Benson's chums – to Plaisance.

Then came the sensation of King Edward's abdication, which formed a subject for animated and juicy discussion at Naomi's.

Susie Peters and Greta Soodeen and Clothilde Pumba were strongly in favour of King Edward's decision. Jerry and Gregory Brandt, while not against, indulged in obscene and slanderous attacks. Naomi was herself – shruggingly indifferent. "I don't know who is right and who is wrong. I would have to be in Mrs. Simpson's place before I could tell you what I think." Jack Sampson crowed and cursed by turn. "Good so! Ah glad it happen Blue blood don't act no different from common red blood!... De stinking capitalists! Let dem watch good and see what scandals their system bringing about! When you trace back, you'll see it's de capitalists who really cause dis abdication..."

A few days before Christmas, she went to a cantata in the Town Hall with Beryl Dell and her parents and brother. The Dells came for her in their car. It was the first time she wore an evening gown. Charlotte made it, and took pride in making it, forgetful that it would be a means of furthering her daughter's rise in high-colour circles. Nowadays Charlotte was losing her interest in matters pertaining to class and colour; she seldom made bitter remarks to

Janie and Sarah and Aunt Clarice about "de high-colour people"; it was as though, because of the easy life she led, she were spinning about her personality a cobwebbed sheath of indifference and quiescence. As one frictionless day succeeded another, the cooler grew the spark of her fretful belligerence.

Sylvia turned round and round for Russell to inspect her. He was in a Berbice chair in the gallery reading Rodway's *History of British Guiana,* a motheaten and water-stained copy obtained, after much trouble, by Robby van Huisten; some pages in the third volume were missing. He lowered his horn-rimmed spectacles, smiled and nodded approval.

Charlotte fussed around, tapping and adjusting.

David appeared from the sitting-room, fountain-pen in hand; he had been doing his homework. "So much fuss," he grinned.

Russell glanced at him, grinned, too – and winked.

The Frances' Alsatian was barking. Deep whuff-whuff barks.

"I bet you you trip up when you're going down the stairs," said David.

"You go and hide your face."

In the Town Hall she felt as good as any of the other coloured people present. Beryl did not seem any better (besides, Beryl's hair had small waves; it was not as good as her own). Nor did the Dowdens or the Baynes who sat in the row behind; the Dowdens were dark-complexioned, and the Baynes, though sallow-complexioned, had definitely bad hair; the two Bayne girls had had to use a hot comb to straighten theirs.

Tonight, felt Sylvia, she had arrived. Tonight she had become a lady of the good coloured middle-class. She had nothing to fear now for the future. She would live down the shoddiness and nonentity of Mother's pedigree. The thought of Benson, however, troubled her. Of course, she was not in love with him, but – well, just suppose he did, some time in the future, ask her to marry him. Could she? He was only a Portuguese.

She looked round the hall with its dark, varnished walls. She could not see a Portuguese or a Chinese or an East Indian. A few black people. All the rest coloured people of the respectable middle-class. Good-family people. How would Benson be able to fit himself into a crowd like this?

She pulled herself up. What was this she was doing? She was almost admitting that she was in love with Benson and had hopes of marrying him one day. Hadn't she vowed that she would not marry? Hadn't she decided that her father would always be the one man on whom her heart could be set?

The cantata bored her. This kind of music did not appeal to her. She liked dance music and sentimental airs. Nevertheless she applauded enthusiastically because everybody else did. She was a lady of society and must do what was considered the correct thing.

They had left the sitting-room light on for her. As she ascended the stairs to the front door she heard the sound of voices, and frowned. It was unusual for her father to have in friends for bridge or poker on the nights when he settled down after dinner to read any serious book.

She paused with her hand on the doorknob and listened.

The voices were in the sitting-room. She recognized them. There were only two – her father's and Mr. Knight's. There was something about the tone of them that made her want to eavesdrop. An earnestness and a seriousness. It might have been a tragedy they were discussing.

She opened the door quietly a trifle and listened. She heard Mr. Knight saying: "You've known me long enough, Grantley. Have I ever swindled you?"

Russell said something in a murmur which she could not make out.

There was a silence. The scraping of a shoe along the floor.

"This is the first time I've been caught napping," said Mr. Knight.

"Serves you damned right," she heard her father murmur. Another silence. Her conscience troubled her. This was mean. She remembered Miss Jenkins. But she had to listen.

She heard her father grunt. A shoe scraped again.

"Very well. Twenty thousand it is. I want a note for it, too."

"I'll give you a note." Mr. Knight's voice was relieved; it was a whining relief. She felt contempt – and then fear. Was he trapping her father into some shady scheme? She had a vision of a policeman coming up the stairs. Knocking at the door. Was Mr. Russell at home?... He presented a bluish paper... "This is a warrant for his arrest."

She entered and slammed the door hard, hurried into the sitting-room. They were sitting in the corner near the Victrola. Mr. Knight smiled at her – a rather artificial smile. He was getting stout – especially around the waist. He wore a pale brown palm beach suit. She hated palm beach.

"Starting to keep late hours already? What are things coming to?"

"I went to a cantata with the Dells."

He leaned forward in his chair. She sensed the new gleam in his eyes, and began to move toward the dining-room.

"Not coming to tell me good night – and looking so sweet?" She changed direction and approached him. Held out her hand. He gave a low grunting laugh, ignoring her hand. "Nowadays you think yourself too big to kiss me, eh, young lady?"

Russell was staring fishily before him.

Sylvia giggled self-consciously and bent and kissed Mr. Knight on the temple. He smelt of tobacco and moth balls. He caught her wrist.

"Who made the dress? Mother?"

"Yes." Her wrist began to burn. A lump turned over in her stomach.

"Grantley, you're going to have to keep an eye on this child."

She tugged, and he released her wrist. She said good night in a stammer and hurried out and upstairs to her room. Nowadays she had a room to herself. David, too, had his own; it adjoined hers to the west. Her father's adjoined hers to the east.

A feeling of trouble lurked in her as she looked at herself in the wardrobe mirror. She kept rubbing the spot on her wrist where Mr. Knight had held her. She felt soiled and yet remotely excited in a not unpleasant way. A warm shiver – also not unpleasant – passed through her at the memory of Mr. Knight's eyes on her body. She wanted to despise herself, and yet she felt flattered. She recalled Beryl's brother in the Town Hall. All through the cantata he had watched her surreptitiously – and with desire. Yes, with desire. The desire of a man.

She turned off from the mirror, shy to see herself. She smiled and experienced a deep elation and self-satisfaction. But the trouble-feeling persisted; it was like a cloud-jelly that shifted in and out of her, quivering and making her quiver, too. Her father. Benson. Beryl's brother. She tried to relate them each to herself, and found that she was up against a problem; it was like trying to establish an affinity with shadows – even in the case of her father, she realized, and the realization alarmed her, gave her a feeling of despair, of being lost and deserted, so that she found tears coming to her eyes.

She heard footsteps. Her father came in. He was still blank-faced, still stared fishily into space. He was sucking at his pipe, but it was out, for no smoke came from it.

"He's gone?"

He started, his hand stretched out to open the door that connected with his room. "Eh? Who? Oh. Yes, he's gone." He began to smile, moved over to her bed and sat down. "Enjoyed the cantata?"

"Not much. I don't like that kind of music."

"Thought you wouldn't."

"Daddy, what was Mr. Knight discussing with you? When I came in I heard him saying something about swindling and being caught napping."

"Been doing a little eavesdropping?"

"I couldn't help it." She took off her earrings. "I was curious. Is he in trouble or what?"

"Yes." He began to fiddle with his pipe – poking at the contents with a forefinger. His mouth looked tight-set and grim.

She pulled off her dress. She still undressed before him without shame, though tonight she felt a slight shyness coming over her.

"He's not in it now, though. I've pulled him out. I've had to do it before." He might have been addressing an invisible presence crouching on the floor at his feet. "I find it pays me to get him out of scrapes. Can't afford to have him go to prison."

"I don't like him at all – nowadays."

"I've observed that."

"He looks at me in a way… you know?"

"I know." His face was noncommittal, inscrutable.

"And he likes to paw me up."

He glanced up and guffawed. There was an obscene note in it, and she found herself getting warm in the face. She had just shed her brassiere. She turned her back hastily and pulled on her nightgown.

When she turned to face him again she saw that he was regarding her seriously – not indulgently or ironically as his laughter had seemed to indicate. "If ever," he said quietly, "I'm not present and he paws you up in any way you think he shouldn't, you slap him so that he feels it."

"I don't like to seem prudish," she said hurriedly. "I've known him since I was small. He might be my uncle. It looks so stupid..."

He rose and gripped her shoulder. His thumb sank hard into her flesh, and hurt. His eyes were cold; he might have been about to murder her. "It doesn't matter how long you've known him. You slap him if he gets fresh. Hear me? Lam into him. He's foul."

He released her and went into his room.

On New Year's Eve – Old Year's Day – he told her: "I'm going to take you to the dance at the B.G. Club next year. How would you like that?"

"That'd be great! You mean it?"

He nodded, and gave her a solemn wink. In his dinner-suit he reminded her of Clark Gable. He looked hard and strong – an iron man. She could feel the strength of him shivering through her as though it were an icy ray he were focusing upon her. The thought of having him as an escort at a dance at the B.G. Club created a breathlessness in her. She would live for next year this night. The New Year's Eve dance at the B.G. Club was a big function. Everybody who mattered in the coloured middle-class attended. It was exclusive. You had to be a club member, or be invited by a club member, before you would be admitted. And to think that next New Year's Eve she would be one of the crowd – an attractive, olive-complexioned young lady of good class in a long evening gown, accompanied by her English father – a hard, dashing Gable in a dinner-suit winking solemnly at the ladies, and, perhaps, snarling at them and rough-handling them.

She laughed at her fancies.

"What are you doing tonight?" he asked. They were in the sitting-room. He was waiting for Mr. Knight and Mr. Ralph and Mrs. Jarrow.

"I'm going round to Naomi's to see the New Year in. I promised her I'd drop in. She's having in a few friends."

He grunted, rubbing a thumbnail against the silk of his coat lapel. "I can't say I'm too much in love with the idea. Who will see you home?"

"Gregory Brandt is coming for me. He'll see me home, too."

"Who is Gregory Brandt?"

"He's a coloured chap. About twenty-nine or so. He's very educated. He comes of a good family. He's an accountant at Wheeler's Garage."

He shrugged. "Let's hope he'll prove a good chaperon." He coughed and added: "And also a eunuch of good conduct."

He crossed over and switched on the wireless, tuned in to London and brought a roar of voices into the room. He glanced round at her and said: "The Chelsea Arts Ball," and his voice sounded nostalgic. A reminiscent look came to his face. His whole manner softened. She went up quietly behind him, curious, and heard him muttering: "London. London." Instinctively she knew that this was a moment when he must be left alone, and just as quietly she withdrew and went into the dining-room.

Charlotte was dining, dressed in dark green and black. This was a special occasion, hence her deigning to eat in the dining-room. She was going out in a few minutes to Aunt Clarice's place. She and Aunt Clarice were attending watch-night service.

An explosion sounded in the kitchen.

Charlotte scowled: "Sylvie, tell David and Henry not to fire off dose t'ings in de kitchen, for Jesus' sake!"

"I think they're on the back stairs, Mother."

"Well, tell dem to go out in de yard and do it."

Sylvia found them on the back stairs. They were preparing another carbide bomb. She heard the clink of the cigarette tin, and smelt the carbide. "Off into the yard, boys! Mother says her nerves can't stand it."

"Tell her to go and bury her face," said Henry Madhoo. He was seventeen and in long trousers, had passed his Pupil Teacher's examination and had hopes of being successful as a primary-school teacher – at least, Aunt Clarice, his mother, had these hopes; Henry's predilections lay with motor engines.

There was a bang and a flash, and Sylvia recoiled with a gasp, hearing the tinkle of the cigarette tin cover on the stairs.

"Let me set the next one," she offered – and Henry let her.

Gregory Brandt called for her at half past ten. He came in a car which he told her he had borrowed from a friend for the night. He was handsome and sophisticated, and she looked upon him as a full-grown man whose business was to protect her. She had no fear of his being fresh. And he never attempted to be. She had remarked that, despite his smutty wit, he was a most moral and strait-laced young man. He never pawed at girls as she saw Aubrey Deleon and Jack Sampson often doing. He was in love with Naomi, but Naomi had told her that because of his friendship with Jerry he would not touch her. Naomi would have let him, and had given him opportunities, but he kept himself primly in check.

Naomi's sitting-room was so small that when six couples were dancing the room seemed packed. But it was good fun. Everybody was in a riotous mood. People kept coming and going continuously. Eustace Frank dropped in for a few minutes. He said he had to have a drink with his uncles before midnight. He and his people had become Christians; they had been confirmed in the Church of England a few months ago, two weeks after having been baptized; they went to church every Sunday without fail.

Greta Soodeen came in with her baby wrapped in a pink blanket; it was a boy, and they drank a toast to it. Sylvia stuck rigidly to ginger-ale and orange crush. Aubrey Deleon more than once tried to get her to take a rum-and-ginger, but Naomi held up her hand and shook her head; Naomi was keeping an eye on her to see that none of the men got fresh with her. "Now, Aubrey! Now!" Naomi would exclaim. "Nothing like that, please. Don't you go trying to tempt the girl to take anything strong. She's still at school, you know."

Gregory agreed. He always agreed with Naomi's pronouncements.

"Whenever Aubrey tempts you," he told Sylvia, "tell him to get behind you – but be damned sure you look round to see what he's doing behind you!"

"Greg, you have a bad mind," said Aubrey, who had had several rums. "You always suspecting evil in people." He added an obscenity so original that Gregory had to compliment him.

Somebody set the gramophone going again, and Aubrey grabbed at Sylvia and said it was his dance. Sylvia allowed herself to be grabbed. She did not mind the drinks he had had, and there was something dangerous about him that appealed to her.

Smoke mingled with the toy balloons and sprigs of artificial holly and mistletoe that hung from the rafters. The room was a welter of music, brawling voices and laughter and the clink of glasses. The aroma of rum and whisky triumphed above the smell of sweat and human flesh. And beyond the dark squares of the windows sounded the remoter density of voices and traffic noises of the city. Once Sylvia looked around and wondered if it were happening, whether perhaps she might not find that these faces were fading and the sounds with them. A sensation of ephemerality gripped her. But she did not puzzle over it; she simply shook her head as though to steady herself, and forgot it. She tried to merge herself into the riot; would not merge, but convinced herself that she had. She laughed at Aubrey's jokes, she jerked her head and sang whenever any of the others sang. At one point, however, she felt intensely lonely and wanted to sob. Part of a wall seemed to collapse inside her and a voice howled through the opening. Mournfully. "You'll always be lonely!" it howled. "You'll never be a good mixer! Why do you keep trying! Oh, you lonely, lonely, lonely thing!"

In the bedroom Greta's baby began to squawk, and Greta, who was getting drunker and drunker – she had no head for strong drink – called out to Susie Peters, who was in the room with a black young man named Harold. Greta called out and asked Susie to see what was the matter. Harold withdrew his hand from Susie's bosom, and Susie investigated, and called back: "De diaper wet! Ah going change it for you!"

"T'ank you, chile!" Greta sighed. "Oh, Jesus, Ah drunk!"

Jack Sampson was telling a girl called Henny Logan and a

Portuguese young man whose name Sylvia did not know a joke about a farmer, his wife and four virgin daughters. Henny uttered gusty shrieks, grey eyes sparkling, cheeks flushed from too many whiskies-and-soda.

Presently, a tall, lanky coloured fellow called Bam – Aubrey greeted him so – entered, threw up his arms and made animal sounds. He swayed backward and forward and bawled at Henny: "Henny darling! Come to my arms, lovey-dove!" And Henny rushed into his arms. He embraced her with swaying enthusiasm. And hiccuped. "Oh, gawd! Henny! Henny, Ah drunk, man!" He pushed her off and opened his palm before her. "Tell me fortune, Henny. What coming for me in 1937? Prosperity, sickness, death, travel? Read me hand and tell me what de stars say, child."

"Plenty prosperity," Henny assured him, after a brief reading. "Plenty, plenty, plenty."

This, however, did not satisfy Bam. With an unsteady backward pace, he put out his hand again. "You didn't read me palm good. Look at me palm again and tell me how de stars hang tonight. Go on. Read me fortune, man!"

Gregory, who was passing, told him: "Jupiter is in conjunction with Venus, Bam. You're going to pick up a hell of a dose next year."

Bam turned to Gregory. "Greg, you're my friend, or you're not my friend?"

"I'm your friend," said Gregory, holding out his hand.

Bam gripped it, held it. "Greg, where Naomi? Call Naomi and tell her her good friend Bam here." It was at this point that his eyes fell upon Sylvia who stood by the gramophone pick-up tapping her foot in time with the music. He started. He pointed a shaking finger. "Oh, Jesus! Greg, who is dat pretty girl?"

Sylvia turned her gaze away and felt her cheeks getting warm.

"Greg! Introduce me to dat girl. I never see a girl so pretty in all me life." He went down on his knees and bowed his head. "Oh, Lord, now lettest thou thy servant depart in peace." He looked up. "Henny! Benny, where you gone to? Benny, you desert me? You leff your old friend Bam?"

"I'm coming, darling!" came Henny's voice from the kitchen. Gregory led him off to the kitchen.

Presently, he went out with Benny singing "Rule Britannia" at the top of a raucous falsetto. Jack Sampson shouted after him: "Rule Britannia me backside!" Jack turned back toward the room and proposed a toast to the Government forces in Spain. "Down wid de Fascist dogs! Come on, Naomi child! Leh we drink to de enemies of Mossulini!"

At about half past eleven Jerry came in with some friends, and Sylvia realized with sudden dismay that the relations between himself and Naomi had changed. She was dismayed because she had somehow come to feel that the bond between Naomi and Jerry possessed the quality of eternity; it had never occurred to her that anything could corrode it.

Jerry had his arm around a dark-complexioned girl with artificially straightened kinky hair. He introduced her casually as Cora Barclay, and she waved with an air of sophistication. Waved at everybody.

Sylvia stared at her, fascinated, then turned to look at Naomi. Naomi was laughing at something Gregory had said, and seemed in no way disturbed. She turned her head briefly and called: "Hello, Manny boy!" to the Portuguese man of about forty-five, with a small moustache, who had come in with Jerry. Manny – he was later introduced as Manny Correira – smiled back and waved; he seemed shyish and unassuming, though, otherwise, he was perfectly at ease in the company. He stood chatting quietly with a Chinese young man who was also one of the party Jerry had brought; a very well-dressed young man who probably came of a wealthy merchant family. He and Manny, it was discovered, were doing the town and could not stay long, but before they left Sylvia was introduced to him. His name was Gerald Tai Fook, and he told her in a short chat that he was at Queen's College up to a year ago but was now in a Civil Service job. He knew Benson Riego; he had played against Benson at soccer, and thought Benson one of the best centre-forwards St. Stanislaus had ever produced.

She was sorry he had to leave so early. She liked him. His quiet, cultured manner contrasted markedly with the loud crudity around her.

Cora Barclay stayed on, and kept with Jerry continuously.

Once Sylvia heard Susie Peters saying to Naomi in a stage whisper: "But, Naomi, where Jerry pick up dis piece o' skin?"

Naomi smiled – it was a forced smile, Sylvia noted – and returned: "My dear Susie, it doesn't worry me what Jerry does. I'm not interested in anything he picks up." But from her tone Sylvia knew that she was hurt and jealous; she was only concealing her feelings in the manner of a sophisticated lady. Sylvia felt a deep compassion for her. A sense of tragedy invaded her. The music sounded portentous and empty with the emptiness of a coming horror. It was as though she could detect a trembling in the air. Something dangerous, she felt, was brewing for an explosion.

Jack Sampson caught her arm and asked her for a dance. She danced with him, but all the while she was aware of his shining dark-brown face and his close-cropped woolly head. She realized that her attitude was undergoing a change; she was becoming conscious of race and class differences. She remembered herself sitting in the Town Hall with Beryl Dell and her people – people of good family, olive-complexioned, with Good Hair. Jack Sampson was black and kinky-haired, of no family; she liked him as a human being, it was true, but she knew that in the years ahead she would have to exclude him from her society. It would be impossible for her to be a success with the coloured middle-class if she kept the company of black people like Jack.

Pity and regret came alive in her. Jack was such a gay, friendly chap. She had a real affection for him. Somehow, she never thought of him as black and different; he was just a human being, virile and obsessed with Communism, who could give them good jokes and laugh as though he really enjoyed living, who could be cursing the capitalists one minute and the next guffawing over a smutty story, or slapping somebody on the back as though nothing mattered save the conviviality of the immediate moment. She heard the deep whoof-whoof of a euphonium somewhere outside, and the merry squeaking trill of a flute.

At ten to twelve – she saw the time by Aubrey's wristwatch – she was dancing when it abruptly struck her that somebody was missing. She began to frown about the room. "Aubrey, I sort of feel – oh! It's Naomi. I haven't seen her for a while. Has she gone out somewhere?"

Aubrey winked. "With our good friend Greg."

"Greg! But..." She wanted to say: "But Greg wouldn't be so dishonourable as to make love to Naomi," but the words refused to become sound.

"What's wrong wid Greg? He got a car at his disposal tonight, you know."

She made no reply. She began to watch Jerry and Cora dancing. Aubrey's arm tightened about her. "I feel like a drink," he said.

"No, let's go on dancing. I don't feel like a drink."

He told her to behave herself, and led her into the kitchen which, at the moment, was empty. There was a trembling in her belly, and she felt a yearning for something she could not define.

"Take a rum-and-ginger. Just one."

"No, thank you. Coca-cola for me, please."

"Shame on you, Sylvie. Big girl like you!"

She shook her head, unmoved. Just a coke, please. No rum."

"Awright – if you say so." He winked at her. "I can see I'm going to have to initiate you into one or two things, girl."

"What things?"

"Don't worry. You'll find out. Look, here's your coke."

As they were drinking the pandemonium of midnight broke out. The whole city seemed to dissolve in a wail of sound. In her fancy she could see the sirens of the ships in the harbour sending up long mooing toots into the night – pink columns going up and up into the cloudy sky and showering down in flakes of confetti on all the car-honking and shrieks of whistles and the boom-boom of carbide bombs. She heard the church-bells, and thought of her mother and Aunt Clarice at watch-night service. They must be kissing now and saying: "Good luck, child. God bless you. Happy New Year."

She was aware that Aubrey's arms were round her. She began to resist and protest, then remembered that it was the custom to be kissed.

"Eh-eh You mean you want to refuse me my New Year kiss, Sylvie?"

She gave an uncertain laugh and held up her lips. But he was not content to give her a perfunctory peck. He did it as though for a Hollywood camera. He encircled her with his arms, pressed her close. There was a low drumming inside her as she realized that this would be the first time she would be kissed by a man in this deliberate and luxurious manner. She felt saturated with a deep weakness and let her body relax. The next instant, however, she was stiffening in disgust. She wrenched herself free and glared at him. "You're mad or what! What's the idea of licking me with your tongue!"

He looked dismayed – then began to laugh. Good-naturedly, affectionately. Like a big brother. "You never get kissed before, Sylvie? You don't know how people kiss?"

"What do you mean? Heaps of people have kissed me – but they never tried to – to push out their tongue at me."

He regarded her and jerked his head. "Ah, boy! I can see you're green. Never mind, Sylvie. I should have remembered your age." He explained to her how men and women kissed. It was a revelation. She knew she would remember this moment always.

His manner was still that of a big brother as he gripped her arm and said: "Come and let's go back and dance."

"No, I've got to go home. It's twelve."

"You're Cinderella, or what?"

"Oh, heavens! But Gregory isn't here. He was to have taken me home."

"I'll see you home. Come. I'll borrow Jerry's car."

He broke into song when they swung into High Street. "Should old acquaintance be forgot..." He had quite a good baritone, and she congratulated him. In getting out, she said: "Tell Naomi I'm sorry I didn't see her at midnight. Wish her a happy New Year for me – and Gregory, too. And to you, too."

She watched the car move off, and heard him break into song again. This time it was a Trinidadian calypso. The sirens and church-bells had stopped. But the roar of voices remained – and the shrilling of whistles, the boom of carbide bombs. She found David and Henry on the front stairs, Henry preparing a carbide bomb.

"Happy New Year, Sylvie!"

"Happy New Year, Dave!"

Henry's greeting was lost in the flash and boom of the carbide bomb. The tin-cover tinkled on the stairs.

Up in her room, she stood at the wardrobe mirror and looked at herself, remembering Aubrey's kiss. She turned this way and that, admiring her body, patting her cheeks and hair, making adjustments to her dress. All at once she saw infinite possibilities in herself for the future. But the realization brought with it fear. It was as though a finger from the years ahead had been laid on her forehead, warning her of shadowy terrors. She began to hug herself and shudder.

The Brown Jumbie-men swooped down from the cabbage palms. "Perhaps you think Benson Riego will propose to you this year."

"How could I think anything so stupid. We're still at school!"

"Now, don't go and get dear Daddy jealous!"

"You're big fools!"

She turned off and began to undress.

4

During the first days of January she would often look out of the window and try to induce herself into feeling that everything was fresh and different in the scene. "This is 1937," she would say to herself. "There must be a new look about things." But she was always disappointed. The street went on being High Street with cars rushing past. The Hammonds' house remained a drab pink. At the gateway the fan-palms looked dark green as they had always done, the fronds glistening in the sunshine and rustling with a hollow sound in the breeze. And the Brown Jumbie-men in the cabbage palms sounded as cynical as before. The routine of the house continued as in 1936. Charlotte sewed, Russell came in and went out – read books in the Berbice chair in the gallery, played bridge or poker with Mr. van Huisten and Mr. Ralph and Mr. Knight. Of an afternoon he took her for drives to the Sea Wall.

At Naomi's nothing seemed changed, either. Naomi and Jerry laughed and behaved in their usual casual, sophisticated manner; Cora Barclay and Old Year's Night might never have existed.

Sylvia could not bring herself to ask Naomi about Gregory: how Gregory stood in the picture now since he and Naomi had gone for a drive on Old Year's Night. And Naomi made no reference to the event, nor did she hint that Gregory had become her lover. Gregory, too, was his old self – smutty, worldly, good-natured.

School started on the second Monday in January – and school, also, proved only too monotonously the same as in 1936.

When something new happened – it happened in late February – it lacked freshness, and merely seemed part of the banal process of living. Agnes Feria announced that she had tuberculosis. She had spat blood several times, and when the doctor had examined her he had said that it was T.B. He did not think, Agnes told them in a low voice, her eyes getting moist, that she would recover. "Ah delay too long, he say."

"Child," said Charlotte, "dis is a hard world on poor people. I know for meself, because Ah suffer. My mudder dead of T.B. too." And after some more conversation: "Anyway, look, Agnes, if you got to dead Ah would like to know you dead in comfort. Ah had a lil' money put aside, and Ah want you to take it and make arrangements to go to de sanitarium across de river. You will get decent food and some comfort over dere. You work you' bones hard enough, girl. You deserve a lil' rest and good food for de last o' you' days."

So Agnes went across the river to the tuberculosis sanitarium, and Sylvia reflected, for days after, upon the generosity of her mother. People were so queer and inconsistent, she thought. They behaved like viragoes today so that you loathed them – and tomorrow they did something that made you respect and admire them.

Even Janie Pollard. She was loudmouthed and detestable – more so nowadays when age had begun to overtake her. Thick layers of powder and rouge failed to conceal the wrinkles forming down her cheeks and around her eyes, and her breasts had drooped; her teeth were in holes; she smoked too much and her breath smelt like a man's; her bones jutted prominently at the shoulders and hips. In her own words, she was "breaking up"; her laughter was brave and defiant, but the ring of despair could be detected like a grim, reaching shadow behind her tissue gaiety.

Yet Janie one day brought in a dirty kitten which she said she had found on the pavement; she asked Charlotte for some milk for it, and when it was hungrily lapping up the milk Janie watched it and bit her lip. The next minute she was crying.

Charlotte had several grey hairs. Every day she became more negative. Every day she lost a little more of her fire. She seldom cursed and scolded Sylvia. The servants were impertinent, defrauded her of the house-money, filched things from the cupboard or the refrigerator, and all Charlotte would do would be to mumble to herself about the ingratitude of some people... "But never mind. God can see all. A thief can hide from man but he can't hide from God. Everyone must pay for 'e sins."

May was a big month. Apart from the Coronation celebrations, there was the picnic. One of Beryl Dell's elder brothers was twenty-one on Whit-Sunday, and the Dells planned to hold a picnic – a house-picnic – up the East Bank on Whit-Monday. Sylvia was invited.

"And, child, guess what!" Beryl told her. "Jim knows Basil's brother" – Basil was Beryl's daydream boyfriend – "and Jim has invited Basil, too. And I hear Basil managed to get Dick and Benson invited!"

"What!" Mabel Earle exclaimed, for Dick – in the world of her adolescent fantasies – was her boyfriend. "You don't say! I can see we're in for a time, girl."

Sylvia said nothing, though her heart seemed to have receded. She could hear it beating a mile off. It always did that when doubt attacked her, when a conflict of loyalties arose within her. Ought she to be excited at the news that Benson would be there? Did she like Benson as Mabel and Beryl liked Dick and Basil? What about the way she felt toward her father?

"They're going to ride up on their bikes," Beryl was saying, "but we'll go in the bus with Daddy and Mother and the rest of the party."

"Where's the house, you said? On the East Bank at Houston?"

"Yes, it's the Laverys' place. A nice punt-canal is just near by, so we can take our bathing-suits and have a swim if we want."

Henry Madhoo lent Sylvia an alarm-clock, and on Whit-Monday morning it woke her at half past five, but the first thing she heard after the tinkle had died away was the dribbling roar of rain on the roof. She sat up and looked through the window at the damp, gloomy scene: the cabbage palms and the trees in a ragged black pattern against the muddy-hued eastern sky. Just her luck, she told herself, that rain should fall this morning. Yesterday had been a fine day with hot sunshine.

She hugged her knees and watched the dawn sky lighten to concrete grey and then to an indefinite buff. And suddenly she forgot her disappointment. A slow smile spread over her face.

The patch of sky over the housetops and the trees assumed a mauve tint, and the edges of the clouds – long, horizontal clouds – glowed with a soft pinkness as though fairy-lights had been switched on behind them. The cabbage palms stood out stern, jet-black, against the clouds, but the shorter trees seemed to absorb some of the colour of the dawn; their leaves glistened; they acquired a misty-mauve aura along the ragged outline of their foliage. The housetops, too, glistened, the galvanized iron cool-looking and wet in the drizzly air. The rain was visible as flimsy threads; it made a shifty lattice across the scene; it looked unreal, unconvincing and weird; it was melting away. She became aware that the sound of it on the roof had ceased. Only the drip-drip of the trees came to her hearing – and the running of water in the gutters. Everything grew pinker and more singingly resplendent as the seconds passed. The clouds split and spawned deeper reds and new yellows that shot up fanwise so that even the cabbage palms exchanged their jet-black for a soft greenness. The chill air drifted in at the window; it smelt leafy and earthy; she could feel it tingling in her lungs like sprays from a network of jumbie-fountains.

She felt alert and buoyant and tremblingly happy. And yet troubled. Troubled? No, not quite that. Moved. It was as though something, a ghost voice, wanted to tell her that a scene like the one out there ought not to be taken for granted or simply appreciated and forgotten; it ought to be held and closely welded to the central core of her life-experience, and allowed to influence her future. Colour the days to come with mauves and jet-blacks and weird pink lattices. It should be stored away within the very intimate parts of her being so that one day, when she was on the point of despair, she could bring it forth and let it comfort her, spread a coolness over any heated thoughts and grey feelings that happened to be plaguing her.

She uttered a breathing giggle and told herself that she was being silly. Yet the baffled, half-troubled feeling persisted, and she sat for a while longer, hugging her knees, and listened to the cock-crowing and the distant barking of a dog, the slow rattle of a donkey-cart coming through the damp early-morning air.

The Laverys' house proved to be not on Plantation Houston but somewhat higher up the river bank. It was a one-storeyed place badly in need of a painting (not a three-storeyed mansion painted pink and white, as she had seen it in her fancies). Inside, it was well furnished and decorated with taste, and cosy. The furniture was a mixture of ancient and modern: bentwood rocking-chairs, tables with carved legs, a wall mantelpiece with mirror, and Chesterfields, Morris chairs, divans and a wireless set on a low bookcase.

Mr. Lavery was an olive-complexioned gentleman with European features and bristly, greying hair, Mrs. Lavery, of a darker tint, with dead-straight hair like an Indian's. They seemed a quiet, pleasant couple, and greeted the party with smiles and cordial commonplaces. Mr. Lavery slapped Beryl's father on the shoulder and made a joke about the Civil Service. He told the young men to take off their coats.

"No formalities. This is a picnic!"

As it happened, only three of the young men had come with coats, but these three immediately took them off.

The girls giggled and babbled. Olive girls and sallow girls, some fair-creamish, some almost Caucasian pink. Some with natural straight hair, some with kinky hair straightened, some with hair that rippled attractively in a mass of smallish curls. All young ladies of the respectable middle-class. Typists and telephone girls. Stenographers and sales assistants in the big Water Street firms. Daughters of Chief Clerks and Chief Accountants; of doctors and solicitors and Sub-Comptrollers of Customs. Young ladies of old and established coloured families.

But for the presence of Mabel and Beryl, Sylvia would have felt awkward among these young people, especially as they were all in their twenties and full of airs and affectations. Mabel and Beryl and herself were the only teenage girls present, and Freddie, Beryl's brother, the only teenage boy. Benson and Dick and Basil had not yet turned up, though they were expected at any moment. Basil's elder brother had told Mabel in the bus that Basil had said he and the other fellows would come up some time around nine o'clock. Basil, who was a Boy Scout, had had to go on a hike with his troop – he was a patrol leader – but he ought to be back in the city by eight.

Now and then the breeze brought a whiff of cane-juice – a sweet, rich smell – and Mabel said that as soon as the boys came they would set out on a jaunt toward the punt canal on the nearby sugar estate. Meantime dancing had begun to the music supplied by a radiogram. The clink of bottles and glasses sounded in the pantry.

A thick-set young man with a cheerful round face came out into the gallery and put his arm casually around Sylvia. "Who is this pretty little girl, Beryl?" he asked. "You haven't introduced me."

Beryl told him: "Her name is Sylvia Russell," and giggled and tossed her head, glancing from Sylvia to Mabel with an air of but-who-does-he-think-he-is-at-all?

"Oh, this is Grantley Russell's kid?"

"Kid?" said Mabel. Beryl gave him a cutting look and murmured "She's no kid. A kid is a young goat."

"Cheeky young devils, eh? Come, let's dance, Sylvia."

Sylvia found she could not refuse, though she knew she should have done so at once, if only to support the tacit disapproval of Beryl and Mabel. The young man, however, had a charm that overpowered all other considerations. She let him lead her into the sitting-room. A foxtrot was on at the moment, and as the two of them moved off cries went up from the three other couples already dancing... "Ralph, that's a sin!"... "Cradle-snatching!"

Sylvia bit her lip sensitively, but Ralph merely chuckled, in no way put out. He danced perfectly. He murmured: "You dance well, Sylvia. Who taught you?" She said in a shy voice: "Daddy and I dance a lot – on Saturdays and Sundays, mostly. And I dance with other friends." She caught herself in time and refrained from mentioning Naomi and her crowd.

"You dance like a dream," he said – and said it as though he meant it. She dared not glance toward the gallery, because she knew that Mabel and Beryl must be watching her, and she was sure she would have wanted to giggle if she had caught their eyes. That would have seemed silly and girlish, and she must behave grown-up and with dignity to impress him and his friends that she was no green slip of a thing. He kept introducing abrupt variations – precarious swings and backward steps and sidewise staggers – but she responded to every one immediately, so much so that he complimented her again.

"You know your stuff, girl!"

She felt proud and elated.

When the music came to an end he said: "Come and have a drink."

"No, thank you. I'm not thirsty," she said hastily. She smiled and rushed off back to the gallery where Mabel and Beryl received her with giggles. "You danced with that big ass, child!" said Mabel. And Beryl sniffed: "You mustn't bother with him. He likes too many girls. He's too fresh, if you ask me!"

Sylvia learnt that his name was Ralph Gennarty, and that he was a Customs Officer. His father was Mr. Tom Gennarty, the manager of Wheeler's Consolidated Groceries. "He went to Queen's College with Jim," said Beryl, "and he's an Artillery man. He plays football for the Artillery Club."

Sylvia remembered that Russell had told her that the Artillery Company – a unit of the local militia – accepted only young men of good coloured families. The lower middle-class and the black fellows had to be content with the Infantry.

Beryl suggested that they should take a stroll out to the road, so they set out. The sun glared down from a sky patchy with grey-white clouds, but a steady wind was blowing from the north-east, and the heat was not unbearable. The grass was wettish, and, here and there, pools of water glittered in the sun. The smell of cane-juice drifted into their senses often, and presently Mabel pointed to where there was a punt-canal with slow-moving black punts laden with sugar-canes. They had to cross the road to reach it, had to brave patches of grassland squelchy with water, but they took off their shoes and found it good fun splashing through. The water in the canal was muddy and had blue and red whorls of oil on its surface in places, but Mabel said that farther east the water was not so dirty, and good for bathing in. They stretched across and pulled out a length or two of canes from the punts, and the East Indians who were in charge of the oxen pulling the punts smiled at them indulgently.

The factory was not far off. They could see its tall brick chimney against the clouds in the south-east, and the cane-juice smell was stronger here. From the east, along the muddy dam that bordered the canal, came a sunburnt white overseer on a mule. He touched his sun-helmet to them as he went past, the suggestion of a smile on his face, but only Sylvia smiled and waved in response.

These sugar-estate overseers, as Mabel put it, were not men you should notice. "They have an awful reputation! Oh, Lord!" Beryl agreed, and told them in murmurs how she had heard of an overseer who had had three illegitimate children by different East Indian women on a certain estate on the West Bank. Oh, heavens! And that's nothing. When they get drunk the things they say and do! Daddy says they're just white trash who come out here from England and Scotland."

But," said Mabel, "I know one or two respectable coloured girls who go mad over them. Low-minded girls," she added.

Beryl confirmed this, tearing at the piece of cane in her hand. She said between sucks: "I know of a girl who had a baby by an overseer. She went into the country to have it on the quiet – but everybody knows it's an overseer who is the father – and she's a nice girl. But now not a respectable coloured chap will look at her."

Serve her right!" said Mabel. "Who told her to chase after any cheap white man!"

Sylvia pretended to be very engrossed with the piece of cane she was sucking. Fortunately, Mabel and Beryl had no chance to notice her embarrassment. A hawk passed overhead pursued by two kiskadees and a blue sackie, and Mabel exclaimed: "A chicken-hawk! Good! Worry it, birds!" She shook her fist at it. And Beryl suddenly said: "But look, we'd better be getting back now. Perhaps the boys have come."

The boys, however, had not yet arrived.

A tall, thin girl saw them with the cane, and cried: "Those girls have some cane. I want a piece." She came hurrying down the stairs, a shortish, plump girl after her. "Just what I want, Beryl. Give me a piece like a good girl. Oh, but wait! You're Sylvia Russell, eh? Ralph was hunting all over the place for you."

A handsome young man with a small moustache came down and said: "Come, Sylvia, let's go up and dance. I hear you're a professional." He held Sylvia's arm and led her toward the stairs.

"My hands are sticky with cane-juice."

"We'll soon fix that, no fear." He took her into the kitchen. "Mother Lavery, where's the tap? Let Sylvia wash her hands."

"Oh, no, Charlie, take her into my bedroom!" Mrs. Lavery began to make concerned, fussy sounds, but Sylvia smiled and told her it was all right, and washed her hands under the tap at the sink.

As Charlie took her into the sitting-room, Sylvia found her shyness melting. Even when she realized that they were the only couple dancing her self-possession did not desert her. She was being stared at and admired. The young men were noticing her. She was definitely on her way to being a lady of society. In the ecstasy that seized her she forgot to be concerned over the non-appearance of Benson.

When the record came to an end and hand-clapping broke out she did not get flustered but stood aside and smiled while Charlie bowed deeply, his hand on his stomach, in acknowledgment of the applause. She felt like a screen star.

Almost at once another record was put on, and a wiry young man with classical features darted up and held out his arms. "My dance, I think, madam!" he said with mock ceremony while Charlie tried to jostle him off. But she was already in the arms of the wiry young man. She smiled at Charlie: "The next one."

At the end of the piece, however, somebody called: "Intermission, everybody! What did the Governor of North Carolina say to the Governor of South Carolina?"

"It's a damned long time between drinks!"

"Forward to the dining-room!"

While the crowd went babbling and jostling into the dining-room Sylvia hurried out to the gallery to find that the boys had arrived. Benson was red and perspiring from the long ride in the hot sun.

Sylvia felt a breathlessness – then it passed. She gave Benson a bold smile – the sort of smile, she thought, a screen star might have brought off – and said: "Hallo, Benny! What kept you so late?"

This was the first time she had ever addressed him with such a lack of self-consciousness, and Mabel and Beryl stared at her. Benson's face grew redder; he, too, seemed surprised. He shifted about his feet and replied: "Basil was on a hike with his troop, and I had to play in a football match the fellows arranged this morning." He spoke without looking at her directly, and she could sense the gauche schoolboyishness in his manner – the masculine bravado struggling to triumph over his bashfulness. He glanced at Basil quickly before Sylvia could say anything and said: "How about a swim, Basil? Where's this canal you told me about?"

"It's over yonder," said Basil, pointing. "You have to cross the road and walk toward the factory."

"Oh, yes, we went there this morning," Sylvia interrupted. "Why not let's all go and have a swim! How about it, Beryl? Mabel? Game?"

Beryl mumbled something in an uncertain voice. Mabel smiled and bit her lip and glanced at Beryl as much as to say: "But what's come over Sylvia all of a sudden like this? Why this brazenness? Even the boys seemed somewhat taken aback at the suggestion. They grinned and shuffled their feet, though Dick tried to show a daring spirit by saying: "Yes, let's go if your old people won't say anything. I don't mind at all."

"We brought our bathing-suits, so what's wrong?" Determined to show how grown-up and sophisticated she was, Sylvia smiled from one to the other of them, "You brought yours, too, boys, didn't you?"

"Yes, of course," Benson nodded, still without looking at her. He glanced at Dick. "Let's go, then – it's all right with me."

At this point Ralph Gennarty came out and asked them if they had had anything to drink. He put his arm around Sylvia and squeezed her arm in his easy, urbane manner. "This girl can dance, you know! Sylvia, come in and have a Coca-Cola with me."

Sylvia exclaimed: "Sure! Let's go. I don't mind."

An inner voice told her that she was behaving like an affected fool, but she could not help herself. The temptation to show off was too great. To be noticed by a chap like Ralph Gennarty was something. It showed that men must find her irresistible. It was not only her dancing. It was her face and her figure. After all, Mabel and Beryl were nowhere in her class for looks and a lovely figure. She had sex appeal. Yes, that was it. Sex appeal. So she let Ralph keep his arm about her while she accompanied him into the dining-room. She could feel the eyes of the boys and Mabel and Beryl staring after her, but she did not mind. There was a lightness, a lilting elation, in her head.

In the dining-room the usual comments concerning cradle-snatching were thrown at Ralph, but he smiled them off and poured a Coca-cola for her. He handed her the glass, and then poured himself a rum.

"Here's how, Sylvia!"

"Here's how!" she said, and smiled at him as they sipped.

She heard one of the young men say: "Hot young piece, that." He probably had not intended her to overhear, but, all the same, the blood came to her face. In a minute shyness would have taken control of her, but Ralph saved the situation by asking her whether her father were going to the Artillery dance that night.

"I don't know," she replied quickly. "But he ought to be. He's always at some dance or the other. He never misses anything."

"A real sport, Grantley Russell." He spoke as though her father were a contemporary of his. "Always game for a good time. Let's go out on the back veranda. It's cooler out there."

She finished her drink – he had already gulped his down – and they moved out on to the veranda, his hand resting, as though for guidance, lightly on her shoulder. She discovered that he had a quality about him that made it impossible for her to refuse him any request.

The back veranda seemed a fitting place for romance. It was cool and twilit. There were four windows, each separated from the other by latticework. A luxuriant tangle of correllita and morning-glory clung to this latticework and shut out the light, even at the windows, for it extended past the upper part of the windows, the foliage and stems of the vines drooping down curtain fashion. In a corner stood an old bookcase containing dusty, motheaten volumes. The smell of rotting books was mingled with the smell of vegetation from the vines and from the kitchen garden that could be viewed from the windows.

As they leant out of one of the windows, Ralph asked her about her dancing, how it was that her father had come to teach her to dance. He spoke in a matter-of-fact voice, and did not give the impression that he wanted to be flirtatious.

"You seem to have a natural talent for dancing," he said.

She made no comment. Only smiled and watched the kitchen garden.

He was rubbing a tendril of morning-glory idly between his fingers. And, just as idly, it seemed, he took her hand and began to toy with it – almost as though he had mistaken it for a tendril of morning-glory. "I mean it," he said. "You have talent. Born grace."

"Miss Jenkins said I had born grace," she mumbled.

He asked her who was Miss Jenkins and she told him. His fingers played along her wrist and forearm now – gently, as though he were perfectly unaware of what he was doing. A mere accident, it appeared.

After a brief silence, he said: "Has anybody ever told you you're a nice girl, Sylvia?"

She hung her head, saying nothing.

"No joke. I think you're very pretty." He touched her hair lightly. "Look at your hair. Lovely hair." He was staring at her. "And your eyes. Unusual colour. I don't think you have your father's eyes."

"Daddy's are bluish green."

His fingers – how it had happened was a complete mystery – had climbed to her upper arm. He seemed to be testing her biceps. "Such smooth skin," he said in a musing manner. His face took on an expression of slight deprecation. He glanced down at his own arm. "Look at my ugly hairy skin in contrast. Big difference, eh?" he grinned.

She giggled. There seemed to be a ghostly sponge inside her; it kept quivering. She watched the clumps of lettuce in rows on the bed directly beneath the window; they, too, seemed about to turn into ghosts; at any second they would tremble and disintegrate. She could feel his eyes looking straight at her forehead. They burrowed warm holes into her brain. She felt dizzy and unreal.

"Yes, you're a very nice girl," he said. His finger was on the point of her chin. She knew the pressure would come – and it came. She resisted, but only for a second. She let her face tilt up. She tried to avoid his gaze, took a swift breath. And then it happened, though this time she knew what to expect. She had a flashing memory of Old Year's Night, and she parted her lips as she knew was expected of her. Her breath seemed to recede a hundred miles along a cone of wind, and her body dissolved in a warm shudder – afterwards, she was not sure whether it were a shudder or an ache. Her breath returned like a prong of lightning and she jerked her head aside and gasped: "Why did you do that?" But her voice sounded unnatural and hoarse, and she could feel herself trembling in actuality now.

He held her wrist and talked – talked in an easy, unflustered voice. She did not listen to what he was saying; she was too upset and enchanted. She could sense new rivulets of emotion trickling through her limbs. It was as if some hitherto unsuspected machinery in her had been set into motion, and all the cogs and gears were being lubricated in spasm after spasm of some thin, delightful magic oil.

Mrs. Lavery's voice destroyed the magic. "Time to eat! Come along, everybody!" He squeezed her arm and said: "Let's go and eat. We'll come back out here in a little while."

The rest of the day, for Sylvia, moved past as though it were a tense cloud filled with small strutting blue Jumbie-men. They kept marching by in a misty pageant of triumph – but a triumph that, at moments, seemed tinged with omen. Throughout the meal, Ralph sat next to her – she sensed them tramping past, mingled with the magic-cloud of unreality that permeated her consciousness. Their faces were reflected in rum bottles, and she heard their chuckles amid the chatter of voices and the laughter and the clink of glasses. They dodged between the young men as the young men competed for her as a dancing partner. She was for ever in demand. If one of them did not want to dance with her he wanted to sit with her on the steps to hold her hand and tell her how pretty she was, or to take her on to the back veranda to kiss her. Jumbie-men or young men – often she was uncertain which was which. Often she tried to shake herself in order to banish the dreamlike feeling that enmeshed her, but her efforts never succeeded. It was not until about three o'clock when she felt sick while dancing and asked her partner to take her quickly to the back veranda that it came upon her what was the matter. She had been taking too many Coca-Colas doctored with rum. She was tipsy.

After she had been sick out of the back veranda window she felt much clearer in the head, and a dull regret came upon her. The blue Jumbie-men turned grey – and then faded altogether. She looked out and saw that a drizzle was falling and that clouds had banked in the sky at all points.

Charlie, her partner, was uttering coaxing words. He told her to wait out here a moment. He would go inside and get her something. "It'll settle your stomach and make you feel better."

In a moment he was back with a bottle and spoon.

"What's that? Medicine?"

"No. Worcestershire sauce." He poured out a teaspoonful and made her take it. He laughed and said: "See if that doesn't work wonders! I don't know of a better remedy – you ask anybody."

A gust of rain-laden wind blew in upon them, so they went into the dining-room and squatted on the floor, like two coolies, near the sideboard. Charlie made a joke about it, and began to sing a tuneless song in mock Hindustani. She laughed until tears came, then stopped, remembering that tomorrow was school again. How would she face Mabel and Beryl and the other girls after this?... "Child, Sylvia behaved terribly. Ran after all the chaps, and got drunk..." How about Daddy? He might hear of it... Oh, stop thinking about it. It was a grand adventure. Let anybody say what they wanted to say about her. What did it matter? She was getting a thrill out of it, wasn't she? It was a new experience. It was exciting. And it proved that she had charms every other girl didn't have. Men didn't notice dull, plain girls. You had to have a pretty face and figure before they paid any attention to you.

On the way back to Georgetown, in the bus, she sat with Ralph Gennarty in the two back seats. Everybody noticed them – and did not. Only eyebrows and sniggers told what everybody really thought. But she stuck it out – defiantly. She was Joan of Arc, she assured herself. Or Boadicea. A fearless warrior who didn't care a damn. She even let Ralph stroke her knee, and, later, her thigh. She let his hand creep round her waist – so lightly and unobtrusively – until it came round and cupped one of her breasts.

She did not regret any of it. On the contrary, she went up in her own respect. She had braved the sniggers and raised eyebrows. She had had a good time with the boys as any of the grown-up girls had had. She had shown that she was no shy, blushing virgin like Mabel and Beryl, afraid of sex and men. She was glad that her father had not treated her as other fathers treated their daughters. More than ever she saw what a grand chap he was. More than ever he seemed a dashing hero. He was no smug, narrow-thinking middle-class father. He was different. He was unique.

Another thing. She had gained a much better picture of this famous coloured middle-class she had been hearing so much of since she had come to an age where she could understand class differences. The highly respectable people of old families! She had had a chance to see them at close view – and she couldn't rave over what she had seen. In fact, she assured herself, she was more inclined to sympathize with Naomi and her crowd than with these artificial people. Naomi and the people who visited her might have their artificialities, too, but, somehow, they seemed sounder at heart. Was it because they had to struggle so hard to live whereas these middle-class people had everything secure and safe for themselves?

She broached the subject with her father, and in the course of their talk together he raised his brows and said: "Mabel and Beryl have actually taken up a different attitude toward you since Monday, have they?"

She nodded. "Yes, they're quite different now. You can't help noticing it. They would have gone skating with me this afternoon, but they made an excuse about having somewhere else to go."

He grunted. "Typical. Typical. Yes, the middle-class have some ways that are rather irritating, and your theory is not far off the mark. It is because they haven't got to struggle as hard as Naomi's friends. Their security breeds smugness. Oh, it's nothing new, Goo-goo."

"But I don't care. I expected them to behave like that. Their parents must have told them to cut me. I saw Mabel's mother giving me queer looks on Monday when I was sitting with Charlie on the floor in the dining-room. She sniffed and said something to Mrs. Lavery. Let them cut me. I still have Naomi and her crowd. And you." She wanted to add: "And you're the most important of them all. You make up for all of them rolled into one." But a shyness prevented her.

He was staring at his shoes. His feet rested on one arm of the Berbice chair in which he reclined. She sat on the arm of the chair near to which his head inclined.

"What of the Portuguese chap you say you have a leaning toward?" he asked suddenly, as though emerging from a reverie. "Has he, too, treated you coolly?"

"I've only met him once since – and he just smiled and waved in his old way. I wouldn't know what he feels because I've never really been chummy with him. We were all shy of each other."

He lit a cigarette. "You haven't got to worry about it. It will straighten itself out before long. I know it must seem terribly important to you now, but the day will come when you'll look back on this and smile." He gave a loud sigh. "Same old story, Goo-goo. Nothing in it that's new. Same, same old story. Happens to all of us."

She watched him. His face had taken on that tired look. He was staring at the drop-cord of the electric light, his eyes slightly narrowed. His lips began to move but no sound came. Then he glanced at her and grinned, reached up and tickled her playfully on the cheek. "Don't think I'm laughing at you. I'm not."

"I – I know you're not," she stammered.

There was a long silence which she broke by saying: "Remember one afternoon long ago you told me you'd prefer to see me marry a fellow of the coloured middle-class? Suppose I don't see one I like, or suppose I prefer somebody like Benny or even an East Indian or a Chinese chap?"

"Marry him – without hesitation." He shifted slightly and focused his gaze on her. "Don't let what I told you that afternoon in the Garden bias you. You've got to battle your own way through things. I won't always be here to advise you and solve your problems. And even if I were it would be damned impertinent of me to try to run your matrimonial affairs for you. Understand this. I only suggested that you would be more likely to be happy with a coloured man of the middle-class because I think the standard of living he would favour is the one to which you're accustomed, but you can adapt yourself to anything if you try. Above all, don't rush into any alliance simply for the sake of establishing yourself as a lady of the better set. That would be foolish. Marry for love! There's an axiom for you!" He slapped her thigh and sat up. "Getting late. Daphne will fancy I've been unfaithful. Go and get me a drink of water – good long drink – then I'll run upstairs and have a bath."

"Who is Daphne now? A new one?"

"Afraid so. Brand new." He winked. "Delicious, too, warrant."

"But why do you go on taking them to Dixie if you say – if you say you find them monotonous?

He guffawed in that way that always seemed obscene. It repelled her and yet excited her, made her heart beat fast in an anticipation of unknown delights. "A man has to have a woman once or twice a week, Goo. You're accustomed to my un-English crudity, so that won't shock you. Now, run off and get me that water. Put a lot of ice in it for me, there's a good girl!"

5

For Sylvia, after 1937, Hallowe'en held a different significance from what it does for most people. Before 1937 it had meant virtually nothing to her. She had simply heard of it as the night at the end of October when you held dances called Hallowe'en dances, the dance-halls being decorated with paper witches and owls and bats and lighted pumpkin-like objects called Jack o' Lanterns. It was generally a fancy-dress dance, and some people wore masks which were taken off at midnight. She had never attended one herself, so carried no very definite impression in her imagination about the occasion. After 1937, however, Hallowe'en took on a real, not fanciful, weirdness; for her it became the symbol of something actually ghostly and sinister – a time always to be associated with horror and ugly deeds; a time to shudder and be afraid.

At about five in the afternoon she had just come home from music lessons when Russell called out to her from upstairs. She went up and entered his room to find that he was standing before his dressing-table mirror in the costume of an Elizabethan courtier. She giggled but was not surprised; he had told her that he was going to the Hallowe'en dance that night in the Assembly Rooms and had mentioned what costume he was having made. He asked her what she thought of it.

She went round and round him, giggling and grunting. "You do look a sight!"

He scowled. "That doesn't sound very complimentary." He wriggled and dug at the ruffles. "Damned hot around the neck, I can tell you."

"You'll have to keep a portable electric fan on your shoulder."

"I didn't call you in here to make any of your nasty quips. Does it fit all right at the back?"

"Perfectly. You look like Raleigh about to spread the cloak for Elizabeth. Why don't you wear it at the B.G. dance on Old Year's night?"

"One occasion is enough, thank you," he said, taking off the ruffles.

"You're taking it off? Why don't you keep it on until it's time for the dance so that you can get accustomed to it?"

He gave her a cutting look. Then suddenly he laughed. "I wonder what Daphne would think if I turned up in the car in this outfit to take her to Scandal Point."

"You mean you have a date with her for Scandal Point before the dance?"

"I have. And don't speak in such an admonitory tone. Of late you've adopted a manner, when referring to my amorous adventures, that almost makes me feel I'm in the presence of your mother."

She laughed. "You do need a scolding! And, Daddy, look! That cigarette! Don't leave it alight in the ashtray there. I don't know why, but the whole day I've been dreading fire."

"Too confoundedly imaginative!"

She left him and went for a ride on her bicycle, eventually dropping in at Naomi's. She found Aubrey Deleon and Greta Soodeen there. Greta's baby was on the floor, its nose sticky with phlegm; it had a cold. It looked up at her and smiled.

Aubrey was relating how he and another chap had nearly had a fight the other night on the Sea Wall. Greta lay sprawled in an easy chair, smoking a cigarette, her long black Indian hair in a thick plait hanging down her bosom. She was flashily made up, for nowadays she frequented the Viceroy Hotel; force of circumstances had driven her to start hiring out her body. Jack Sampson had disclaimed fatherhood of the child, and it seemed as though his disclaimer might be just, for Greta never made much show of contradicting him; she always shrugged the subject off whenever it was brought up. Naomi felt certain that the child was not Jack's.

Naomi, also smoking, reclined with grace and abandon in a collapsible deck-chair which Jerry had recently bought for her. She waved to Sylvia casually. "How's it, girl?" She was listening to Aubrey's account of the fight that had nearly come off. She uttered low, mellow gurgles, her loose dressing-gown threatening to open wider and reveal more of her bosom than was already revealed.

Sylvia, with the familiarity of a seasoned friend, crossed to the wireless set and tuned-in to see what she could get.

Naomi's son, Garvey, came in and slunk shyly into the bedroom, and a few minutes later Gregory Brandt appeared and asked who were the witches and bitches coming with him tonight to the Hallowe'en dance at St. George's schoolroom. Naomi looked up at once, a new sparkle of interest in her eyes. She waved her cigarette and said: "Count me for one, Greg! I'm with you."

Aubrey exclaimed: "But you let de man insult you like dat, Naomi? What are you? A witch or a bitch?"

"Tell him which, Naomi," said Gregory gravely.

Naomi laughed, and her dressing-gown parted a little wider in front. Aubrey said he had "a lil' piece o' flesh" he was taking to a private dance. He moved his hands through the air in descriptive curves, and Gregory took the opportunity to tell them a story about two black girls just come to town from the East Coast. He lapsed into creolese for greater effect.

It was nearly seven, and darkness had already fallen, when Sylvia got home. She found David alone in the dining-room at table.

"Anybody upstairs with Mother?" she asked, as she took her place.

"Janie, I think," he said. "I saw her going upstairs."

During the course of the meal he told her that Henry wanted to join the Infantry. "He applied, but they say he must be eighteen first, so he has to wait until next year."

"I wonder what he'll look like in uniform."

"I'm joining the Scouts. I asked Daddy and he said I can join. I went to see Mr. Darke, and he said I can come to the next meeting and start studying for my Tenderfoot badge."

"I can join the Guides, but I would hate having to march through the streets. And standing at attention before the War Memorial on Armistice Day! Not for me. I'd feel like a real fool."

"What's foolish in that! Everybody does it – the Infantry and the Artillery and the police and the Militia Band."

"Not for me, though. I'm not orthodox."

"You like to repeat every big word you hear Daddy speak."

"That's silly. Orthodox is a word we've met with in school several times. And I *don't* repeat everything Daddy says. I think for myself."

"Fancy you're so big, eh? And look how short you are!"

She laughed. "I may look short, but I know a lot!"

"You *think* you know! Baa-aa-aa!" He thumbed his nose at her, rose and went upstairs, breaking into a shrill whistle as he sprang up the steps, taking them three at a time.

She felt a slow affection rising in her. Often she had told herself that her father must have been just such a boy: cocky, self-assertive and full of jeers for everyone who disagreed with him.

The telephone rang. Somebody – it was a male voice – wanted to know if they could speak to Mr. Russell.

"I think he's out. Wait a bit and I'll make sure." She put down the receiver and called: "Dave! Is Daddy at home?"

"No! He went out about an hour ago!"

She took up the receiver. "No, he's out. Is there any message you'd like me to give him when he comes in?"

"No, thank you." The voice sounded a trifle curt, she thought. It was not the voice of anyone she knew, but she was not good at recognizing voices over the 'phone.

"By the way, who is it? If you leave your number..."

There was a faint click at the other end. The line went dead.

She went back to the table frowning. Most peculiar sort of man. He could do with a few lessons in politeness. She dismissed the matter.

After dinner, she went upstairs to do her homework. Lessons were still a bore. She wished for the day when she could leave school and stay at home and read *True Story Magazine* and the film magazines she borrowed and bought. She could see herself waking every morning, bathing and dressing in an ordinary house frock, and, after breakfast, settling down in a Berbice chair in the gallery with a stack of magazines. No more Caesar Book Two, no more French idioms and irregular verbs, no more Theorem Five and Construction Seventy-two.

Doing the French exercise, she could hear the mumbling voices and husky giggles in her mother's room – and the whirr of the machine. She was frowning over a passage of Caesar when she heard Janie Pollard leave. She heard her call: "So long, Charlotte!" Then her footsteps sounded on the stairs.

When she was undressing she thought of her father. He ought to be home any minute now to get rigged out for the Hallowe'en dance. Perhaps next year she would be able to go with him. She would have to think up a good costume.

She settled down in bed to read, but more than once her thoughts strayed. She pictured her father at the Hallowe'en dance – saw him in her imagination smiling and winking at the ladies; uttering his obscene guffaw. Persuading his dancing partner to leave the dance and go with him to Dixie. How they all fell for him! Not surprising, though. He was so male and attractive.

An irritation came upon her. There she went again. Thinking

about him as if – as if he were her boy friend. She tried to switch her mind off to Benson Riego; it was a habit she had of late been trying to cultivate. She had decided that it was the only way to cure herself of this obsession with her father. She knew it would not work but she kept on trying.

Since Mabel and Beryl had stopped skating and going for bicycle rides with her she had seen little of Benson, for Benson had to go where Dick and Basil, his chums, went – and Dick and Basil always went after Mabel and Beryl. Whenever she did happen to pass him in the street, however, he smiled and waved at her in the old way. Some intuition told her that what had happened at the house-picnic on Whit-Monday had not affected very much his attitude toward her...

The telephone was ringing again.

She sprang out of bed and went down to answer it. It was Delly Simpson, and she wanted to know whether her father was at home.

"No, he hasn't come in yet. He ought to be in at any minute to dress for the dance, though."

"Is he going to a dance?" Her voice sounded surprised. Even dismayed.

"Yes. The Hallowe'en dance at the Assembly Rooms. Aren't you going?"

"No. No, I don't think so." Her voice had gone lame. A pause. "All right, Sylvia. Ask him to give me a ring when he comes in." Quickly: "No, don't bother. Don't tell him I rang. It doesn't matter."

Sylvia gave a malicious smile as she hung up. So that was it! He must have spun Delly some tale about not going to the dance when all the time he had arranged to go with some other lady. Served her right!

Her conscience troubled her. Delly was a fine person. From what I saw of her at that picnic long ago I know she's good. Too good for Daddy even... Upstairs again, she tried to go on reading, but within a few minutes was nodding. She dropped the magazine on the floor and settled down to sleep. She did not switch off the light. Her father would do so before he left for the dance. Uneasily she thought: I would have liked to see him dressed up again. Hope

I wake up when he comes… Sleep sent the thought curling toward the rafters. A curling streamer… The streamer straightened out… The telephone was ringing. Oh, bother! Could it be Delly again? What did she want this time?

She hurried downstairs.

"Is that Mrs. Russell?" It was a male voice.

"No. Would you like to speak to Mrs. Russell?"

"Yes, please – right away." She detected a note of urgency in the "right away", and was on the point of asking if anything were the matter, but checked her curiosity. One must be polite. Cultivated.

"Very well," she said. "Just hold on a minute. I'll call her." She took the stairs two at a time. Charlotte looked up irritably from her machine.

"What you want in here, Sylvie?"

"The 'phone, Mother. Some gentleman wants to speak to you."

"Some gentleman?"

Sylvia could have laughed. The expression on her mother's face was decidedly funny. She seemed so bewildered – so clubbed. If she had been told that a giraffe had called to see her she could not have looked more blankly incredulous.

"Yes, it's a male voice, Mother. I didn't recognize it. I'm never any good at recognizing voices over the 'phone."

"But which gentleman could want me on the 'phone?" She kept exclaiming "Eh-eh!" softly as she went down. Sylvia, curious, followed her. Charlotte seemed unaware that the tape-measure was still draped over her wrist. She exclaimed "Eh-eh" for the last time as she took up the telephone receiver.

Sylvia watched her face.

"Yes. Who is dat?" said Charlotte into the phone. Her dark negro-Indian face looked really stupid, thought Sylvia. Stupid and weak. No character at all.

"Mr. Ralph? Oh… What's dat?"

The high cheekbones. And her eyes were so dull and passive.

"What!… What's dat?"

The coffee-brown complexion began to lighten to a muddy grey.

Sylvia moved closer, trying to make out what the voice in the instrument was saying. It was like a thin amber wire. A human voice – Mr. Ralph's – in another part of Georgetown communicating something to her mother so that her mother's face turned muddy.

"Mother, what's it? What's wrong?"

"Oh, Jesus! Oh, Jesus... when? When dat happen, Mr. Ralph?"

"Mother, *what's* wrong?"

Charlotte dropped the receiver. It hit the wall with a clack.

"Oh, Jesus! Oh, Jesus God!" She grabbed Sylvia and hugged her. "Oh, Jesus, Sylvie! You' fadder dead!"

6

In Sylvia's fancy, it was as though a mist – a long, smoky-blue swathe of mist – swirled out of the sideboard and enveloped her. Through it Charlotte's face appeared bluish-muddy. Everything in the room took on a bluish tint – the light, the walls, the chairs and the dining-table. She heard, as if through a filter, her mother's low exclamations.

Charlotte did not shriek. She did not throw herself on the floor and thump the floor with her fists. She did not indulge in obscenities. She wrung her hands and muttered: "Oh, Jesus! Oh, Jesus God!" That was all.

"But, Mother, what happened? What *happened?* You haven't told me."

"They find him cut up bad on de road. De East Coast. A lady was wid him."

"Cut up? How do you mean cut up?"

"Somebody attack him and murder him. Oh, Jesus! Oh, *Jesus!*"

A car in High Street plonged a bell's note through the house as it droned past. An unknown car with unknown occupants. Perhaps bound for the East Coast. The telephone sent out scratching noises.

"Answer it, Sylvie. Somebody talking."

It was Mr. van Huisten.

"Yes, we've just heard, Mr. van Huisten. But how did it happen? Who was it attacked him?"

He said he was coming at once. She must brace up, there was a good girl. He would be with them immediately. Yes, immediately.

She found herself going upstairs through the blue mist. She tried to jump forward so that she might precipitate herself out of it. Once out of its influence and she might enter again the real everyday world where everything was normal, where there was no telephone ringing, no Mr. van Huisten telling her to brace up, there was a good girl. She was sure it must be her plaguing imagination. Her imagination was forever building up some absurd situation. She was too romantic, that was the trouble. There was nothing to bother over. Nothing terrible bad happened on the East Coast. Mr. van Huisten would tell her when he came that everything was all right. Let her brace up, there was a good girl.

She shed her pyjamas and put on her clothes. She put on her dress back to front, gave a breathless giggle and pulled it off, put it on the right way. Then she discovered that she had not put on her brassiere. She began to pull off her dress, decided not to bother about the brassiere. She giggled again. Should she powder her cheeks? Yes. No. She found herself moving about the room in aimless agitation. She heard a car stop outside the house. She rushed out and went downstairs.

Charlotte and Sylvia stood while Mr. van Huisten told them about it. He tried to get them to sit, but they stood. So he stood, too, and told them about it. With restraint. Not excitably. With soothing, sympathetic nods and in a low, calm voice. With dignity and poise. A coloured gentleman of good family. One of Daddy's best friends.

About a mile from Plaisance. The car was parked by the parapet, and the bodies were found a few yards off, partly on the road, partly on the grass border. Yes, the attack must have been sudden and savage. The bodies were badly mutilated... No, no one seemed to have seen the assailant... "The lady? Oh – eh, Mrs. Teller – Mrs. Daphne Teller." He flicked at a fictitious speck of dust on his sleeve. "But don't let it upset you too much, Mrs. Russell. I know just how you must feel. It's a shocking affair."

"Shocking." He squeezed Sylvia's arm, sympathetic, perturbed – but restrained.

He looked at Charlotte, and his manner implied: Try not to make a scene, my dear lady, I implore you. Try to be well-behaved for this once in your low-class existence. He could not say it aloud; he simply had to imply it. He patted Charlotte's shoulder. Wagged his head. Charlotte continued to whimper and wring her hands. And call upon Jesus.

Sylvia murmured if he would care to have a drink. She had to be the well-bred hostess, fantasy or no fantasy. Couldn't let Daddy down.

Mr. van Huisten thought he could do with one. "A spot of whisky, thank you, Sylvia."

Before he left, he promised to take care of all arrangements. They must not trouble. "Yes, all arrangements," he said in answer to a question from Charlotte. He frowned and wiped his forehead. Sighed softly.

"You'll see de funeral people, too, Mr. van Huisten?"

He winced. "Yes. Yes, of course. All funeral arrangements, too." Really, she must not trouble. She must try to be calm. He knew what a terrible, terrible strain it was going to be. The shock of the whole thing. He himself was benumbed – horrified. But please, she must try to be calm.

He kept patting her shoulder and moving toward the door – a man in a blue smoke-cloud. So Sylvia saw him. A man who used to come to the house here – only two evenings ago he was here – to play bridge and poker. A man she had known from her earliest childhood as a good friend of her father's. She had sat in his lap when he was playing bridge, had had her hair stroked by him. Mr. van Huisten of the well-known van Huisten family of doctors and barristers-at-law and Mayors and Members of the Legislative Council. Tonight he was a man in a blue smoke-cloud.

After he had gone Sylvia began to walk up and down the dining-room. She squeezed her wrists and stared about her. No thoughts would come. No feelings. So she had to walk up and down and squeeze her wrists. She heard her mother upstairs talking hysterically to David. David, a tall boy who resembled his father in features. He had said at dinner tonight he was joining the Scouts... "I asked Daddy, and he said I can join."

The air in the dining-room began to close in upon her. All the atoms and gases she had learnt about at school. She was suffocating.

She must do something about it. She must get out of the house. Go somewhere where the air would not press in upon her like this. She would go and see Naomi. That was it. Naomi her good big-sister friend.

When she was on the street she remembered that it was night and that nice girls of her age were not supposed to be out alone at this time... Daddy himself had once warned her... Let her go back and get her bicycle... But she remembered that her bicycle was in the garage... Daddy and herself in the garage when she was eight. Early in the morning, with the cocks crowing and water dripping from the star-apple tree. He was showing her a child's bicycle – his birthday present... No. She must walk. She could not go into the garage. Memories would smother her in there.

She walked fast. Near the War Memorial, a man called at her: "What's the hurry, girlie!" but she ignored him. Another one whistled at her when she was under a shop awning, and began to approach casually. She kept her head straight and quickened her pace. He did not follow her, but she heard him whistle again.

The Stabroek Market clock was striking ten.

It was a long way to Sussex Street, and she began to get breathless. She had to slacken her pace. The night was hot and she perspired. Her hair kept falling across her forehead. She kept brushing it back. One or two wisps felt damp with perspiration. At her armpits, too, it was damp. The sweaty-perfume scent of her body seeped into her sore lungs. *Soir de Paris* and sweat. Trickles of moisture ran down between her jolting breasts and down the middle of her back. One trickle ran down her temple on to her cheek. It might have been a tear. She wondered why she was not crying.

At last, she was in Sussex Street. The tailors' shops and cake-shops, the tenements, the shoddy two-storeyed houses, the nigger-yards – all were smoky-blue with the mist of fantasy.

She plodded her way slowly up the stairs to Naomi's quarters. Her rubber-soled sports shoes made no sound. It might have been a jumbie ascending. Her lungs felt so sore from her rapid walking that somebody might have pumped sand down into them. She felt she was going to collapse with fatigue. Her leg-muscles ached. Her heart thumped a mile away behind the sticky-clinging dampness of her dress and underclothes.

A wireless somewhere in the neighbourhood was playing "Thanks a Million".

The sitting-room was in darkness when she entered. She sank into an easy chair by the small table where Naomi kept her highbrow papers – *The Times Literary Supplement,* the *New Statesman and Nation,* the *London Mercury.* Gregory Brandt brought them for her.

She looked toward the bedroom and saw that the door was ajar and that there was light in the room. Her gaze steadied. She was looking at the bed – Naomi's comfortable Simmons bed. Two people were in it – two people naked and locked together, the male on the female. She recognized their engrossed faces, then turned her gaze away quickly, got up and moved over to a window, leant against the sill and looked down upon the dense gloom in the nigger-yard. Jerry and Susie Peters naked in Naomi's bed. Yes, this certainly was fantasy. No doubt about it... Hallowe'en. A witch had cast a spell on her so that she was hearing and seeing queer things.

She turned from the window and called: "Naomi! Are you at home?"

She heard gasps, a violent creaking of the bed's springs. The light in the room went out. The door slammed shut. Jerry called: "Sylvie! That you?" And she replied: "Yes, Jerry! Where's Naomi?"

"But, Sylvie, what you're doing here at this hour? What's wrong? You come alone, or somebody with you?"

"No, I'm alone, Jerry. Where's Naomi?"

"She's out. She gone to a dance with Gregory."

"Oh. Yes – at St. George's schoolroom. I – I forgot."

He came out and shut the door after him, switched on the light in the sitting-room. He was wearing a dressing-gown. There was a smile of embarrassment on his face. He was a good fellow, Jerry. Had his weaknesses – like Daddy. The ladies. She must not think ill of him.

"I just came to see Naomi," she said – and something in her manner must have struck him as odd. Something about her perspiring body, her disarranged hair. For he frowned and asked: "What's wrong, Sylvie? Anything happen?" His tone was soft and sympathetic. Jerry, the motor-mechanic, big and crude and car-grease-smelling, trying to comfort her, looking at her in a big-brother way.

She told him what was the matter.

Susie came out, dressed now, though her hair was in disarray.

Sex became an unimportant issue. It ceased to be embarrassing. They questioned her, speaking together, their faces amazed, animated. How did it happen? Where did she say? Did she know who were the attackers? Oh, Christ! Oh, heavens! Who discovered the bodies? She shook her head to every question and exclamation. No, she couldn't tell them anything. She didn't know anything. She didn't want to know anything. She never wanted to hear how it had happened or who had done it – never, never. She only wanted – she only wanted... Here she had to break off. For the tears had come. They mingled with her perspiration, made a stickiness on her cheeks. She had forgotten to bring a handkerchief. She lay back in the chair and could not see the room, could not see Jerry and Susie.

"Sylvie, I really sorry, man." That was Susie.

"You have my deep sympathy." Jerry.

She heard them saying other things, but the fuzz had grown too thick. The night buzzed and ticked and made a circling round her. Nothing was coherent any longer. She felt a hand on her forehead. She heard footsteps and murmured voices. Exclamations shooting up to the rafters like cones of colour on Old Year's Night. Muffled carbide bombs human in tone.

Once she opened her eyes after what seemed two years' sleep and found the room soft with light from a reading-lamp near the wireless, but there was no one but herself present. She did not trouble. She shut her eyes.

She must have slept again, for nightmare whistles sounded from near a tall grey obelisk – a mighty war memorial that towered into the clouds. Smoky-blue clouds. A black dog leapt at her and threw her to the ground where she somersaulted to a standstill, accompanied by innumerable somersaulting old men.

"Alone at this time of night on the street?" snarled one of the old men. He breathed rum-fumes into her face and made affectionate sounds. He had a round face, and told her that she was a pretty girl, did she know? She could dance well. She had born grace, did she know? He held her hand and rippled his fingers along her arm. She kept smelling old books and vegetation and hearing dance music. Then a man's voice came menacingly from the gloom under a low flamboyant tree... "That bloody rake! One day he's going to get a shot in his backside!"... The drone of traffic and the babble of voices pressed around her so that she felt as though she were blind and staggering helplessly in the street.

She awoke, and looked around. The light was still on near the wireless. After a while she heard a clock strike four. Somebody seemed to have thrown a flannelette blanket over her. She felt a weakness in her limbs, and her head ached.

She would not be persuaded. Naomi and Jerry, Gregory and Susie, and even Greta, spoke to her, but she refused to go home. No, she told them, she must not see him dead. "I must remember him as he was alive. I don't care what people say. People's opinions don't matter to me. I'm not going to the funeral. Daddy always hated funerals. He said funerals are obscene. People in black in cars, and a hearse and flowers. Nothing but hypocrisy. I tell you, I don't care what anybody says. I'm not going to the funeral. I want to stay here. When it's all over I'll go home...

"No, thank you, Greg. I don't want to see the papers. They have it in headlines? Very well. I don't want to read about it. Don't tell me any of the details. I don't want to know anything at all...

"No, nothing, thank you, Naomi. I don't feel hungry. I couldn't eat a thing. Just give me some water, please. No, no food. Nothing..."

In the same clothes in which she had come the night before, shiny-faced and unwashed, hair in a tangle, she lay in an easy chair at five o' clock, alone in Naomi's sitting-room, and watched the sky above the housetops and trees. Watched it turn yellow and pink and orange. Watched smoke rising blue from the nigger-yard. Smelt the old smells of cooking food, and knew that somewhere, about a mile away, a funeral cortege was moving slowly toward the avenue entrance of Le Repentir cemetery. An avenue lined with cabbage palms.

There were long, wispy clouds in the sky, and at about a quarter to six they were a vivid orange. Lovely. Soothing. Peace-giving.

The breeze came in at the window in soft, cool puffs, leafy and earthy, tinged with the smell of something frying.

PART THREE

1

And now the new era. The reports in the newspaper that she could not avoid reading. They were morbidly compelling. Footprints had been found in the vicinity. Signs of a struggle on the grass border. The doctor was certain that a sharp cutlass must have been the weapon used – but a heavy stick covered with clotted blood was found about a hundred yards from the scene. The pathologist had certified that it was human blood. The mystery as to the identity of the murderer or murderers. Mr. and Mrs. Teller had been living apart for some months. Mr. Teller had a perfect alibi, however, and, in any case, his physique was small. He was not an aggressive man – just a mild, bespectacled, highly placed official in the Education Department. Absurd to think of him in connection with a brutal murder.

The inquest was the worst ordeal... No, she did not recognize the voice. It might have been one of her father's friends – or it might not; she was not good at recognizing voices over the telephone... It must have been about half past seven when the call came. Yes, she was pretty sure, because it was seven when she got home, and she had been taking dinner when the 'phone rang. Yes, she was still eating... No, he had never told her much about his friends – or about his intimate affairs. He had told her about Mrs. Teller, but he had never gone into details about his friendship... Just mentioned her name, and that he went to Dixie with her, but nothing more...

Mr. Knight called. He assured Charlotte that everything would be all right; she had nothing to fear concerning her financial situation. As always, he was charming. He was sympathetic and kindly. He patted Sylvia on the shoulder and told her to keep her chin up. It comforted her. She felt mean for having thought ill of him in the past. The Chicken Hawk. Widow-fleecer. How could people have invented such names for him? Such a kind, considerate man. She could have kicked Janie Pollard and Sarah Johnson for advising her mother to go carefully with him... "He's a rogue, Charlotte. Don't let him rob you. Careful what you sign. Don't sign no papers he give you to sign. He noted for robbing widows, child..." It seemed so unfair, so petty to say such things about him when he was taking care of their affairs for them as a good friend of her father's and not merely as a solicitor.

Then there was living down the minor disgrace of not having attended the funeral. "So heartless," said Charlotte. "I can't understand the child. She and her daddy such good friends, and when he dead she won't even show her face at 'e funeral."

Sarah and Janie and the others agreed. "It's unnatural," said Sarah. "She ain' got no feelings."

All that, however, could be ignored. It hurt to hear such things said, but she could shrug it off without much trouble. So long as she herself understood her reasons for not having been in the house to see his battered corpse. He, too, would have understood. He would have agreed with her that with her impressionable nature it would have made the event doubly horrible for her had she beheld him lying still and bruised in death. As for the funeral, she could hear him laughing and telling her how right she had been to shun so obnoxious and barbarous a ritual – so farcical and hypocritical a performance. It was true he had attended funerals himself, but he had always done so under protest. More than once he had said to her: "I'm already trapped in the social animal-pit, Goo. Don't let them get you, too. Be yourself. Live in your own world and do as *you* feel you ought to do, and in the long run you'll be a satisfied person."

That was what she intended to do – to live in her own world, to be herself, to act in accordance with her own convictions.

If only she could dispel this feeling of fantasy, though. Nothing seemed solid and substantial now. Even the buildings and trees might have been things made of mist. There was that persistent lightness in her head that made her want to stare about her with a sensation of instability.

She told Charlotte that she wanted to leave school, and Charlotte said that she could do as she pleased. "I got enough to worry me head, child, and you is a big woman for yourself. Do just as you like."

So she did not go back to school. A feeling of independence blossomed in her. She felt free to mould her own fortunes and her own schemes for living. More than ever now her mother appeared to her a cypher; she did not count. Her father was dead – and only he had mattered. He had been her one rock of respect, her one idol of interest. She had no one to disappoint or hurt now, so she could do whatever she felt inclined. She had nobody to reckon with but herself.

One afternoon at Naomi's, Gregory commented on the fact that she was made up more brilliantly than usual. "You dazzle me with your reddened cheeks, lady. And your lips would make the cherries bow with shame."

She gave a hard laugh, and told him to go to hell. He stared. He asked her since when she had begun to use such language. "Our dear unspoiled Sylvia!" She experienced a twinge of shame but outwardly preserved a brazen face. "I'm my own mistress these days, Greg. I can swear if I want to – and use all the lipstick and rouge I please."

But that cured her of her newborn daring. She realized that it was not in her to be crude in her speech and vulgar in her appearance. Whether her father were alive or not, there was her own self-respect to consider. Revolting from the old way of life simply for the sake of revolting would be foolish – and pointless. It came upon her that how she had viewed life before her father's death was how she wanted to view it now. To be clean in every respect; to be generous and considerate toward other people; to be balanced in her outlook; to be sane in her attitude toward people, and tolerant of their weaknesses. These were the precepts her father, directly or indirectly, had instilled into her; occasionally she even framed her thoughts in his language. Very well. She did not mind if she was considered an echo of him. She was proud to be his echo. She would carry on his teachings and shut her ears against the jeers of the world. But she must not be cocky. Her father had often told her that she had a noble spirit. She must remain noble – not degenerate into a poor specimen like Mother. Even Mother she must try not to think too harshly of. After all, everybody could not be strong and full of character; there had to be weaklings. The strong must help the weak, not sniff at and despise them.

When she suggested to Charlotte that Russell's things ought to be gone through to see what documents and papers he had that might be of value Charlotte said: "All right, Sylvie, you go through dem. I ain' know nutting about documents. You tek de matter in hand." She did not speak in her usual surly manner. She spoke as though she recognized that she had a daughter who was more capable than herself.

But when Sylvia went through the documents in the drawers of her father's desk she saw, with humility, how very little more capable than her mother she was. These legal papers and sheets of foolscap with close typewritten words baffled her completely. She had to put them away.

Her dream of an idle life did not materialize as she had fashioned it in her fancy when she was at school. She read so much that her eyes grew tired and sleepy, and the magazines themselves began to seem dull. She became surfeited with stories of love and love and more love and rape and murder. She found that time began to prove a problem – so much of it and so little to do in it except the same old things day after day. Go for a ride on her bicycle, read, come home, read, go and visit Naomi, come home, read. Nor did the cinema help to fill the emptiness and pointlessness of existence. Nothing she indulged in seemed capable of replacing the chats she used to have with her father, and his companionship. She told herself that she had been a fool to leave school.

Gregory suggested that she should find some hobby. "Poultry rearing, gardening, sewing – anything."

"Why don't you let your mother teach you to sew?" said Naomi.

"I hate sewing. Nothing I hate more than that machine of Mother's buzzing all day long. The very smell of dress material annoys me – and all those fashion magazines! *Weldon's, Mademoiselle, McCalls* – I hate them! I can burn them all and stamp on them!" Her voice rose hysterically.

She grew depressed and irritable. She sulked and spoke snappishly when addressed. And her mood was made darker by the people who came to the house to see Charlotte. Foster relatives from the country who brought fat loads of sympathy, who wagged their heads and moaned and gave long-winded sermons on the suddenness of death in the midst of life, who expatiated on the subject of the Hereafter – "dat place of rest above", as Cousin Benji called it. They quoted comforting passages from the Bible... "Ah, me child! Dat book! Dat great book!" sighed Dear-aunt Betsie.

She could have screamed sometimes when she heard that droning, mournful display going on in her mother's room. And Charlotte accepted it all in passive silence, only grunting or sighing occasionally, her face a long mask of self-pity or mock grief.

When Sylvia could stand it no longer she would go down into the gallery and recline in the Berbice chair and stare at the rafters. Stare until thoughts of her father made her eyes burn and spill out tear after tear.

One afternoon, about three weeks after his death, she was halfway across the sitting-room, on her way to the gallery, when she came to a halt with a gasp, her eyes wide. The blood pounded through her body.

There he was! In the Berbice chair in the gallery reading the *Strand Magazine!* So ghosts were real, after all... Her skin began to prickle. Then she uttered a quavering laugh and went hurrying forward into the gallery.

"Oh, heavens, Dave! I could have sworn it was Daddy!"

David turned his head and lowered the magazine.

"What's wrong?"

"It – it must have been the way the light was striking in. I – I..."

She gulped and sat down on an arm of the chair.

At any other time David would have scowled and told her to hang off and not disturb him. But he let her sit where she was without protest. A silence had come upon him since Hallowe'en. Often she had seen him, red-eyed, staring into nothingness. The depth of his grief had surprised her. She had never thought of him as being capable of any but the slightest of emotions. Of a sudden he ceased to be a boy in her sight. She put out her hand and stroked his hair. "You resemble Daddy so much."

He gave a deep grunt, and his features twitched in an uncertain scowl. He adjusted himself and held up the magazine before him. But she knew he was only making a pretence of reading. She saw the strained look on his face, and how rapidly he was blinking.

"Let's go for a walk," she said, rising hastily. She had said it merely to save him from embarrassment – according to his boyish code of pride it was a disgrace to be caught shedding tears – but he surprised her by rising and saying in a quick, low voice: "Yes, let's go."

They went to the Sea Wall, and were silent all the way. They found a vacant bench not far from the bandstand, and seated themselves.

"Did you join the Scouts?"

"No, I didn't go back after – after what happened to Daddy." He stared straight before him, out to sea. The tide was coming in, and the grey waves crashed tumultuously on the beach. A strong wind was blowing. Children screamed and frolicked all about them – on the grass embankment and on the wall promenade. Nurses with prams and couples went past. The sun was low in the west, and the sunshine mild, the air pleasant and exhilarating.

"You should go back. It's a good thing, the Scouts."

He rubbed his hand self-consciously along his thigh. "Mother says we've got to be careful how we spend. She's sure to say she can't afford to buy my uniform."

"What! She couldn't say such a thing. We're not poor. Mr. Knight told her we have nothing to worry about." A protectiveness arose in her. She gripped his elbow and said: "You go back to Mr. Darke and tell him you still want to join. I'll speak to Mother and get her to buy your uniform."

"You'll speak to her?"

"Of course. You go ahead."

A sparkle came into his eyes. She could see that she had raised his spirits. He had confidence in her power to get things done. For the first time since Hallowe'en a warmth of interest stirred inside her. She studied his profile and remembered how she had mistaken him for the ghost of her father. She had never noticed before how close the resemblance was. She felt a sudden regret that she had taken him so much for granted in the past. Perhaps this was just how her father had looked when he was twelve – except, of course, that he would not have been so tall. The colour of the eyes was the same. And the hair. David was fair-complexioned, too – not pink as her father had been; David's complexion was sallowish. Still, in certain lights, and especially after exertion when the blood was in his face, he could have passed for pure white. He showed every sign, too, of being as masculine as her father.

The warmth in her increased, spread through her limbs. Her heart beat faster. The impulse to run her fingers through his hair burned in her. Her hand jerked slightly in her lap, then subsided. She decided that she must restrain herself.

2

One morning toward the end of November Mr. Knight came up the stairs and surprised her in the Berbice chair. She sprang up, drew her gown about her and opened the door for him. She could feel his eyes on her, and knew that he was seeing her as a woman. It reminded her of the night when she had come home after the cantata. After she had asked him to be seated, she hurried inside and upstairs to her mother.

Charlotte frowned and uttered a whining sound. "You talk to him and ask him what he want. I busy here now, and Ah not dressed to see nobody."

"What about me? I'm in pyjamas."

"You can't haul on a dress quickly? It must be money matters he want to talk over. He say he would give me a cheque at de end of de month." Her manner was appealing. "I ain' know nutting about money matters, Sylvie. You had more education dan me. You go down and talk to 'e. It's in your interest, too."

"But, Mother, you're Daddy's widow. It's your place to see him. Suppose it's something he has for you to sign. I can't sign for you."

Charlotte sighed and rose. "Ah suppose Ah will have to see him, den. I only hope it's nutting to sign, though, because Ah not signing no paper for him to defraud me. Clarice and Janie and Sarah, they all warn me against him. He's a very clever man."

Sylvia uttered a sulky sound and went into her room, but when she heard her mother going downstairs she followed her. She did not go farther than the dining-room, however. She ensconced herself between the sideboard and the curtain that hung partly across one of the doors that opened into the sitting-room. She heard her mother greet Mr. Knight in her weak, whining voice, heard Mr. Knight greet her in his soft, charming voice. Then there was the scraping of chairs, and Mr. Knight began to talk about money and death duties, about property and bonds and securities. Charlotte punctuated his remarks with assenting monosyllables, though it was evident that she understood not a word of what he was saying.

It was not until he came to what seemed the real reason for his visit that she understood. He said: "Well, what I dropped in about, Mrs. Russell, was to have this little chat with you, and while I'm about it I thought it would be as well if I took a look at Grantley's papers. No harm sorting them out and putting them in order."

Sylvia peeped through an aperture in the folds of the curtain and saw his pleasant, smiling face. His paunch seemed larger every time she saw him. A feeling of distrust swept her. Was he, at heart, as kind and generous and understanding as he wanted to make out?

Charlotte hung her head hesitantly and mumbled: "You want to look through his papers, you say?"

He leaned back easily in his chair. "Yes, I might as well. He kept them upstairs in his desk, I think, didn't he?"

"Yes, in his desk upstairs," said Charlotte. There was caution in her manner. She must be recalling the warnings of Aunt Clarice and the others.

"I don't suppose there's anything vital among them," smiled Mr. Knight." It's more or less a formality, you see. I have to assess his estate and submit the returns so that we can clear off the death duties, and there may be one or two vouchers and receipts and little odds and ends of a useful nature among the papers in his desk. The quicker we get everything settled the better for you. Don't want your allowance held up, do you?"

Charlotte sniggered and fumbled sheepishly with her skirt. "Yes, I understand, Mr. Knight." She hesitated, then went on: "If it's any special paper in de desk you want to see, Ah can go up and get it for you. Sylvie can help me to search for it."

"Oh, no, no, no! Nothing special. Nothing at all special." He sat forward abruptly, and his manner now was a trifle stiff. "Do you object to my looking through your husband's papers?"

"Oh, no, Mr. Knight! I didn't say I object." She sniggered again. "All Ah had in mind – Ah was just wondering if Ah couldn't save you de trouble of going upstairs."

He laughed, as though the situation had just been made perfectly clear to him. "Ah, you housewives!" He wagged a playfully scolding finger at her. "I know what the truth of the matter is. You've dusted and tidied everything on that desk so carefully that you're afraid I'm going to make a mess. But don't let that upset you. I can promise you I'll preserve order. My vice is tidiness. My clerk will tell you that."

Charlotte now seemed thoroughly defeated. She rose and said: "Very well, Mr. Knight. If you want to come up I will take you." Sylvia dashed across the dining-room and up the stairs. By the time her mother and Mr. Knight had entered Russell's room she had climbed on to a ledge over her dressing-table. From here she could watch them through the latticework at the top of the wall, for the wall, in tropical fashion, did not reach to the ceiling.

Charlotte unlocked the desk – it was a roll-top desk – and also the drawers in the desk, and Mr. Knight sat down and began to go through the papers. Charlotte stood aside and watched him, a silly, fixed smile on her face, her manner nervous and anxious. Once she said: "You not taking away any paper, I hope, Mr. Knight?"

Mr. Knight shook his head reassuringly and smiled: "No need to fear, Mrs. Russell. I know you must attach a lot of sentimental value to everything that belongs to Grantley. I simply want to check through to make sure there's nothing of importance in here."

After a while, Charlotte showed signs of restlessness. Mr.

Knight glanced up and remarked: "Hope I'm not keeping you from your house duties."

"No, no, Mr. Knight. Ah not very busy dis morning."

She watched him continuously – and with a sly, catlike keenness. She kept squeezing her hands together as though they were cold.

Presently, Mr. Knight glanced up again. "Could I trouble you for a glass of water, Mrs. Russell?"

Charlotte, not being a lady, did not rush off downstairs to get the water. The desk was near a window that looked down upon the back stairs – the stairs that led down from the kitchen. Hardly removing her gaze from Mr. Knight's agile hands, Charlotte leant toward the window and bawled: "Kathy! Katey! Bring up a tumbler of water! Ice water! In de master' room!"

Mr. Knight winced, his upper-class sensibilities evidently jarred upon. Or it might have been for another reason that he winced. Annoyance and frustration, perhaps. Sylvia was not certain.

When Katey brought the water, he took a few sips, then put down the glass and turned his attention to the papers again. After a moment, he appeared definitely uncomfortable. He frowned and shifted about in the chair. But Charlotte kept her post, her eyes never leaving his hands for one instant.

Abruptly – after he had stacked away most of the papers neatly in the pigeonholes and in the drawers – he rose and said that he supposed that would have to do for today. He would probably call again another day.

"A lot more work in this than I'd bargained for," he murmured. Casually he bent and took up an oblong slip of paper from a right-hand drawer which he had omitted to shut. He glanced at Charlotte and said in a bantering tone: "You know, I've always had a weakness for tasting paper, Mrs. Russell." He crumpled the slip of paper into a ball, put it into his mouth and began to chew it up.

Charlotte gaped. After a moment she said: "But why you do dat, Mr. Knight? What paper is dat you put in your mouth?"

"Nothing of particular importance. Forget all about it." He chuckled and went on chewing. Took a sip of water.

As Sylvia watched through the latticework, a picture shivered through her memory… Herself as a girl of eight or nine seated near one of the doors that gave into the dining-room, eavesdropping on her father who was speaking to one of his lady friends over the telephone… Late afternoon… Was it Jessie or Delly? No, Jessie… "Nowadays it's Jessie, though – but mum's the word!"… She shut her eyes and fragments of his side of the telephone conversation came back… "Was Knight with them… I've heard those tales about Knight… A promissory note for six thousand… No, I don't believe that, Jessie. Chewed it up and ate it – the promissory note!… Sounds tall to me. I can't see Frank doing such a thing…"

She was trembling. She had to clutch the lattice tight.

After he had gone, she told her mother: "He's done it before, Mother. He's done it before. I remember Daddy speaking to someone over the 'phone –"

"But, Sylvie, why he should do it to us! And what is dis paper he eat? It's a important paper? Ah ain' understand nutting –"

"It must be some important paper, or he wouldn't have eaten it. Of all the dirty dogs!" Her head trembled with rage. Suddenly she snapped her fingers. "I know what it is, Mother! I remember! That night I came home from the cantata I heard him telling Daddy something about his being caught napping. He wanted Daddy to lend him some money to help him out of some scrape – and Daddy lent him twenty thousand dollars on a promissory note. It's that! It's the promissory note he ate. He's robbed us of twenty thousand dollars!"

At midday, when David came home from school, she told him about it, and he said: "I wish he could come back here again. I'd kick him in his big stomach and stamp on him." His face grew flushed and he clenched his hands until the knuckles turned white.

Sight of his rage calmed her, made her forget Mr. Knight. She discovered that she was watching him with admiration. His lean young masculinity stirred up a strange excitement in her senses. She felt a little ashamed of herself.

"I'd kill him if he came back here."

"He's a – he's a demon. Have you been to the tailor yet to be measured for your Scout uniform?"

"Yes."

She wanted to give him a hug and tell him not to let it bother him. A wire of intense feeling burned its way through her. It took all her will to restrain herself. She was breathing fast.

A few minutes later she sat on her bed in her room and stared out at the hot, white noon, and tried to sort out her thoughts and feelings. One thing piled up on the other. Her father's death. This fraudulent act of Mr. Knight's. And David, the way she was beginning to feel about him. She looked down at her hand and rubbed a finger along the back of it.

"I'm just trying to imagine myself abnormal," she murmured. "Daddy said one day that I liked to dramatize myself too much. He was right."

She watched the cabbage palms that showed above the Hammonds' house, remembering her fantasy concerning the Brown Jumbie-men. "See that," she murmured. "It's my imagination. I have too much imagination."

She looked slowly around the room, feeling intensely lonely.

There was the matter of mourning. It was a question that caused much unpleasantness. Up to now she had compromised by wearing white, but when Charlotte produced two black silk dresses and said that they were Sylvia's mourning dresses, Sylvia said: "I'm sorry, Mother. I'm not wearing black. I warned you before, didn't I? I told you not to make anything black for me. I don't believe in mourning."

"You don't believe in mourning? What stupidness you talking, Sylvie!"

"It's not stupidness. I mean it. Daddy always said mourning is a farce, and he was right. You haven't got to put on black to feel sorry over the death of anyone you care about."

"But everybody wear mourning when their relatives dead. What you mean? You going walk about in public wid white dresses all de time when your fadder only dead a month ago?"

"And what if I do! I don't care what people think. It's what I feel inside myself that counts. In fact, I'm going back into colours next week."

"Into colours! Eh-eh! Child, you can't be right in your head."

Sylvia stuck to her decision. She refused to wear black, and the following week was back in colours. Charlotte was very hurt. Janie and the others agreed with her that Sylvia had no decency to be wearing colours and her father only dead a few weeks. She ought to be ashamed of herself.

To Sylvia's surprise, Naomi, too, frowned upon her decision.

"No, Sylvie man, I don't think you're acting right. You should wear black. After all, it's your father. We have certain things we must do."

"Certain things we must do? Why must, Naomi? Mourning is only a custom – and a hypocritical one."

Naomi smiled. "That may be so, but, you see, we're living in a society where these things are looked on as important, and you can't brush aside the customs people reckon as important. If you want to be popular with people and get on in the world you have to do a lot of things you mightn't want to do in your heart."

"Oh, I see. You mean, just so that people should smile and say what a nice person you are, you have to – to pretend you're what you're not."

Naomi laughed. "I suppose you can put it that way if you like. Sylvie, you think this is a sweet world we're living in? I don't like to sound cynical, but take it from me, you can't be honest and sincere if you want to get on."

Sylvia was silent. She felt ashamed and foolish, as though she had behaved like an impulsive child of eight and had been reproved. She felt Naomi's eyes on her, nonchalant and amused – and affectionate. Naomi was laughing at her, but doing it inoffensively and good-naturedly. Naomi the imperturbable, who faced life always sprawled back carelessly in an easy chair, a smile on her face, a cigarette between her fingers, who took pleasure and adversity with the same casual wave of a hand.

"Anyway, I'm not wearing black, Naomi. I'm wearing just what I wore before. I'm sure Daddy would have approved."

Naomi's shoulders came into play again. "You must please yourself, of course. Always please yourself, Sylvia. Good rule, child." After a pause she lit a cigarette from the end of the one she had just smoked, put out the end in an amber ashtray on a table near by, then took up the matchstick and flicked it at Sylvia. She laughed: "You look so serious, Sylvia."

"I am serious."

"It's good to be serious – but I think you're living too much in a dream these days. And you have your father too much on your mind. Everything you say you have to quote him. That isn't wise."

Sylvia nodded, pensive.

"You hinted at something once not too long ago – it was before your father died. But, as I told you then, I think you were only imagining it. You're not a pervert."

Sylvia continued to be silent.

"How about Benson? Haven't you seen him recently?"

"Not for a long time. He doesn't matter to me, Naomi. What can I do? I can't force myself to like him. I've tried but it's no use. I've done everything I possibly could to get my mind away from – from what you're talking about, but it made no difference."

"But now that he's dead can't you stop –"

"Yes, but there's David. David resembles him a lot. I'm almost beginning to feel about David… Oh, I'm a mess, Naomi!" She rose and uttered a distracted laugh. "I have a twist! I'm abnormal!"

Naomi told her to sit down. "Sylvie, it's only your imagination, child. Look, take it from me, you're as normal as anybody can be normal. In fact, Greg was saying only yesterday how ordinary you are. He said you're pretty and attractive but mentally you're very ordinary."

"Ordinary?"

"Yes. What he meant was that you're the last person anybody could accuse of being a pervert. I've noticed it myself. You're a sweet person, but you couldn't indulge in any kind of vice even if you tried."

Sylvia laughed. "Why do you say 'but'? You mean I'd be better off if I were able to indulge in vice?"

"I don't mean it that way. Look, child, I'm awful at explaining anything. Greg is trying his best with me but I haven't any brain, that's the truth of the matter." She sighed and laughed and stretched herself lazily. "What I want to say is you're a nice child, but you don't know how to attract men or make your presence and your charms felt. Sometimes a little wickedness can be a virtue, you know. Well, you haven't got that, Sylvie. You're just a good, sweet, ordinary person. That's why it sounds so absurd when you try to make out that you might be going the way of a pervert. Forget that, child! Don't be afraid of any such thing!"

3

The situation crumbled more rapidly than they had feared. In January Mr. Knight's cheque was for a hundred and fifty – seventy less than the previous one. When Sylvia said to him: "But, Mr. Knight, this is a big house. How can we keep it properly on a hundred and fifty?" he replied: "My dear child, things are bad all round. This is the best I can do this month. The death duties were high, and your father's estate is not as secure as it could have been." He patted her shoulder. "But don't let it upset you. There may be an improvement before long."

"How do you mean the estate is not as secure as it could have been? I thought Daddy's affairs were – were quite prosperous before he died."

He looked at her with surprise, as though not expecting her to show so much intelligence and interest. "Quite a big girl now, eh? You think you understand finance and stocks and shares?"

She said coldly: "I don't say I do, but I'd prefer you to tell us exactly what you mean. You can't just say that Daddy's estate is not secure and not explain why you say that."

He continued to be indulgent and bantering in his manner, but she could see that he was perturbed. Her aggressive stand had impressed him.

"My dear girl, it would be pointless my trying to make you understand anything concerning your father's estate. It's too involved. All I can say is that I'm doing my best for you. Your father left no will, and I can assure you that if you handed over your affairs to another solicitor you'd find yourselves in very desperate straits. Much of what I've given you in this cheque I've had to supply out of my own pocket –"

"You mean it's only charity, then?"

"Oh, don't be foolish." His face darkened; it might have been an evil shadow, and not the blood coming to the skin, that had fallen on him. "I'm advancing you money – not giving it to you. Your father was a good friend of mine, and what I do for you I do as a friend –"

"Is that why you ate that promissory note that day?" He went grey about the lips.

"What do you mean!"

"What I mean is that you're a thief, Mr. Knight. A common thief." Her head was trembling. "That promissory note was for twenty thousand dollars, and you ate it so we couldn't make any claim for the money. Get out of the house! Get out, you – you filthy thing!" She fled upstairs, for she could no longer keep back the sobs.

In February he gave them a cheque for the same amount – a hundred and fifty. And then in a quiet voice – he did not attempt to be indulgent and facetious this time – he told Charlotte that he was afraid they would have to go and live in the Fort Street cottage. The High Street house they were living in now had been heavily mortgaged and the person involved intended to foreclose within a few days and take possession.

"But why?" Sylvia interposed. "Haven't we enough to meet the mortgage?"

Mr. Knight looked past her, his manner frigid. "There's isn't enough – that's why the interest on the mortgage cannot be met. Or perhaps I may say that if the interest and all monies due were paid you would be left without a single cent to feed and clothe yourselves. If you go to the Fort Street place you will still have a shelter over your heads, and you will have the income from your bonds and shares to exist on –"

"Why couldn't we sell the car?"

"The car has to go back to the firm from which your father purchased it. Remember, it was virtually a new one he acquired only a few months before his death. He bought it on the hire-purchase system, and not even an eighth of the cost has been paid up."

They had to give the people living in the Fort Street cottage notice to leave. They had to have a sale of those pieces of furniture in the house here which could not be taken to the Fort Street place, for the cottage was a small one of two bedrooms, a sitting-room and a dining-room, all tiny and incapable of accommodating much furniture. Mr. Knight arranged everything.

Two days after Hitler marched into Austria they moved into the Fort Street cottage. Wireless sets in Fort Street kept blaring out the B.B.C. news bulletins all day.

From the window of the bedroom Sylvia and her mother decided to share the Demerara River could be seen, shimmering and amber-white, in the space between two cottages on the other side of the street. When the sun was going down Sylvia watched the water turn orange and red. From the tiny front portico the Sea Wall was visible in the not-too-far distance. At night, in bed beside her mother, she heard the sea – a continuous, lulling, muffled roar.

To Sylvia, these were consolations. Not to Charlotte. Charlotte took the change hard. She moaned and wept. She said that this was the beginning of the end of her; only the grave was left for her now. She even overcame the sentimental codes of her class which ruled that naught but good should be spoken of the dead. She cursed Russell, threw the blame of everything upon him. It was his wickedness, she declared, that had brought this upon them. His sinfulness. But for his adulterous doings, they would have been secure and comfortable today. "It's God who punish him! He and dat woman he was in de car sinning wid – God punish dem! Dat's why de police can't find de murderers. It's de hand of God dat strike dem down – and now me and his children got to suffer!"

One evening, David was so disgusted that he got up from the table and stamped out of the house, and Sylvia rose and followed him. She caught up with him at the bottom of the front stairs, and gripped his arm. "Don't take any notice of her, Dave. She's been in this mood all day."

He shrugged off her hand. "Don't hold me. You're always holding me."

She opened her mouth to speak but remained silent.

He sat down on the bottom step. "I can't do any homework with all that stupid talk going on. Mother is a fool. A big fool!"

Sylvia hesitated – then the impulse won. She sank down beside him. She said nothing. Only watched the red flame of a candle in a window across the street. A poor family. They could not afford electric light.

David kept mumbling to himself.

"You want to let's go for a walk?" she suggested.

"Go for a walk? But I've got my homework to do. Why is it you're always wanting to go for a walk with me? You're afraid to go out alone since Daddy died, or what?"

"Don't be silly. Of course I'm not afraid. I just want company, that's all." She was aware of a sense of panic... He's beginning to find my behaviour odd. Before long he won't want me to come within a yard of him.

He grunted. "I can't always be going out with you. Get some of your old school friends. Look! Hear how she's going on! Still cursing Daddy! I'm getting really fed-up with her!"

"Same here." She rose. "I'm going for a walk. I can't stand it."

She moved toward the gateway – and trembled as she heard the scraping of his shoe. The next instant he was beside her and they set out in the direction of the Sea Wall.

It was a night of pale moonlight. The moon, a thickening crescent, hovered low in the west, serene but sinister. Rain had fallen during the afternoon-half of the day, and the air was chilly and leaf-scented. Tree-frogs kept up a chorus of chirruping on both sides of the rocky street. There were pools of water to be avoided, and their progress was a zigzag one. Once she collided with him, and felt a pleasant shiver go through her. But the next moment she was hot-faced with shame. She hated herself.

She tried to concentrate on the sound of the frogs. A lovely sound. She saw it in her fancy as a soft, greenish glow – a multitude of tiny, greenish pips of light making one big, soothing glow in the night. She let it soothe her. It seemed so detached, so far separated from human problems. It was not cruel and mocking like noonday sunlight. It had nothing to do with Brown Shirts tramping and stamping in the streets of Vienna. It might have been death. Could death be like this: the cool, peaceful, other-world chirruping of tree-frogs? It almost made her want to be dead.

By the time they had reached the Sea Wall she was calm inside. There was hardly any breeze. The sea was far out, on the ebb. But the air, as always, smelt fresh and sea-rank. Fishy but invigorating. She suggested sitting on a bench, but he said he preferred to walk. "No, let's sit down," she insisted. "Here's a vacant bench." He made an irritable sound and agreed.

They said very little, and she took care not to touch him. His presence gave her comfort. Gradually he was filling the place her father had occupied. Gradually. If she tried to hurry the process, however, she might ruin everything. She must go softly, delicately. She must not alarm him. Once he got a hint that her behaviour was in any way abnormal it would be the end. For he himself was so normal – just what a schoolboy should be.

When he rose without warning and said that they had better be going back home she agreed at once. "Yes, we'd better go," she said, trying to make her voice as casual as possible. "You've got to finish your homework."

Charlotte and her sewing began to prove irksome as the days went by. Charlotte used the dining-room as a sewing-room, and all day there was the whirr of the machine, and the mumble of voices when Sarah and Janie or Aunt Clarice Madhoo called. It was useless trying to listen-in on the wireless, for the sewing-machine caused electrical interference. And, in any case, if Sylvia did persist in listening in defiance of the grating noises interposed, Charlotte would inevitably call out irritably and ask her to stop playing "all dat stupid dance music!" And Sylvia, in order not to make a row, would stop it. Sometimes she stopped it because she herself had become tired of it.

A heavy depression closed in around her. She saw it as a fog of dust-particles. In the morning when she got up it would be a thin mist of drifting fluff and lint, but as the day progressed the fluff and lint took on a buff tint. By noon it was grey, and had thickened: by mid-afternoon it hung blackly about her, a menacing curtain.

Many mornings she lay in the one easy chair in the sitting-room in her pyjamas and stared up at the grimy rafters. Hour after hour. Now and then she would stir and sigh. Now and then rub her eyes when they burned with the threat of tears.

Janie or Sarah or one of the others would come in and give her sneering glances. One morning Janie remarked to Charlotte: "Charlotte, you got a play-girl of a daughter. In pyjamas at half past ten in de morning and lolling off in de sitting-room. Ah wish I was so lucky!"

Charlotte sighed and returned: "Sylvie is her own mistress, Janie. Ah weary telling you dat. Let her do just what she want to do."

Sylvia ignored them.

One morning she dressed early and went to see Naomi. She told Naomi that she felt like drinking poison or taking a swim out to sea.

Naomi, in no way alarmed, laughed. "I understand, Sylvie. You're not the only one who gets such feelings. Don't think your case is singular, child. Far from it." She began to hum "Love is the Sweetest Thing", then stopped and said: "Up with your chin, Sylvie. Hope for brighter days. They might be just round the corner, for all you know."

"There'll never be brighter days for me."

"Why don't you look for a job, Sylvia?"

"What sort of job?"

"Anything. A store job, or a job in an office."

"An office? But I don't know typewriting or shorthand."

"All office clerks don't do typing and shorthand. You could keep books. I know a girl who keeps books and does filing work at Wheeler's. Mr. van Huisten or Mr. Ralph – any of your father's friends – would get you a job. That's all you need, really – some good backdoor influence."

"I should hate to have to go to any of Daddy's friends for help."

"Forget your pride, man. You're going to get more and more despondent if you sit at home and mope. In a job you'd have something to do, and you'd meet people. That would make all the difference in the world."

Naomi set her thinking. She was not in need of money, but she certainly wanted some form of occupation. This sitting idle at home would eat into her system and cause her to do something desperate. Even the sight of trees and the sound of the sea and of birds – even the occasional spells of David's company she enjoyed – she found not enough to sustain her and keep her from brooding. One late afternoon, when she went to the door and saw the lovely vivid reds and yellows of a sunset over the housetops across the street, she clicked her tongue and turned away.

She had been accustomed to watching the sunset from an upper-storey window where she could see it beyond a panorama of housetops – not from a doorway twelve feet from ground-level. She was suddenly saturated with the full significance of the change that had taken place. From High Street to this – this contemptible little hovel with its two bedrooms that could barely hold a bed each and a dressing-table and clothes-rack, a sitting-room fifteen feet by ten, a dining-room the same size, a mere coop of a kitchen – and, worst indignity of all, the bath and toilet outside in the back-yard; a tiny, rickety detached hut, dark inside and grimy-grey with a permanent dinge, a thin wooden wall, unpainted, separating bath from toilet.

No. This, she decided, would not do. Her outlook was becoming warped. Idleness was breeding a vast discontent. She must take Naomi's advice and look for a job of work to do.

After reflection, she decided that she would not go to any of her father's friends. Her pride forbade that. She must find work on her own. It would be better so, too – more interesting. Already she could visualize herself walking into a store and asking to see the manager… "I'd like a job. Have you anything?"… She was sure her attractive looks would work the trick immediately. An "ordinary girl" she might be, but men could not resist her.

She simply had to smile at them – as she had smiled at them at the picnic – and the battle was won. Just wait and see.

It was a drizzly April morning, and the prospect did not look so bright when she was actually jostling her way along the crowded pavements in Water Street. And when she was ascending the long, dim stairway of the first office – the office connected with a large hardware store – a brume of shyness came down upon her. She found herself heavy-footed and at a loss to know what she was going to say when she got upstairs.

On the top step she stood and stared, awed by the reality of the office. A railing and a counter and a cage in which a cashier seemed busy with money, desks and desks and typewriters clicking and young men and oldish men and attractive girls engrossed with books and papers, bending over desks or sitting at desks or standing in corners working adding-machines, all in a sacred hush – an absence of voices – as though it might have been a religious ceremony.

She felt like an intruder, felt that at any instant a man with a spear or a battle-axe would materialize and threaten her with death if she could not give a good enough reason for her presence here.

A young man with a quiet, polite smile approached the counter and asked her what he could do for her. He was fair-complexioned coloured.

"Could I see the manager, please?"

"The manager? I think he's engaged at the moment. Wouldn't anybody else do?"

"No, I'd like to see the manager, please."

"Very well. As soon as he's disengaged. Will you be seated?" He indicated one of the three chairs on her side of the counter, and she smiled and thanked him and sat down to wait. Her spirits rose. To be invited to have a seat was something; it showed that she was going to be given a chance. The man with the spear or battle-axe seemed a less likely bogy.

After about half an hour the young man smiled and beckoned at her, and she followed him past several desks until they came to a frosted glass door with *Managing Director* in gilt letters across the top panel. As the door closed behind her she became aware of the humming of an electric fan and the sweetish smell of ink and paper and something else she could not place – and then, vividly, of the manager's bowed head. He seemed busy scribbling on a sheaf of pinkish papers. He glanced up quickly over pince-nez and smiled: "Please have a seat, won't you?" in a preoccupied but pleasant voice. He was a sallow coloured gentleman of about fifty, with thin, greying, black bristly hair. Presently he put down his fountain pen, shuffled the papers together with precision, and looked at her. He clasped his hands lightly together.

"Well, what can I do for you, young lady?" His voice was brisk but had a fatherly note. His brown eyes were sympathetic.

"I came to ask you if there's a job I can have in the office here."

"A job?" He pursed his lips. Took off his pince-nez and began to polish them. He frowned at her consideringly. "May I ask your name?"

She told him, and a look of interest came to his face at once. "Oh, you are Grantley Russell's girl?"

She could not meet his gaze, and he seemed to detect the sudden rigidity that had come into her manner, for he hastened on: "You want something to do, you say? Can you type or do shorthand?"

"No. But I thought I could write up books, or – or something."

He put on his pince-nez and examined the palm of his hand, toyed with a signet ring on his little finger. He had a musing air. "Well, my dear girl," he said, at length, "the truth is, at the moment, we're, if anything, overstaffed. I should like to do something for you. I knew your father very well" – he gave her a kindly glance – "but I really don't see any opening for you at present." He put his hand to his forehead and frowned thoughtfully, as though determined to find some way out of the problem. After a moment be said: "Have you tried anywhere else?"

"No. This is the first place I've come to."

He pursed his lips. "H'm. Well, look here, I tell you what. If you don't succeed in getting anything, say within a week, come back so me and I'll see what I can arrange." He broke into a broad smile, tucked his thumbs under the lapels of his coat and sat well back in his chair. He rose, after she had murmured her thanks, and saw her to the door.

She felt more confidence when she went to the next office. It was the office connected with one of the most well-known dry goods stores in Water Street. The manager was creole white; he probably had a great-great-grandfather or grandmother who was pure black but whose blood had become invisible amid the bucketfuls of white blood supplied by succeeding forebears. She thought he might have been curt and huffish, but she was wrong. He proved as charming and sympathetic as the coloured manager. He did not claim to have known her father, but he said he would have liked to help her in some way. He stroked his chin and rubbed his cheek. What she could do, he told her, was to send in a written application which would be put on file for reference in case they needed any assistance later on.

The next office was a commission agency run by a firm of Portuguese – Portuguese of the third generation after the original Jose-and-Maria immigrants of the middle nineteenth century; educated, newly arrived upper middle-class Portuguese; not white people yet, but on the way to being white, as Gregory Brandt had commented once. Portuguese to whom the Portuguese language was as foreign as it was to her. British Guiana Portuguese who spoke and thought like creoles because they were creoles.

The manager was a young man of about thirty with a small moustache. He made her sit down, and smiled and asked her whether she could type or do shorthand… She couldn't? Then he was sorry there was nothing doing.

He was businesslike. He did not clasp his hands or purse his lips or rub his chin or finger signet rings. Unlike the coloured manager and the white manager, he did not create an atmosphere of sympathy. She was conscious of a difference – a lack of something seasoned and easy. He was a perfect gentleman, but an alert, efficient, practical one; there were no soft edges or rounded surfaces to him.

Her fourth try brought success. The office manager, a coloured gentleman who had known her father, gave her a note to the departmental manager, a Mr. Jarvin, and when Mr. Jarvin – the manager of the grocery department – interviewed her he said yes, he thought they could do with another girl. Of course, he was afraid the salary would be very small for a start, but he was sure that with good service she would soon get a raise.

That would be all right, she assured him. It was not the money that mattered so much as the work. She couldn't stand being idle at home.

Mr. Jarvin smiled and nodded, very genial, very amiable. He had an olive moon-face, and reminded her of Ralph Gennarty on the picnic. "You can start tomorrow morning if you like, Miss Russell. The salary will be fifteen dollars a month."

"You see these sons of bitches!" cried Jack Sampson. "Fifteen dollars a month! They going to work you to de bone, sweat you till four every afternoon – and pay you fifteen dollars a month! You know what's their takings on an average for one *day*? Anything like two or three thousand dollars. A big grocery department like dat! Oh, shit! When I sit down and think of dese suckers! Sylvie, look, tek my advice and join de Clerks' Union. See Mr. Hubbard and get enrolled. De union will watch your interests."

She was so happy that afternoon that she wanted to laugh without stopping. "Jack, you're making fun. What have I got to join any union for? Suppose I'm satisfied with the pay they're giving me – why should I join a union and make a big fuss?"

Jack shook his head and groaned. He made a gesture of disgust. "You see dat! Same old story! Passivity! Indifference! Look, Sylvie, you know why we in dis colony can't develop all de jungle-country we got? You know why over eighty thousand square miles of dis land lying fallow and untouched? It's because we mesmerized. It's because we walking about in a dream. And dat's why we'll always be kicked around and exploited by dose imperious sons of bitches in de Colonial Office in London. We got to wake up. We still dazed. We still stupid. Look at you and your upper middle-class! All you-all strive to do is to be cultured and polished – cultured and polished like de English. I don't say culture and refinement isn't a good thing. But de English people clever. They encourage you-all coloured people to be cultured and refined – to be cultured and refined like *dem!* Because de more English culture you imbibe, de more loyal you will be to de British throne! Yes! *Dat's* where they got you by de balls! Dat's why it will be hard for us in dis West Indian zone to be independent. De Australians, de Canadians, de New Zealanders, they all rule themselves – and why? Because they are politically conscious in a big sense. They didn't achieve self-government by just being good British subjects and licking de boots of de big men in Downing Street. They had to struggle for their independence – de same as India struggling now. But we in dese West Indian colonies, all we bother about is a few petty Town Council and Legislative Council elections, and we ignore de bigger world issues – de capitalism dat strangling de working-man. Dat's a big issue – but we forget it. We still hypnotized by English culture and English easy-going ways. Even our trade unions we don't support as we should. We all afraid of offending de big-money men – de sugar-estate bosses and de big-business creole whites. We won't wake up and get togedder and fight dem. *Fight* dem! Dat's what's wrong wid us!"

Naomi clapped her hands. "Good speech, Jack! Good speech! Encore!"

Aubrey Deleon stamped. "Oh, hell! Jack man, why de devil you don't walk around wid a portable platform?"

Jack grinned good-naturedly. He was perspiring. His ebony face shone. His white, widely spaced teeth glistened like refined porcelain specially wrought and planted in his dark gums. "Go on! You-all laugh at me. One day you'll realize Ah was right. You don't see what happening in Europe? You don't read de signs? War coming. War just round de corner. De Revolution at hand!"

"Wise words, Jack!" Gregory agreed. He had just appeared at the door. "I have a bet with a fellow war breaks out before the year is over."

But all the talk about war and world unrest did not trouble Sylvia. Politics and world affairs did not interest her in the slightest. Tomorrow there was the job at Brankers' to look forward to. A new adventure. An exciting adventure.

Going home leisurely on her bicycle, she could appreciate the soft fleecy array of clouds in the sky. She watched them change from bright yellow to purple, then to grey-brown, the fan-like rays of sunshine behind them dimming all the while. The breeze felt cool on her cheeks and smelt leafy-chill from the showers that had fallen during the day. The traffic sounds and a cock crowing in a back-yard beyond the gloomed foliage of an orange tree made a pleasant nostalgic glow in her. A soothing sadness passed through her spirit as though it were mist that emanated from the residences of Main Street, and in the deep twilight she could feel the solid presence of the saman trees, rough-trunked and aged, guarding her with a secret umber intelligence.

4

The actuality, however, disappointed her – though not very much, for, intuitively, she had known that the actuality would not live up to the dream.

Five pounds of butter... two tins of pears... three pounds of sugar.

"Get up this order at once, Miss Russell. It has to be sent up by the van within the hour."

"Can I get you something?"... "A tin of Capstan cigarettes..."

"Miss Russell! What about the Harrisons' order?"

"I'm afraid I'm attending to someone now, Mr. Bradley..."

That was the actuality. A rush – a rush all the time. A jabber of voices asking you to do this or that or whether you had got up this or that order yet. Why didn't you hurry? Mrs. Smith was a very fussy person. Always making some complaint to the office.

The telephone rang every few minutes. The traffic droned and honked and tooted in the street from eight in the morning to four in the afternoon. The smell of butter and raisins and cheese and tobacco amalgamated into a sweetish-rancid cloud that hovered about you incessantly. Mr. Bradley was never tired of scolding you. He did it as a matter of habit. He was the assistant manager, and all the girls hated him.

No, it was not the kind of adventure she had hoped for. No young men fawned upon her. No male customers offered to take her to the cinema or to dine at the Park Hotel.

There was an exciting moment one day, however, when Benson Riego came in to buy three slabs of Cadbury's chocolate. He opened his eyes when he saw her. "I didn't know you were working here, Sylvia!"

They had a brief, friendly chat. He made no reference to her father's death, probably considering it an awkward subject. His voice had deepened, and he seemed more a man in every way. She found a dull admiration moving in her. A swift image of him taking her into his arms trembled in her fancy – and as swiftly melted. He asked her where she was living now, and when she told him he said he liked that part of Kingston because it was near to the river. His manner was self-conscious as he said it, and she suspected that he was only trying to make polite conversation. More than once she caught that old gleam of interest in his eyes. She could feel that he was still attracted to her.

She went home thinking about him, but her thoughts were detached and uncoloured by any deep emotion. David had promised to go to the cinema with her, and the anticipation of being with him swamped all other considerations. She gave him a shilling pocket money every week, and took him to the cinema whenever she could coax him into going. It was always a delicate business coaxing because he had told her bluntly that he did not like going with her. He preferred to go with Henry and the other boys. She did not care for cowboy films, but she tolerated them in order to have his company.

Of late, she had come to look upon her affection for him as something normal. Deep within, she knew that she was not being honest with herself, but she refused to ponder on the matter. If she did not think about it, she reasoned, it would not bother her.

Many times the issue did force itself on her attention and would refuse to be put aside – especially on the occasions when David rebuffed her – and these were her black moments. She would shudder in self-revulsion and be depressed for hours. She would stare around her, baffled and distracted, and introspect on her affliction. In such moments she saw herself as two beings – one ugly and deformed, the other lovely and striving to be good and clean. Then invariably she would remember Frederick March in *Doctor Jekyll and Mr. Hyde,* and laughter would spread like a golden cloud over her, and she would see herself as an absurd romantic trying to make herself into an ogress. In this way she often escaped from her gloom.

In September, when the Crisis that everybody was discussing seemed at its most exciting – she could hear about nothing but the Sudetenland and the Czechs – Charlotte fell ill. Sylvia came home from work one afternoon to find her in bed shivering with ague and whimpering.

It was another nervous breakdown, but this time, said the doctor, Charlotte had succumbed to an attack of the malarial parasites that must have lain dormant in her system while her vitality had remained high. "She's overworked herself," he said, "and the result is a breakdown as well as an attack of malaria. I warned her not to kill herself out over her sewing."

The doctor was a short black gentleman with an air that inspired confidence. He prescribed a quinine mixture and another mixture which, he said, contained a bromide for her nerves. He treated Sylvia in a manner that made her know that he appreciated the fact that she was an intelligent girl. She liked him and assured him that she would do everything she could to carry out his instructions.

Had Charlotte been a good patient the situation might have proven a simple one to handle. But Charlotte lived up to the reputation she had established in October 1934. She moaned and called upon God, and insisted that she must have someone to take care of her. "You won't do, Sylvie! You won't do! Get in a nurse, child. Oh, Saviour! Oh, God! Dis time you' pore mudder going to her grave, Sylvie!"

"Don't be silly, Mother. You'll be well in a few days. I'll take care of you and see you get better."

"No, Sylvie! Go and get a nurse. You can't see after me. Let me die in comfort. Oh, Jesus! Ah feeling too bad. Go, child! Go and get a nurse to see after me pore carcass properly."

"We can't afford a nurse. You know that very well. Last month Mr. Knight only gave us seventy dollars, and he said at the end of this month it might be fifty. A nurse will want to charge at least two dollars a night. The one you had in 1934 charged four dollars a day."

"Godma! Ow, Godma! You see ingratitude! Look down from above..."

Sylvia went into the sitting-room and told David: "Go and call Aunt Clarice, but don't tell her anything about bringing a nurse. Mother's nerves are bad, that's what's making her behave like that."

"I thought it was some stupidness like that," he grinned, and went off to fetch Aunt Clarice.

Aunt Clarice came. Nowadays she was fat and broad and unhappy. Her husband was not behaving as he should.

"Clarice! Ow, Clarice! You' pore cousin dying! Send for a nurse. You didn't bring a nurse wid you?"

The same performance began again, but Aunt Clarice agreed with Sylvia that a nurse would be a needless expense. "Don't trouble yourself, Charlotte. I will stay and look after you. You must keep quiet and rest."

"Ow, Clarice! Dis is de grave facing you' good friend. You can't grant me dis one favour before Ah dead? Send for a nurse. Ah want to dead in comfort, Clarice."

There was no sleep for Sylvia and Aunt Clarice that night. David was not affected; he would have slept through a hurricane.

Sylvia got into pyjamas after ten o'clock and stretched out in the easy chair in the sitting-room.

Charlotte moaned and talked incessantly. She cursed Aunt Clarice when Aunt Clarice tried to sponge her down with bay-rum. She ordered Aunt Clarice to hell. She called Russell a whoremonger, and referred to the private parts of the ladies with whom he had been friendly. Once she laughed hysterically and broke into song.

"Oh, madam, I hear that cocks do crow-w-w-w! Do *crow-w-w-w*!
"Oh, madam, I hear that cocks do crow-w-w-w!
"Around your *cunt*...ree-ee-ee-ee garden!"

Sylvia dozed off, only to awaken to hear her mother screaming.

"Murder! MURDER!" Charlotte screamed.

Aunt Clarice was begging her to be quiet. "For Jesus' sake, Charlotte, keep quiet. You'll disturb the neighbours. Sylvie, come quick, child! Come and help me here wid her!"

Charlotte struggled when Sylvia and Aunt Clarice tried to get her to lie down. Eventually they had to desist and let her remain sitting up.

"I can't stand dis no more, Sylvie. Ah sorry. You better get a nurse for her tomorrow as she want. Dis will kill me out. I not young no more."

Meantime Charlotte wagged her head and in a shrill voice called down God's curses on all who had done her ingratitude. "Ah slave! Ah slave, oh, God! Ah work out all me pore strength to help people – and dis all de t'anks Ah getting. But, God, you dere on high to witness all de wrongs men commit on earth. Godma! You' soul in heaven listening to me? Witness, Godma!

Witness and intercede wid God to curse dose dat spit on me. Curse dem! I CURSE DEM!"

"You hear dat, child? You hear what she talking?"

"She's delirious, Aunt Clarice. She's not responsible for what she's saying."

"Ah know what Ah talking!" Charlotte blazed. "You, Clarice, you! You is a snake in de grass No wonder you' husband take up wid de Chinee woman in Albouystown! You' husband lost to you! De Chinee woman got him good! She got him by de balls! You hear me? She got him by de BALLS!"

Charlotte broke into loud, obscene laughter. She rolled about and yelled. Beat the bed with her clenched hands. Then burst into tears. Sob after sob tore through her slight frame.

Aunt Clarice strode out of the house.

When daylight came Charlotte implored Sylvia not to go to work. She was weak and in a profuse sweat.

"Very well, Mother," said Sylvia. "I'll ask Dave to take a message to Mr. Bradley and say I'm not well and can't go to work this morning."

She remained at home three days so that she could take care of her mother. They were three days of misery. Charlotte whined and whimpered and complained. She kept calling for things, kept protesting in a feeble voice how she was being neglected. Fortunately, however, there were no more delirious outbursts of obscenity.

On the second day, freakish dry-weather rain poured from mid-morning until after one o'clock. Sylvia got sprinkled in going down the back steps to take a bedpan to the toilet, and by afternoon she was sniffling, her throat on fire and her whole body achy and feverish. She knew she was in for an attack of influenza. On the following day only her will kept her going. That night was a fantasy of burning throat and nostrils and fevered dreams in the easy chair. Old men tumbled about on the floor and tugged at her toes, black dogs leapt at her from bushes, telephones rang, and Mr. Bradley scolded her in gruff barks. Soon he was a black dog barking and chasing her along a tunnel-way the walls of which were equipped with interminable shelves of tinned meats, marmalade, butter, tinned fruits...

The next morning, after a bath – to the horror of David who said she would get pneumonia – she felt a little better, though she knew it was a false feeling. Her throat still itched and burned. But she was determined to go to work. She could not afford to lose her job. In April the financial situation had seemed fairly secure, but now that Mr. Knight kept cutting down their monthly allowance the job had suddenly become very important.

Charlotte begged her not to go, but Sylvia paid no heed. She told David when to administer the medicine and how much to measure out. It was Saturday and David did not have to go to school.

When she arrived at Brankers' and was going to her locker to get her apron, Mr. Bradley called her and said: "So you decided to favour us with your presence again, Miss Russell! Well, before you put on your apron, go and see Mr. Jarvin. I have a feeling he has something to tell you."

Mr. Jarvin received her with a cold curtness that dismayed her. He told her that her services were no longer required.

"But I don't understand, Mr. Jarvin. I sent a message by my brother to say I wasn't well."

"The message your brother gave us was that your *mother* was ill and that that was why you couldn't come to work. We can't take excuses like that, Miss Russell. Any girl can stay at home when she pleases and send to say her mother or her aunt is ill as an excuse for slacking. You can go to the cashier and collect what salary is due to you, and you'll probably get something in lieu of notice."

The next week taught her what she had not fully realized before. She learnt that despite illness the human body can still perform acts of great endurance if pushed on. Coughing and sniffling, blowing her reddened nose, tiny flames of fever dancing over her skin, she remained on her feet, seeing after the running of the house and taking care of her mother.

5

There could be no doubt at all, she told herself, that the easy, carefree days were over. It was a certainty now that life for her would be one day-to-day, week-to-week struggle. She had to forget her dreams of being a lady of the upper middle-class. She had to suppress her illusions. The High Street times lay irrevocably in-the past.

Only the active present mattered, only the swift curve of Now held any significance. The future? Whenever she thought of the future a tide of ghost-ripples shivered over her skin. She conjured up events to come in terms of groans and sighs and the rolling of thunder, sobs and the bitter staring out at trees in hot sunshine. Perhaps the desire for death. She would have given anything to have been clairvoyant, to have been able to view the panorama of the future *now* so that she could know whether it would be worth putting up a struggle in its cause. She would hate to struggle and not win, to go through a welter of agony and then fade out like the tints in a sunset sky.

"We've just got to go on, Sylvia," Gregory told her. "Everything in life is without point, my dear girl. The best of the best philosophers can't tell us the *raison d'être*. Why do we live? For what purpose? We're born, we struggle like hell to get Somewhere – a somewhere we call success. So what! Even if we do achieve success haven't we got to die and putrefy like any stupid fool who turned out a failure? We don't get extra rewards in the form of prolonged youth or the power to flap our arms and fly. Take it from me, all that matters in this life is to fill in the in-between between birth and death with as much fun as you possibly can. 'The rest is silence'."

She was one of them now – one of Naomi's crowd – irretrievably one of them. A struggler like Greta Soodeen or Susie Peters or Aubrey Deleon. Jack Sampson. Nowadays a shilling was a big sum. She had to think before deciding to spend it, plan, and distribute the cents and pennies contained in it with the utmost care. Cinema or no cinema? Or would Aubrey or Naomi or Gregory ask her to go and thus save her having to spend the amount under consideration?... Should she sell her bicycle? Yes, sell it and walk. The days of joy-riding were over.

She did not get another job until early in January 1939, and this time it was at a dry goods store in Lombard Street run by Syrians. Hook-nosed Syrians who spoke with a foreign accent and told her that the most they could pay her was seven shillings a week.

"Seven shillings! But how could I live on seven shillings a week!"

"Well, Meess Russell, zat ees ze best we can do. Business not goot. How we can pay you beeg salary? Seven shillings ze most we can offer. We got to say, 'Take eet or leave eet'. Nodding help for eet!"

So she had to take it, for, with her too, there was no help for it. The big offices and shops had turned her down one by one. Even the friendly coloured manager – the first one to whom she had gone that drizzly morning in April last – could find no opening for her. Others said they were overstaffed or were considering cutting down staff. And her pride still forbade her going to Mr. Ralph or Mr. van Huisten or any of her father's friends. Mr. Knight gave them only thirty dollars a month now.

One afternoon, not long after she was in this new job, Naomi gave her a shock. She said that she was moving into a little cottage in George Street.

"Why?" asked Sylvia.

Naomi shrugged her renowned shrug. "Everything changes with time, child." She hesitated an instant, then added: "Greg and I have decided we're going to live together from now on."

"You and Greg! But, Naomi!"

"You're surprised? Surely you must have seen how the wind was blowing." She glanced up and laughed. Her gown fell away and revealed a full drooping breast. "Sylvie, what have I got to live for? Only fun. Jerry and I had no row. We've just made up our minds we'll part. He and Susie are going to stay here together, and Greg and I will go and live by ourselves."

"But do you love Greg?"

Again the lifting of the shoulder. Naomi was silent a moment, polishing her nails. She looked up and said: "Sylvie, some things I never discuss with everybody. But you're different. You're only eighteen in years, but you have the intelligence and understanding of a woman of thirty. I can tell you this – just between us as we're alone. I don't love Greg – and I've told him so. I like him as a good friend. He's educated and can talk to me about philosophy and music and books. I like that kind of man, because you know how I've always wanted to improve myself culturally. But, as a man, I love Jerry. I don't think I could ever love another man as how I love Jerry. He's rough and he hasn't much intelligence, but I still love him. He loves me, too – he's admitted it to me. But he still wants to go to bed with Susie, so we just had to make the best of the situation and decide on this step."

"But if you don't love Greg, how can you bring yourself to live with him and – and be intimate with him?"

Naomi laughed. "Sylvia, some things you'll only understand by experience. All the books won't teach you. And not a soul can explain it to you."

She did not like her new job – nor her employers. Mr. Dikran, especially, was a loathsome man. He was the half-brother of Mr. Zekkel, who owned the dry goods store, and was a kind of assistant boss. Mr. Zekkel, for some reason she could never discover, seemed to place a lot of confidence in him, and was generally influenced by him. She knew this, so had to put up with Mr. Dikran when he was fresh toward her – put up with him and wish that a flash of lightning could crackle out of the sky and slice his gross, greasy body in half.

During a slack period when the store was empty of customers, and when Mr. Zekkel and his sister happened to be in the back store, Mr. Dikran would stroll up and pat her buttocks and say: "How ees ze leetle girl today? She looking goot."

Without a word, she would move away, her breath like a petrified cloud within her.

"One night ze leetle girl got to come for ze dr-rive weet me. Heh?"

Mingled with the traffic noise in Lombard Street, his chuckles sounded weird and menacing.

Fortunately, his opportunities were few, for Mr. Zekkel and Miss Zekkel very rarely left the outer store at the same time to go into the back store, and she could sense that Ms. Zekkel would have disapproved strongly had he caught Mr. Dikran taking liberties with her. Mr. Zekkel, though as greasy and sweaty and repulsive to look at as Mr. Dikran, had a kind heart – a miserly but a kind heart. She could sense also, however, that should Mr. Dikran recommend her dismissal, Mr. Zekkel would probably tell her to go.

She was in the bath – soaping herself – when she heard quick barefooted steps on the back stairs. The bathroom door, ajar, was wrenched wide open, and David, in his pyjamas, his face excited, told her: "Sylvia, you've heard? Hitler has invaded Poland!"

"What! How did you hear that?"

"The news just came through the radio across the way!"

"You're sure you heard right?"

"Of course. They say Warsaw was bombed."

"And only yesterday Miss Zekkel was saying she was certain everything would blow over like last year when the Czech crisis was on."

David did a jig. "Henry might have to go. He's a lance-corporal."

"The local forces won't go abroad. They have to remain here for home defence. So Gregory said last week when we were discussing things."

"Whoops! If I was old enough I would have joined the R.A.F."

A chill struck through her. She went on soaping herself. "You think it's fun, eh? War is terrible. The poor Poles!"

"See me in a bombing plane over Berlin. Zooo-ooom! And then let loose a bomb on them. Booo-ooom!"

She watched him, something hard rising in her throat. "You can join the Red Cross. You're old enough."

She gave a brittle laugh and turned on the shower. "Go back upstairs, Dave!"

"You're a coward, man! You're afraid!" He rushed off upstairs.

A few minutes later, dressing for work in her mother's room, she heard a newsboy going past on the street calling out: "War! Hitler gone into Poland!" A black boy on a creaky bicycle.

Today, the first of September. Friday. This was the day she had to go to Mr. Knight's office in Croal Street to collect the monthly pittance he saw fit to dole out. Nowadays it was twenty dollars. Perhaps next month he would tell her it was only ten... The war. World conditions...

The war. Could it really be true? Men got killed in wars. There were big guns and bombing planes... And David seemed so keen.

She shut her eyes, a sense of great weight upon her. She observed the whorls of blues and reds in the gloom behind her eyelids. They seemed to represent life and its mysteries and infinite complexities. She felt her body swaying, and wondered if death would be like this. Darkness with red and blue whorls gradually turning green and grey and a disembodied swaying in space. Only she was not disembodied nor was she swaying in space. This was actual. The instant she opened her eyes she would see herself in the mirror – the dressed-up human body called Sylvia Russell.

She opened her eyes. What was the use trying to unravel anything? It would always be a mystery. What did Gregory call it? The *raison d'être.* Who would ever discover why men had to be born and had to go through this long, tiresome torture called living

I'm getting to be a regular cynic...

Black women who came into the store to buy dress material discussed the war. "Watch how prices going to go up! All-we pore people is de people who going to suffer. De rich ain' got to worry..."

"They call up all de Militia..."

"Me son in de Infantry. He's a corporal..."

"Well, chile, if they send 'e abroad and he get killed what to do? God will it so..."

A wireless across the street kept pounding out military marches. It was the German station. Hard, lusty, ranting sounds. Brassy and ominous.

Miss Zekkel was still optimistic. She said she did not think England would fight. Mr. Chamberlain would find a way out.

"You na 'member last year? Chammerlan move out soft, soft, soft! Englant na fight. Me sure Englant na fight."

About mid-afternoon Mr. Zekkel went out to the Customs to see after clearing some goods. Miss Zekkel went into the back store to unpack a new assortment of silk threads arrived during the morning. Mr. Dikran, as though on the alert for his chance, sidled up to Sylvia who stood by a drawer behind the counter engrossed in sorting cards of fancy buttons.

"Ze leetle girl, she working hard, no?"

She started and glanced up, for she had not heard him approach.

He did not touch her, however. He said: "Ze beeg war come now. Job going to be hard to find. If you come out wit me for ze dr-rive it might profit you beeg. You might eefen get more raise in pay. How much you get now? Nine shillings? You might eefen get twelve. But if you go on play pr-roud you na profit so much. You might eefen na got na more job. So you better listen good and agree to come out one night for ze dr-rive wit me."

She took no notice of him. It was as though a wire kept twanging in her head... Nine shillings a week. Two shillings raise from July last,... "Yes, Meess Russell, you is a goot worker," Miss Zekkel had smiled. "Meester Zekkel say we giff you two shillings more"... Nine shillings a week – to keep her in a dress a month and to contribute to the house money for food. To give David pocket money...

"You too pr-roud, Meess Russell. You na prosper dat way. You better t'ink over what I tell you. Ze *beeg* war come now. Zis no play-play war. Zis ees ze *beeg* war."

The big war.

"Times going to be hard now. Dave better sell his bike same as you sell yours. Ah getting in debt more and more every day."

"He couldn't sell his bike, Mother. You know how fond he is of that bike. He takes so much care over it."

"It's easy for you to talk so, Sylvie. Ah can't open me mouth to say a word about David but you want to fly down me throat. David got to remember we is pore people now. He can't have what he had before."

Sylvia did not argue. She went for a walk.

... My new policy. No argument. Just take a walk.

From a coconut palm, with a chortling swoop, came the Brown Jumbie-men. Nowadays they lived in the fronds of a coconut palm; there were no cabbage palms in Fort Street.

"This new policy – is it a sign of defeat? Are you trying to run away from adversity?"

"I like peace, that's all. That's why I go for walks instead of arguing. Who doesn't like a little peace?"

"Especially as we're at war now, eh? Ze beeg war!"

"That dirty beast!"

"But he's going to get you before long! How are you going to fight him? It's either that or you lose ze job!"

"Then I'll lose it! I prefer to die than have him with me in a car."

"Hee, hee! You're a poor girl now, though. Don't forget. And how about Dave? Pocket money. No use! New policy or no new policy, he'll get you. Ze dr-rive! Straight to Dixie – Daddy's old haunt. Down with the panties! Present arms! Legs!"

"Oh, leave me in peace! Leave me in peace! Go away!" They went scooting and chortling back to the coconut palm. She took deep breaths of the fresh, cool air as she walked. Once she shut her eyes tight.

On an open space, not far from the Lighthouse, white robed figures were gathered. On a table before them stood a bottle with a smoky flare. The red flame moved restlessly in the soft wind, and lit up the group with a shifty weirdness. It was as though at any instant they might vanish into the darkness around them. They were Jordanites – the new sect that had recently sprung up in Georgetown. Bearded negroes who wore white, flowing gowns, and preached a mixture of politics and religion. They were treated by everyone as a huge joke.

One of them was bawling and gesticulating at an audience of three or four who had collected by the grass border.

"Dis war was prophesied! It was prophesied in de Book! You look good and see! Turn to *Ezekiel*..."

Sylvia laughed out of habit, but before she had gone out of earshot a phrase burnt itself into her awareness.

"... we all got to suffer in dis war. Mankind was born to suffer!

De Bible tell us dat, and I tell it to you dis night. We got to suffer like Job. But remember dis! Out of suffering cometh salvation..."

Out of suffering cometh salvation...

All the way to the Sea Wall and all the way back home that phrase kept making circles in her imagination. It teased her. Troubled her. It drew strange passions out of the night. Intensified her loneliness, urged her into new depths of introspection.

She found David sitting on the bottom step. Even in the dim reflection of the street light she could see he was not in a happy mood. He said he had been waiting for her.

"What's the trouble?" she asked, seating herself beside him.

The war. Mr. Dikran. Their poverty. All the bogies fell dead and were submerged in the trembling wave of pleasure that engulfed her.

"Mother told you about my bicycle?"

"Yes. Don't worry. I've told her what I thought about that." She put her hand on his knee. He scowled but did not brush off her hand.

"She says we're heavily in debt with the grocery people."

"I know – but that doesn't mean you've got to sell your bike."

A certain relief came into his manner, but he still looked troubled. He uttered a deep male sound. His voice was changing – like his whole being. Every day he seemed to grow more gnarled and masculine.

"I don't like to know things are bad with us and I can't help out. I was wondering if I shouldn't leave school and look for work."

"Oh, no! You can't do that, Dave! Education is important – especially for a man. You're just over fifteen. How could you leave school now!"

"I'm tall and big for my age." He spoke in an offended voice. "A lot of people say I can pass for seventeen or eighteen."

She laughed. "I know you can – but you're fifteen, all the same. You've got to go to school until you're at least eighteen. You don't know how I'm hoping I can get a good job so as to make enough to send you to Queen's College. I'd really like you to go to Queen's."

"That's all well and good, but you can't go on working all the time to keep me at school. And what about the Scouts? I had to miss the last camp because Mother couldn't afford to give me my subscription. And another camp is coming off next weekend. I asked her if she could give me the sub and she said no. She said if I want to go camping with the troop I must agree to sell my bicycle."

"I see. So she's been putting on pressure." She sat still for a moment and stared out at the street, then asked: "How much is the sub?"

"Five shillings."

She was silent again, then said: "I'll give it to you."

"You? But – have you any money put aside?"'

"Not a cent. But I'll give it to you out of my salary next Saturday. Will it be in time if you get it at midday?"

"Yes. Mr. Darke stands all expenses himself, and we pay him our subs the day before or the very day of the camp. As long as I can tell him definitely I'm going it will be all right." A throb of excitement had entered his voice. "But, Sylvie, you're sure you can manage it? What about the house money?"

"I'll give four shillings to the house instead of the usual six. But you'll have to do without pocket money this weekend."

"Well, of course. Oh, whoops! Thanks a lot!" He squeezed his hands together. "I really didn't want to miss that camp. We're going up the river in a launch Mr. Darke managed to get. A good friend of his at the Public Works Department lent it to him. We're going to land and go exploring in the bush – and Mr. Darke says he's going to show us how to do tracking – like the Red Indians."

Later, in her pyjamas, she lay in the easy chair and felt the darkness melting into her as though it were etherized down. A low, cool wind seemed to hum delightfully in her lungs. She could hear the sea swashing remotely, and it might have been within the distance of her own being that the sound had its existence...

Out of suffering...

I can suffer anything – *anything* – in the cause of one moment like this!

Can I? I wonder.

It was Tuesday night she asked that of herself. Again in the darkness, in the easy chair.

At about two o'clock that day, she was alone in the back store unpacking hats. Broad-rimmed straw hats that could be trimmed with flowers. Black women from the country were especially fond of them. On Miss Zekkel's instructions, she was selecting certain of them for immediate showing in the front store. Miss Zekkel was sure they would sell fast.

Like a ghost, Mr. Dikran approached – like a ghost with a shiny, beaked nose and an oily smile. She turned her head and saw him. The sour-sweat smell that always surrounded him smote her senses. She continued to bend over the packing case, ignoring him but rigid inside.

"Ze leetle girl na decide yet to go out wit me, eh?"

There was a sliding warmth along her right thigh. She straightened up. "Mr. Dikran, *please* don't do that!"

"Why you so pr-roud, Meess Russell?"

Her head trembled slightly. She bent and continued to unpack. He moved round so as to stand in front of her. The neck line of her dress was low. It was an afternoon dress she had pressed into service as a work dress. She could hear his breathing. Her own breathing, too.

The rustle of the paper wrappings took on a significance that had no relation to reality. It became a symbol of the shivering inside her: of the channel between her breasts which she could glimpse at odd seconds.

She straightened up, and, with an armful of hats, hurried toward the front store. She deposited them on the counter and said to Miss Zekkel: "I think these are the ones you want, Miss Zekkel."

"Yes. Aha. Yes, dese goot. But plenty more dere in ze case. Go pick dem out for me. Two dozen more at ze least."

"You – you want them right away, Miss Zekkel? I thought perhaps I could arrange the show-window –"

"No. Mr. Zekkel, he doing dat now. You go back unpack ze hats. Pick out ze ones wit ze pink and blue straw like me tell you. Two dozen more."

"Very well, Miss Zekkel."

He was still there. He laughed softly. "I know you had to come back, Meess Russell. You want to – how they say? Geeve me ze sleep? I like to watch you work. Go on. Do ze unpacking."

She went on. This time she stooped and pressed herself against the side of the packing case. But to no avail; her arms were not long enough to reach down to the bottom. She had to rise and bend over.

The channel...

And into the channel swooped the clammy hand, and squeezed. She straightened up so abruptly the front of her dress nearly ripped.

"If you do that again I shall have to tell Mr. Zekkel."

The words came out of her in a croak. She felt as if she were being strangled. Her head sang.

"What Meester Zekkel, he can do? Meester Zekkel tell you to leaf ze job eef I tell heem so. And if you na like me touch your skin I can tell heem so. Which you preffer? To let me touch you, or tell heem to send you home?"

Remotely a voice kept asking her whether this were actual or shadowplay in a dream... A ghost with a lascivious sneer on its face.

She swallowed, bent again and resumed her work. But her hands moved now as though controlled by a brain not her own. A machine brain. A radio brain, perhaps. She no longer had any interest in what her hands were doing.

"You gotta learn to like me, or you can't work here. Me beeg boss."

She would always remember the smell of these wrappings – dryish, sweetish. Reminiscent somewhat of Christmas. The lifting out of a doll from a box. In the far-off, dulcet days.

"Eef you na want me touch your skin you will have to go. I tell Zekkel to pay you off at ze end of ze week – or eefen zis very day. Pay you three shillings for yesterday and today send you off."

He was panting softly. She saw the shadow of his hand as it approached. Into the channel – and it squeezed.

She did nothing. She let it squeeze. At one instant she thought the singing in her head would grow so intense that she would faint...

Out of suffering... a bearded negro in a white robe gesticulating.

Nine shillings... five shillings... "I really didn't want to miss that camp"... "I tell Zekkel to pay you off at ze end of ze week – or eefen zis very day. Pay you three shillings..."

Strain forward slightly, or the front of the dress might rip. That was better. Only a mere instant in time. Everything must pass. Only a globe of human flesh being massaged by a human hand. Rationalize it… *Out of suffering*… I can suffer anything – *anything*…

Now, again in the darkness, in the easy chair, she wondered. Under the thin muslin of her pyjamas she could feel her breasts shrinking. Shuddering as separate entities with a memory of their own.

Only a clammy hand fumbling and squeezing. Two minutes. Three – and all over. That could be endured, surely. There were worse things.

She laughed. But her laughter did not reassure her.

Friday at mid-morning.

This time it was bolts of coloured prints… "Pick out ze nice patterns," said Miss Zekkel. "Ze nice patterns you think will sell queek."

She had hardly begun to unpack when he appeared.

"Ze leetle girl…" The old formula.

She had worn a dress with a high neck, so he had to content himself with operating on the outside… "Always working so hard – ze leetle girl." And a panting laugh, deep, low… "When we go for ze dr-rive she got to wear different dr-ress. Neck too high." Flip! He undid the button at the back.

The colours of the prints blurred into a dizzy blaze. She straightened up and let him have it. On both cheeks – hard. Once – twice.

"You slimy, filthy beast!"

At midday, Miss Zekkel interrupted her as she sat eating her bread-and-cheese lunch. Miss Zekkel's face was grave. And sad. She held out an envelope. "Me gal, I na like tell you zis, but Meester Zekkel, he say to geeve you your week' pay and tell you not to come back. I sorry, Meess Russell. I too sorry. You such a goot gal. You work so goot."

"I understand, Miss Zekkel."

Miss Zekkel tugged at her fleshy chin and glanced around cautiously. "Zat man Dikran! Ow, Meess Russell! He terrible Tay-rible!" She moved away shaking her head and groaning softly, mumbling in Arabic.

The wireless across the street was playing airs from *Snow-white.*

Miss Zekkel came back after a few minutes. She held out a small box. A box of Ashes of Roses face-powder. "Take eet, Meess Russell. Take eet. It's for you. I give eet to you."

"Oh. That's very nice of you, Miss Zekkel. Thanks."

"Na cry, me gal. Na cry. You will find more work."

"...some day my prince will come..." The soprano voice shrilled out the words with earnest fervour, and the lisp of footsteps and the buzz and hum of humanity on the pavements, the traffic in Lombard Street, made a webbed filter through which the sugary sounds squirmed grittily.

6

"That settles it. I've got to leave school and look for work."

"No, David, please! Not yet. Give me a chance. I'll find another job."

"But you've been trying now for nearly two weeks and you can't get anything. Mother is grumbling. She says I ought to look for a job."

"I know. But give me a few more days. To – to the end of this week. I think I know someone. I'm almost sure I'll get something this time."

She put her pride to one side and went to see Mr. Ralph.

He was smiling and affable. He rubbed his chin, grew grave and concerned all of a sudden. It was terrible, terrible, he said. He really wished he could do something for her, but the employment situation was extremely difficult at the moment. If she could have typed and done shorthand he might have been able to place her at Hart & Stephens'.

He sat for some time grunting and rubbing his chin. Eventually he shook his head and said that he was afraid there was nothing he could do to help her at the moment. But (my dear girl) from time to time she must call to see him, just in case anything should turn up. Yes, just in case he should hear of something to her advantage. It was terrible, terrible.

Mr. van Huisten was equally concerned. He, too, rubbed his chin and grunted. Went further and massaged the tip of his nose with a thumb nail. Finally, however, he had to admit that he could not think of any opening for her. He would keep an eye out for her, of course. He could promise her that. Oh, certainly, he could promise her that! He would drop her a line at the first opportunity that offered. He would not forget her. She could rest assured that he would not forget her.

She held out her hand and thanked him. With a smile.

The September heat was stifling. There was dust in her right shoe, let in through the hole in the sole.

She would not bother to go to Mr. Jarrow or any of the others.

"Look out, Miss!"

She sprang out of the way just in time.

The boy lost his balance temporarily, and his foot scraped along the asphalt. He paused and looked back and grinned. He had perfect teeth, white and even, in a shiny, dark brown face. She liked him.

"I'm so sorry! I wasn't looking where I was going."

"It's nutting, Miss!"

She watched him ride off, and remembered that David's bicycle would have to be sold. And David would leave school and look for a job.

I've failed him.

She felt very exhausted. There was an empty singing in her head, and her skin grew clammy. All the way home she willed herself not to faint.

"Sylvie, you heard the news?"

"What news?"

"Aubrey is engaged."

"You're joking."

"Serious. He brought her round to see us last night."

"What sort of girl is she?"

"Half Chinee, half coloured. A nice girl. Plenty curves. You know how Aubrey likes his curves."

"I can hardly believe it. He's given her a ring?"

"A ring with diamonds and rubies. He'll be here with her in a few minutes. Sit down and wait."

That was in October – after David's bicycle had been sold. He got twenty-five dollars for it. He had left school and had secured a job as a printer's assistant at five shillings a week.

Early in December, Henry Madhoo told her that he had heard that Beryl Dell was engaged to Wilfred van Huisten, a nephew of Mr. van Huisten's. Beryl, her old school friend. Next it would be Mabel Earle. And it seemed only yesterday they had been riding through Murray Street on the way to school.

Everywhere something was happening to somebody. Aunt Clarice had gone to New Amsterdam to live. Her husband had got a job there with a big firm. He was a motor salesman now. He used to be a Singer sewing-machine salesman, but he had made a failure of that. He drank too much. Aunt Clarice was happy now because he had given up the Chinese woman in Albouystown, and going to New Amsterdam meant that there would be little chance of the friendship being revived.

Everywhere, thought Sylvia, something is happening to somebody. Only I can get nowhere. Only I remain always at a standstill.

She found herself lapsing into a state of self-pity. Felt her will going. And Charlotte accused her of laziness. "Morning after morning you dump you'self in dat chair and stare out de window. Why you don't stir you'self, Sylvie, and look for some work to do?"

Sometimes Sylvia would go for a walk. Sometimes she would blaze at her. "My shoes are in holes! My dresses are getting shabby. What's the use of my tramping the streets when nobody will give me a job!"

"How David manage to get a job so quick?"

"That's unfair. There are more opportunities for men than for girls! I've tried and tried. It isn't my fault!" Daily her nerves grew more and more frayed.

One evening, desperate with misery, she stood by the gateway, after a row, and David came down the stairs and said: "Don't let her get you riled, Sylvie. Why bother to argue with Mother!"

"But, David, didn't you hear what she said? She called me a loafer. She said I have no pride to be living off her and you. I feel like killing myself. I don't feel like living any longer."

The struggle to keep back the tears hurt her in the pit of her stomach. She could feel David's gaze upon her, could sense his sympathy.

A stray dog, thin and ugly, went past the gateway.

"That's what I feel like. Like that dog."

She looked at him and saw that he was frowning out at the street, his face troubled. A lock of his hair hung loose over his temple.

A tight bubble of emotion burst inside her. She uttered a moan: and pressed herself against him, clutched him and buried her face into his shoulder. "Dave! Oh, Dave!" He tried to push her off automatically, embarrassed, but she continued to grip him, her body in a desperate tremble. "But for you I'd have nothing to live for! I wouldn't want to exist if you weren't here." She said much more – in an incoherent stammer. He did not try to repulse her now, but she could feel from the tenseness of his frame that he was awkward and at a loss what to say or do. She did not mind. She continued to hold him to her.

She relaxed against him, and shut her eyes. Felt as though a jet of bay-rum were running through her, assuaging the loneliness of her spirit, reducing the accumulated iron of bitterness that had gathered in her these past weeks into cool, fragrant dust.

"I – I think some people are coming up the street," he murmured – and put her from him. But he did it gently. She was not hurt. She gave him a look of gratitude and said: "You're a good boy. I must seem very stupid, I know."

Without meeting her gaze, he mumbled: "You're worrying your head too much." He went upstairs, and she watched him until he had disappeared inside, the lassitude of relief still sweet and heavy in her.

After that, she took to leaving home every morning – but instead of looking for a job she would go to George Street to Naomi's and spend the half-day there. Some mornings she helped Naomi to dust and clean, or to cook. But she never accepted Naomi's invitation to stay and have lunch. Her pride would not let her; it would have been too much like sponging. On the days when Naomi prepared a good steak or roast, the temptation was great

– but she disciplined herself to resist and return home to her bread and cheese, or bread and sardines, or rice and salt fish, whatever modest meal Charlotte had got ready.

One morning, on returning home, she was about to ascend the stairs when the sound of footsteps attracted her gaze to the street. A shortish, thickset man – he was a European – paused at the gateway and looked at her. He was dressed in white duck. His blue eyes narrowed with uncertainty, then he smiled slightly and asked:

"One Mr. Russell lives here, can you tell me?" He had an accent that was a trifle foreign.

"Yes. Mr. David Russell."

"Yes, that's right. Mr. David Russell. Is he at home?"

"No. He won't be home until four or five this afternoon. Have you a message for him?"

He hesitated, then said a little hastily: "No, but I wanted to see him. I thought I would have found him at home. I'll call again."

"Could I – what name shall I tell him?"

Again the hesitation, then: "It's no use my giving you my name. He doesn't know it. I met him – just casually, you know and we got talking. I'll call back later." He raised his hat – a new-looking felt hat – smiled and moved off, his manner obviously uncomfortable.

The whole afternoon she puzzled over the incident. It worried her. It was so mysterious. Where could David have met this man?

She approached him the moment he came in. "Dave, you didn't tell me you expected a visitor."

Was it her imagination, or did he grow a trifle pale?

"A visitor?"

"Yes. A shortish white man stopped at the gate this morning at about eleven and asked if you lived here. He wouldn't give any name."

"Oh. I –" He broke off and turned away – but not before she had seen the frown of irritation and alarm. "He's a fellow I met in Water Street on my way to work the other morning," he said in a voice that was too offhand. "He did mention he might drop in some time."

"You met him in Water Street?"

"Yes." He began to whistle, stopped and said: "I've got to run off to a Scout meeting. Better get into my uniform right away."

She asked him no more questions, for she knew he would have flared up in annoyance and told her not to be so inquisitive.

She remained at home for the rest of that day in the hope that the man might return, but he did not show up. At about seven, David came in from the Scout meeting. He put his pole in the corner near the hat-rack, then began to whistle shrilly as he moved toward his room door. She was in the easy chair, but he did not glance at her. She could sense that his whistling was the result of self-consciousness. He was concealing something, and was aware that she knew he was doing so.

She did not sleep well that night. She had dreams of large grey ants that came crawling into the cottage to attack her. She woke the next morning with a dull headache. It was early when she woke. She could see the sky, greyish-white, at the window – the colour of a dirty concrete pavement. She watched it until it turned grey-blue, until the sun began to thrust orange shafts through the foliage of the trees. She heard an alarm-clock tinkling in the cottage next door. The sound brought back some dim memory – a pleasant memory. She sat up and looked at the old Westclox clock on the dressing-table. Two minutes past six. Beside her, Charlotte slept on, a frail, ineffectual skeleton covered with a dark-brown skin. Her skin seemed to be darkening with age.

She got out of bed carefully so as not to disturb her mother. She went to the window and looked out at the morning. Wondered vaguely why it was she got a certain peace from looking outside. She had to look through the glass, because the window was shut. Charlotte would not hear of the window being opened while they slept. She was afraid of taking a chill. The room, as a result, was hot and stuffy, but that was a circumstance that must be tolerated, like many another.

David always slept with his windows open.

Her head throbbed. And the new day, though soothing in its peace, did not allay the many deeper aches within her. A sudden yearning swept through her – a yearning to be comforted, to be held close within safe arms and whispered at that everything was all right. A weakness saturated her being. She began to tremble from sheer self-pity.

She looked round the room, and abruptly moved toward the door that connected with David's room. She went in and stood by the bed and watched him asleep. He lay flat on his back, his arms thrown back. She smiled and wished that she could have slept as he did – with such complete relaxation, so deeply. She bent and kissed his cheek, and told herself that this was how she would kiss a child of hers one day – with this same tender, possessive feeling.

The very soundness of his sleep was like that of a child. If he could know the number of times she had come in here at night and kissed his cheek while he lay in absolute unawareness of the affection she was lavishing on him!

That guilty feeling came over her. It had not troubled her for a long time. Suppose her mother discovered about this secret obsession. Suppose one day she heard her whispering to Janie or Sarah: "Her own brother! Sylvie ain' got no shame. It's unnatural..."

She was about to turn off when her foot touched something soft. She glanced down and saw that it was David's Scout haversack. The end of it was visible under the draped sheet. She stooped and lifted the sheet.

The haversack was packed tight and bulging, the top secured with cord. Beside it lay what looked like a pillowcase also tightly packed and bulging. A grey fear drifted through her. She rose and stared at her brother, and found that her throat had gone dry: She sat down on the edge of the bed and shook his shoulder gently. He did not stir. She shook him again, bent and whispered: "Dave. Wake up."

He grunted, turned on his side away from her, then opened his eyes, and rolled over on to his back again. He blinked at her, still dazed with sleep. She rose quickly, crossed to the connecting door and shut it softly. She returned and sat down again on the bed.

He was fully awake now. He sat up and gave her a puzzled look.

"David, what are you up to? Your haversack – and that pillowcase under the bed here. Why have you packed them?" She spoke in a hoarse whisper.

His face took on an expression of alarm. He glanced toward the closed door. "What haversack?" He, too, spoke in a hoarse whisper. "What are you talking about?"

"You know what I mean. What are you planning to do, Dave? Tell me."

"I – how did you find out? – look here, don't bother me. Why have you got to be questioning me like this?"

She gripped his arm. "Please. Tell me, Dave. I won't tell Mother. Just tell me what's wrong. Are you in trouble?"

"Trouble? No, I'm not in trouble. Why can't you leave me alone?" He shrugged her hand off, and sat glaring at her, his arms hugging his drawn-up legs.

She was trembling. Her throat felt choked.

"I'm going away," he said. "Everything is settled. You can't stop me."

He began to tell her about it. It was a cargo ship. It was sailing for Canada tonight – Halifax. He had met Mr. Tompkins on Wheeler's wharf two days ago. He was the chief steward on the *Falconer,* and he had said yes, they did need someone in the galley. He would see about it. "I gave him my address, but I told him if he dropped round here he wasn't to say what he had come about if he didn't find me at home. I forgot to tell him I wouldn't be home during the day. I – I was so excited. Oh, whoops! Sylvie, don't tell Mother. She'll want to stop me. I gave them a fake age. I said I was eighteen. Last night I went aboard the ship and they signed me on. I have to go aboard by eleven o'clock tonight. I thought I'd be able to sneak out when you and Mother had gone to bed –"

"But, Dave, the war! They're torpedoing ships all the time. And you're so young. Dave, what am I going to do without you?"

"I can't go on living like this, Sylvie. Mother makes me sick. And I'm only getting five shillings a week. What's five shillings! They're going to pay me over a hundred dollars for the trip to Halifax. And I want to go for the adventure. Oh, you'll never understand. You girls are all so softy and silly."

"But I do understand. You mustn't think I don't. I'm not like Mother. I understand how you feel. But you could have waited until you were a little older, Dave. I know you're big and strong for your age, but – but – oh, I'm so afraid for you. Please don't go.

Please. Just for me. I'll die from missing you. I won't have anything left to live for. I'll – I'll – oh, my God! I can't believe this. I can't believe it."

This time he was silent. He sat with a scowl on his face, uncomfortable, troubled. He kept plucking at the bed-sheet.

An aeroplane was passing high overhead. The sound of it made a dark-blue shadow in her fancy – a conical shadow of doom that burrowed into her. It foretold inconceivable agonies, inconceivable aches and tortures. It was the future conspiring against her, showing greenish fangs. At last, the sound faded, and the spell was broken. A cool rain seemed to invade her. A voice murmured distantly: "This is it, Sylvia. Take it and make the best of it." And she took it.

She stretched out and patted his cheek. "Don't look so upset. Go and make good. I don't blame you for not wanting to stay in this place."

He gave her a look of incredulity and gratitude. "You won't tell Mother, then?"

She smiled and shook her head.

He uttered a muffled chortle. "You're a real sport, Sylvie. I wanted to tell you but I was afraid. I wasn't sure."

She nodded. The smile on her face had become fixed.

"I meant to leave a note for you on the dressing-table."

The sun was coming in at the window. There were shadows on the bed, on his pyjamas, on her right hip. The shadows of leaves, shapeless and shifty.

"I'll help you. Today when you're at work I'll pack my old suitcase for you. The one Daddy gave me after the Berbice trip."

"But suppose Mother sees you."

"She won't. I can be sly when I want."

PART FOUR

1

Charlotte took it with indifference. The note she found on the dressing-table addressed to her made her exclaim: "Eh-eh!" a few times. Then she called out to Sylvia who was in the bathroom: "Sylvie! Sylvie, you see dis note on de dressing-table from David?"

"No, Mother! What note?" In a loud, over-surprised voice. "Has he left a note on the dressing-table? Isn't he at home?"

"No! His bed empty. I just been into his room. He say he gone to sea!"

"To sea!"

"So de note say. He must be off his head. Eh-eh!"

And during the day, the usual murmured monologue about ingratitude.

"Not even to tell me he was going. Very good, David. You right. You right to treat me so, boy. But never mind. God can see all. Ah leave you in God's hands. God will know how to deal wid you..."

Sylvia gave up altogether trying to find a job. She began to accustom herself to lazing at home or at Naomi's. At Naomi's she listened-in to the news every evening. The B.B.C. sometimes announced the names of ships sunk. One morning the postman brought an airmail letter addressed to her. It bore a Canadian stamp.

"Dear Sylvie,

"I arrived safely at Halifax..." (half a line cut out by the censor)... "and I'm quite well, only it's very cold here, I had to buy two wool pullovers and an overcoat. I was seasick the first day out but after that I was O.K. The sea is great. Whoops! I like it a lot..." (a line and a half censored)... I went aboard one of them, and now I really think I'd prefer to be in the Navy, I'm thinking it over. See me firing off one of the big guns, nothing I'd like better. Roger, he's a cook, I'm going with him to see a show tonight, he says it's a good show. Well that's all the news for now, I'll try and write you again when we arrive in..." (word cut out)... "and I'll tell you if I managed to join the Royal Navy.

I remain,

Yours truly,

David."

"... me his mudder, and not a line to me. He won't even ask after me. It's all well! God knows how to deal wid ingratitude..."

Janie came in at about ten one morning and found Sylvia in the easy chair. Janie sucked her teeth and muttered: "Some people really lucky in dis world. While odder people slaving some people jest got to lie back and do nutting."

Sylvia overheard but ignored the remark.

Janie and Sarah began to put up Charlotte to quarrel with her. Between the whirr of the machine Sylvia often heard them telling Charlotte not "to stand for no idleness".

"Put her out de house if she can't go and look for work. Who she t'ink she is at all dat she can squat down on her backside every day and do nutting! She must be a queen or a countess. Don't stand no stupidness, Charlotte. Talk to she. Make her see how you got to kill you'self to make two ends meet. She had life too easy when her daddy was alive – dat what spoil her."

One day in December – it was shortly after the *Graf Spee* affair – Charlotte said: "Well, look, Sylvie, Christmas on awready. De stores and shops always want extra help. Yet you still sitting down in de house day after day and won't stir you'self to go and look for somet'ing to do. You t'ink dis is fair to me? I got to work so hard to make a few cents, and all you can do to come out in de sitting-room in you' pyjamas and lie down in de easy chair."

Sylvia made no reply. She knew that, in a way, the censure was deserved.

"Anyway," her mother continued, gaining courage, "I decide upon dis. If you don't go out and look for somet'ing to do today you not getting no food to eat at midday. Understand dat I not standing for no more idleness."

Without a word, Sylvia rose and went inside. She dressed and left the house, but did not go job-hunting. She went to the Sea Wall and seated herself on a bench. The sky was overcast, and the heat unpleasant. Sticky and steamy. Now and then the sun showed itself amid the grey-white pall overhead – dimly, like a gob of yellow glue.

She kept wriggling uncomfortably. She looked around slowly.

The waves swished softly on the beach, far out. Very little wind was blowing. Not a single person was in sight anywhere along the wall-promenade. Everybody was at work. Everybody was shopping, planning what presents to buy for Christmas. Thinking of the parties and dances, of the toy balloons and Christmas trees decked with artificial holly and fairy lights.

She heard the drone of an aeroplane, and tilted her head. What memory did it bring back, that sound? Some tiny but vital event. She frowned and pulled at her ear, but the memory would not be nailed. She had to give up. A feeling of defeat descended upon her. A cold finger seemed to press on her cheek. She wanted to scream. She must scream. She would suffocate and die if she didn't. Panic attacked her. She must run. Get up now and sprint along the wall. Whimper and cry out as she ran.

She jerked herself to her feet. She clenched her hands.

Life. If only she could discover why it was she had to go through this agony. Why had life been given to her if eventually it was to result in this? This what?… This near-death. She was dying. She looked down at the concrete. Turned and saw the bandstand. Glanced up at the banked clouds. Why?… She stood waiting… No answer. Only blank silence. The clouds remained banked clouds. The concrete was still concrete; she could see no message etched upon it. And the bandstand – there were no hieroglyphics in the bandstand's roof. The wall, the beach, Georgetown… only silence everywhere. Yet… she looked about her. Yet it was as if she were being watched – by a presence. Or an intelligence. An unseen mind near by – or partly within and partly without her. A living shadow that was herself plus an unknown quantity. ... This is madness. I'm going off my head. I'd better walk. Go for a long walk to Kitty or Plaisance.

She was about to move off when she hesitated.

I'm making a fool of myself. I'm admitting defeat. If I can walk aimlessly to Kitty or Plaisance I may as well walk to Water Street and look for a job. If Daddy were here now he would have told me not to be a romantic idiot. "Be a realist, Goo. Don't get lost in a fog of fancies and morbid imaginings. Keep your chin up! Up!"

So she set out for Water Street.

It was the old routine… "Sorry, Miss Russell. Nothing doing here, I'm afraid. Overstaffed as it is."

"No, we have all the help we need for the season. If you had come in last week, perhaps. We took on two girls at the beginning of the month for the season…"

"No, we're filled up now. You've come too late. We did need some help earlier in the month…"

"Well, let's see…"

The rubbing of a chin. The world swayed.

"Yes, I think we can do with an extra assistant. Sit down; Miss Russell. I'll see Mr. Beecher…"

The world continued to sway…

"No, I'm sorry, Miss Russell. Mr. Beecher says he's already arranged with somebody to come on…"

The world righted itself.

She went into a restaurant called the Red Mavis – the name had always amused her – and the smell of food reminded her that she was getting hungry. She remembered, too, that Charlotte had said that there would be no food for her if she did not look for a job

Well, she had earned her meal, surely. She had tried.

She asked to see the manager.

He was a tall, slimmish Portuguese. He smiled at her rather sympathetically as he approached. Perhaps he was mistaking her for a customer. The place was crowded. The girls in their light-blue uniforms hurried about as though serving people with food was their sole interest in life. All of them were fair-complexioned coloured girls – or Portuguese. All of them were attractive.

"I came to ask if you needed any help for the season."

"Yes, we do need help," he said, and his smile remained. "Very badly, too."

The world swayed again...

He hesitated, and appeared thoughtful, but she sensed that he was appraising her. He was thinking of her in terms of her face and her figure and her complexion, possibly her height, too. So far as height went, she had failed the test already. Five feet two... she might as well go home.

He was asking her name. She stammered it out.

"Do you think you could manage this kind of work, Miss Russell?"

"Manage it? Oh, yes, I'm sure. I – I could try. I'm sure I'd do it well. Quite sure!"

"Very well. Will you come into my office and let's discuss everything fully?"

"And the pay is four dollars a week, Naomi! Think of it! After that measly nine shillings I used to get at Zekkel's!"

"Greed, greed!" said Gregory, wagging his head. "Four dollars isn't all. You'll probably make ten a week, salary and tips."

"Ten! I'm rich, then!" She did a jig. "And guess what! It's not only for the Christmas season. Mr. de Jaires says he wants me permanently. Business is increasing every day, and he wants bright, attractive girls. Naomi, am I really attractive?"

"Can you look in a mirror," said Gregory, "and watch that trembling balcony you've got and then ask if you're really attractive?"

When she got home she stood naked before the dressing-table mirror in David's room which she now occupied... A trembling balcony. She smiled and tilted her head, shook her hair about and watched it gleam in the electric light. Cupped her breasts in her hands.

Perhaps it was the dim memory of that occasion in the Strand Hotel when she had stood before the mirror admiring herself – it might have been that that made her suddenly sober down. The hysterical jubilance abated.

She let her gaze move slowly about the room. The world was

still the same. Let her not be fooled by this success. Gloom was still within her, ready to take control at an instant's notice. Today she had been dying. Her spirit, her mind. Now she was alive again. But death crouched always in the offing. A shadow-hound waiting to pounce on the shadow-self that was the real being contained within the solidity of one's shapely body.

She laughed… Madness again.

She sobered down again… Is it madness? It may be growing up.

2

Men noticed her, and the girls, she discovered, were not machines whose sole interest was serving people with food. They were human. They laughed and chatted with her when they were in the big kitchen with the aproned cooks and dish-washers. One or two were catty, but not unbearably so. One or two were big-hearted and confiding – talked about their boy friends and cinema dates and the Sea Wall. One or two were smutty in stage-whispers. Human girls, all of them; not brilliant or poetic or bookish. Their chief aim was to get married and have homes and babies and good times at parties and dances. She got on well with them, because – she realized with dismay – she had much in common with them. She was not as abnormal as she had imagined herself to be.

The men smiled at her, leant their elbows on the ice-cream counter and talked to her in quiet, trying-to-get-friendly voices. They tipped her, though it took her some time before she could accept tips without a sense of outrage to her pride.

It was hard work, but she enjoyed it. The cooks and the dish washers and the lady in charge of the kitchen could be irritable and snappish at times, but she saw that it was only the rush that made them so. They liked and respected her. It was because of her soft manner and her speech. The lady in charge once commented with a smile: "You speak very well, child. I wish some of these other girls could imitate you."

It seemed, somehow, not the thing to reply that her father had been English and had been an unusual father from whom she had learnt many ways of speaking and of looking at the world that other Georgetown daughters could not have learnt from their fathers. She smiled and let the comment pass.

The manager, too, made life pleasant. He was unbelievably considerate toward them. He was always inquiring whether they had had anything to eat yet, or expressing the hope that A or B was not working after her hour for going home. "I don't want you girls to collapse from fatigue, you know." His methods of making them feel at home and happy struck her sometimes as so studied that she wondered if he could be some sort of psychology faddist.

She had no time now to introspect and indulge in romantic or morbid fancies. She became so extraverted that she even wondered how it had been possible that she could have thought and felt as she had done only a few weeks ago. She began to worry less about David. He seemed hazier in her fancy – not so obsessively important a factor in her life as she had thought him to be. She ceased to see herself as a pervert. Her sense of shame left her.

She still saw Naomi and her crowd. Aubrey Deleon and his half-Chinese girl got married and set up house in a cottage in Bent Street, not very far from Naomi's. The wedding (a formal affair with veil and train and bridesmaids and speech-making, for the bride's people were middle-class and thought much of themselves, though they came of no family that counted) took place on a day when Sylvia had to work – on Saturday, the Red Mavis's busiest day – so she had to miss it. She sent Aubrey a present, however – a hairbrush set – and after a week or so received a piece of black cake wrapped in crepe-tissue paper with a small white card which announced in silver letters that Mr. and Mrs. Aubrey Deleon sent their compliments. Gregory and Naomi attended, and Naomi told Sylvia that Gregory's toast was a masterpiece. He had everybody in roars of laughter. Champagne glass in hand, he suddenly emerged from under the long decorated table on which stood the wedding-cake, and in a low but dramatic voice cried: "Ladies and gentlemen! I rise from the direst obscurity to do justice to this delicate occasion!" Aubrey and his bride spent a two weeks' honeymoon in Berbice, on the Corentyne Coast – the proper and correct honeymoon for a middle-class couple.

Life kept drumming on. Jack Sampson had left the Government service. He was no longer an engineer on the ferry-steamer. He had bought a cottage out of the savings of years, and had set up on his own as a boat-builder. Gregory laughed: "But, Jack man, you're a capitalist in embryo – and a vigorous embryo! Buying property and setting up a boat-building concern! You're on the way to wealth. You're a hoax!"

Jack, however, had convincing arguments to support his new actions. Why should he always be an underdog? Why should he not be a man of independence? "I got a purpose, Greg. You wait till I make some money! Den you going to see dose bitches on top squirm. It's a campaign I'm working on, boy! I'm going to bring dem down by using their own tools. Ah got a five-year plan all worked out to handle dem capitalist dogs…"

In Berbice Aunt Clarice seemed far more happy than she had been in the city. She wrote often, and told them that Charlie was still "good friends with the bottle", but was trying to do his work properly and she did not have so much to complain of now. What she meant – but could not say in plain language – was that the Chinese woman had not followed him to New Amsterdam and that he was doing his best to be a faithful husband. She was always inviting them to come and spend time with her. It was a very quiet town, New Amsterdam, she said, but the people were friendly and nice to get on with. She was lonely, that was the truth of the matter. Henry, since the outbreak of war, had been on active service with the Militia, and she had no other child on whom to lavish her affection. Sylvia decided that as soon as she got her two weeks leave she would go to New Amsterdam and spend some time with her.

Benson Riego came in often for ice-cream, but it was not always that she could find it convenient to serve him and chat with him. Every time she saw him she felt a dim tugging excitement. But as always in the past, it was transitory; it never lasted more than a second or two.

Whenever he looked at her his eyes would grow bright and a queer twist would appear at the corner of his mouth. He had a bated intensity of manner when he said anything to her. It was no imagination on her part, because when he spoke to any of the other girls he was casual and at ease.

The more the image of David receded, the more interest she took in Benson. So much so that she never liked him to come in when she was working the cash-register, for his presence unnerved her and was inclined to put her off the business of giving change.

She and two other girls, Esmé Peterson and Belle de Geira, had been given the job of working the cash-register. They took it in turns. While one worked the cash-register, the others served. They arranged things to suit themselves. Mr. de Jaires gave them a free hand. Sylvia found it a nerve-straining task. She was for ever in fear of giving wrong change – especially during rush periods. And what worried her, too, was that Esmé and Belle took advantage of her willingness to please and left her at the machine much longer than the agreed upon time. Then there was the temptation to be dishonest. Sylvia never yielded, but she knew that Esmé and Belle often did. It was easy to receive money and pretend you had forgotten to press the keys. When business was quiet you could not do it, because the girls came one at a time with the money received from customers. But when three, four, five of them were clamouring around you, pushing coins and notes at you and demanding change, not waiting to see you register the amount but itching to hurry off with the change to get their tips, there was no difficulty at all about putting aside your own little pile. The system was faulty, but Mr. de Jaires, despite his psychology – or perhaps because of it – seemed to prefer it this way.

She received another letter from David – this one from England. He was still on the *Falconer* which, so far, had not been torpedoed. He said he had not been allowed to sign off so that he could join the Navy. Merchant seamen, he had been informed, were as important and as necessary to the war effort as Navy ratings.

There were moments when anxiety for his safety reached an unbearable degree of intensity, moments when the old passion rose up to torture her and bring back the sense of secret shame – but these moments were rare, and grew rarer as the days turned into weeks and then months.

Benson Riego took her to the cinema one evening. He stammered when he asked her, and she could tell that he had rehearsed for the occasion. He fiddled with his ice-cream and kept shifting about on the stool.

In the cinema they hardly spoke, and he did not try to hold her hand. But a silent something came and went between them. More than once she felt a glow rise up in her like thick, warm ribbons, and once when he shifted in his seat her heart seemed to turn to mist and recede in a green cone of yearning. It was on this night that she realized that, basically, she had not changed from what she had been a month or two ago. She was still a romantic, still possessed of odd poetic fancies and illusions.

On the third occasion she went to the cinema with him she nearly blurted out that nowadays she only enjoyed seeing a film when he took her. But she checked herself. He might think her forward and brazen.

After the show, they walked along the avenue in Main Street on their way to Fort Street. He could have afforded a taxi, but she always turned down his offer, telling him she preferred to walk – which was no hypocrisy; she did, indeed, prefer to walk.

On this particular occasion the palish light from a half-moon slanted down between the house-tops and through the foliage of the saman trees that lined the avenue. It was nearly midnight. The air held a slight shivery chillness. For no reason that seemed apparent, a deep peace moved through her, and she began to sing in a soft voice, "Thanks for the Memory". He glanced at her and asked if that was one of her favourite song-hits. She nodded, and after a moment broke off in the middle of the refrain and laughed. "One day I'm going to Hollywood!"

"You ought to do well there."

"Why do you think so?"

"Because you have everything." He kept his gaze on the street. His tone was strained and unnatural, and she sensed that he was struggling to express something but felt afraid of making a fool of himself.

"You really think so? You really think I have everything?"

"Yes." He hesitated, then said: "I was going to tell you something, but it will sound stupid."

"Why should it?"

He shrugged.

"Tell me," she said.

"It's a big thing. I don't know if I should."

She could say nothing to this. She, too, had to stare down at the street and watch the grey-black asphalt swim past under them in the pale moonlight. The night air whirled with a freshness of leaves and flowers and tree-blossoms. Now and then a car glared whitely at them, droned coming at them, rushed past gone, a savage, ruthless monster vanished in their rear.

"I've always liked you," he said, his voice deep and shaky. "Since we used to go skating. But I could never bring myself to tell you."

She made no response.

"I always knew you had something the other girls didn't have. I – I always wanted to ask you to go out with me, but I thought you might have had some other friend already."

"Me? I've never had a boy friend. None at all."

"Oh, I see." She could note the relief in his manner. He took a handkerchief from the top pocket of his coat and wiped his face. Despite the humility in his manner, she found herself overpowered by the vibrant maleness of him. She wanted to be sorry for him because of his shyness, but it was impossible to feel pity. Instead she felt a little afraid of him – as though he were about to hold her and hurt her, but hurt her in a way she would like. A weakness of surrender spread through her whole being.

"I wanted to be friends with you for a long time," he said, after a silence. "I only wish – oh, I don't know what to say!"

"What's it? What do you wish?"

He said nothing.

"Is something on your mind, Benny?"

"You see," he said, after a hesitation, "nothing ever works how we want it to. I mean, I want to be friends with you, but – but I want to go abroad."

"Go abroad? Go abroad where?"

"To Canada to join the R.C.A.F."

"You want to go to the war?"

"Yes. Pa doesn't want to hear of it, but I think I've managed to persuade him at last. He sort of agreed last night."

It was she who fell silent now. A patch of numbness was widening slowly inside her, despite her efforts to tell herself that she was not shocked at the news... I'm hardened to things like this now, surely. No need to get worried and morbid... But the numbness would not be denied.

"When are you going?" she asked, at length. "Have you decided?"

"I'm not too sure. The boats are so upset nowadays. But if everything goes as I hope it will, I ought to sail in two or three weeks' time."

"As soon as that!"

"I can't be sure, I tell you. That's if everything works out as I hope." He began to say something, then broke off. After a moment he tried again. "You see, Sylvia, I really like you, but – but I couldn't miss this war. I'm determined to join either the Navy or the R.A.F. I sound like a fool, eh?"

"Not at all. I understand. How old are you?"

"Two months over twenty."

"You ought to pass your tests. You – you look so big and fit."

"I had a medical test already, and the doctor said nothing could stop me from being selected."

After that, there seemed nothing more for them to say. She listened to their footsteps on the hard surface of the street.

"I'll still go on liking you," he said abruptly. "If you think you can wait I'll be prepared to wait. They can't kill me. I'll get through."

"I can wait. Any time – however long you want me to."

A breathlessness possessed her at the thought of the decision she had just made. The bigness of her commitment gave her a dizzy feeling. She could see whorls going up into the moonlight. Cones and towers.

"I don't know if you'd like a ring."

"A ring? An engagement ring? Not at all! I should hate that. Daddy always said that that kind of thing is so farcical. Engagement and wedding rings. You won't have to be afraid for me. I won't let a soul touch me while you're away, ring or no ring. I can promise you that."

"I know. I'd trust you anywhere. I always knew you were tops."

It sounded like an American word. Tops.

When they entered Fort Street, she asked him about his people. "You think your father and mother will approve of me?"

"Mother is dead. She died last September – a few days after the war broke out –"

"She did! And I never heard! You've told me so little about yourself and your people, Benny."

He suggested going to the Sea Wall so that they could sit down and talk. "You think your mother would quarrel with you?"

"Mother? It wouldn't matter to her if I didn't come home until midday tomorrow. So long as she gets the money I work for." She had not intended to put so much bitterness into her voice, and regretted it at once.

"You don't get on with her, eh? I knew it must be like that."

On the Sea Wall, they sat on a bench west of the Round House and not far from the site of the old Dutch fort. The Round House nowadays was out of bounds to the public. It was surrounded by barbed wire, and sentries kept guard, and there was a gun in it whose muzzle pointed menacingly out to sea.

They talked about themselves, though she had to draw him out to get him to discuss himself. He said he never liked talking about himself. She learnt that his parents were of poor education – especially his mother. She was a de Fuega, he said; her family belonged to Plaisance on the East Coast. His father was a little better educated. He was doing well in the rum business; he had three rum-shops, one on the East Coast and two in the city here.

"I suppose he'd like you to carry on after he has died?"

"Yes, he would like that, but I have a younger brother and two sisters who could handle the business, so he hasn't got to worry about that."

"Oh, you have a younger brother?"

"Yes. He's ten. There're nine of us in all."

"Nine!"

"Yes. I have two elder sisters who help Pa with the rum-shops, and a string of others after me – all girls except Manny."

"That's short for Manoel?"

"Yes."

"By the way, I always wondered how you came to be called Benson. It's not a Portuguese name."

"It's some name the old man saw in a book he was looking through, and he got it into his head to call me that."

She asked him what were his ambitions, and he grinned and told her she would think him stupid if he said what they were. After a slight hesitation he went on: "My first ambition was to make sugar. It used to seem wonderful to me how people could get sugar from canes, and I wanted to try to do it myself. But that was when I was very small. Nowadays I'm thinking of taking up electrical engineering. But that will have to wait until after the war."

"How long do you think the war will last?"

"Not more than a year, I'm sure – I mean a year from now. The British have them well blockaded. They'll soon have to give up."

"Then by next March you should be coming back?"

"Yes. I can't swear it will be next March, of course – but around then. Hitler can't last. In fact, that's why I'm so eager to go. I sort of feel the war might come to an end and – and I'll have missed it. Nothing I'd like better than to dive down on Berlin and drop a few bombs. Or stand behind a big gun in a battleship and fire a few salvoes."

He was leaning forward, his hands clenched. He reminded her of David now. He was just a boy. An ache moved in her, and she told herself that she must be in love with him. The image of David tried to obtrude, but she put it aside without any trouble.

She began to look around her slowly. The moonlight looked unreal and jumbie-weird on the wall – and on their persons. She could feel it drifting through her as though it were a cool ghost. The ache dissolved out of her, but she still tried to assure herself that she was in love with Benson. A panic seized her… Am I just forcing myself to feel this way? Is it another illusion I'm deliberately trying to build up?

"It must be late," he said, breaking the silence. He glanced toward her wrist. "Didn't you have a watch when you were at school?"

"Oh. Yes. Daddy gave it to me as a birthday gift." She hesitated, then said in a rush: "I had to sell it" – and turned away her face.

He mumbled something in an embarrassed tone. Then, as though on impulse, he gripped her wrist and said: "I know you've been seeing hell. I really would have liked to help you out, but – well, I know how you'd have felt if I'd offered, so I didn't say anything."

"That's nothing," she muttered, the blood hot in her cheeks. She withdrew her wrist from his grasp and laughed briefly. "I'm accustomed to having a tough time, Benny. But I can take it. I'm not soft."

"I know you're not."

After another silence, he rose and said that they had better be going. It was a shame to keep her out of her bed when she had to go to work at seven tomorrow. She asked him to sit down again; she said it did not matter. "I could stay here the whole night and talk to you."

The panic had left her. An exuberance possessed her now. She became talkative and described the dawn she had witnessed on Whit-Monday morning of the picnic in 1937. She could see, how ever, that he was not impressed, though he tried to seem appreciative. In this instant she knew that he had no poetry in him. He was not a romantic like herself. Something inside her sank a few degrees,

She rose and said: "Let's go now. Perhaps you're right. I ought to go home and get some sleep."

As they descended from the wall, he held her elbow lightly as though to help her down the embankment, but when they were in the roadway he did not release it. His manner was still tentative and shy.

At her gateway, he made no attempt to kiss her, though she sensed that he wanted to. She gave him no encouragement. A rigid pile of rocks seemed to dam back the warm feelings in her that struggled for expression. When he held out his hand she squeezed it tight and murmured: "Cheerio. Sleep well."

She waited by the gate and watched him stride off along the street. After he had disappeared around the corner, she wrapped her arms slowly about her body and hugged herself. The shiver that went through her, she knew, was not from the chilly night. It was caused by the uncertainty in her.

When Naomi told her how glad she was to hear of it, her voice sounded sincere – not polite as the voice of anyone else might have done. Naomi's cool, sweet good-nature filled the room as though it were some lovely spirit-smoke.

Gregory, the realist and cynic, however, shook his head. "I may as well be frank, Sylvia. I'd never like to see any child of mine get linked up with a Portuguese. I daresay it sounds provincial, but I can't help it. Those mean, salt-fish-shop Jose-and-Maria people! No! It will take a long, long time before they'll come to appreciate the living standards of us coloured folk. Benson may be a Stanislaus boy, but his parents and grandparents viewed life in terms of two-bits and half-a-bit make the world go round, and eventually he's going to have to bow to the urgings of Pa. Pa doesn't think in progressive terms, you know. He has a peasant mind – which is even worse than a bourgeois mind. Pa wants security for his family above everything. Safety and security. Electrical engineering is a gamble – and a city occupation far removed from rum puncheons. Rum puncheons are safe..."

He said much more in the same vein, and she did not attempt to argue. She was not in the mood to argue – only to listen. A strange neutrality pervaded her spirit. After a while, she could feel Naomi watching her. Naomi must be wondering why she should be so calm. When Gregory stopped speaking Sylvia nodded and murmured: "Yes, I understand, Greg."

Naomi said: "Sylvia, you're not yourself. Is it because he's going to the war?"

Sylvia fidgeted. "Yes, that – and – oh, I don't know myself." Gregory chuckled. "I think I probe the trouble. You're not in love with that fellow, Sylvia. He's in the sad position of yours truly in relation to our maddeningly seductive friend sitting over there."

Naomi uttered a shriek of laughter, then sobered and said: "But I'm sure that isn't true about you, Sylvie. Aren't you in love with him?"

Sylvia hesitated, embarrassed. "I'm not too sure," she murmured, at last. "Sometimes I think I am and sometimes I feel I'm fooling myself."

A brume of unhappiness settled upon her as she said this. She had a feeling of shame as though she had committed a dishonourable act.

Naomi said: "Child, if you'll take my advice, don't bother your head about whether you're in love or not. He's a good, handsome fellow, and his people have money. If he marries you he'll put you into a good house and you'll have all the comforts you want. Love will come afterwards. You only have to put your mind to it."

"Great God! What a philosophy! You see the kind of monster I'm living with, Sylvia!"

Sylvia laughed. "I don't know, Greg. Perhaps she's right. I've made myself such a fool over ideals and all that silliness. Ideals don't pay when you're starving and unhappy in a dilapidated cottage."

"You never said a truer thing, Sylvie," said Naomi, leaning forward so that her long black plait fell down into her lap. There was an intensity, almost a hardness, in her manner that surprised Sylvia. "Life is cruel, child. Cruel. If you let yourself be a martyr to ideals you'll always be miserable. If I were you I'd do my best to get him to marry me before he goes away. You never can tell what might happen when he gets into these big cities. Some white girl can easily turn his head and trap him into marrying her. You think these English and American girls have any ideals! Their idea is just to get a husband, at all costs!"

Gregory grunted. "Reluctantly I must admit that there is wisdom in that, yet I feel Sylvia's integrity won't permit her to be happy if she married him now – especially as she isn't certain she's in love with him."

"Integrity!" Sylvia snapped the word at him. The scorn in her voice dismayed her. "I have too much integrity, Greg," she heard herself saying. "I believe that's what's wrong with me. That's why I suffer so much. If I were more cold-blooded and didn't try to be so honest with people I'm sure I'd have got far more out of life than I've got now."

"That," said Gregory gravely, "is where you delude yourself. You can't escape from yourself, my dear girl. Whatever you are you are, and there can be no happiness for you if you transgress your own inner personal codes."

"But suppose you have no inner personal codes!" Naomi fired at him.

"You may imagine you haven't, but the most unscrupulous of us possesses some personal code, some individual philosophy, however loose, however haphazard, it may be."

Naomi threw back her head and made soft gurgling sounds. "I

mightn't know much about philosophy and science, Greg, but I've seen life, boy. All that you're saying there is just glib talk. When you find yourself up against hardships – real stinking hardships – you don't give two damns for codes, unless you're a fool. All you're concerned about is to get out of your misery the best and fastest way you can."

The argument lasted nearly an hour. Sylvia ranged herself on Naomi's side, and eventually Gregory had to stop talking and begin to whistle an operatic aria. This was always his way of indicating his surrender when he was opposed to Naomi in any conflict of words. He was perfectly unruffled, and Sylvia knew that though he had surrendered he did not consider himself defeated. An odd mixture, Gregory. A cynic with ideals.

She went home in a thoughtful mood. In bed, she could not sleep for a long time. It was as though a chilly wind kept blowing through her. Her heart felt cold, and her brain spawned one argument after the other, machine-like and detached. Before she fell asleep she decided on a plan of action... If I wake tomorrow morning, she thought, and look outside at the trees and still feel the same way I'll know that my decision was sound, and I'll go ahead and do exactly what I plan to do.

She woke at a quarter to six. It was raining. Not heavily but steadily. She shivered and wriggled her toes, and listened to the sound of running water and the drip-drip that mingled with it. She sat up and looked at herself in the dressing-table mirror... Can I ever change, I wonder? Will I ever be a cold, calculating realist?

Last night seemed unreal. She had lost all enthusiasm for carrying out her resolve... It would have been wrong. I couldn't have been happy.

A gust of rain-laden wind came in at the window, and she hugged herself and shivered again. A whiff of frowsy, unhealthy air from her mother's room assailed her senses. The connecting door was ajar.

She looked around her. What shabby walls! Right above the dressing-table there was a spider with an egg. Perhaps it had crawled over her last night while she slept. She became aware of a dull spatter of water in the dining-room, and remembered that there was a bad leak in the roof in there. Another in the sittingroom. Soon there would be one in this room. Her hands clenched slowly. In the mirror she saw her face twisting into a scowl.

I'm going through with it. I'm quite resolved now. I don't care how wrong it may seem. I'm going to see it through, personal codes or no personal codes.

3

Two nights later, on the Sea Wall, she asked Benson if he would not postpone his going away for a month or two.

"Postpone it?"

"We've only just really got friendly, Benny. I want to see something of you before you go off."

"Well, as a matter of fact, it's doubtful if I can go next week as I'd hoped. I was inquiring a day or two ago and the shipping people say they haven't a single berth to spare this trip. And the next boat won't be going for another month, at the earliest."

"I see."

He turned toward her with a sudden movement. "Sylvia, why do you – is it because you think you like me a little that – that you want me to postpone going?"

She steeled herself and then said it. "Not a little – a terrible lot. I love you."

She observed that his hands were tightly clenched in his lap. He was staring out at the waves. Then she saw his lips move and heard him murmur: "I can hardly believe that. It seems – too good to be true."

Her mouth began to quiver, and she had to brush her cheeks quickly to dry off the tears. She could not suppress the sniff, and he glanced at her and exclaimed: "What's the matter? You're crying!"

"Oh, it's nothing. I suppose – I suppose it's because I feel so happy." She averted her face and shut her eyes.

"I love you, too, Sylvia – like – like anything."

He gripped her wrist and then released it, and she could sense that he was trembling. The breath in her seemed like a tight ball of steel strands that had become hopelessly tangled. But after a moment there was a relaxation, and she told herself that the worst was past. She had weathered the crisis. She had committed herself to deceit; there was no going back... "You can't escape from yourself, my dear girl. Whatever you are you are, and there can be no happiness for you if you transgress your own inner personal codes..." Let Gregory go to the devil! Gregory didn't have to live in a leaky cottage with a soured old hag who quarrelled all day... She sidled closer to Benson, and put her hand in his lap.

"Benny, do you realize you haven't even kissed me once?"

"I know. I – you'd like me to kiss you?"

"Of course."

She did not let her lips part, because she knew that it would have puzzled him – and probably disgusted him. He was so utterly green. Even as she felt his mouth pressed against hers a wave off contempt moved through her. But she forced herself to appear convincing in her fervour, and put her hands behind his neck and pressed herself against him.

It was in the following week that Charlotte said to her: "Sylvie, Ah got somet'ing to say to you, and Ah don't want no long talk, please."

"What's it?"

Charlotte bent her face over the machine – a face haggard and fragile with fear, frustration, irresolution. A face that twitched nervously. Without raising her gaze, she said: "Ah been discussing a matter wid Janie and Sarah. They is old and true friends, and friends scarce dese days. It ain' every day you is find friends like Janie and Sarah. When odders desert me in me troubles Janie and Sarah keep by me, and Ah always got to remember dat. Dis a world, it full of ingratitude, chile –"

"Mother, what is it you want to say? Why not say it and be done!"

"But why you got to speak to me so sharp, Sylvie! I is you' mudder, you know. Even for once you can't speak to me properly?"

Sylvia sighed. "I'm waiting, Mother. I want to go out. Just say what you want to say and be done, please."

"Well, Janie and Sarah was having a lil' talk wid me. They not doing well dese days. They in bad circumstances, and they ask me if Ah couldn't help dem out by putting dem up here –"

"Putting them up here! How could we put them up here!"

"And why not, Sylvie? You can come back in my room like before David went away and give dem your room. You mean it's too much for you to do for de pore girls! Look how Janie and Sarah used to help you when Ah was sick dat time and you did ketch dat bad cold –"

"Is that any reason why I must give up my room to them? Look here, Mother, please don't bother to go any further. I'll never agree to that. Never. Life in this house is terrible enough without making it more beastly by bringing in those two creatures. I simply won't stand it!"

"Since when you is mistress in here, Sylvie! Eh-eh! You properly ketching you'self since you get dis restaurant job!"

"I don't care what you say. I won't have them here. I have a right to object. I'm helping to keep this house, please don't forget. How much is Mr. Knight giving us now? Five dollars a month. He might soon stop giving us that. And now you calmly suggest that we take in these two girls. If you expect me to support them you're mistaken. I won't!"

"Awright, Sylvie. Ah see now what sort of person you is. You ain' got no heart. Ah always feel you was a ungrateful child. Ow, me God!" She raised her eyes to heaven. "Saviour, look down and witness! Watch de t'anks Ah getting for all me slaving. Look ingratitude..."

Sylvia left the house. She was almost halfway to Naomi's before her rage subsided. But with calm came a heavy gloom.

Naomi, however, saw no reason for gloom. "You take it from me, Sylvia, Janie and Sarah know that your mother is a weak fool, that's why they can suggest such a thing to her. If you took them to live with you there, before a week went past they would be the mistresses of the house. They might even want to put you and your mother out."

"You've seemed very quietish these past few nights," said Benson one evening, about a week later. "Anything worrying you?"

They had just come out of the cinema and were on their way to the Sea Wall. She made no response except to squeeze his hand.

They walked in silence for about three blocks before she said: "All sorts of things are worrying me, Benny, but what's the use of pulling a long face."

He made no comment, but she saw out of the corner of her eye the frown that appeared on his face. A grain of irritation moved inside her. He was so dumb. Why couldn't he ask her what was the matter, what was worrying her, press her for details and try to be sympathetic?... "You're only handsome and that's all. You're no man. You can't even kiss me properly!" That was what she wanted to shout at him, but the vision of that rainy morning returned. In her fancy she wrinkled her nose at the foul aroma that emanated from her mother's room. The faces of Janie and Sarah rose up to menace her.

"I want to get out of that place, Benny," she said, instead. "It's killing me. I'm sick of it."

"Yes, I know."

He knew. That was all he could say. She barely restrained herself from clicking her tongue and telling him to go to the devil. Suddenly, however, she realized that she was being unfair to him. He was only twenty. He had just left school. He was inexperienced in the ways of the world. In his place, David would have been gauche. More so.

A baffled distraction assailed her. She looked around at the trees and the houses and the stars, and, as before when her spirit was sorely troubled, she found herself appealing to the scene for an answer. Why this agony? Why the necessity to go through all these events – events the sum of which was called living? Why did she have to live?... No answer. Always there was no answer. The trees remained rigid-trunked; the foliage glistened in the street-light. The houses reared up dark and solid, dumb wood shaped into angles by men. The stars blinked impassively, more aloof and dumb than the houses. Oh, for death! A fade-out. A knowing-nothing. Death must be so soothing.

She came to a halt.

"What's wrong?"

"I – oh, nothing," she said. She laughed. "Let's go on."

"You feel tired?"

"Tired? Yes, very – no, no! I'm not tired." She stifled back the sigh. Tried to make her voice cheerful. When they were climbing up the embankment to the Wall, she caught his hand and said: "Benny, what are you doing this weekend?"

"This weekend? Nothing particular. Why?"

"Couldn't we spend Sunday on the East Coast or somewhere? Just the two of us? It's my Sunday off."

"Oh." His voice had an awed sound. "You mean a sort of picnic on the beach?"

"Yes. We can take a lunch-basket and catch the eight o'clock train, and return in the evening."

"Just the two of us?"

"Of course. Why should there be anyone else?"

"Yes, I know, but..."

"But what?"

"No, I was just thinking what people might say."

"What can they say? Is it immoral to go on a picnic?"

He gave her a puzzled glance, and then grinned uncomfortably. "I don't say there's anything in it, but – but you think your mother would agree?"

"Haven't I told you that Mother has no say in my affairs? It wouldn't matter to Mother if I went to Timbuctoo with you alone."

"Well, let's go, then." He spoke with enthusiasm, and as they seated themselves he began to squeeze his hands together as though in pleasurable anticipation. "We can take our bathing things and go swimming."

"You can leave the lunch-basket to me. I'll fix that up."

"Good. Oh, and look I've got it! Instead of going to the sea let's go aback of Plantation Ruimveldt. I know of a good canal there. Dick and Basil and a lot of the boys used to go there on Saturdays to swim. We've had some great times there!" He was leaning forward, exuberant and voluble. He went on to relate some of his Saturday escapades with his school friends. He forgot his diffidence, forgot he was in love with her. He was a schoolboy revelling in country-rambles and tree-climbing and swimming. To her dismay, she caught herself staring at him, fascinated, a hand clutching at her thigh. A warm mist seemed to drift through her stomach.

A kiskadee woke her. It was perched on a branch of the custard-apple tree in the next yard. "Kisk-kick-kadee!" it cried, fierce and tyrannical, and then fluttered off as though in pursuit of its mate. The sun made patterns on the wall over the washstand – shifty patterns. Some memory tried to take shape in her head, but sleep blurred it, smothered it.

She listened to the sounds of Sunday morning. A remote car-horn. The cooing of pigeons from across the street. The gobble of a turkey. She pressed her knuckles hard against her chin. If only I could make up my mind how I really feel this morning.

She turned her head and saw the lunch-basket in the corner near the dressing-table. Packed and ready. Ready for what?... Inside her, as though midway between her stomach and her heart, there seemed to be a feather, and she felt it quiver and stop, then quiver again and stop.

She went with him by bus to Ruimveldt, then he took her along a track strewn with dried sheep-dung toward a ramshackle two-storeyed house from which the shingles were falling and the windows of which were without glass.

"What house is that?" she asked.

"I don't know. It must be one of these old plantation houses."

"It's falling to ruin. A pity."

"Yes," he said.

"It looks so sad and tragic."

"Sad and tragic?" His tone and the glance he gave her were such she might have said: "It's an alligator, isn't it?"

"Yes, sad and tragic," she repeated, and a sense of loneliness came upon her. She might have been in a foreign land and he a stranger who had offered to show her around. He did not understand her language very well, so she must repeat whatever she said and try to explain her meaning.

He led her past the house and they skirted a rusted boiler-tank that at one time must have been used as a rainwater storage-tank. The path became grassy now and ill-defined, and wound between mango and jamoon trees. The air smelt of cow-dung and swamp-water. Now and then a chit-chit noise startled her as a grasshopper or a cricket bounded out of the grass at their feet. It made her think of snakes. Snakes were supposed to hiss. He said there were no snakes about here. He and the boys had never once come upon any.

"Once we killed a salampenter, though. About two feet long."

"But they're harmless. Why did you kill it?"

"Only for fun." Again the tone and the glance that made her feel she had said something extraordinary and baffling.

They emerged suddenly into open pasture country. Cows were grazing lazily, and here and there the sun glistened on shallow pools of stagnant water. She gripped his hand and asked him about the cows. Was it safe to venture here? She didn't trust cows.

He laughed and said: "They're tame. They won't notice us. And for the first time that morning she felt inferior to him. They were in a province where she was afraid and he unafraid.

It was a relief when they left the pasture behind and entered upon another grass-grown track amid *courida* trees and an odd coconut and cabbage palm. As fear oozed out of her, humility took its place. A new confidence in him took possession of her. She saw him as a protector.

"It's over that way," he said, pointing. "The canal."

She saw a fringe of shrubs to their right. A low wall of black sage that seemed so regular that there could be no doubt it bordered water.

In less than a minute the canal came into view. It was about twenty yards wide, and the water looked black and dangerous. The vegetable matter in it made it black, but it was clear when she dipped some of it up in her hand – clear and cool.

"You're not a good swimmer, you said?"

She shook her head. "Not very. Is it deep?"

"About seven or eight feet. You'll be out of depth."

He had put down the lunch-basket he was carrying. They stood side by side and stared at the water, abruptly awkward and undecided. After a moment, he bent and plucked off a few leaves from a black sage clump, crumpled them slowly in his hand. The strong aromatic scent assailed her nostrils. She looked around and said: "You want to go in right away, or shall we sit down a bit first?"

"Whatever you like." He looked at her, then looked away quickly.

"Let's sit down and talk first, then. Look! There's a nice shady mango tree. Let's go under there." Her voice was loud and self-conscious.

"Good," he agreed. "We can make that a sort of headquarters and leave the lunch-basket there." There was relief in his manner at her decision. He grew talkative and told her about the times he and the boys used to come here. He pointed to a tamarind tree about fifty yards along the canal's bank, and said that they used to undress under there. One afternoon Dick climbed into the tree and dived off from a branch. It was a low-hanging branch, though, and the boys laughed and asked Dick if he thought he was doing something so marvellous. And just to prove it was nothing marvellous, they all climbed up and dived off from the branch.

They sat under the mango tree and talked. He did most of the talking, and she found that she liked listening to him. Somehow, he did not seem very aware of any sex difference between them; she might have been one of his male cronies. She could feel the force of his masculinity to better effect when he was in moods like this.

Abruptly a restlessness came alive in her, and she said: "Let's go and bathe now, Benny." It was as though this were a cue. Some voice within her seemed to say: "Horses off!" Her fingertips felt cold as she stretched out to the lunch-basket and raised the lid. Their bathing things lay on top. Dark-blue bathing pants with a white belt and a green-and-red flowered two-piece suit. Their propinquity took on, in her fancy, the nature of a symbol. She whisked her own out quickly and rose, tense.

"Well, we've got plenty of bush to undress in," she said, and knew that her voice sounded falsely gay. Unnatural. She felt a fool.

"Oh, yes, no trouble about that. I'll go over that way, near that clump of palms."

"Good. I wonder where these palms came from. Do you know?"

"They must have been planted in the old days, I suppose. Perhaps these were the grounds of the manager's residence."

"Or the overseers' quarters," she laughed. "The manager's residence wouldn't be so near to a punt canal."

"You're right. I didn't think of that."

Neither of them made any move to leave the spot. He seemed

to have caught some of her tenseness. They stood toying with theirs bathing things. She became aware of the wind in the foliage above them. The tree made soft creaking sounds. Two branches must rubbing against each other. Straining together. Again her fancy fashioned a symbol. She began to tremble.

"What are we waiting for?" she laughed.

"You're right," he laughed, and moved off toward the palms.

"I'll go behind those lime trees," she said, her voice a croak.

"Righto!"

When she had shed her clothes and was about to slip into her bathing suit she glanced above the lime trees and saw the plume of a cabbage palm – and down swooped the Brown Jumbie-men, chortling in their most ironical manner.

"Is this the way you're going to carry out your wonderful plan?"

"No fear, I'll do it still."

"Well, hurry up. Run out naked like this before him and tempt him."

"I'm not as crude as all that."

"Bah! Don't make excuses. You know as well as we do you're as green and shy as he himself is. Can't you realize you're not equipped for a game of this sort?"

"I have the physical equipment, though."

"Thousands of women have it, but temperament defeats many. Many!"

"Oh, go away and leave me in peace. Even here I'm to be plagued!"

"I was having an argument with the Brown Jumbie-men," she laughed, as she joined him under the mango tree. He had black hair on his chest. In her fancy she had always seen him as clean-chested. She felt light-headed. He laughed, too – shakily.

"The Brown Jumbie-men? What's that?"

She explained, trying to keep her voice serious. There had been too much laughing. If she laughed again she would fall in her self-esteem. She must control herself or she would never succeed with her plan.

"I have all sorts of strange fancies," she said. She stretched out her arms and then dropped them suddenly to her sides as though about to indulge in warming up exercises before going into the water. Her breasts jolted violently – just as she had known they would have done.

"It's better you should know from now what queer ways I have."

"That's nothing so queer." He changed from one foot to the other.

She began to whistle "Stormy Weather" in order to create an effect of ultra-sophistication. She tapped her foot on the grass to the rhythm of the tune. But a memory took shape... On the train on the way to Berbice. A lump in her throat prevented her from whistling any longer. She caught his hand and said in a too-casual voice: "Well, what are we waiting for? Let's go in and bathe."

The sun had gone under a heavy cloud, and the water looked blacker than a moment ago. Fear wrapped a chilly scarf around her heart.

"I'm not accustomed to swimming out of my depth, you know, Benny. The only swimming I've done was with Mabel and Beryl off the Sea Wall, and we never went out of our depth."

"Oh. But – but I thought – well, it doesn't matter. I'll keep by you all the time and see that you're all right."

"You plunge in first and let me see how you can swim."

She sat on the bank, with the black sage tickling her legs, and watched him disporting himself in the water. He was an easy and expert swimmer, and swished through the water with a grace delightful to watch.

"Aren't you coming in?"

"In a little while. You go on."

She was in a funk. Her imagination hatched nightmare dangers. Suppose she were to sink out of sight when he was not looking; how would he find her in this black water? Suppose a hidden tangle of weeds caught her feet. Or some sharp-toothed fish might attack her. Perhaps at this very minute it was swimming towards this spot, attracted by their presence...

"Water lovely!" he shouted. "Nothing to be afraid of! Jump in!"

"Who said I was afraid? I'm not afraid."

That settled it. She rose, took a deep breath and plunged

forward. She emerged gasping. Her feet had touched the slimy bottom and there had been weeds down there just as she had visualized. Panic seized her. She struck out for the bank. Then to her horror, she realized that it was the farther bank she was heading for. She hesitated, tried to tread water, sank. She rose and spluttered, called for help. She sank – but almost at once an arm encircled her and she was gasping and blinking at the sky.

"Relax. Don't struggle. It's quite O.K."

In less than half a minute she was on the bank, blowing and sniffling and trying to laugh off the incident, though it was useless. The damage to her pride was already too great.

"Oh, I'm a real fool!" she exclaimed angrily. "I – I'd better get dressed."

"You don't want to bathe any more?"

"No, I don't think I'll bother. You go on. Don't mind me. You hear me? Go on and have your swim."

"O.K.," he muttered, and plunged in again.

Behind the screen of lime trees, she had just taken off her bathing suit when she remembered that she had no towel to dry off. The towel was in the lunch-basket. She was so infuriated she could have run to the basket naked as she was and not have bothered to haul on her bathing things again. When, at length, she was dressed she was taut and smouldering. She sat by the edge of the canal, a frown on her face, within her the bitter realization that Gregory was right. What she was she was. It would serve her no useful purpose to try to transgress her inner personal codes. In this instant she saw that her plan had been doomed to failure from the outset. It was not in her nature to carry through such a deceitful undertaking.

Such a wave of remorse rushed over her that she felt like calling Benson out of the water and confessing everything. "You know what I brought you here for, Benny? I wanted to get you to seduce me so that I could use that to press you into marrying me before you go abroad. You have such a high sense of honour you would have agreed without hesitation. And if your father had refused to give his consent you would have waited until you're twenty-one in January next and married me before going away to the war. Yes, I'm sure you'd have done that if I'd succeeded today."

She had to bite her lip hard to prevent herself from calling him. For the rest of that day she was quiet and inclined to sulk. He endured her moods without protest, tried to entertain her by narrating schoolday escapades, was obediently silent for nearly twenty minutes on a stretch when she interrupted him once and told him irritably that she wanted to listen to the wind in the trees.

At about two o'clock, she had grown so bored, and the heat of the day had intensified to such a degree, that she began to feel sleepy.

"Benny, I want to sleep. This heat is terrible."

"Of course. If you want to." He looked round searchingly. "Over there looks like a good spot. It looks dry and hard and shady."

"There may be ants there," she yawned. "I'll stay right here."

"But what are you going to rest your head on? Oh, I've got it. Let me take off my shirt and roll it up in a bundle like a pillow."

"How could you remain half-naked all the time I'm asleep?"

"It won't give me a cold. Is that what you think?" He laughed and hauled off his shirt and proceeded to roll it up neatly. "There you are. You don't bother about me. I'll be all right like this."

As she lay down and rested her head on it a cool feeling of gratitude toward him flooded her. Within ten seconds she was asleep.

When she awoke the shadows were long on the ground. A deep sense of refreshment saturated her being. There was a humming as of ghost-bees in her head. She took deep breaths of the leafy air, and it entered her and spread within her like a honeyed mist. She saw Benson standing by the canal's edge. He was throwing black-sage leaves into the water, a tall, forlorn-looking figure. It occurred to her that perhaps he, too, had felt sleepy. But he must have considered it his duty to remain awake to watch over her.

Her vision abruptly grew misty, and a deep, tender ache began to move in her. She called to him, and he turned with a start.

"You're awake, then?"

"Yes. Come and sit with me."

He came at once. After a silence she touched his hand and said, without looking at him: "You haven't kissed me for the day."

He still had not learnt how to kiss; he was still awkward. But, to her surprise when it was over, she found that, for the first time, she had not had to force herself to respond. She continued to grip his arm, watched a blue vein and traced its course up his arm. A great peace descended upon her. It might have been the wind in the foliage of the mango tree showering down a spirit-rain.

4

On Wednesday Charlotte fell ill and took to her bed. The doctor said it was her nerves again, but that there were also complications involving her menopause. On this occasion she seemed too weak to indulge in hysterical outbursts of obscene language. She could not even sit up. But her groans and whimpers filled the cottage without cessation. And Janie and Sarah, quick to seize an advantage, decided that they would sit up with her at night, which meant that they had to be provided with a meal in the evening and breakfast in the morning.

This new development in the home situation made Sylvia so miserable that the following afternoon she said to Naomi: "My head is in such a whirl I feel I could take a walk into the sea and not come back."

Naomi said nothing.

"I feel as if I'm gradually dying. I'm longing to die. Is it possible to die while your body lives on, Naomi?"

Naomi sat before the dressing-table combing her hair. "Don' be morbid, Sylvia," she said. After a pause she went on: "I think you're making a mistake about Benny. If even you can't bring yourself to get him to be intimate with you, you can, at least, tell him you'd prefer him to marry you before he sails. Your pride shouldn't worry you, because he's already asked you to marry him."

"I see what you mean, but something else has arisen that I haven't told you about. Since Sunday night I could have told you, but I didn't."

There was a silence during which only the swish-swish of the comb in Naomi's hair and the twittering of a wren outside were audible. Then Sylvia changed her position on the bed and said:

"On Sunday before I left him I discovered that – that I'm beginning to care rather deeply for him."

She had intended this to be in the nature of a dramatic announcement, but Naomi seemed quite unimpressed. She said: "Well, that's the trouble, then? All the more reason why you should broach the question of marriage before he goes. If he married you he could put you in a cottage of your own. I'm sure his father must own a few properties around town."

"But, Naomi, don't you see this makes it impossible for me to tackle him about marrying me right away? If I didn't care for him, I might better have been able to do it, but I'd feel now I was taking advantage of his youth and inexperience. I'd prefer to die than force his hand. You have no idea how soft I've felt about him these past two or three days. I couldn't do it!" A tear ran down her cheek.

On Friday, Charlotte was much better but still prostrate in bed. Sylvia told Janie and Sarah that it would not be necessary for them to sit up that night, and Sarah snapped: "You ain' got to tell me twice if you want me to get out de house!"

Charlotte groaned for an hour after they had left, but Sylvia ignored her, though her conscience troubled her. Janie and Sarah had rendered whole-hearted service toward Charlotte during the past two days. At best, Charlotte was a tiresome patient, but Janie and Sarah had never once grumbled in Sylvia's hearing. In the middle of the night they would wake, when Charlotte called, and attend to her wants, and they had made no fuss about sleeping on the floor. Moreover, they had kept the room clean; the smell that came from it now was far less nauseating than it had been before Charlotte had fallen ill.

On the Sea Wall, Sylvia told Benson: "That's just it. Nothing in life is completely black or completely white. They have their good sides as well as their bad, those two girls, and it worries when I have to treat them shabbily. But it couldn't be helped. Once I let them get a foothold in that house there'd be no shaking them off."

Other couples moved past them on the wall promenade. The wind droned. The sea was coming in, and the waves thundered on the beach in the starlit darkness. She turned her head and looked back upon the city – at the vast array of lights and trees. The muted rumble of traffic and human voices seemed to rush at her in a wave that was almost palpable. How many thousands of dramas were being enacted amid those trees and lights! How much laughter and how many groans and sighs must go to make up that low murmurous wave of sound! That car dashing past now on its way east might contain a couple on their way to Dixie – on their way to death at the hands of an ambushed murderer, who knew?

Benson shifted about and said: "I know it will sound stupid, but I'd wondered if we couldn't have got married before I went away."

"Oh."

Another silence, then: "I couldn't expect you to want to marry me off so abruptly, of course. We've only been engaged a couple of weeks. And to make it worse, the old man wouldn't want to hear of it. I'm still a minor, and – and – well, he won't agree, I'm certain."

"Have you told him about our being engaged?"

"Yes."

"And what did he say?"

"He ripped hell. Sorry. I didn't mean to use such language. He's a bit narrow-minded, you know. He still has the old idea that a Portuguese should marry a Portuguese and all that nonsense."

"I see. You mean because I'm coloured."

"Yes. But don't let that bother you. It doesn't make the slightest difference to me what he feels about it. It couldn't stop me from marrying you when the time comes."

She found herself smiling – a smile of irony. She remembered what Gregory had said when she had announced her engagement to him and Naomi.

"I know it wouldn't matter to you," she murmured, squeezing his wrist. And to herself she added: "That settles it once and for all."

During the following week a letter arrived from David. He had been torpedoed but was safe and "only badly shaken up, no limbs broken or anything like that". He was in hospital.

The news set back Charlotte's health. She wept and moaned for more than twelve hours without a break – from six in the afternoon until six the following morning. She kept Sylvia awake the whole night. At one point she sat up and prayed aloud to her Saviour on David's behalf. She lamented his going away, blamed herself for not having treated him as a mother should have done, cursed her friends – as usual – for their ingratitude; it was their ingratitude that had brought her to the state she was in now. Had she not given so freely in the old days she might have had "a lil' somet'ing put aside" for herself in these hard times.

"Ah getting what Ah deserve. It's God speaking to me. He put dis illness on me as an affliction to punish me for me sins."

She got out of bed and stumbled across to the dressing-table. She took up a ragged Bible, stumbled back to the bed, collapsed shakily, and lying on her side, began to read aloud passages from the Old Testament. She read from *Isaiah.* She announced it, chapter and verse.

"*In all their affliction he was afflicted, and the angel of his presence saved them; in his love, and in his pity, he redeemed them, and he bare them, and carried them all the days of old. But they rebelled, and vexed his Holy Spirit...*

"Yes, Lord," she interposed, "thy humble servant has rebelled and vexed thy Holy Spirit...

"*Therefore he was turned to be their enemy, and he fought against them. Then he remembered the days of old...*

"Yes, Lord! The days of old when thy humble servant was young and foolish! Ow, Lord! Ow! Look down on me, Saviour!" Her cheeks streamed.

From across the street came the sound of music from a wireless... "A Pretty Girl is Like a Melody..." A soprano voice sang the words with syrupy fervour while Charlotte hugged her knees and blubbered.

It was at the end of that week that Benson told Sylvia he had succeeded in getting a passage to Canada on a cargo ship. "I heard from the shipping office this morning. They say it's not customary to accept passengers for that boat, but as I'd asked them some time ago they thought they could see their way to offer me a passage."

"And when do you sail?"

"Over the next weekend. They wouldn't give me a definite day. They say it's against regulations because of the war, but I must have my baggage aboard by Saturday afternoon at five and be aboard myself by eight."

"Oh."

"It's – it's sort of sudden, eh?"

"Yes."

He touched her knee – cautiously. "I'll write you," he said.

Every night after leaving the Red Mavis she walked with him to the Sea Wall, heavy-eyed with sleep though she was.

On the night before he embarked she told him: "I'm not going down on the wharf. I think I could get a permit, but I won't. It would be – you know what. Vulgar. I hate farewell scenes."

He nodded and said he understood. He, too, wouldn't like a farewell scene on the wharf.

There were many silences that Friday night. The wind was strong and chilly. It would not have been chilly if she had suddenly learnt that he had not to sail, after all, and that next week they would get married and go to Berbice on their honeymoon. More than once she looked up at the sky at the inky clouds that kept obscuring the stars off and on. More than once the old questions shaped themselves…

"No answer. Always no answer."

"Eh?"

She laughed. "I was speaking to myself. Being romantic."

"Romantic?"

"Or philosophic. It doesn't matter. Oh, Benny, don't look so puzzled! Please! I warned you how queer I am." She pressed herself against him and burrowed her face into his shoulder, and he gripped her arm but made no attempt to kiss her. She always had to make the first move when she wanted to be kissed. A few weeks ago she would have been contemptuous of his inhibitions, and impatient, but now she loved him all the more for them. "Tonight I feel full of premonitions," she said.

"Premonitions about what?"

"About the future, of course, silly! What else?"

"Oh, well, don't worry. I'll come through safely, no fear. I think I'm going to decide definitely on the Navy. I must fire a big gun. Have you read of the naval actions going on now near Norway? We're cleaning them up. Hitler didn't reckon with the Navy when he invaded Norway."

"Yes," she said.

"You're shivering. Feeling cold?"

"It's the wind. Doesn't it feel cold to you?"

"No. No, I can't say I find it cold."

She held his hand. It was warm. She pressed it between her two cold ones to see if she could extract some of its warmth. A large male hand. An urge to slip it down her bosom came upon her. He had not once fondled her since they had been friendly. But she resisted the urge, though the ache of longing made her dizzy. It would embarrass him too much. She must accept his greenness and hope for what the future would bring.

All the same, she trembled in her frustration.

She listened to the roar of the waves, and tried to let the sound – it had a dramatic grandeur – distract her senses from the physical.

PART FIVE

1

"By the way, what's your name?"

"Sylvia Russell. And yours?"

"Copps – Milton Copps."

After they had danced in silence again for a while, he said, "It would be interesting to know what you're thinking of me."

"Thinking of you?"

"I mean for my unconventionality in asking you to dance without knowing you from Eve."

"I think well of you for that. I'm not conventional at all."

"I had a feeling you weren't. That's why I risked it. Who is the big stout lady you were sitting next to? Relative of some sort?"

"No, not exactly. I call her Aunt Clarice, but she's only a kind of foster relative of my mother's."

"How long have you been in New Amsterdam?"

"I came last week. I'm spending three weeks."

"About a fortnight more to go, then, I take it?"

"Seventeen more days, to be exact."

"Must be pretty dull for you, after the city."

"A little – but I don't mind."

He turned his deep-set eyes down upon her from his height of six feet or more, and she felt as though his gaze were boring into her forehead.

"Something is the matter with you," he said.

"The matter?"

"You have a vacant air. Dreamy. Yet you're not a negative personality."

She laughed.

"I liked the look of you. I've been noticing you for some time from the veranda over there."

"You seem to have been the only one doing that," she said.

He smiled slightly, and his olive face looked more villainous than when it had been in repose. A long, oval face with a long high nose and sunken, intense dark eyes that always looked into, rather than at her. He would have made a good screen bad-man – of the sinister kind who plotted and nodded and gave curt, callous orders in a quiet voice, who twisted the heroine's arm and narrowed his eyes in sadistic pleasure as she winced and gasped. He even had the dark hair sleekly brushed back and the precise, clipped tone of voice. He did not have a creole air, but might have been foreigner – a Spaniard or an Italian – who had been dropped by parachute this very evening, before the dance started, on to the streets of New Amsterdam. His clothes did not fit him well. He seemed uncomfortable in them. He had broad shoulders, but, for his height, he could have had more flesh on his wiry bones. Two things upset the perfection of his villainous looks – the ironic humour in his voice and a certain indefinable sympathy in his manner.

"With a body like yours," he said, "you couldn't help being noticed anywhere. But this is New Amsterdam. You're a stranger here. Your Aunt Clarice is the only black lady in the hall. You haven't been introduced to anyone. The result is that, despite your devastating looks, you remain a wallflower. It's only because I happen to be totally lacking in respectability that you've succeeded in finding a dancing partner."

"Your family wouldn't like to hear you saying that you lack respectability. They're pretty well known, aren't they?"

"Pretty. One of the oldest of the oldest families. But they won't mind. I have the reputation of being a lunatic."

She asked him if he believed in God, and he looked at her in surprise.

"What on earth could have prompted you to ask that?"

"A whim. I'm very unpredictable."

"Interesting. Extremely. No. God, Miss Russell, has no greater detractor than myself. I've instituted a campaign against God and the Church."

"What kind of work do you do?"

"I paint pictures."

"Oh, you're an artist?"

"I spend my life trying to convince myself I am."

During another silence she looked about the large auditorium. Before this evening she had never seen the interior of New Amsterdam's Town Hall. She liked the silhouettes of local birds and beasts and scenes painted on panels along the lower section of the ceiling. And the stage was tastefully decorated with palms and ferns and softly floodlit so that the members of the orchestra, in their shell-jackets, appeared as detached jumbie-figures spewing out their music beyond the fragile green of the artificial garden.

But for these middle-class folk and their exclusive cliques which relegated her to her own and Aunt Clarice's company, she mighty have enjoyed herself. Well, Aunt Clarice had warned her what to expect from this New Amsterdam crowd.

It was a Red Cross dance, and supposed to be open to the public, but, in actuality, intended only for the elite. Jeanne de Groot was among the crowd. She was dancing with a white sugar estate overseer – a tall, well-groomed young lady who had forgotten the orchid-shed and the rabbits and the *Children's Cyclopedia* and the long talks lying flat on their stomachs in bed, the walks and the rides to the Sea Wall and the Botanic Garden. Jeanne had simply looked at her and raised her brows, and then smiled in polite, chilly recognition, thereafter looking through her. She seemed to be confined to the exclusively fair-skinned clique who worshipped English sugar-estate overseers. How she posed and simpered and preened herself and Behaved!

When Milton Copps escorted Sylvia back to her seat – under a picture of a former Mayor of New Amsterdam; by a coincidence, an uncle of Milton's – she introduced him to Aunt Clarice, and he shook the hand Aunt Clarice held out as though he might have been an old friend. He asked them what they would have to drink and when they refused, said: "Nonsense! You must have something. What about ice-cream, then?" So they agreed to have ice-creams.

Presently, when he was moving off with Sylvia in a waltz, he said: "Your accent and idiom don't go along with Aunt Clarice. Tell me something about your origins." His blunt, forthright manner disarmed her, and she gave him a brief sketch of her early life.

"Interesting," he said – and looked at her as if she were a

laboratory specimen. He asked her whether she went anywhere in the evenings.

"Nowhere at all. I don't know anyone in this town."

"Then I'm going to come and see you. Where does Aunt Clarice live?"

"In King Street." She described the place and how to find it, for in New Amsterdam houses have no numbers. You are expected to be a good detective. "I'd be glad to see you," she said. "I'm always alone and rather bored in the evenings."

That was how her friendship with Milton Copps began. Every evening, for the rest of her stay in New Amsterdam, he came to see her at Aunt Clarice's cottage in King Street. He said her presence revitalized him. They had long chats by the wireless set in the tiny sittingroom. He did not like dance music as a sedentary form of entertainment, he said, but he would tolerate it if she liked it. He went on to make brief, ironic comments on tolerance.

"What kind of music do you like?" she asked.

"Good music," he replied. "Wagner is my composer above all others."

"Daddy was very fond of Beethoven and Brahms."

"I, too. Especially Beethoven. Anything from the Eroica onwards. I have no use for his first and second symphonies. Too much of Mozart and Haydn in them. Music for me, Sylvia, must be strong and passionate – flaming. The louder and more thunderous, the weirder and more dissonant, the better I like it. The drums and cymbals are my favourite instruments. And I rave about trumpets."

"I'm afraid I can't find anything in heavy music."

"Strange. You have so much of the poet in you."

"I'm a queer mixture, I've told you."

He gave her the scientist-specimen look. "You've told me about your childhood, but you haven't yet given me a picture of the past few years. You're not in a job, you say?"

"No. I used to work at the Red Mavis as a waitress, but I left in November last. It's three months now I've been out of work."

"The Red Mavis? A restaurant, isn't it? I know the Brown Betty. I generally go there when I'm in Georgetown."

"It's much like the Brown Betty – only the girls wear pale blue uniforms. Let's forget it. I don't care to talk about the Red Mavis."

He shook his head. "Never dump into Lethe what is unpleasant. Turn it around before you, probe it, analyse it and get to understand the anatomy of its unpleasantness. Why did you leave the Red Mavis? Resigned, or did they send you off?"

The way he asked it destroyed her reserve. "They sent me packing."

"Broke a plate on the boss's head?"

"Nothing quite so drastic. Oh, it's a long story."

But she told him, just the same. She and two other girls used to run the cash-register, and the two other girls were in the habit of putting aside cash for themselves during rush periods instead of registering everything on the machine. "I never did that. I would have died before I did anything so dishonest. But the manager began to suspect after a time that Esmé and Belle were carrying on this racket. He included me, too, because he couldn't trace anything definitely to any of us in particular. But he was clever – I'm sure he was a psychologist. He kept a secret check without our knowing, though even then he couldn't find out which of us was doing it. He just discovered from the check-up that money was not being registered which ought to have been. Anyway, upshot of the whole thing was that he called Esmé and Belle and myself into his office one morning and told us he was sorry but that he had decided to make a cut in the staff and that he would have to dispense with us. He never mentioned anything about the cash-register, and the way he smiled at us you'd never have dreamt that he suspected us of anything shady."

"I see. And since then you haven't been in employment?"

"No."

She began to sing in a soft, unconcerned voice, "Balalaika". She could feel him looking at her, puzzled, interested, attracted.

He grunted. "Sometimes you can be a regular Buddha, Sylvia."

She smiled – but went on singing.

"Your outer air never deceives me," he said. "I can tell there's something big behind your inscrutable mask."

"Do I look inscrutable?"

"Most times."

"And the other times?"

"Falsely gay."

She laughed. "You're certainly frank, Milton. Oh, what's the use of worrying! Forget the blues. Sing and be happy. That's my philosophy nowadays."

"Unfortunately I can't sing, so I've got to look my blues in the face and punch them on the chin to stop them from getting me down."

"How about the war, Milton? When do you think it will be over?"

"I'm not a member of the British Secret Service. Somehow I've gathered the impression that the war means more to you than a mere struggle between the powers."

"You're good at guessing. I have a friend in the Canadian Navy."

"Officer?"

"No, just a rating. He started out as an Ordinary Seaman, then he rose to A.B. Now he's a Leading Seaman. He's on a corvette."

"I can see he's also a leading interest."

"He is. That's why I'm so anxious about the war."

"What about your brother? Didn't you mention something to the effect that he ran away to sea on a cargo ship?"

"Yes. He's still alive and somewhere at sea. He was torpedoed twice. The last time he was on his way to America. He seems to have a cat's lives."

"H'm."

"How old are you, Milton?"

"Thirty-one."

"Thirty-one and you're not married yet?"

His plans and ambitions in respect to his art, he told her, precluded marriage from his programme of living.

"But suppose you're not a success till you're forty or fifty?"

"Then I won't marry until I'm forty or fifty."

She regarded him a moment, then asked: "What's your outlook on life?"

"My creed is simple: I believe in Destiny – and myself. Work like the deuce on my own schemes, and leave the rest to Destiny. I'm an adventurer at heart, Sylvia. That's why I detest bourgeois society. That's why I don't work in an office like a respectable young man of good family. That's why I live by my wits and ignore the barrage of contumely from my relatives and fellow townsmen." He wagged a forefinger at her. "Always please yourself, my dear girl. Snap your fingers at the mob. Take notice of public opinion and you'll never be happy."

"Haven't you a girl friend?"

"Not in the sense you mean. To have a girl friend in New Amsterdam one must conform with the code of the herd, because a girl friend in New Amsterdam expects marriage as an inevitable climax. I keep mistresses, instead."

She laughed. "You have a philosophy much like Naomi's."

"Naomi? I like that name. Have you Jewish friends?"

"She's a Eurasian." She told him about Naomi and her crowd. "She was living with Gregory Brandt in a little place in George Street, but she left him last August and went back to Jerry."

"She did?"

"Yes. But Greg took it quite well. I thought he would have been upset, but he took it like a man. He said he knew it had to come eventually."

"Your friends seem interesting. When I'm in the city I must get you to introduce me to them. Where do Jerry and Naomi live? In the same Sussex Street place you mentioned?"

"No. They're in Bent Street – two houses from Aubrey Deleon."

She stirred in her chair and began to hum. Hum and keep time with her hand to the music from the wireless. Outside, a mango tree kept brushing the side of the house. A soft, mysterious, night time sound. A cool peace sifted through her being.

"What of this brother of yours? Has he never sent you any money to help you out?"

"He sent twenty dollars once – but nothing after that."

Toward the end of her stay she found herself feeling soft inside when she thought of Milton and his nightly visits. But for him this stay in New Amsterdam would have been barren and dull and she would have introspected more than she had. She would have sunk into lower pits of morbidity. It had been to escape the screaming drabness and misery of the cottage in Fort Street that she had accepted Aunt Clarice's perpetually open invitation and come to New Amsterdam to spend these three weeks. To prevent the utter decay of her will and endurance, of her ideals and few surviving illusions. To create a respite whereby she could review things and insulate herself for further periods of endurance and suffering, inoculate her mind and her will against desperate acts and rash resolves. To stave off the dying of her spirit. That was why she had come.

During the last two evenings she became talkative and overflowed with confidences. She told Milton how she hated to hear the word Hallowe'en mentioned, but still went on to relate in detail the events of that large-looming day in 1937. He listened with grunts and nods, and frowned often. But he did not interrupt her once. He looked like a gaunt cloud settled there in the chair, his legs crossed, long and slim and gauche in his ill-fitting clothes, his deep-set eyes alert yet tinged with a troublous dreaminess so that she knew he was absorbing everything she said but at the same time weaving his own colours and incense around it.

The mango tree kept scraping against the wall outside, and the lonely toot of a car sounded now and then. The magic-eye on the wireless set winked stably in green soullessness, and dance music came in soft tinkles out of the set, irrelevant and unheard by either of them, forming only a background for her voice and his punctuating grunts.

She told him, too, about her mother's last illness, how Charlotte had taken to bed, it seemed, for good. "She hasn't been able to do any sewing since she fell ill. Milton, if you know the hell I've been going through since she took ill! Many mornings I had to go to work with my head heavy and aching from no sleep the night before."

Her voice trailed away.

After a silence, she said: "Then when I was dismissed from my job, Janie and Sarah, at last, had their way and came home to live with us. I couldn't resist any longer. I was too sick in spirit. They took David's room, and I had to share Mother's room as I used to before David went away. Most nights I have to sleep in the easy chair in the sittingroom because of Mother's groans and mutterings

– and the stench in the room. And all day Janie and Sarah keep plaguing me. They're trying to get Mother to agree to starve me out if I don't find another job –"

"Why don't you kick the bloody sluts out of the house!"

"You don't know what viragoes they are! If I tried that I would be the one to get hurt. Nowadays they're the mistresses in the house – not Mother or myself. It's exactly as I'd feared. Oh, you don't know how utterly fed-up I am with the whole business."

"I wish I were in your place. I like dealing with viragoes." He drummed on the arm of the chair, his lips set in a thin line.

"I suppose I'm too soft, that's the trouble. I hate ugly, vulgar scenes. I've had to put up with enough of them from Mother –"

"On some occasions we have to be ugly and vulgar. There's only one effective policy in a world fashioned as this is. When you're dealing with people of genuine culture and breeding, be a gentleman; when you're up against raw brute humanity, be a savage – act like a savage. Otherwise you get crushed."

"They come in at all hours of the night and morning. Sometimes when I've just managed to drop off into a doze they come in and disturb me, and if I say anything they suck their teeth and ask me what do I care if I'm disturbed; that I have the whole day tomorrow to sleep. They're always dropping some remark about my being at home during the day. And it's not that I haven't tried to get a job. I've tried again and again. I've tried until I'm tired, Milton. I've tried until my shoes became worn out and – and my dresses – they're shabby..." She broke off abruptly.

"What about the American contracting companies which have recently arrived to start building these military bases? I hear jobs are being shared out pretty freely. Have you tried them?"

"Yes. Four times I tried them. But they say unless I can type they won't have any opening for me, and I've never typed in my life."

There was another outburst of fury from him when she told him of Mr. Knight and the promissory note. "He's done that to you, too, has he? He has a reputation for eating promissory notes, the son of a bitch! Most people think it's just a joke on him, but I heard on good authority that it's true." He spoke with an intensity and restraint that frightened her. She laughed uneasily and said: "What's the use of worrying about it now! It's happened already. Nowadays I don't let anything worry me, Milton. I just sing and forget the blues."

"A negative attitude! You're being almost like your mother. Look here, doesn't Knight give you anything at all now?"

"Five dollars a month, and I have to go to his office on the first of every month to get it." She laughed. "Don't look so fierce, Milton!"

"I have reason to look fierce."

"Let's change the subject. Please. I got a letter from Naomi today. She says Gregory Brandt has published a booklet of poems. He sent her a copy, and she bought one and sent it for me."

He gave her a look of interest. "Poems? He writes, does he?"

"Casually – but I didn't know he did poetry. It was a surprise to me. She says he's leaving his old job to go into a new one with the Americans. As a costing clerk or something. He's going to get treble what he was getting in the old job. The Americans pay big salaries."

"Where's this booklet of poems?"

She went inside and brought it. He went through it with nods and frowns. There were more advertisements than poems; advertisements must have paid the printing bill. Milton thought one or two of the poems very good – unusual imagery and individual in expression. "On the whole, they're slight, though," he said finally. "Emotional orbit too narrow."

"You write poetry, too, don't you?"

"Nothing of any value whatever." He uttered a bark of contempt. "Speaking in this year 1941, there's only one poet of any substance in this colony – perhaps in the whole Caribbean area – A. J. Seymour. The rest are like sand-hills, with Seymour a Mount Roraima looming in dark and jagged solemnity in the rare and remote distance."

"I'm afraid I don't read any poetry at all."

"Only interested in *True Story Magazine,* eh? Deplorable! Oh, but what does it matter? Poetry! Art!" He snorted. "The futility of things! Have you ever wondered why you're living, Sylvia? What purpose are you serving on earth? What purpose am I serving? Or Churchill? Or Hitler? Or Bernard Shaw? What the devil are any of us alive for? Simply to produce others like ourselves and continue in perpetual monotony throughout the ages fighting and building and singing and dying?"

She stared at him, fascinated. It was strange to hear him voicing the very questions she had posed so often in her moments of desperation. The questions to which the sky and the trees always replied with a poker-stare.

She nodded. "Yes, I know. I know all about that. You don't know how many times I've wished myself dead!"

"We should all look forward to death, my dear girl. It's the one dream that, once having come true – and it always comes true – will cause none of us any disillusionment. The final emptiness. The final cessation of all pain and striving and backbiting and anxiety. What greater heaven could one desire! I live for death." He threw out his legs and guffawed. Wagged his finger at her. "Come, come! No morbidity! You must fight, Sylvia. Keep your gaze steadied on the rail tracks. No matter if you look ahead and see the tracks disappearing into the haze of infinity. Keep on. That's my policy. Frustration and disappointment only make me more angry and defiant, more determined to slam my fist into the ugly visage of life. Keep moving on. You must get to some destination eventually, even if it's only a wayside station. Fight Move on!

> "*Then to the rolling heaven itself I cried*
> *Asking, 'What lamp had Destiny to guide*
> *Her little children stumbling in the dark?'*
> *And – 'A blind understanding!' Heaven replied.*"

He rose and said that he would come and see her off tomorrow. "I'll probably cross the ferry with you."

2

Now she had the will to fight and the courage to stand up to Janie and Sarah. So she kept telling herself on the train. Milton Copps had brought alive again in her the militant spirit. She would fight back and win. A new era was about to begin. It dismayed her now that she looked back on what she had been three weeks ago. She had become indifferent, lethargic. She had been on the down-path to absolute despair and annihilation.

When she arrived home, Janie and Sarah laughed and remarked that the grand lady had returned from her holiday in the country. Sylvia snapped at them: "And what of it! What the devil have you got to do with it if I went on a holiday! I can do as I please I'm in my own home. I'm not a sponger!"

"Eh-eh! But who talk to you, Sylvia? Who address you?"

"The remark was intended for me, whether you addressed it to me or not. I think the quicker you remember that this cottage doesn't belong to you the better. You've forgotten yourselves!"

"I've just had a bath," she told Milton later in a letter, "and had my sardines and bread and a banana, that was all they had for me to eat, and now I'm in the sittingroom writing this in my pyjamas, they're getting rags now and have thin places down the side of the trousers and over my left breast. Since I was on the train I decided to write you at once to tell you about what I was thinking and my new outlook which you have given me..."

After she had told him of the row she had had with Janie and Sarah, she went on: "Janie and Sarah spoke to Mother, of course, and Mother whined as usual about my ingratitude, I'm sick hearing that word from her, but I don't mind. I'm not going to stand any more nonsense. I'm taking your advice and fighting back. No more soft words and giving in to them. I've been too foolish with all this pity and nobility and my ideals, well, it's got to stop right away.

"You did a lot of good for me by talking to me as you did, Milton, and I'm looking out for long letters from you. I feel really good tonight, just sitting here and remembering our talks, and a lovely night, too, plenty of stars and the air smells of leaves and dew and jumbies hiding under buckets. I can hear the sea plainly, it's loud at the minute and dark blue and brown all mixed together like what I'm thinking and feeling at the moment. But I'm trying not to let too many romantic and poetic ideas spoil my new resolves, though I still can't stop myself asking the old question, Milton. Why? Why must all this happen to me? Why was I born so that I had to live this kind of life? Where is it leading to, and where am I going to end up? Sometimes I sit and tremble when I ask myself these questions. I know you think that that is the best part of me, all my fancifulness and philosophy, but somehow I feel that it's that that makes me soft and weak, and it hampers me. I wish two things now. I wish Benny to come back quickly and marry me, and I wish you could be here with me now to talk to me about books and painting and people, and steady me up. I'm going to start reading the book by John Galsworthy you gave me to bring as soon as I've finished writing this, but I know Mother is going to fret because I'll have to use up oil – I forgot to tell you, Milton. We had to give up electricity in December, we couldn't afford it, so now it's only oil-lamps we use. Not so nice, eh? What to do but sing and not worry? You see how good a mood I'm in this evening? Please go on sending me books and I'll read them and try to appreciate them, mostly by daylight I'll read so as not to waste oil in the lamp. They're going to plague me, I know, and say I'm only sitting at home like a lady reading, but I don't mind, I'm going to fight them. And something must turn up before long as that man the Dickens book we used to read at school used to say, Mr. Mick-something, I forget. Oh, I'm getting accustomed to hardships now, I'm tough. I mean to adjust myself to this beastly life here and yet do my best to get out of it before long. Another thing I didn't tell you, do you know Aunt Clarice helps us with money nowadays? Yes, she sends us five dollars every month. She paid my fare to and from New Amsterdam. Even Henry gives us something from his Militia pay, he's a sergeant now and gets more pay. Mother had to sell her sewing-machine, she sold it the day before Old Year's Day last year.

"This letter is getting longer than I meant it to, hope I'm not boring you. I wish I were a good writer like you and Greg. By the way, I'm beginning already to appreciate good books, especially after those talks with you in New Amsterdam. It's only music now but I still don't think I'll ever care for that heavy groany-grumbling music you like and the opera screeching, I can't see anything in it no matter how I try. Sometimes I hear a lot of it from the radio across the street and Greg has plenty records, but not for me, Milton, I can't stand it. Give me swing music any day and nice songs. Please write soon, and please don't send any stamps as you said you would. My pride can't stand that. The six you gave me in the ferry boat will do for the time being. I know you don't think it charity giving them to me, but still I feel queer about it a little. I'll filch a penny somewhere to buy a stamp whenever I want to write you. Cheerio and sleep well, I'm going to read the Galsworthy now,

"Sincerely yours,

"Sylvia."

The following evening she decided to go and see Gregory so that she could tell him of her Berbice holiday, and especially about, Milton and what Milton thought of his poems.

She found him at home. Though alone nowadays, he still lived in his old artistic splendour, surrounded by his books and the oil and watercolour paintings that hung on the walls. Despite the absence of a female – he only had occasional mistresses now – there was a feminine tidiness and cleanliness about the place that seemed odd for a bachelor's abode. He was never tired of stressing much he detested disorder.

During the past few months she had spent many an evening with him here. Alone, they would sit and talk about people and life – or she would listen to dance music from the wireless while he read some new novel or biography or political treatise. The middle-class neighbours, people of high respectability, considered her, she had no doubt, one of his mistresses, but she did not care.

As she had expected, Gregory was very interested to hear about Milton. When she told him what Milton thought of his poems, he nodded and said: "He's perfectly correct. They're slight pieces No one realizes that more than I."

"What about your new job with the Americans, Greg? How do you like the Yankees?"

"They're a crude lot. They seem to have selected the crudest types to send out here. But I'm fitting myself into their habits. So long as they pay me I won't grumble about their crudities. I'm getting nearly three times what I got at Wheeler's – and for a soft job."

As usual, she enjoyed her visit. An evening with Gregory was never wasted. She was either entertained or edified. Sometimes both. Before she left, he told her that Jack Sampson was campaigning for a seat in the Town Council at the elections this year. "Jack is a chap to be watched, Sylvia. I believe he's going to get somewhere in this community. He mightn't be well educated, but he's got spirit and determination, and what's more, I feel he honestly has the welfare of the working man at heart. At first, I was suspicious of all his ranting about the Revolution and the capitalists, but of late I'm beginning to feel convinced of his sincerity. Well, look, I've got to kick you out this minute. I'm expecting the apple of my seraglio at nine-thirty, and yon dial on the bookstand telleth me it's just about that now."

On her way home she felt a soft dust of affection sifting through her at the thought of Gregory. He was a grand fellow. It occurred to her that she had experienced in his company this evening something that was rich and full. After an evening of such camaraderie she could not feel that life was empty and not worth living – at least, not immediately after. Tomorrow, when the memory had faded, when the richness and fullness had succumbed to the misery and frowsiness of the Fort Street cottage, she would probably feel as she had before. But in this minute life was good. Life was significant and exhilarating.

To keep up her mood, she kept humming tunes, and it was as though the singing freshness in her spirit were oozing out in actual sound.

"Love is the sweetest thing…"

She ought to hear from Milton tomorrow – if he wrote promptly, and she knew he would. She could depend on him… She took deep breaths of the water-vapourish air.

3

Sing and fight…

"I'm reading now, Janie. I wish to hear nothing from you. If you must make such remarks go into the kitchen."

"Oh, Ah suppose you fancy because Ah black I is a servant, na? You proper getting uppish all of a sudden. Reading book –"

"Get out of this sittingroom! Get out, you dirty sponger!"

"Who you calling a sponger? Charlotte! Charlotte, you hear what Sylvie call me! She say I is a sponger –"

"Ow, Janie! Ah too sick dis morning. Don't take no notice of Sylvie. Sylvie ain' got no heart, chile. Come rub me head, Janie. Ow, Almighty Fadder, Ah dying fast! Ow, Godma! Pray for me, Godma! Saviour..."

"When I grow too old to dream..."

Sing. Sing and watch the sunshine on the crotons in the garden across the street... Read over Milton's last two letters and be inspired to further resistance. Milton the fighter... "Don't give in to them. Fight them at every turn. Show them you've got steel in your guts. Civilized men don't like to admit it but it's a cold, harsh fact, Sylvia. The weaker inevitably get crushed; the strong survive. Darwin and Nietzsche knew a few sound truths. They may not be palatable, they may not conform with Christian teaching, but the truth is the truth. Let us never evade the truth. When we smash Hitler and his loutish combine we won't have done it by folding our arms or turning our cheeks in Jesus fashion and being meek and mild. No! Only by bombs and bullets we'll have done it. Force..."

"...I agree with you, Sylvia. They're real upstarts. I always knew it. And they're saying things against you."

"Saying things against me?"

"Yes." Naomi was dusting the furniture. "I don't like repeating gossip, but I can tell you they're doing their best to get you a bad name in this city. Greta told me last week she heard them talking about you at the Viceroy Hotel. They were telling some coloured young man that soon you, too, will have to be like them and go to the Viceroy to earn your living. Some young man who was in the bar having a drink. I think he knows you – he's a cricketer or a footballer – but how the conversation happened to get set on you I can't say..."

Sylvia, however, had ceased to listen. An icy wind seemed to whirl through her stomach. A nightmare fantasy sprang to life and took on full maturity. She was wafted away from Naomi's sittingroom. She was on the veranda of the Viceroy Hotel, and the time was eleven at night. The orchestra was blaring forth in the shoddy dance-hall, and sitting opposite to her at a table was a seaman who watched her with lascivious eyes. He stretched out and pawed her wrist with a grimy hand. He murmured something, and she nodded and rose... Now she was in a dingy bedroom in a lodging house in Hincks Street or Regent Street... *Rooms to let.* Two shillings – short time. Five shillings – all night. From odd bits overheard at various times from her mother's friends, she could picture the whole business... Perhaps the bed had been used by a couple only a few minutes before. The sheet was disarranged, the pillows dented – and there were grey, wet patches here and there. A frowsy smell permeated the room. On a wooden basin-stand was an enamelware basin with water – dirty water; though sometimes it would be clean. The room would be lit by a ten-watt bulb. And there she stood undressing...

"What's the matter, Sylvia? You look so pale."

"Do I?" Sylvia rose. She felt dizzy. "They needn't fear, Naomi. I won't become a prostitute. I'd drown myself first. You hear me? I mean it. I – I –" She could go no further. She pressed her hands to her face.

Naomi made her sit down, tried to comfort her. "I'm sorry I mentioned it, child. Don't let it upset you."

Sylvia stiffened. "Don't be sorry, Naomi. They envy me, that's what it is. That's why they could say a thing like that. I feel like killing them sometimes. Perhaps I will do it before long."

After a silence Naomi said: "Since you've come back from Berbice you haven't been the same person. I believe Milton Copps has done something to you."

"Done something to me?"

"Yes. He's influenced you a lot. You never spoke like this before. All this about fighting and killing."

"But he's right, Naomi. Only force can do it. How else can I prevent them from getting the better of me except by fighting back?"

Naomi shrugged. "I suppose so, but, personally, I only smile to myself when you tell me about Milton and his outlook. As Greg said once, you can't be happy if you try to act against your own codes. This Milton Copps, from what you've told me about him, seems to be a born fighter – but you're not that, Sylvia. You're soft – you're the compassionate kind. It's not natural for you to behave in an aggressive way. You're only going to spoil your life if you try to adopt that attitude."

Sylvia laughed.

"You've always been so nice and soft, Sylvia. That's what I've always admired you for. A lot of people admire you for your soft ways. This harsh attitude you're taking up doesn't become you."

Naomi was taking down the pictures and dusting their frames. She paused and looked at Sylvia and said: "You know, child, I think you let the men in your life influence you too much. First it was your father, then when he died you let your brother obsess you. Then your brother went away and Benson began to take up your whole life. Now it's Milton."

"Perhaps he'll go out of my life, too – soon. Like the others."

It was Naomi now who laughed. "Sylvia, don't look so tragic!"

Sylvia said nothing. She found that she was crying. She could not tell why she should cry, but the tears ran down her cheeks. She looked out of the window at the April sunshine. It thrust prongs through the foliage of a sapodilla tree and made a dappled pattern on top the water-vat next door. In Bent Street a black boy was whistling "Oh, Daddy!", and she could smell guava jelly. Somebody must be boiling guava jelly in the neighbourhood. And not far off a parrot kept squawking. It must be perched on the rail of a back veranda or on the bannister of a rickety backstairs.

The sunshine dimmed. A woman uttered a shriek of laughter. Creole laughter, broad, warm, unrestrained. Laughter of a black woman – perhaps with a basket balanced on her head. Or she might be well dressed and moving along the street with swaying hips, on her way to the Syrian stores in Lombard Street...

Naomi bent down to take up a blue-and-brown rug. Her breasts hung pendant for an instant within the loose kimono They sagged a little too much nowadays. They were not as attractive as they had been a year or two ago. Age, wasn't it? Age sidled in slyly upon you all the time. It pulled down your breasts, made gutters in your cheeks, sucked the brown and the black from your hair, dimmed the gleam in your eyes. Death was always on the way.

Sylvia dried her cheeks. "I'm running off now, Naomi. See you again soon. 'Oh, Daddy!'..."

A slight drizzle was falling... "I want a brand new car..."

The drizzle became a heavy shower, but she went through it. Singing.

At home, she found two letters on her mother's dressing-table. They were both addressed to her. She gave a whoop. "Milton *and* Benny! Oh, boy!"

"Ow, Sylvie! Look how you dripping water on de floor. You soaking wet. You going take cold. Ow, Saviour! Enough trouble in de house..."

"Love is the sweetest thing..." She sang as she undressed. The room reeked of stale urine, stale bay-rum, stale eucalyptus oil and the scent of frowsy clothes...

"... as I told you in a previous letter, don't try to be perfect. The best we can hope to achieve in this world is a balanced outlook. There is no golden peak of goodness. There is no one philosophy, no one path to righteousness. Each individual looks through the kaleidoscope of his imagination and sees right and wrong in tints that are his and his alone. Pilate might well have asked: 'What is righteousness?' Who can dare attempt to say what is *right? 'And a blind understanding!' Heaven replied.* The man who tells you, Sylvia, that he *sees* and *knows* is a charlatan. All parsons are charlatans... Your life rests upon you and you alone. If you act like a weak fool, then you will suffer the fate of all weak fools; if you act with strength, you will enjoy the triumph of the strong. So take my advice. Don't let up. Resist, resist..."

4

A crisis was coming. She could sense it as though it were a chilliness in the wind – the rainy wind of May and June. She could hear it in the long showers that dribbled monotonously on the roof hour after hour, sometimes for a whole day and night without break. It was in the uneven swish and jolt of the tyres of cars in the mud and rocks of Fort Street. Something in the very timbre of the B.B.C. announcer's voice seemed to foretell it amid the trail of depressing news… The Nazis in Yugoslavia. In Greece. In Crete… Hitler had invaded Russia… The very birds chirruped a warning: the thrush that in the early morning sang of rain to come – rain that always came – and the twitter and cheep of blue sackies, the shrill, questioning cry of kiskadees.

On the last day of June she spoke to Janie and Sarah. At about ten in the morning in the kitchen. Janie and Sarah were cooking the midday meal. "I want to know what you two have decided. This is the end of June. Since March you said you were going to look for new quarters."

Janie sucked her teeth and went on peeling the skins off some boiled tannias that sent up a thin wisp of steam. Sarah gave a brief laugh. She was picking and cleaning saltfish.

Outside, there was pale sunshine. Everything looked damp and steamy from the rain last night. The shrill whistle of a train came like a yellow streamer from the east, sickly-bilious, and the voices of Georgetown throbbed in a subdued, inarticulate chorus beyond the trees.

"I've spoken to you, Sarah and Janie. I want an answer." The tin saucepan went clink-clink as Janie lifted the lid to see how the rice was getting on. The starchy smell of the rice pervaded the small kitchen. Janie stirred the contents of the pot with a long iron spoon.

Sarah began to sing "Kiss the Boys Good-bye" in a low voice. Janie sniggered. "Eh-eh! Sarah, since when you learn to sing!"

"What wrong wid me Ah can't sing, chile! You t'ink is one body alone in dis house who know how to sing!"

"Why you don't put in you' name for de Amateur Hour Monday night?"

"Ah going dis very morning to put in me name. You must listen-in and tell me how Ah sound."

"Ah bet you they gong you!"

They burst into loud laughter.

Sylvia went in to her mother. Charlotte lay on her back, her eyes shut. She moaned softly. Not that she was any worse, but it had become habitual now for her to shut her eyes and moan. When she thought anyone was listening she moaned louder.

"Mother, I'd be glad if you will listen to what I have to say."

Charlotte opened her eyes and shifted slightly. Her moans grew louder. The stench in the room seemed to intensify.

"Yes, Sylvie. What's it?" Her voice was like a limp, dirt rag.

"I want you to understand that if Sarah and Janie aren't out of this house by the end of next month I'm going to get a policeman or the bailiff to throw their belongings outside."

Charlotte whimpered. "Sylvie! Ow, me God! Sylvie, tell me, child, what wrong wid you? What happen to you dese past few weeks? Ow, child! You mean you ain' got no sympathy at all for you' pore sick mudder!"

"Mother, I'm tired of hearing that. I'm simply telling you I'm not going to have those two people in this house after the end of next month, and I want you to make them understand I'm serious."

She went into the sittingroom and settled herself in the easy chair, and stared up at the dim, cobwebby rafters. She bit her lip hard and willed herself not to cry. If tears came they would only be tears of rage and frustration, but Janie and Sarah would interpret them as weakness. She succeeded, but the effort made her head buzz and gave her a tight pain in her chest. For the past week she had not been sleeping well. Her nerves were on edge, and the easy chair was developing an uncomfortable sag that curved her spine and prevented her from relaxing and resting as she should. To consider sleeping with her mother was out of the question. At night the room was a plague-spot. How her mother slept through that stench baffled her.

She gripped the arms of the chair and told herself that she must be brave. Phrases from Milton's letters ran through her head... "Above all, never weaken – no matter how desperately weak you feel. Keep at them. Harrow them..." Words. What were words? She shut her eyes and watched the flicker of the spectrum in the red gloom behind her lids. This was the world – the world into which, without asking, she had been thrown twenty years ago... Blue and green whorls converging into each other... This was the earth with trees and striving things. How much longer after twenty years? A blue sackie in the next yard kept twittering. It must be at the guavas. The guavas were ripe... If only it could tell her what lay ahead! But it was interested only in guavas. It was a realist – not a poet or a philosopher.

Sarah had gone in to Charlotte. Their voices issued from the bedroom in mumbles... Like long ago in the old house. In the sewing-room... Janie and Sarah, two attractive black girls... Teresa Feria. Agnes... Aunt Clarice, young and slimmish... Where were Teresa and Agnes?... Who occupied the front room at the old house – the front room where a little girl used to watch from a window the trams in High Street?...

The mumble-mumble went on. Perhaps they were plotting against her. The suspense began to hurt her stomach. She changed her position in the chair. Her forearms and wrists were damp with a fine sweat. They must be hatching some elaborate plan to outwit her. They were all opposed to her. The two of them and her own mother.

How can I alone resist three of them, Milton? I can see myself having to surrender. I can't stand this any longer. I'm not eating well. I'm always with a cold. The weather is so depressing. My clothes are going bad. They're threadbare and faded. I'm getting shy to go outdoors. I'm losing my self-respect. I'm accepting gifts of underclothes from Naomi, a meal from Aubrey Deleon and his wife, a two-dollar note from Gregory "to celebrate my second coming of age at thirty-five". Charity under the guise of pretty phrases... I'm getting more and more afraid every day to pass by the Viceroy Hotel. I'm going down, Milton. Down all the time. Death has set in. It's no use my trying to delude myself any longer. Your letters are very inspiring, but how can you inspire a person who lacks guts?

When I think of you it helps, but even the thought of you can't stop my will from breaking up... I'm sliding down, down all the time. How can I fight if I'm sliding down toward dark emptiness, Milton? How can I nudge myself, as you say, and look ahead along the rail tracks? How do I know that the tracks, for me, don't lead to a cliff-edge?

Milton, I'm beginning to turn my mind towards the Sea Wall. That dark, moonless night is always in my fancy nowadays. That walk out into the waves at about two in the morning when nobody is around. Walk and never turn back, never stop... And still a virgin. I sometimes think of the waste. A good luscious virgin body to be lost in the muddy waves. Perhaps I should offer it gratis to some man first, and then go for the walk...

I'm even beginning to feel Benny won't return. I see a foamy wake in the water – and a clash and thick black smoke rushing up with bits of metal and men in it. The end of a dream.

The mumbling had stopped, at last. Sarah had gone back into the kitchen.

"Sylvie!"

"Yes, Mother!"

"Come in here, if you please! Ah want to talk to you."

Sylvia rose and went in. Charlotte uttered a long whining moan. "Sylvie! Ow, child! Ow! You see how much trouble and worry you causing you' pore mudder! Ow, Sylvie! A porely woman like me who struggle so hard to bring you up – and dis all de t'anks Ah reaping! Ow, Jesus! Ow! Sylvie, you can't try and mend you' ways, child?"

Sylvia watched her and listened. A gauze of unreality veiled the scene, but after a moment she succeeded in tearing it aside... It's real – this room and everything in it. I can see it – and smell it. That thin, filthy caricature lying on the bed there whining at me is Mrs. Charlotte Russell, my mother – widow of the late Mr. Grantley Russell, an Englishman. She was once attractive enough for my father to kiss and fondle. Incredible, but very real.

"... why you don't reason, child? How Sarah and Janie can go away from here, eh? Who will look after you' pore mudder? You can't look after me. Look how you scorn me! If Sarah and Janie go away who will cook lil' food for me? Who will rub me chest down and give me lil' physic? Ow, God! Ow, Almighty! Godma, pray for me and change her heart –"

"Cut out all that, please, Mother. Let's get down to facts. The other day I told you I'd do my best to take care of you if those two women left, and I meant it. I will do my best, but they must go. I won't have them here living on us like – like two parasites."

"Who you calling a parasite, Sylvie? Who you cussing?"

Sarah flew into the room, her eyes ablaze, her gaunt, hawklike form thrust forward, threatening and fierce.

Sylvia turned. "I'll call you what I like. You're both a pair of stinking parasites, and I mean to get you out of here –"

"Look! Look!" Sarah's arm shot out, her forefinger pointing dramatically at Sylvia's face. "Ah warning you, Sylvie! You can't abuse me every day and fancy Ah going stay quiet and take it! Charlotte, warn you' daughter to stop cussing me! Ah not going stay quiet –"

"If you don't like it get out of here –"

"Ow, Jesus! Ow, Almighty! Sylvia! Sylvie! What you making a quarrel wid Sarah for, child! Ow, me Saviour! Ow!"

"Why you don't buss she tail, Sarah!"

Janie had appeared now – like another hawk – a gaunter, more churlish hawk poised to pounce. "She want a good cut-tail!" Janie screeched. "She's a lil' virago!"

"Get out of here, Janie! At once!"

Janie threw out her chest in violent bravado. "Push me out! Push me out, na! Push me out if you call you'self a woman!"

"I could have expected this of you – you vulgar whores!"

Janie darted forward. Her hands reached out, and there was a soft, crisp sound as Sylvia's dress ripped down from the shoulder across the breast. The material was old and threadbare. Sarah screamed approval. "Good so! Good so! Strip she naked, Janie!"

Sarah, however, had other intentions. She held on to the torn dress, and butted once, twice. Her head connected with Sylvia's collarbone, then with her cheekbone. Then Sarah stepped back, and Sylvia staggered against the dressing-table, sobbing. She tried to speak but she could only blubber.

Thus defeat.

Defeat was like mashed wild leaves. Bitterish, astringent... One afternoon she and Henry Madhoo and David were playing housekeeper and guests. She had made a paste out of some wild leaves and served it up in tiny plates. It was supposed to be roast beef... "Another helping, Mr. Brown?"... "Thank you, Mrs. Smith." Then, out of curiosity, she had tasted the mess, and it had tasted bitterish, astringent.

The weather was fine this evening, and that made a difference, of course. The trade wind trailed soft threads past the throbbing bump on her cheek. The stars speared soothing points of light into her nerves. But even this could not remove the astringent taste of defeat, nor destroy the itch for revenge.

They were out tonight. As usual, they had gone to try to attract men at the Viceroy. It would be an easy matter to go into their room and wreck their belongings, fling their clothes into the street – into the soft, muddy puddles. But what would be the use of that? They'd attack me again when they came in. They'd throw my things out, too…

The Brown Jumbie-men: "So, in short, you admit you're afraid."

"I admit nothing of the sort."

"Then why don't you fight back? Why are you sitting here moping?"

The wind in soft threads past her cheeks…

"Sylvia, you've been deluding yourself again. You haven't got it in you to be aggressive. Naomi was right. You've let Milton Copps lead you into bad tactical moves, and now you're paying for your error."

"But I still think Milton is right. Only by fighting you can get the better of people like Janie and Sarah who bully you in your own home. Oh, I'm sick of everything. I think I'd better go and take that walk to the beach."

"Then go and do it. You're weak. The weak must perish. It is the basic rule of life. People like you only clog and retard human progress."

"Progress toward what? Where is anybody heading?"

"Hee, hee! Talking back at us, eh? Well, we rebut by asking you to recall your Miltonic philosophy. Keep your gaze on the tracks. No matter if you look ahead and see the tracks disappearing into the haze of infinity. You must get to some destination eventually, even if it's only a wayside station. Don't try to understand purpose. Don't ask where we're progressing toward – or what. '*And a blind understanding!*'…"

"But isn't that what the church people do? Believe blindly in a myth in the sky? God and the Hereafter? They just accept what the theologians tell them, and have faith. You expect me to delude myself, too, by putting my faith in an invisible goal and in a purpose I can neither see nor understand nor fathom in any way?"

"Perhaps now the true light is beginning to drench your understanding. There is *nothing* to believe in – except yourself. There is no one right way of looking at life; only your own matters – for you. Life is a muddle – a contradictory, aimless, inconsistent phenomenon. It's you who try to give it significance and orientation. You, Sylvia, a human being, with your discontented, probing mind. Do the dogs and cats worry about a *raison d'être?* Do the mosquitoes in Berbice get thin and grey because they can't understand the Real Purpose behind sucking blood?"

Tiny blue-white points of light in dark-blue space... Ten thousand... Ten million... A thousand million of them watching her and blinking inscrutably.

5

The following morning she had to forget the unseemly bump on her cheek and go out. For today was the first of the month.

Mr. Knight's office was in Croal Street, a low-built two-storeyed building painted pink, with dark-green facings. It was called "Lorna Doone".

She took a seat on a long form in the waiting-room where two East Indian women were already settled. Dressed in national costume, long skirts to their ankles and pink diaphanous head-veils trailing down past their shoulders, they were adorned with heavy necklaces of nuggets and sovereigns, nose-rings set with rubies, weighty-looking silver anklets that jingled whenever they shifted their feet, and rings on their fingers. Peasants from somewhere on the East Bank, perhaps, they murmured nasally in Hindustani, nodding their heads and looking secretive and dark with intrigue.

From beyond a varnished wooden jalousied screen came the sound of other voices. Mr. Knight's soft, suave tones – too soft and suave to make out what he was saying – and the fluctuating voice of an East Indian man. Sometimes it was a nasal drone, sometimes a raised, impassioned whine. When it rose she could always hear something about "prapperty" or land or conscience... "Dat was *my* prapperty, Mr. Knight!"... "But de land, Mr. Knight! De land! 'E na want to discuss de *land!* Dat's wha' *worry* me, Mr. Knight!"... "Me conscience won't 'low me to do such a t'ing, Mr. Knight, and 'e *know* dat good! Dat's why 'e t'reatening me!"...

Some months it was the tall, thin black clerk who attended to Sylvia; some months Mr. Knight himself – and these were the months she dreaded.

She kept watching the doorway that opened into the southern room, for it was in there that the clerk worked. After a while she heard a loud rustle of papers, the scrape of a chair, then footsteps sounded and he appeared, his air, as usual, worried and preoccupied. He had a way of showing his teeth when he looked around the waiting-room. Sometimes he tapped them with a dark green pencil. He did that now.

"You here, Miss Russell?" He uttered a pensive sound, as though noting the fact of her presence for possible future reference in a *cause célebre.* "Mr. Knight will attend to you dis month, Miss Russell."

"Very well," she said, and wondered whether he detected the sigh in her manner. Possibly not, for he had already turned off to address some very confidential remark to the two East Indian women in a very hoarse, hushed voice.

Nearly half an hour must have elapsed before she saw Mr. Knight. He glanced up as she entered – then glanced down. He wore pince-nez, and there were many grey hairs amid the black on his head. His paunch seemed larger every time she saw it. His sallow-olive face had a flushed look. It was not a healthy flush, she was sure.

The room smelt of ink and papers and the dustiness of old books, though all the books that were visible in the three tall glass-fronted cases looked new and well-bound in leather or cloth, with gold lettering. Bound volumes of the *Official Gazette* for over fifteen years lined two whole shelves of one bookcase, and perhaps it was from these that the old-book smell came.

Mr. Knight was writing with a Parker pen. Before him on the desk lay a sheaf of blue foolscap sheets. Presently he glanced up, and this time he seemed to take in her presence more thoroughly, for though he lowered his gaze again and went on writing, he remarked: "You seem to have been fighting."

Her hand went to her cheek. She said nothing.

"Sit down."

She took the chair near his desk. It was the only one in the room besides the swivel one at his desk in which he sat. She was so close to him now that she could smell a sweetish pomade scent that must come from his hair.

"Where did you get that bump? Fell down?"

"I'd be glad if you could attend to me without delay, Mr. Knight."

He gave a low laugh, put out his hand, as though absent-mindedly, and patted her knee. "Still on the high horse, eh?"

Her leg did not even twitch. She stared at the inkwell.

"Two or three years ago I used to consider you an intelligent girl."

A fly was playing about on the desk. It hopped from the topmost blue foolscap sheet onto the edge of a small glass bowl with a soaked sponge.

"It seems as if it's going to take me a long time to convince you that you can have much more than the mere dole you're getting now." He took a black Catarrhozone tube from his top coat pocket and inhaled briefly – first at one nostril then at the other.

"You could have a little place of your own in Queenstown, furnished and provided with anything you require. Simply a matter of asking for it. I can't see anything so horrible in the idea. I know of quite a number of fine girls who have done it. In any event, I certainly think it will be a pleasanter alternative to living in filth and poverty. And every girl likes to dress well. I'm sure you're no exception."

First at one nostril then at the other...

"You should consider it. I think you'd be much happier." He interlaced his fingers and looked quizzical. "I'm not such a big bad bear as you seem to think me. I can be nice to you – if you let me."

He gave her a sidewise glance. "You're looking a little thin. Not eating enough, I suppose."

She was gazing at the lattice work at the top of the wall.

"I'm sure your father would have considered it a sensible course of action – in your present circumstances. For inevitably you'll have to do something like this in order to exist. Why do it the ugly, promiscuous way?"

"Mr. Knight, could you attend to me now if you're ready?"

Out of the corner of her eye she could see him smiling. He was absolutely unruffled. She saw him take his wallet from an inner pocket and extract a five-dollar note. He let it fall lightly into her lap.

"There you are. Run off and behave yourself."

"Aren't you going to let me sign the receipt, as usual?"

"No need for such formality this time."

"I prefer the formality, all the same."

He gave his head a slight shake. "I may as well tell you, Sylvia. The money I've been giving you for the past three or four months came out of my own pocket. It was charity."

"Charity?"

"Yes, charity. On the first of March I paid you the last cent you're legally entitled to. All you possess in the world now is the cottage you're living in. Your father's estate is as dead as this desk."

"Why have you waited until now to tell me this?"

He shrugged. "Your father was a very good friend of mine."

She rose. In her hand the note seemed to have caught fire. She wanted to drop it but could not. Instead, she crumpled it tight in her hand and pressed her clenched hands to her face. This way it was easier to keep back the tears. Her whole body vibrated as though a dynamo had started up inside it. She could hear the hiss of her breath.

"Sit down."

Automatically she obeyed. Her knees felt weak. In any case, she would have had to sit. At length, she managed to control herself. She stared out of the window. A drizzle was falling. She could see it slanting across the trees and houses on the other side of the street.

"The cottage I have in mind in Queenstown is a cosy place. Two bedrooms, a sittingroom and a dining-room and a kitchen. In a very quiet street. Several fruit trees grow in the yard, so you could have all the privacy you want from the neighbours. It's furnished and ready for occupation. Each bedroom has a Simmons bed with spring-filled mattress..."

The drizzle was getting coarse... A Simmons bed with spring filled mattress... The shower was getting heavy. In a few seconds the big leak in the kitchen would be causing Janie or Sarah to get the bucket... Day after day they kept pecking at you. Two hawks wearing down your will...

"... and there is an electric stove in the kitchen. No messy stove to smoke up the house...

It was thinning off. The sun was coming out again...

"... what's all this fuss they make over virtue? I've never forgotten how Grantley used to curse these highly respectable prudes. He hated everything prudish and respectable. Most remarkable in an Englishman..."

She crossed her legs for comfort, then uncrossed them, remembering the holes in the soles of her shoes...

"... and then there is my car. It would be always at your disposal. You could do any shopping you wish or take a run into the country for a breath of air. My chauffeur is a reliable fellow. I've had him for years, and he's the essence of discretion..."

The sunshine was getting brighter, and she could see a patch of blue appearing between two houses with reddish roofs... A lovely car to sit back in. She could smell, the leather and feel the humming bliss of being carried along... Into the country for a breath of air...

"... you'd be able to live like a lady. There'd be no convenience you'd lack. And you haven't got to hurry yourself about deciding. Think it over at your leisure. You can go into it today, tomorrow, next week. It's there for you whenever you make up your mind..."

The patch of blue had widened. That must be a plum tree in the space between the two houses...

"... I won't bother you every night, so that needn't frighten you. Your friend, Mrs. Dowden, could visit you whenever she likes – or whenever you care to have her. She could spend days with you..."

She rose.

"I think I'm going now, Mr. Knight – before the rain comes down again. Good morning."

As she walked out she heard his swivel chair squeak. Like vicissi duck flying high at night.

6

A week after Naomi's son Garvey died of typhoid in the hospital, Milton Copps arrived in Georgetown. He turned up in Fort Street at about noon, and when Sylvia went to the door and saw him she gasped not so much with amazement as with dismay and shame at the fact that he had surprised her in her shabby, threadbare house dress.

"Milton! You never mentioned you were coming to Georgetown!"

"I'm noted for doing surprising things."

"Are you making a long stay?"

"Very long. I have shaken the mud of New Amsterdam irrevocably from the harrowed soles of my shoes. Stop fidgeting. You've told me about your house dresses in your letters." He sniffed. "I can smell the smell, too – even from the door here. What about the Harpies? Are they at home?"

"Sssh! Yes, they're in their room."

"I won't stay, then. It wouldn't be good policy to commit murder on the first day of my indefinite sojourn in the city. I'll come back this evening and we'll go for a walk on the Sea Wall. How's that?"

"I'd be glad. Please come."

On that first evening he did most of the talking. He told her the story of the past few months, how it had become more and more obvious that New Amsterdam and its small-town atmosphere was going to suffocate him to death. He told her of how he had quarrelled with his people, of the affair he had been having with a girl whom his people considered to be of no class; it was that which had caused the final break with them. He had come to Georgetown with three dollars in his pocket, and he was staying at a lodging-house in Regent Street run by oily, nasal-voiced East Indians. It was not pleasant, but it was cheap, and to a fugitive from the stultifying prison-camp of New Amsterdam it was not an unwelcome haven.

"I'm not afraid," he said, on their fourth night on the Sea Wall. "In fact, it's exhilarating in a way. But you'll have noticed how brittle I am in manner. It's the being perpetually alert that's done that to me. But for the utter desperateness of the struggle for existence I believe I might have wanted to make love to you despite Benny and all other considerations. But a hunted wolf must eschew love." He guffawed briefly. "The bourgeoisie are close on my heels, Sylvia. They'd like to see me rolling defeated in the dust. But they'll never get me. Ah, no! This wolf is too old a hand at adventuring on its wits. I'll lick 'em yet!"

"But, Milton, I don't understand. How are you living? How do you eat and pay your lodging and all the rest?"

He shrugged briefly – not like Naomi; not with abandon and nonchalance. His was a shrug of confidence. "I just bring it off somehow. Sell a picture here, sell an article to the papers. And, of course, there's my mother. These mothers, Sylvia!" He guffawed again. "You'd be surprised to know the number of treasury notes I keep discovering concealed among the clothes in my suitcase. From a point of human values, my mother really deserves to have had a better son than I have been to her. She is an unfortunate woman.

"Most unfortunate," he said, after a silence. "Perhaps more unfortunate than you have been, because, at least, you had a father who prepared you psychologically for the adversities of the spirit. You can face harsh truths with courage. My mother cannot. Too much of her childhood and adolescence was spent in antimacassared sitting-rooms. No odd circumstance, of course. The history of our British Guiana middle-class is no different from that of the English. You can't know the world, Sylvia, simply by sitting in a rocking chair and looking out of your parlour window. Pardon my banality. I ate raw peanuts and milk chocolate for dinner this evening. Peanuts are rich in Vitamin B, milk chocolate in Vitamin A."

She made no comment. Simply smiled. She thought idly of the

dinner she had had this evening. A penny loaf of bread with a daub of cooking butter. A teaspoonful of condensed milk stirred into a cup of hot water.

"I could have invited you to a posh dinner tonight," she said.

He made no remark, and after a silence she went on: "I never told you about it in my letters." So she told him now. He listened in silence. "For a long time before that he had been trying to get me to go out with him in his car to Dixie, but I always treated him with contempt. I suppose he felt certain in the end I would have to agree to let him have his way, that's why he thought he could get this cottage fitted up and offer to put me in it as – as his concubine."

"I see."

"I can excuse him. He never really knew what sort of person I am."

"The point is, how have you been existing since then? You say you didn't go back the following month to get the usual dole. How have you been balancing your budget at home without his five-dollar note?"

She was silent a moment, then said: "By chucking overboard something I used to place great value on – my pride."

She told him about Mr. van Huisten, how she had gone to him and spun a tale of destitution. An old friend of Daddy's and so on. If he could lend her ten dollars until she got a job, she would pay it back at the earliest opportunity. "And, of course, he gave it to me. He knew he would never see it again, and I knew he would never, but we both pretended. At home, they don't know that Mr. Knight has stopped giving the fiver – at least, that I've stopped going round to him on the first of each month. I handed over five of the ten Mr. van Huisten gave me to Mother at the beginning of last month and kept the other five, and when the first of this month came I gave her the other five."

"But in two or three weeks from today it will be the first of October. Where will the other five come from?"

"Simple. It will be Mr. Ralph's turn. Don't you think it's only right they should pay something for being old pals of Daddy's?"

He nodded gravely. "I can see why you're looking so thin."

She began to bite her little finger hard. She looked slowly all over the cloudless September sky.

He pointed up and said that Aries had just risen.

"In a way, I can agree with Naomi. You're not a born fighter, Sylvia. It was a mistake to have advised you to resist those two harpies. I realized it after the incident you described – at the end of June. What I always marvel at is how it's possible for you to be what you are in spite of your background. Astounding how you sustain this air of composure."

She said nothing. The waves were getting more thunderous. The tide must be washing. She found herself comparing these nights on the Sea Wall with the February nights in New Amsterdam. In February he had been her mentor and companion solely, but now there was the merging mist of friendship as well. Now there was intimacy that was saturating and yet unburdened with the itchy warmth and tenterhooks of passion. The instability of both their lives created a sympathy of desperateness between them which, at the same time, precluded any yielding to sentiment. The feeling of being hunted down, of being cornered, was too strong in them. It shut out soft passages.

On the nights they did not go on the Sea Wall they went to Naomi or Gregory, or Aubrey, who was now the father of a daughter. They had all taken a liking to Milton. His Bohemianism and his candour appealed to Gregory and Aubrey especially, but Naomi liked him for his philosophical pronouncements which she took very seriously.

One day Jerry, as though to test him out – for Jerry did not seem certain about him – asked him if he would like to assist him with a job at his shop, that it would mean a few dollars in his way.

Milton replied: "My dear fellow, anything that means a few dollars in my way is precisely the thing I'm looking for. But, unfortunately, I know absolutely nothing about engines, combustion or otherwise. I'd make a mess of a toy steam-engine if you put it my care."

"You haven't got to know anything about engines to help me. It's only to hold heavy parts and wash and grease. You see, we're short of labour at the shop. The Americans have taken away most of the fellows who used to work with us."

"In which case, simply tell me what time to drop in and where your shop is and I'll be with you as sure as there are bacteria in the air.

He worked for three days with Jerry, and said he enjoyed it. Jerry had promised to send for him again as soon as another big job that called for extra help materialized.

Sylvia liked to hear him and Gregory discuss art and literature, or argue out some philosophical theory. One evening they went on until after midnight arguing about what form the novel should take. Gregory was all for the propaganda type of novel, Milton against.

Another evening it was philosophy – negative as opposed to positive. Milton defended his views that life was too complex for any philosophy to prove workable, that there was no aim, no goal ahead. Men had to act as their conditioned impulses and accumulated experiences directed. Right and wrong were relative. The exigency of the situation must decide the right or wrong of an act – exigency plus an innate sense of decency that everyone of us possessed though many of us deliberately suppressed it.

Gregory shook his head and said that Milton's philosophy was a negative one, and that a negative philosophy cancelled itself out automatically. The negative philosopher was as bad as the cynical philosopher. No system of thought could be built up on cynicism or negativism. The very fact that a philosopher admitted that no system of thought was workable proved that he was defeated; he had given up the struggle of unravelling the mystery. He had become a charlatan thumbing his nose at those who still persisted in trying to find a positive solution.

Did Gregory think, posed Milton, that any philosopher, either now or in the future, would succeed in finding a solution to the problem of living? So far as actual results were concerned – and, in the final analysis, only results mattered – Plato had proved as much a failure as Christ or Buddha or Nietzsche. For instance, take Sylvia. Review her life up to the present and suggest what one stable outlook she should adopt toward living. How was she going to avoid becoming warped and embittered? For the sake of argument, let them say that she was forced to turn to prostitution as a means of keeping herself alive, how was she to adjust her mind to such a degrading occupation? How was she to reconcile her high ideals with a state of things that was the complete antithesis of what she had aspired to in her earlier years?

At this point, Sylvia interrupted to say that the argument did not hold good, because, with her outlook on things, a situation such as Milton mooted could never materialize; she would commit suicide rather than become a prostitute. She had vowed that to herself a long time ago.

"Ah!" said Milton. "Precisely! Suicide! Of course it would intervene and prevent such a situation from materializing. But that's a negative view to take, remember. Gregory is advocating a *positive* solution to the problem, my dear Sylvia. So where do we stand now? Come to our rescue, Mr. Brandt. Tell us how. Unravel *this* mystery."

Gregory smiled and wagged his head with an air of indulgence. "That's a very adroit way of slipping out of the corner," he said. "But there's something else you haven't taken into consideration. The human will. Let us assume that Sylvia, instead of adopting a negative attitude toward her life, decides to solve matters on a positive basis. So long as she is determined in her resolve, her subconscious mind, supported by her will, will immediately come to her rescue and create in her such a resourcefulness that there will be no necessity for either prostitution or suicide. You yourself have given us an example. You've had, and are still having, a tough struggle to make your way in the world, but why haven't you decided to let things slide and degenerate into a beggar or a pimp or a housebreaker? Or why don't you commit suicide? It's your will that drives you on despite frustrations and disillusionments. Without knowing it, you've adopted a positive attitude towards living."

Milton laughed. "With a facile command of language we convince an audience that a pumpkin is a glass marble, or the converse. To begin with, I never said that my outlook on living was a negative one. I said I have no *one* outlook, that I simply adjust myself to a situation as it arises and refuse to orient my code of behaviour in any *one* direction. I consider this a very positive attitude. Your arguments in themselves are sound, Gregory. It's only that you're rushing off at an impetuous tangent. Now, let's discuss this question of the human will. I admit your view that, faced with a black situation, the human will can certainly solve seemingly hopeless problems by urging the subconscious mind to a state of resourcefulness. I, as you say, am an example. Good. But when you pose this question of the human will aren't you taking it for granted that *everyone* has a will strong enough to whip his subconscious into superhuman feats of resourcefulness? Aren't you ignoring the fact that a strong will is the exception rather than rule?

"Let's revert to our specimen under examination, Sylvia Anne Russell – may the Lord, if not ourselves, have mercy on her sensitive feelings! – what line of argument would you take up if we proved that Sylvia does not possess the amount of will power necessary to generate in her subconscious the energy of resourcefulness which, in turn, is necessary to solve her stern problems of living? In vulgar terms, suppose she can't use her wits to the same extent that I can use mine in fishing for a meal and wangling a shelter. And let us say that the sum of her past experiences has bred in her a certain self-respect which, combined with her innate sense of decency, forbids her from going to excruciating lengths to cadge money or food off her fellow-men or to indulge in any shady business deal. Added to this, let's consider the heredity *motif.* Heredity, let's assume, has inflicted upon her a streak of weak character which, no matter what environmental influences have been at work, cannot be suppressed. Despite all efforts on her part, it continues to push up its head, because it happens to be a legacy from dear Mother. It's a part of her make-up, whether she likes it or not. Furthermore, from some remote ancestor came a romantic and poetic twist of mind – she is inclined to dream and live in coloured soap-bubbles; she is imaginative, and introspects, conjures up fanciful situations of terror or blissful ecstasy; she magnifies the ordinary and the commonplace so that it becomes the irrational or the fantastic. Assuming, then, that she is this complex being I've just sketched, where does the human will step in to solve her problems? Can you explain that?"

Gregory replied that as Milton had already taken as his premise that Sylvia did not possess the amount of will power necessary to produce a state of resourcefulness, the argument automatically had come to a stalemate. Everything, therefore, that Milton had said concerning the sum of her past experiences and heredity was relevant. Now, suppose they took a different line of argument. Let them forget the human will...

At this point Sylvia's attention strayed. She found herself staring out of the window at the dim haze of the Milky Way visible in the clear September sky. In this moment Milton and Gregory seemed futile, absurd pedants... The human will, heredity, sum of past experiences... Words. High-flown words cleverly strung together... What concerned her at the moment was what she was going to tell Mr. Ralph in a few days from now, what tale she was going to concoct, how she was going to brazen her story out so that it would sound convincing. Suppose he had too miserly a streak in him and had forgotten his sentimental memories of her father and the old days. Suppose he merely talked nicely and put her off with promises...

A meteor flashed across the sky.

She took a deep breath. The air smelt of jasmines. Or it might be stephanotis. The people next door had a vine on an arbour.

They were talking about Garvey's death now. What was the purpose in such an event? Why did a human have to be born, and then, even before the intellect had awakened, life was sucked away? Why such an aimlessness in the purport of events? What did it portend? Not that everything was blind and without any fixed plan?

She smoothed down her dress, and became aware of the thinness of her thighs. She had reduced a lot during these past few months. Her vitality was not as high as it used to be. Lack of vitamins, of course. Perhaps she should do as Milton did – instead of eating bread and sardines with the customary milk and water, scientifically diet herself on raw peanuts, milk chocolate, oranges, bananas and an occasional egg swallowed uncooked. It was a cheap diet but one that supplied, said Milton, Vitamins A, B, C and D. But to do this would mean having to convince Charlotte and Janie and Sarah that money spent on these things was better spent than on bread and sardines and condensed milk. It would mean waging a war against the ignorance of her mother and those two prostitutes. What did they know about vitamins and calories? They would only laugh at her.

She rose. "Milton, it's late. Time to see me home."

Milton rose at once. He pointed a precise forefinger at Gregory. "That's where we pause and ask ourselves: Is it worth while? Where is the point in proceeding further? Why do I hurt my head over accumulating money? Why do I want to be a successful artist if the Big Nought looms persistently before my inner gaze? Why do I want to marry and bring children into the world if the same monotonous, aimless process is to go on generation after generation, century after century? Well, there you are! *'And a blind understanding!' Heaven replied!*"

Gregory laughed. "I think you deserve a drink for that. Rum or whisky?"

"Your memory is short. I told you Bacchus and I have signed a pact of non-aggression."

"I was forgetting. We'll drink your health in Ovaltine, then. It's supposed to be a good nightcap. Sylvia, you'll join us, won't you?"

"Yes, I don't mind, thanks."

Milton flung out his hand in her direction. "You heard her! She doesn't mind, thanks. Damn it all! And she knows she needs it as desperately as I do. But, of course, she's a sensitive, well-bred lady of the upper middle-class. She can't express her feelings frankly." He tapped her briskly on the shoulder. "Face up to ugly facts, Sylvia. Come on. Shake yourself and remember that vitamins rather than veneer make the world go round."

She laughed and told him he was a scream.

"A piercing one, my dear. A piercing one."

On the way to Fort Street he pointed out one or two constellations, and told her some of the Greek myths relating to them. He said he could not understand why the stars fascinated him so much. He sometimes dreamt at night of new and magnificent constellations.

Before they parted at her gate, he gave her a milk chocolate – a slim six-cents slab – and told her that it would not be necessary for her to go to Mr. Ralph as she was planning to do within a few days. When she asked him what he meant, he told her to be careful in withdrawing the chocolate from its wrapper. He added: "Right-o! See you tomorrow!" He waved briefly and hurried off like a long, erratic cloud toward Barrack Street.

When she went upstairs and lit the lamp, she found a five-dollar note secreted between the tinsel and the outer wrapping of the chocolate slab.

7

One morning early in October he came round at about ten o'clock and told her that he was sailing by the afternoon tide. Just like that.

"But – but I don't understand."

"Always springing these surprises on you, eh?"

He said he had met a schooner captain at the lodging-house, and they had got friendly. He had signed on as a deck-hand.

"But where is the schooner going, Milton?"

"Round the West Indies. First to Barbados, and from there to Trinidad, then back to Barbados with a cargo of gasoline. Then to St. Lucia with a cargo of marl. After that, well, it may be any island. It's the biggest stroke of luck that's ever befallen me, Sylvia."

"I'm glad," she said – in a murmur.

He laughed and gave her shoulder a brisk pat. "Don't look so desperate. I'll write you. You can depend upon me."

"Yes, I know. I'll write you, too." She asked him what was the name of the schooner, and he said the *Russell P. Darrell.*

"Such a queer name!" she commented. She tried to laugh.

That afternoon she sat on a bench near the site of the old fort and watched the *Russell P. Darrell* get smaller on the grey expanse of sea. It was around three o'clock, and the glare from the sun made her squint hard. The sun shone down from a cloudless sky, harsh and without pity, blistering and dazing. But the trade wind droned bravely from the north-east, and that made a difference. Without the trade wind it might have been much hotter. And a ragged saman tree did its best to shelter her. Perched on one of its weathered limbs, a kiskadee kept crying: "Key-y-y! Key-y-y!" piteously. A sympathetic bird.

When the schooner was a mere grey-white dot amid the crested breakers far out she got up, looked around at everything and gave a soft breathing chuckle. She bit her lip and stared around, and wondered how many times she had done this within the past two or three years. Bit her lip and stared around... Her father... David... Benson...

She looked at the Round House in the east. It was solid and satisfying, and grey with memories of childhood. The muzzle of the gun pointing seawards did make a dissonance, it was true. The war. In the west stood the old gasoline bond – and beyond it the shimmering Demerara.

Directly behind her the grassy embankment sloped down from the wall to the rough swards and the roadway.

The sun. The sun was so hot and dazzling that it made the sky grey-blue and hazed. It brought water to your eyes. Not tears. No, not tears. Only water. There must be no tears.

Straight on. Toward death? Never mind. Straight on she had to go. There was no purpose. No aim. No goal. Yet from day to day she must exist. She must exist, no matter if she could see ahead only umber emptiness.

One day she threw back her head and laughed. "You *might* get to some destination, Sylvia – even if it's only a wayside station." Other people around her got to destinations, so why not she? Jack Sampson, for instance. After a hard battle against two candidates, Jack was elected to the Town Council by a majority of seventeen votes.

"Now you will see some fireworks on dat Council, Greg! Watch out!"

They were celebrating at Gregory's cottage on the night of the election. Everybody was drunk. "We all drunk," Aubrey remarked once. He glanced at Sylvia. "Sylvia! Only you alone sober. Our saintly, dear beloved Sylvie. Sylvie, I should have married you, but I look on you as a sister..."

"Three cheers for Stalin!"

"Over the top, boys!"

"Jack, I betting heavy on you for de Legislative Council. And when you get elected Ah want you to piss on dem! You hear me? *Piss* on dem! Dose sons of reactionary bitches!..."

"... Sylvie, remember the night – de Old Year's Night – I took you home from Naomi's?"

"Yes, Aubrey, I remember. That *was* a night."
"Yes, man. Dat *was* a night."
"Don't talk about it, or I might want to cry."
"Oh, hell! Sylvie, your friend Aubrey drunk. Have a rum-and-ginger with me. Break your rule for once, Sylvie."
"No, thank you, Aubrey. Soft drinks for me – all the time."
"Oh, Christ! Sylvie, what sort of nature you born with? You're a funny girl. Up to now Ah can't understand you."
"That's nothing strange. I myself don't understand myself."
"Ah get a job wid de Americans, girl."
"You have?"
"From next week I'm going up to de air-base up de river to work for de Americans. Have a drink to Uncle Sam, Sylvie."
"Aubrey, you really *are* drunk."
"Sylvie."
"Yes."
"Why you don't look for a job?"
"Don't let's talk about jobs. Let me sing you a song. 'A pretty girl is like a melod-ee-ee...'"
"Dat's right, Sylvie! Sing for us, girl!"
"Clap hands for Sylvie!"
"Girl, you should go to Hollywood!"
"Boys, it's time to elevate de new Councillor!"
"Push him up! Push him up!"
"For he's a jolly good fellow..."
"Hear, hear!"
"One burroo tiger! Brrrrr!"
"For he's a jolly good feh-low-w-w..."
"... feh-LOW-W-W-W... And SO say all of us..."

They were all getting to destinations. Wayside stations. Yet true, they every one had to die some day. No matter if Jack eventually got into the Legislative Council, he would die – and others like him would be born and would go to school and grow up and do what he had done. Generation after generation. There was no purpose. No aim. No golden point stop. You simply had to go on and on and on and take what came to you. Lovely gardens and fine houses, cars and rich carpets. Or leaky cottages and sardines and bread, and holes in your shoes.

About the middle of the month, Naomi told her that she had big news for her, and when Sylvia asked her what was the news Naomi said: "I'm getting married." Just like that.

"You're joking."

Naomi smiled wanly. These days she had become quiet. Not so much nonchalance lurked in her shrugs and gestures. The death of Garvey had shocked something alive in her – a something that had lain dormant these past years. She had gone into black after Garvey's death. Naomi the carefree Bohemian in mourning. She was a sadder, more thoughtful Naomi nowadays. Garvey's death seemed to have brought into being her latent maternal love. She had treated Garvey in life with total, almost brutal, indifference. But in death Garvey was her beloved son. She took flowers to his grave every Sunday.

"No, Sylvia, I'm not joking," she said. "It's true. By special licence next week. A quiet ceremony at the Registrar's Office. No fuss."

"I'm glad – but surprised. I never thought Jerry would ever come round to marrying any woman."

Naomi shook her head slowly. "I'm not getting married to Jerry, Sylvia. It's Gregory."

"Greg!"

"Jerry has joined the Navy."

"The Navy?"

"The Trinidad Royal Naval Volunteer Reserve. He enlisted last week and passed his medical Monday last. He's sailing Friday for Trinidad."

"But I can't believe this."

"They advertised in the papers for volunteers, and he enlisted. He says his shop isn't paying since the Americans came. His best workmen have gone to work with the Americans for big pay, and he can't get labour. The recruiting officer said that with his engineering experience he ought to rise quickly in the Navy. He's joined up as a stoker rating."

"I see." Sylvia was still staring at her. "And, Naomi, you mean you still love him – Jerry?"

On a similar occasion, even less than a year ago, Naomi would have shrugged her famous shrug and laughed. Now she merely nodded and replied: "Yes." In a quiet voice.

After a silence, Sylvia said: "Anyway, I'm glad, Naomi. Really. I think it's much better like this. Greg is nice. He's solid."

"We would like to have you as a witness."

"Of course. Certainly."

Gregory gave Sylvia a "wedding present" of five dollars. It was enclosed in an envelope, and on the envelope was typed: "From the Bridegroom today – in token of all the pleasant yesterdays". It was signed in green ink "Greg".

She looked at it a long time and smiled.

Pretty words. Pretty gesture. But, nevertheless, charity in disguise. Charity done so that it would not hurt her pride too much. Like Milton and his slab of chocolate. Like Milton again and the postal order from St. Lucia for twenty-one shillings – the equivalent of five dollars and four cents. He attached a slip of paper with two words: "No comment". His letters were very interesting. He was finding sea life tough but exhilarating. It was not suited to his temperament, he said, but he had fitted himself in to it, and the "rhythm of his soul" was responding. He had painted two pictures. He would send her one of them – the one in which he had "captured the tinge of the Caribbean". It was the best thing he had ever done, but he was fearful that if he kept it too long within his sight the glory would depart. "There is nothing more terrible and tragic, Sylvia, than to create in heat and then watch the slow smoke-rings shaping *Ichabod* across the wondrous, towers of your fancy."

Anyway, that solved the question of November the first and December the first. It postponed the hard-luck tale for Mr. Ralph or Mr. Jarrow. With what Henry Madhoo contributed and what his mother, Aunt Clarice, sent from New Amsterdam, the budget was secure for November and December. Unless sardines went up in price, which was not such an impossibility with this war on.

In November there was a letter from David, the first they had had from him for over six months. He had been torpedoed again but was safe, though he was in hospital suffering from slight burns and shock.

At David's letter, too, she looked a long time and smiled.

The past... Was there really a time in her life when David was real, when David meant the beginning and end of existence to her? Was there really a time when she desired him with a perverted passion? Where had all those feelings gone? It was unbelievable that they could have been in vain.

She moved to the window and watched a star-apple tree. A soft breeze was blowing, and the star-apple tree swayed a trifle, its brown-and-green leaves hissing quietly.

One day in December she sat on the Sea Wall and watched the breakers. Today was no different from yesterday or the day before. Wake up, have a shower, dress, eat. Then sit on the stairs and stare out at the morning. Or take a walk to the Sea Wall, sit on a bench and stare at the waves. Or read a book just in case the waves proved too fascinating. *Swan Song* by John Galsworthy, or the last number of the *New Statesman* Gregory had passed on.

You must do something. You couldn't sleep during the day as well. And evening soon came. Evening, like death, always came true. Evening settled in violet around you and turned the air soft and leafy-smelling. How could anything seem sordid when such pinks and yellows were blending together over the river and the insects were cheeping in the grass? And look at the saman trees in Main Street, patterned in spidery sepia against the skyline of housetops. Sniff the invisible fragrance of flowers that rose from the gardens of the comfortable residences. Could anything seem miserable when you could stand near the railway crossing and take in such a scene?

Hardly anyone walked on the Sea Wall during the hours of the white day. You could sit by yourself on a bench for hours. Even if anyone strayed along they would not know that you were wearing no panties, or that your brassiere was patched in five or six places so that it had hardly any shape. Nor would they bother to scrutinize your faded dress and wonder how long you had had it. To them you would be just another stray girl. Of no interest whatever.

That was why it came as such a surprise on this December day of pale sunshine and cloudy sky when the black young man in the livery of a chauffeur appeared beside her bench and halted. He touched his peaked cap and smiled. A rather handsome black chap, and his livery made him seem more handsome still. Smart. Yet, somehow, his eyes had a sly, untrustworthy glint, and his smile seemed ingratiating and toady. You noticed it all in one enveloping, intuitive flash.

He said in a soft, respectful voice: "Miss, I'm sorry to trouble you, but Mr. Knight asks you if you would see him, if you don't mind."

"Mr. Knight?"

"Yes, miss." He made a gesture with his hand toward the road. She looked and saw a long car parked near the bandstand – the bandstand where the Militia Band played every Saturday afternoon from five to six. A dark-blue car.

"But I don't understand," she said. "What does Mr. Knight want with me? Why should he come here to try to see me?"

"I think he has something to talk over wid you, miss."

She closed *Swan Song*. Soames had been fighting the fire in his picture gallery... The sea was far out. It trembled softly. There was hardly any wind. "But if he wanted to talk over something with me why did he have to come *here?* I don't live on the Sea Wall."

He said nothing. He plucked at the seam of his khaki breeches.

"Tell him I'm sorry. I have no desire to see him."

"Very well, Miss."

She listened to the tip-tip-tip of his footsteps on the stone stairs, then rose and began to walk leisurely in a westerly direction. Behind her she heard the hum of the dark-blue car. Receding.

It was not such a bad Christmas, considering everything. Gregory and Naomi took her to a dance. She wore the new evening dress which was Naomi's Christmas gift. It was good to look at herself in it – good and sad. And Milton's painting of a scene off St. Lucia, and a postal order, added to the sweetish-brackish cheer of things. She bought a new Bible for Charlotte, and Charlotte was bleakly happy. She only called upon Godma and her Saviour twice for the whole day.

Aubrey's gift was a five-dollar note tucked into the left side of a pair of shoes (she suspected conspiracy between him and Gregory and Naomi). When she was dancing on Christmas Eve night she did not have to worry about January the first. The budget for January was safe. She felt so easy in mind at the dance that whorls swam lightly through her head – dark-blue and purple ones like those she saw sometimes in the darkness of her shut eyes.

On Old Year's Night, at a party Aubrey and his wife took her to, she felt so dizzy and singing with carefree bliss that she let an unknown drunk young man kiss and fondle her in a dark part of the gallery.

8

The extra energy she spent on the Christmas festivities, especially on Old Year's Night at the party – where there was a lot of wild trucking and jitterbugging – and a drizzling she got on New Year's morning proved too much for her resistance. She contracted a cold. So the first few days of 1942 were not pleasant ones. They were spent chiefly in the easy chair in the sittingroom.

And the old men came. They tumbled about on the floor in grotesque somersaults, tugged at her toes, squeaked and grinned up at her so that she shivered and woke up, sneezing, to find that it was raining and a draught full of damp and earthy smells was blowing in upon her.

When she dozed off again she dreamt of Milton and Gregory arguing over her dead body... "See! Tell me! What was the purpose in this creature called Sylvia Russell having been born and having lived! Her life ended in a Grand Nought..."

"But think," said Gregory, "of the pleasure her existence gave to her friends and many other people who knew her. Isn't that an end achieved? Isn't that alone a purpose fulfilled?..."

She opened her eyes and saw the stars framed in the window, and though her head throbbed she thought of Milton and his constellations and the Greek myths. She felt relieved and consoled a little. In Milton's last letter he had told her he had left the schooner and signed on on a tanker in Trinidad. He had decided to chance the U-boats.

She took a deep breath, and tried to adjust her mind to the reality of the moment. She touched her stomach, looked up at the blackness where the rafters were. The air smelt fresh and filled with night dew, leafy and full of earth and flower scents... I'm really here, active in the darkness. I'm dying but Death hasn't touched me on the shoulder yet.

She watched the stars again. They looked so passive. Cool-blue and aloof. Like the earth and its waterish smells, and the leaves unmoving in the night. Like cabbage palms and breadfruit trees, the star-apple trees. Like long purple clouds at sunset. Silently intelligent. Always *silently.*

It was nearly February before her cold was better. February was Mr. Ralph's month. Or Mr. Jarrow's. For nobody had been prettily charitable. No five-dollar note had turned up yet discreetly concealed in a slab of chocolate, or in the one side of a pair of shoes. There had been no postal orders.

When she went to Mr. Ralph's office, one of the clerks told her that he was sorry but that she would not be able to see Mr. Ralph. He was busy preparing for a director's meeting. He would not be able to see anyone for the next week, at least. But next week was February. She could not risk waiting. She must see Mr. Jarrow.

Yes, Mr. Jarrow would see her in a few minutes. "Please have a seat," smiled the pleasant-mannered coloured young man.

The clock ticked indifferently on the other side of the room. An old-fashioned clock with a window at the bottom so that you could see the pendulum wagging, brassy-grey and relentless. The wall was green, and one or two knots in the boards looked like varnished spiders.

Typewriters clicked in the sacred hush.

Take a deep breath now. Here was the young man again.

"This way, Miss Russell. Mr. Jarrow will see you now."

Mr. Jarrow listened, nodding now and then. He pursed his lips and frowned, toyed with an ivory paperknife, the handle of which was shaped like a dignified eagle, its wings partly open for flight. Once or twice he said: "Mm". Once he said: "Tch, tch, tch!" very softly. She knew that the hard-luck tale was sinking home. It was working.

It was not until she got outside and opened the envelope that she knew the amount. A ten-dollar note. Full of creases but crispish, strong, so that she could crackle it... *Damus petimusque vicissim.* And the frigate. The coat of arms of the colony of British Guiana. The King's head. Yes, it was a genuine note.

She clutched it tight in her hand and tried to fight back the rivers. But the tower of the Museum building blurred in spite of her efforts. She blinked it clear again, strode firmly along the pavement, her chin well up. Fiercely up.

So everything was fine for February and March. All you had to do was shut your mind against the past and your pride. Forget the pendulum of the clock and the varnished spiders on the green wall. Forget the ivory paperknife. And forget the death in your spirit.

On the nineteenth of February everybody was talking about the report in the newspapers concerning the U-boat attack on two ships in the harbour of Port of Spain, Trinidad. How far off was Trinidad? Only three hundred and fifty miles. The U-boats had arrived in the Caribbean.

Your thoughts went to Benny and Milton. David you did not trouble about. David, you were convinced, had a cat's lives.

Aruba attacked by U-boats... A schooner attacked and sunk a few miles off Georgetown. The war had come to British Guiana, and you began to compare your own petty troubles with the wider troubles of the world.

The trees here were still green. The cabbage palms still had dignity, and the breadfruit trees splayed calm hands against the blue. Here you saw no up-sprouting plume of black smoke, no rubble, no people on stretchers. Your flat coastlands remained grey and green and yellow in the March sunshine, and the birds cheeped and twittered and dived at chickenhawks, the coconut palms sizzled in the trade wind, and it seemed hard to think of tanks and bombs when you smelt the flower-fragrances in Main Street and watched the stolid saman trees, when you listened to the ice-man's whistle or the kee-keeing of a kiskadee. But the newspapers and the B.B.C. announcer could not be wrong. It must be true about the bombs and the tanks and the Messerschmidts. And here it was you were worrying about a mere five-dollar note that wasn't there to give to your mother on the first of April. What did a five-dollar note and sardines for Sylvia Russell matter when you put them alongside the bombs and the Spitfires and the Eighth Army and Kharkov? What significance did they bear in relation to the rest of the world?

She quickened her pace along the pavement, and told herself to stop posing questions. She must be a realist. These cars that droned past in High Street were metal driven by engines. Only small children and poets conceived of them as monsters that rushed past with a whoom and a whoosh. Gasoline exploding in metal and driving pistons and cylinders...

Had this one run out of gas? Why was it slowing down?

"Good morning, Miss!"

Oh.

"What is it now?"

"Miss Russell, Mr. Knight ask if you could drop round at his office some time after one o'clock. A very important matter he have to discuss wid you, Miss. Somet'ing to do wid your father' estate, he say."

"But why did he have to send a message in this way?"

The discreet smile, the sly glint, the ingratiating blandness. "Miss, I was on my way to your house, but as I happen to see you walking here I say I will stop and give you de message."

"Very well. Thanks. There is no answer."

She moved along the pavement.

In Barrack Street, she decided against, but as she turned into Fort Street she decided she would go... "Somet'ing to do wid your father' estate."... One never knew. It might be his conscience, or it might be that something really had turned up.

Never would have thought, he said, that she could be so strong-willed. Well, well! Only the other day a mere tot wandering around in Water Street so that he had to rescue her and take her home – did she remember? – and now look what a stubborn young lady she had grown into!

She would be glad if he would take his hand off her knee. She objected to his putting his hand on her person.

But why such an attitude? My dear girl! My dear girl!... The Catarrhozone tube. First at one nostril, then at the other.

"I understand it was something to do with my father's estate you wanted to discuss with me, Mr. Knight." She rose, stiff, dignified.

He beckoned her to be seated again. "Sit down and compose yourself, Sylvia." He laughed softly. "It is something to do with the estate. You'll hear about it in a moment."

She sat down.

He indulged in more irrelevant commonplaces, then suddenly began to tell her about the mortgage. Yes, he was afraid that that was the position. The little place they were living in in Fort Street was mortgaged and the party concerned intended to foreclose if the amount was not met by the seventeenth of next month...

But she didn't understand. She had never dreamt that the Fort Street place was mortgaged, too. How could... she had to break off. The inkwell and the bookcases had gone hazy.

"I may mention, of course," she heard him saying, "that there's no need whatever for you to be alarmed. The matter can be arranged so easily. As I've often told you before, my girl, I'm an old friend of your father's. It's natural I'd have your welfare at heart. Come, come, don't be upset!"

His hand reached out toward her knee, arrested itself in midair and returned to his stomach, rejoining the other in a light clasp.

"It's a good thing to be patient, Sylvia, and I think I've shown a great deal of patience. It's months and months I've been containing myself and waiting for you to see reason. I mean, I simply can't understand your attitude. I'd really credited you with more intelligence. You know what position I hold in this community." He was toying with the Catarrhozone tube, his gaze on the blotter. She knew that he was nervous, diffident, despite his attempt to appear worldly and nonchalant. In this moment she could see through him as though he were a piece of cheap bottle-glass.

"With all modesty, I think I may claim to be unassailable. There aren't many people who have succeeded in getting the better of me. I simply mention it by the way, of course. Don't imagine I'm trying to intimidate you. This is a hard world, Sylvia. Everybody likes to strike a bargain. I'm only human – and you're a very attractive young lady. I've always had a weak spot for you – ever since you were a little thing."

He put down the tube and changed his position in the chair. He looked up at the ceiling and rubbed his cheek. "I do think it would be wise to consider my proposition, don't you?"

She said nothing. Let the burden of speaking be upon him. Let him writhe in his diffidence.

"I could settle this question of the mortgage without a thought if you would only be sensible. How are you going to exist if the cottage is taken away from you? I understand your mother has been ill for some time – bedridden. Surely you don't want to see her put out on the street. And think of yourself. I'm certain you can't be very happy where you are now. You see, it isn't my fault that this mortgage exists. I'm afraid Grantley gambled far more than was wise –"

He broke off at her laugh, then, after fidgeting, went on: "Oh, I don't mean the bridge we used to have at the old place in High Street with Robby van Huisten and Bertie Dowden – and Jack Ralph and Archie Jarrow. We hardly ever played for more than sixpence a hundred at bridge. Oh, no. I'm thinking of the Club. Grantley didn't play bridge at the Club. It was poker – and I can assure you, many nights his losses went into several hundreds. Both Robby and I used to warn him to go easy. One night he nearly knocked down Jack Ralph because Jack attempted to get him away from the Club. There's much that occurred that you never heard of, Sylvia. But let's not go into that." The Catarrhozone tube. First at one nostril... That's a closed chapter. Your father might have had his faults but he was a fine chap. A fine chap."

She listened to Georgetown. All the old sounds that had impregnated her deep, deep self. The honk and drone of traffic, the trees in the trade wind, dogs barking, creole voices broad and drawling, poultry cluckings. At this very instant she could hear a cock crowing...

She scraped her foot along the floor.

The click-click of a typewriter sounded in the office next door. Another solicitor's office. No, it was a barrister's. Mr. David Ramsanny, LL.B. An East Indian.

She rose and murmured that she would think it over. Would let him know before the seventeenth of next month.

9

Once, on their way to cinema, Sylvia began to whistle "A Pretty Girl is Like a Melody", and Gregory glanced at her and asked her what was it she found in that out-of-date tune. She made no reply. Only tilted her head roguishly and went on whistling.

"It's a nice song," said Naomi. "I like it myself."

"You would. Damned lowbrow," said Gregory.

Sylvia stopped whistling. A car went past with a whoom… There was the smell of blossoms in the wind. Jasmines. Or stephanotis. Or honeysuckle. After they had walked a little way, Gregory grunted and asked Sylvia why the sudden silence. Had Mr. Irving Berlin failed her?

She laughed. "Nothing. I'm thinking. You know me. Always thinking."

"Always." He gave her a playful nudge in the ribs that made her giggle. In a moment she would begin to whistle again.

She generally confided everything in Naomi and Gregory, but she had not been able to tell them about Mr. Knight and the mortgage crisis, about how she had been thinking things over: the cottage in Queenstown and Mr. Knight and herself in bed. She had told it to Milton in her letter to him yesterday. The written word could thunder within the silence of oneself. The trees could not hear it, nor the kiskadees, nor the watching angles of the house tops. But furniture would listen to the spoken word. The window panes might rattle in ghostly portent, the sapodilla trees might shiver to their roots. And who knew if the traffic noises would not fade into a waiting silence?… "I'm weighing the matter, Naomi. Greg, I'm trying to make up my mind whether to walk out into the waves or lie on my back and listen to Mr. Knight panting over my naked body in that little cottage in Queenstown." The sound-vibrations, if she had said that aloud, would have broken windows. Caused the kiskadees to stutter. Interrupted the local broadcasts.

Tonight, Wednesday the twenty-eighth of March. How many more times would she see the sun rise before the seventeenth of April. How many times would she tilt her head and whistle or hum a tune?... "A Pretty Girl..." "Balalaika..." Would she be able to breathe music on the night of the seventeenth of April?...

"Daisy! Daisy! Give me your answer, do!

"I'm half-crazy, all for the love of you..."

The days at Miss Jenkins'...

The show did her a lot of good. She was talkative and giggly on the way to Fort Street. Naomi and. Gregory always saw her home after taking her to a show. A warmth had invaded her inside, and the frozen gloom had thawed. It had been a pleasant respite. These two people were really good friends. She loved them with a deep, deep love. Naomi and Gregory.

The Smell smote her at the front door. She was well inured to it nowadays, however. She generally undressed in the dark, but this night her mood was such that she decided she would like to see herself in the mirror. Stand before the dressing-table and gaze at herself naked. As in the Strand Hotel in 1935. As on many other occasions in the High Street place. Milton had mentioned some word in relation to this weakness of hers. A Greek myth was attached to it... Ah! Narcissism. That was the word.

Charlotte would probably wake up and moan. Let her!

Why have I got to be considerate of her every time? Why can't I indulge my whims now and then? Heavens! Life is tough, tough, tough. If I can't even indulge a whim... No, please. No hysteria. Calm, Sylvia! Calm!

Her head felt a little light. It usually did, nowadays. When you ate light meals your head felt light. She laughed softly.

She stood before the dressing-table mirror and watched herself naked in the lamplight. Turned this way and that. The bed creaked. The Smell made invisible coils and tentacles... Not so bad, you know, despite starvation. I'm not really thin. Only people who have known me for years can tell I've reduced. She cupped her breasts. They were still upright. Still jutted far out. Oh, I'm attractive. I know I'm attractive.

A car tooted distantly.

Mr. Knight... Did he have hair on his paunch? Oh, heavens! Oh, *heavens!*... Please, Sylvia. Calm!

The bed creaked again. The snores came uneven. Rasped and stopped.

A fat paunch rubbing slowly...

"Eh-eh! Sylvie, dat you, child?"

"The unique one, Mother. The only Sylvia Anne Russell."

"What you doing dere? Eh-eh! You mean you naked?"

"Admiring my fruity body by lamplight." She did a jig. Charlotte sighed. Turned over so that her face was away from the light. She moaned and said: "Somebody been here to you when you was out."

"To me? Who was that?"

"Some young man. He knock on de front door, and Ah call out and ask him what he want. Ah tell him you not at home, and he go away."

"But who could he have been?"

Charlotte sighed again. "Ow, God! Dis pore sick body. He say he come off some ship, child. I ain' know who he is."

"A ship?"

"Yes. Some Navy ship he say he come off. Ow, Saviour! Dis head! Day and night, day and night!"

"Mother, what do you mean? What ship? Didn't he tell you anything else? Didn't he say who he was?"

"De door was lock, ent you know dat? He could only talk to me from outside. He say he off some Navy ship and de ship going away in de morning, dat's why he come to see you."

"Mother, you don't mean it was Benny who came and – and – Mother, what else did he say? Did he – you didn't hear where he said he was going when he left here? Didn't he leave a message for me?"

"No, he ain' leave no message. Ow, child! If you know how me head hurting! Ow, loving Saviour! When you calling me home, Jesus?"

"Mother, didn't he tell you his name? Try and remember. He must have left a message for me, I'm sure. He – he must have."

"Ow, Sylvie! Ow! You ain' got no consideration for you' pore mudder! I'm a sick woman, child. Put out de light –"

"Did he say his name was Copps? Milton Copps? Or Riego?"

"Yes, Ah t'ink dat was de name he call. It was a Puttagee name. Ow, child! Leff me in peace and put out de light. Me whole body suffering wid pain. Ow, Godma! Ow, loving Saviour! Call me home, Jesus! Tek me to your dear bosom, heavenly Fadder..."

Sylvia dressed. Her hands were so shaky she nearly tore the dress in hauling it on. She blew out the lamp and hurried out the house. After locking the door, she tucked the key under the ragged door mat so that Janie and Sarah would find it when they came home.

She wondered what time it could be. Long after eleven. And he was sailing in the morning. At five? At six? At seven? Trees, tell me something. Where is he? Must I 'phone his home? Whose telephone must I use? I have no money to speak from a public call-box. Tell me what to do. I'm desperate. Fate, why did you have to do this to me? Me of all people, Fate. Why couldn't you have remembered my many past hells and given me this *one* consolation? I could have died after and not minded. Oh, but I must see him before morning comes. I'm going to will it. I'm going to pull him to me by hypnotism. I *must* see him!

The Brown Jumbie-men: "Hysteria will get you nowhere. Remember the calories and the vitamins. If you go rushing through the streets you'll feel faint in a few minutes. Your resistance is dangerously low. You have no energy to waste. Walk at a leisurely pace and don't be a fool."

"You're right. I mustn't get panicky. I must control myself. But it's hard. Oh, it's hard. I'm human, you know."

"We know you're human. But you can't evade facts. Facts are cruel. Life is cruel. Life is purposeless. There is no goal."

"Oh, stop that! Life *isn't* purposeless. And there *is* a goal. Benny. He's my goal – and I don't care about any other!"

She hurried. Walked fast, trotted, walked fast. Gasped. Listened to the dup-dup-dup of her heart. A skeleton did a dark-blue dance in her singing stomach. Bones waving and kicking up and bending in dark-blue twilight.

"Let this be the end of me. I must find him. I'll go home to where he lives. His people will tell me if he's at home. Or perhaps he's at..."

Her muttering trailed off into silence. She came to a halt.

These seamen often went spreeing at the Viceroy Hotel. He might have gone there with some of his friends – his Canadian friends off the corvette. It must be the U-boat activity in the waters around here that had caused the corvette to call at this port.

She could watch her deliberations making blue-black snakes about her. Green now... She was going to faint... No! Please! No fainting!

She jerked her head. Fought the darkness that tried to envelop her. The skeleton danced. Her will sent out orange feelers. The snakes retreated. Blue. Pale blue. Now they were gone. She had won.

She would have to go to the Viceroy. She might run into Janie and Sarah there, but it could not be helped. Let them think what they liked. Let them say whatever they wanted to say about her. To the Viceroy!

She moved on – uncertainly, testing her feet, listening to her heart. She could do it. It was the will that counted.

...The railway crossing. The old, friendly samans... Her mind began to mutter again within its swirling gloom. How many dramas have you seen, samans, in all the years you've stood here? I wonder how many loves have melted under your silent, warped limbs. The grass borders of Main Street must be piled with ghosts of dead aches and the agonies of wretched lovers... It's the emptiness in my stomach. It's making me think in poetry... She giggled.

The *Chronicle* office... Booker's Drug Store... The Public Free Library... The Hotel Tower... You've watched me so often, you Main Street buildings. It's Sylvia Russell again. She's got away from home. But she's not six years old. Tonight she's a full-grown young lady, and it's not the Stabroek Market she's going to. She's not looking for Naomi Herreira. Tonight it's her beloved she's in search of – and she's going to the Viceroy Hotel where all the best-known whores gather nightly with seamen and other revellers to drink, dance and go to bed. That's how Daddy once described the Viceroy to me. Daddy was a grand fellow for irony...

"Oh, Daddy! I want a brand new car..."

There it was. Hear the tinkle and thump of the orchestra. Sylvia, the Viceroy!... Oh, Daddy!...

She could see the figures on the veranda – seated around tables drinking. As on any other night. Thump-thump and tinkle went the band.

Up the brightly lit stairway. But not too quickly. Remember the skeleton. Remember the blue-black snakes. There must be no passing out.

Two East Indian girls, flashily made up, were on the top step giggling and talking to a young man, but he was not a seaman. He was a well-dressed coloured middle-class young man of about twenty-five. To her surprise, neither the two girls nor the young man paid any attention to her as she brushed past them and stood irresolute in the corridor. Surely they must recognize that she was *different*!

Somebody jostled past her and headed for the dance-hall. The smell of rum and beer swirled around her, and the jabber of voices and laughter streamed out of a room not far off down the corridor. That must be the bar. She had better go that way first. If he was not in there she could try the dance-hall. Or the veranda.

The noise hit her like a solid hand as she got to the doorway. She looked in and saw two Portuguese young men and a black young man playing billiards at a large table. The black young man was chalking his cue in preparation for another stroke. He bent over, played. Click-click! Red darted for the cushion, white slammed into the pocket.

At the bar-counter girls and men lounged drinking and laughing. Tall glasses of stout and ale stood before them, though one or two drank off small glasses of whisky or rum. A fat girl was laughing riotously. She had bad teeth – black, short stumps. Another girl, Portuguese, reminded her of Teresa Feria, only she was taller. She showed gold teeth when she smiled. A white seaman in uniform was chatting with a short black man with a green felt hat and a white bow-tie. Both of them looked grave as though they might be discussing the death of a close relative. This could have been a night in 1920, so much did the scene coincide with the description her father had given her of the Saturday night of that spree in 1920 when he had bought the sweepstake ticket.

The billiard players were shouting applause at a successful stroke. She did not see who had brought it off. She left the room and hurried back along the corridor, for there was no sign of Benson in the bar. On her way, a slim, oldish man tried to stop her, but she hurried on. She saw a shaft of light coming from an open doorway. The music sounded in that direction, so she went toward the doorway and looked in. It was the dance-hall. Only three couples were dancing. She had expected to see a crowded floor. The eyes of two coloured girls seated near the farther wall became fixed on her in curiosity. Her gaze flashed past them toward the veranda. Seamen and one or two fairish girls – there was a black one, too – sat at the tables she had seen from the street. There was no sign of Benson. Nor of any Canadian naval men.

It came upon her that she had come in vain. She had made a fool of herself. Had used up valuable energy to no purpose. Her head began to feel light again. The snakes threatened her. She clenched her hands. There must be no fainting. She must not relax. She felt a clammy sweat breaking out on her arms and neck. A voice murmured: "Dance this one with me?"

She staggered round. "Eh? No! No, I'm sorry."

He was a half-Chinese-looking chap, and seemed well bred. She turned and half-ran along the corridor, down the stairs. She took the steps two at a time. The singing in her stomach rose to a ghastly crescendo. The skeleton clacked in jagged lunacy. She found herself on the pavement panting. Her heart prattled in her throat. She was certain that this time she would pass out. The scene around her swayed and reached out lassoes. But she steadied it. She evaded the lassoes. She felt dismayed at the strength of her will.

When she moved off along the street she discovered that it was drizzling. A wave of despair rushed through her. This is too much. Too much, Fate!

She set out aimlessly along the street. She seemed to drift rather than walk. Her bones felt hollow. Bird bones. At any instant she expected to rise and sail over the house tops. When she was going round a corner she heard the Stabroek Market clock striking midnight. She counted the strokes... Clang! Clang!... They came at her like purple blobs of water.

She was in High Street now. Which way should she go? His people lived a good way off – in Brickdam, the street where the houses were white and lovely and set amid pleasant gardens. But suppose she went there in vain, too. In any case, I haven't the energy to walk so far. I'm hungry. I must go home. I'm defeated.

She leaned against the iron rail of a bridge. The headlights of a car dazzled her in a brassy sheet of brilliance. She began to walk north. Slowly. She felt the sweat on her skin – clammy, unhealthy. Not the kind of sweat she used to ooze after hockey in the old days. What old days? She gave her head a shake. Had there really been a time in the past when she was comfortable and well fed? It seemed incredible that it could have been so. She had to think hard to convince herself that the past had actually happened.

At the railway crossing she thought she would have to collapse. She stooped down, her head drumming, nausea in her troubled stomach. She retched but nothing came up. She rose and moved on. Through space and time. Milton had once told her about Einstein. Could Einstein, she wondered, have told her what was the space-time coefficient involved in walking from the railway crossing to Fort Street?... She moved on. After ten years she came to Barrack Street... Then Fort Street. She had arrived.

And Benny rose from the lowest step and came to the gate to meet her – a tall sailor in a dark-blue uniform that matched the darkness so that his face and hands seemed jumbie objects floating toward her.

10

He had come at about eight o'clock, he explained, and her mother had called out and told him that she was out, so he had guessed that she must have gone to the cinema with Naomi, for in her letters she had told him how Naomi and Gregory often took her. He had gone away and decided to come back at eleven, but he dropped in at the Cuyuni Bar with two of his pals – a petty-officer and a leading-seaman – and he had not been able to leave them until a few minutes after eleven. When he got here he had found the place still in darkness and had thought she must be asleep, but he had still knocked. Her mother had called out and asked him who it was, and when he told her Riego she had replied that Sylvia had gone out again. He did a few deductions like a detective. He guessed that she must have gone to search for him, so he decided to stay right here and wait. They were sitting on the lowest step while he made these explanations. Suddenly he looked at her and said: "Sylvia, you look thin."

"Didn't I tell you in my letters how thin I was getting?"

"Yes, but I didn't think it was so bad. Hell!" The Navy had given him a few imprecations – "Hell" and "Jesus". And a moment ago she had caught him trying to smother back a "shit". He was still the big, gauche boy, though. His breath smelt of whisky but he was not drunk. If anything, he seemed shyish and not perfectly at ease. He had not even tried to kiss her yet.

She said abruptly: "Benny, I'm hungry. Could we eat somewhere?"

"Hungry? Didn't you have dinner?"

"Yes, of course." She tried not to sound exasperated. "But it – it wasn't much of a meal. And I'm a bit exhausted after searching around for you."

"Sure. I get you." He scratched his cheek irresolutely. "But the restaurants are closed up now. It's after midnight."

The drizzle had stopped, but now it began again. A very fine drizzle like some icy powder being dusted down upon them.

"It's drizzling again," he muttered. He got up slowly, but she sat on, too weary to move.

"Benny, couldn't you take me to your home? We could sit in the gallery and talk in the darkness without disturbing anybody. By the way, you've been home to see your people already, haven't you?"

"Yes, I spent about three hours at home. Our boat arrived since three o'clock, but I couldn't get shore liberty until five. I spent from five to about eight at home. You want me to take you home, you say?" He hesitated, then went on: "Sure, if you like. Yes, let's go. I'll get a taxi. It's too far to walk."

"What time are you sailing in the morning?"

"Well, I'm not supposed to say. Strict orders." He gave an uncomfortable laugh, lowered his voice and told her: "Say, don't whisper it to a soul, for Jesus' sake. We're after U-boats. We're sailing at half past seven, but we're only going to cruise around the coast for a while. After that we'll go on either to Port of Spain or Curaçao. Look, you wait here a bit and I'll run go get a taxi."

"But, Benny!"

"Yes?"

She looked at him poised there at the gate, and wanted to ask him if he was not going to kiss her, but a sudden reserve chilled her impulsiveness. She said: "Never mind. Go and get the taxi. I'll tell you later."

"I won't be long," he said, and hurried off.

He was not absent more than fifteen minutes, but it gave her time to make a few spiritual adjustments. She had come home after her rampage to the Viceroy Hotel fully resigned to not seeing him, and the sight of him here had shocked awake a new confidence in the scheme of living. The cheated feeling, the bitterness and frustration, had abruptly been neutralized. She had forgiven Fate for a dirty trick. But now she wondered... It was useless to tell herself she felt exactly the same about him as she had done a year or two ago, before he had sailed. She knew that she had outgrown him. He had not developed, except superficially, whereas she had climbed far ahead of what she had been two years ago. From his letters she had already gained this impression, and now that she had met him again in the flesh she knew just how he stood in relation to her. She knew that he attracted her only physically. Her body responded to him – but her spirit regarded him with a sneer.

She took a quick breath. She must not do this. Let her not analyse the matter too minutely. If her reason put the final veto on her love for him her illusions would melt. The process of death in her would be accelerated. She must guard her illusions fiercely tonight. She must let tonight be the one bright patch in the dreary panorama. There might never be another.

When they got into the taxi she found herself wanting him with a pain that came from deep in her stomach, while her heart beat with a cool, tender pity. The illusion must depend upon pity, she told herself. She must remember that. And she must remember not to think upon it too much. This night was too precious to be annulled at a mere gesture of her reason. She had been pushed into too sweltering a corner to dismiss enchantments like this. On the seventeenth of April it might be Mr. Knight's paunch – or the muddy waves.

"Benny, you haven't kissed me yet."

"Eh? Oh! Well, everything's got my head in such a whirl I just don't know what I've done and what I haven't."

So he kissed her – with intensity but still with the awkwardness of two years ago. Later, when they were in the darkness of the gallery of his home – a white two-storeyed Brickdam place – she asked him what he had been doing in other ports. "Didn't you have a woman now and then?"

The question astounded him, she could see, though he did his best not to show it. He reacted like any orthodox middle-class young man. He gave a muffled snigger and told her: "I didn't like to go messing around. The other chaps used to try to get me to go into these bad spots, but I always steered clear."

She knew he was lying – trying to build up a tower of virtue to impress her, unaware that a tower of virtue would only evoke her contempt. She wanted him at admit that he had indulged. It would have increased her respect for him as a man if he had confessed to one or two orgies.

During the uncomfortable silence that followed she looked round slowly and noted the outlines of the furniture in the gallery. The street lamps threw a vague radiance over everything, in the sittingroom as well as in the gallery. The floor was not polished as a good floor should have been in a well-kept dwelling. And she could smell a certain second-rate shoddiness about the place. The furniture was not uniform. Here and there an old-fashioned table or chair loomed amid modern pieces, and the walls seemed overcrowded with pictures. She could tell, even from this dim midnight impression of his home, that his family had not yet arrived socially. If anything, however, this awareness of ordinary, though monied, people produced a sympathy and peace inside her. She did not feel out of place sitting with him on this Chesterfield. She could imagine this place as the High Street house which had fallen on bad times. This was what the High Street place might have come to had they not lost it.

"You don't believe me, eh?" He took her hand and squeezed it.

"No, I don't, Benny. You're a man, aren't you?"

"Well, the truth is," he mumbled, "I don't say I didn't indulge a bit, but, after all, I had to think of you. I mean –"

"Look, you mustn't think I'm trying to seem superior. I'm not. But I do like to get at the truth of things. I've reached a stage in my life where I detest hypocrisy. We mustn't pretend, Benny. We must face ourselves as we are. What's there to hide in sex indulgence? Why should you be ashamed if you had one or two women? Or why should you imagine it as a disloyalty to me?"

"Yeah, I know you're broadminded. Well, I did go once or twice to women in Halifax, and once in Montreal. I didn't want to mention it..." He broke off in utter confusion.

She squeezed his hand. "I understand. I don't mind. I like to know you've done things like that. I wouldn't think much of you as a man if you hadn't. Don't look so depressed." In an uncontrollable spasm of desire she rubbed herself against him. He responded at once by holding her and kissing her. Her head began to go empty and dizzy from the excess of emotion, and the dull fact that she was hungry slammed itself through her consciousness. She withdrew and said: "We forgot what I asked you before we came here. Haven't you got anything I can eat? I'm hungry."

"I forgot. I can get you something from the pantry. What would you like?"

"Whatever you have. I don't care. I'd eat anything. I feel a little faint or I wouldn't bother you."

He took her into the pantry, and they ate biscuits – Wieting & Richter's soda crackers with guava jelly and butter. The pantry smelt of sour fruits and lard, but that did not matter. The big refrigerator with its automatic light that came on as soon as you opened the door and the cool air that rushed out from amongst the eatables was all that had any solid significance for her. And he made her feel not too great a glutton by saying as he crunched the biscuits in his mouth: "Good thing you mentioned eating. Only now I realize I myself was hungry, kid."

"You're quite a Canadian in the way you speak. Or is it American?"

"What! You really think I've changed in my speech?"

"Well, it's only natural, I suppose. You've been mixing with Canadians and only Canadians for the past two years. No, that's enough butter. If you pile it on so thickly your sisters and brothers won't have any tomorrow." As she took the biscuit from him the sight and smell of the butter made her head whirl. Lord! When last had she eaten of butter so lavishly! When last had she eaten *fresh* butter at all!

She sipped the large tumbler of cocoa-malt slowly – not in large gulps as he did his. He lost his shyness to such an extent that he laughed and said: "Shit! You're drinking it like a goddammed mouse!" He did not even seem aware that he had uttered a "shit", for he emptied his own glass and nodded and said: "Good stuff, this."

When they returned to the gallery she felt heavy in the middle; as though there were a lump of metal inside her. It was an uncomfortable feeling. She had gorged, and her stomach was not accustomed to such burdens. She sidled up against him and tried to forget the discomfort.

"Tell me about yourself, Benny. Let's talk about you – just you and your adventures. Have you sunk any U-boats yet?"

"Sure! We got two of them – one off Bermuda and one off Tobago." He went off into an enthusiastic account of the corvette's adventures. But she had to interrupt him. "Excuse me," she said, and got up and rushed to the window – one of the two he had opened when they had first come in.

Most of it came up. She hoped not all. Valuable calories and vitamins to go to waste like this!

She discovered that he was holding her forehead. She took a deep breath and tried not to moan. She straightened up and rested her hand on the window sill. She felt much better of a sudden, though light-headed, shaky. He held out a big white handkerchief, and as she wiped her mouth she smelt tar and tobacco. A fear of returning nausea curved greyly down her throat, but she held herself tense and the fear passed. The nausea did not come back.

"I gorged too much," she said, and gave a husky chuckle. She felt better and better – empty in her stomach but relieved and trembling and wanly soothed. She handed back the handkerchief, and in the pale light from the street she noticed the red anchor on his dark-blue sleeve. A shiver of desire went through her. It was so urgent that she had to ask him to kiss her. She pressed herself against him.

The strength of him and the thick uniform-cloth rubbing against the femaleness of her awoke a passion of which she had not thought herself capable. Her knees felt wobbly, and the aching infinity that saturated her being projected itself in cool streams down into the dark, untouched places of her spirit.

When they went back to the Chesterfield she told herself that the moment had come. Nothing could stop it now – not even his shyness. For they were both ripe and warmed for it. Lightning sparked in the touch of flesh, in the rustle of clothes, even in the humidity of breath. The feel of his hand with its leathery palm was good as it slipped down past her throat and closed over one breast – briefly at first, then more voluptuously and confidently. She remembered the Sea Wall nights two years ago. This was what she had wanted him to do then, but he had disappointed her. Anyway, that was then. What mattered was now. A few more gasps – lips again – and it would happen. The fumbling with clothes and the stab of fearful, blissful anticipation. How often hadn't her imagination conjured up this event! Sometimes it would be a Simmons bed. Sometimes under a tree on a dry-weather night. Or the cabin of a ship. A large, soft rug in a sittingroom that smelt of jasmines. A divan with purple silk coverings and beside it a brazier of incense – this when she had fancied herself the wife of a Pharaoh.

Yes, the moment was here. Far inside, she heard herself trying to recall the words of the *Nunc Dimittis.* She had read it once or twice in a prayer book at Aubrey's. Aubrey's wife went to church... *Lord, now lettest thou thy servant depart in peace...* and something about mine eyes and salvation. They were good words. Lovely words. She could watch them in blebs juggling themselves in the purple gloom of her fancy. They were the right words for her now. After this had happened she could depart in peace. She would have seen salvation.

The exploring hand suddenly retreated. She heard him mumble something in an unsteady voice. She rubbed her cheek against his shoulder. In a moment the hand would return. She could feel him trembling. She was trembling, too. In a short while – mere minutes – it would happen, and the final dream would have been realized. *Lord, now lettest…*

"Sylvia – say, let's go for a walk. How about it?"

"A walk? Why?"

"I can't – we mustn't…"

"But we're here now, Benny. There's nothing to worry about."

"Yes, I know, but…"

"You have to go in the morning. I don't mind what you do to me now. And I want it. Really. I want it."

"I – but we aren't married yet. I couldn't – it wouldn't be right. I'd feel like a hell of a beast." He rose.

"But I don't – what do you…?"

She could go no further. The old men had come. They somersaulted on the floor. They squeaked and tugged at her toes. A limp weakness began to invade her limbs. She could hear a bell tolling in her fancy. The knell. Even on the very brink – defeat. The biggest defeat of all. The bitterest.

"You understand, Sylvia, don't you?"

She wanted to say: "Only too well," but she had to be kind. She murmured: "Yes, of course."

"You've always been the one girl I've honestly respected, and – well, you can see what I'm getting at. I couldn't do a thing like this to you. I couldn't let it happen between us now –"

"I understand, I understand, Benny! Don't say any more. Look, what's the time? It must be late."

He pushed back his sleeve and held his wrist to the street light.

"Twenty past two! I didn't dream it was so late." He paced off, and she saw his hands open and shut. He turned and came back. Gripped her arm. "You don't know how much I want you, Sylvia. I'd do anything – oh, hell!"

He released her arm. He was trembling again. "I'd better take you home," he said. "You'd like something more to eat? You brought up everything."

"No, no, don't worry. My tummy feels queerish. I don't think I could keep anything down." She asked him to sit, and he obeyed, and gave her a nervous look. He seemed very upset and awkward.

She stared at the furniture. She felt relaxed, but knew it to be an unhealthy feeling. It was not simply a physical lassitude. This lassitude had infected the silence of her inner quiet self.

A slow bourdon of monologue moved round and round inside her... No possible means of retrieve? Suppose she took his hand and put it down her bosom. Suppose she explained, tried to make him see, the urgency, the subtleties of the situation. Suppose she told him about Mr. Knight and the seventeenth of next month. The mortgage. Suppose she begged him, told him that it was the one thing that would compensate for the misery she had been suffering these past months. Suppose she washed him away with sentiment, roused him beyond reason so that he would be helpless to refuse... But that would be an "excruciating length". Her pride... But suppose... No, stop. It was futile to go on supposing like this. The knell had sounded already.

He was biting his thumb.

She must write and tell Milton of this night. Describe it to him in detail. It would be a consolation doing that. The sublimation of the written word. And she must do it before dawn. Milton would understand fully. He had suffered himself. At times she wondered whether she could be... No, she was not in love with Milton, but she could have lain under a saman tree, say at eleven o'clock on a moonless night, and let him point out constellations and talk about the Greek myths and about music and psychology and vitamins and then break off in his startling way and make love to her. Overwhelm her in a rush of vitality, fondle her, kiss her and give her the climaxing bliss that she was not to get tonight.

She could hear the drip of rain.

He was still biting his thumb. He looked solemn and browned with wonder and perplexity. It was not his fault that he had a stilted middle-class outlook, not his fault that he looked upon the sexual act with dread and exaggerated awe. It was all part of the paradox of the civilized world in which supposedly enlightened people upheld the taboos of the savage.

"It's raining," he said.

"Yes."

A car went past.

"Benny, I think I'd better go now." She rose.

He rose, too. "I'll 'phone for a taxi."

"Good."

He looked at her. "Sylvia, what's wrong? You don't seem – I don't understand you, somehow. I feel..."

She touched his sleeve. "Don't worry. I'm not easy to understand."

"But you can see what I mean. I don't want anything to happen between us now. I'm only here for this one night, and we're not married. Suppose you went and started to get a child – look at the trouble for you. And you're not in good circumstances –"

"Don't say any more! Please!"

She moved over to the window and put out her hand. "I think I'll walk. Don't bother with a taxi. I prefer to walk."

"All the way to Fort Street! And your dress is so thin. You'll take cold, Sylvia. Why don't you want me to get a taxi?"

She squeezed his arm. "Look on it as a whim." She tried to laugh. "I feel like walking. Let's say good-bye now and I'll go."

"Well, let me see you home. I'll go with you."

"No, please! Please! I want to go alone."

He stared at her, then shrugged. "O.K. If you want it like that."

When he kissed her she responded. It was hypocrisy to respond, she knew, but she could not go away with the knowledge that she had hurt his feelings.

She hardly felt her feet on the stairs as she went down. Her body seemed weightless. The rain made her shiver. She had the feeling as though it were drizzling through her. Through her flesh and bones.

FINALE WITH CYMBALS AND LOW DRUMS

One – clang! And two – clang! The world whirling – clang!

Three o'clock and all not well. Three o'clock with rain. The sackies and kiskadees were silent amid the leaves. The leaves dripped dismally in the dark. What a shame to disturb your good friends at three o'clock on a rainy morning! But they would understand, because they were your very good friends. The knell, you would tell them, had sounded. Clang! Did they hear it? They would excuse you.

Dup, dup dup! She knocked thrice. Solemnly. That was how a knell should sound. The dull thud of a hammer on a coffin lid. And I'm tired. Tired after a long walk from Brickdam. After a long journey from babyhood. Twenty-one panting years. I have a right to knock slowly. Deliberately. Virgin Sylvia. Dup, dup, dup!

Clang! The knell. I can hear that clock striking still. It will never stop striking... I can hear somebody stirring. A murmuring. I wonder if I've disturbed them in a love clinch. Virgin Sylvia. Hee, hee! No, no! No giggling. Calm, Sylvia. No hysteria.

A footstep in the gallery.

"Who's that?" Gregory's voice through the jalousies.

"Me, Greg."

"Sylvia?"

"Yes, me. Sylvia."

The light went on in the gallery. The key squeaked in the lock. The door opened, and she saw him in his purple-and-brown rayon dressing-gown, his hair tousled. Naomi must have tousled it in bed while they were making love. Virgin Sylvia. Hee, hee! No, no! Calm. There was enough hysteria in the dark behind me, and there may be more in the dark before me.

"Good God Sylvia! What on earth! You're soaking wet! Come in out of the rain."

As she entered she saw Naomi. Naomi appeared from the tiny sittingroom, in pyjamas – pink pyjamas – one long black plait of hair dangling in front. Like a bell-rope. Clang!

"But, child! Oh, my Lord! At this time of night! What brought you here?"

"The knell. I've heard it." She giggled. Stood on the mat, water dripping from her person in a steady trickle.

"You must take off your wet things right away."

"Wet things? Oh, you mean the rain. I walked all the way from Brickdam."

"Brickdam? What were you doing there?"

"That's where I first heard the knell. I'm still hearing it. I'll tell you about it, but I want to write Milton. I've got to tell him first, then I'll tell you. Have you got paper and a pen to lend me?"

"But you'll take cold. Come into the bedroom and get your things off. I'll lend you a dressing-gown until we get them dried off."

"Yes, I'd better do that. I'm shivering. It's gone three o'clock. What clock is that I heard when I was coming up the stairs? Did you hear it striking, or were you asleep?"

"Child, I can see you're not yourself. Come in. Come in and change."

She accompanied Naomi into the bedroom and began to haul off her dress – then paused. "Naomi, I can't undress. I'm – I want to write Milton. It's urgent. Have you a stamp?"

"Yes, I have stamps. But that can wait, man. You must undress first. You'll catch your death of cold."

"My death of cold?" She giggled. "It's too late. I've heard it already."

"Heard what?"

"My death knell. My… oh, I'm talking too much. I didn't mean to tell you… I don't know what I'm saying."

"Sylvia, you're feverish. Don't be silly, man. Undress quickly. Greg is mixing you a hot drink."

But, Naomi, I'm – I can't undress here. My brassiere is patched, and I – oh, I'll be ashamed to undress. Don't force me."

"You're behaving as if I'm a stranger. You think I don't know anything about poverty, Sylvia?"

"Naomi, just give me writing-paper and a pen. I must get that letter to Milton written before – before I go. I've got to tell him what happened this evening after I left you and Greg. Benny came back."

"Benny? He's back? All right, I'll give you paper, but undress first. I'll go out of the room if you like. Here's the dressing-gown. Hurry up before you take a worse chill."

So after Naomi had left the room she undressed, shivering and hearing the clash of metal upon metal. At solemn intervals it came. Clang! The cracking of the final illusion. The tap on the shoulder. She started.

I could have sworn I did feel a tap on my shoulder. Naomi must be right. I'm feverish.

She put on the dressing-gown, and moaned in delight at the feel of the silky material against her bare skin. Luxurious. I could have had one like this a long time ago. If… if… but that paunch. And the Catarrhozone tube. Never! Never! Now careful. Calm. No hysteria.

She went into the sittingroom. Gregory was just coming in from the dining-room with a glass of yellowish liquid. "Drink this, Sylvia. Come on. Right down the hatch!"

"You have paper, Greg? I want paper and a pen."

"At this time of the morning? What's it you want to write now? Come on. Drink this quick."

She drank it. An egg-flip with rum. She drank it in gulps, and heard it gurgling and rumbling in her stomach. Was it a rumble or a ringing?… Clang! Let the knell ring out. I don't care. This hot milk and egg feels nice in my stomach. And the sting of the rum. It arrested the shiver she had seen coming like a scarf of rain from the gallery.

Naomi came in from the dining-room, and said: "Sylvia, come and eat something."

"No, no, I can't eat. I've got to write a letter. To Milton. Haven't I told you?" A sense of panic stuttered through her. Like a shaking cloud of pips. Infinitesimal pips of yellow glue petrified and yearning to clog her spirit. Flatten her down to the floor and flail her so that she would not be able to express to Milton what she had passed through.

She began to tremble. "Naomi, I've got to write now. I can't eat. It's important. I have so much to tell Milton about what happened tonight. I'm still a virgin. I shouldn't be, but I am. I suffered the biggest defeat in Brickdam. The most humiliating. It was the knell. Please! Give me a writing-pad and a pen. I beg you, Naomi. Greg, I beseech you."

They persisted. They tried to persuade her to eat, but she refused. She began to sob hysterically. Pressed her hands to her face and moaned. Besought them to bring paper and a pen. So Naomi gave her a writing-pad and a fountain pen, and Sylvia sat at the small dining-table and wrote Milton.

The paper lengthened and changed from white to pink, and from pink to green, and from green to yellow, then back to pink. But her will kept the pen steady.

"Dear Milton," she wrote, "I'm writing this soon after three in the morning at Naomi's. Clang! Clang! Clang! That was three o' clock striking in the neighbourhood, I heard a clock striking as I came up the stairs. Clang! The cracking of the final illusion. I'm trying to finish this letter and post it before dawn because after posting it I'm taking a walk to the Sea Wall. At dawn there won't be anybody there and I'll be able to take a nice, cool walk into the sea without anyone trying to stop me. It will be so peaceful knowing that all my miseries will be disappearing behind me. All the plaguing problems we've talked about. The purpose in my being alive and if it's heredity or environment that has made me what I am – all that will be going behind me into blankness. I just won't have to bother any more. The Brown Jumbie-men won't snigger at me again. I'll hear a drumming sound in my ears and want to scream for help but I won't, Milton. My will will stop me from screaming. See how morbid and hysterical I am. That should tell you that I really have heard the knell. Yes, I've heard it. Dark blue, and it tells me that I've arrived at a destination. A wayside station, only it's a seaside station and from the platform I'll be stepping into the waves. But let me tell you about tonight, or rather last night and early this morning...

She wrote over nine pages. Shivering and seeing pink and green splotches on the paper. Clanging spectra that spread at solemn intervals over the swiftly scrawled words. Sound and colour in a desperate marriage. Minute after minute, sound and colour merged with curving line until the splotches grew so green, so venomously green, so putridly pink, that the clang of the cold bell went winging wetly away – winging into a deep, deep sea-green void...

"Greg! Quick! Help me! She's fainted. Let's get her to bed."

"You must try and get better, Sylvia. You must fight. Don't give in. You're giving in."

"But I want to give in, Naomi. Why should I want to fight? You've posted my letter to Milton? You didn't forget?"

"Yes, I posted it. Greg posted it. Since yesterday."

"You put the right address on it? You're sure?"

"Yes. You told me the address. Poste restante, Port of Spain. It's gone safely. I even added a note to him telling him you were too ill to finish it. Don't worry about the letter, Sylvia. Try to get better. The doctor says you're not fighting. He says if you don't fight you won't get better."

"Then I won't fight. I'll just sink away sweetly, Naomi. Leave you all to your silly, sickly world." She giggled. And gasped. Clutched the bed-sheet. "Milton will understand. He's like me. He *knows.* He knows what people and the world are like. Sickly. A muddle. He'll know I tried to make the best of it. Nobody can do more than that. Oh, I can die in peace if I know he gets my letter. Naomi, you haven't sent to tell them in Fort Street that I'm ill, have you? You promised you wouldn't."

"No. I haven't told them anything."

"Please don't. I'd scream if any of them came here to see me. Wait until I die to tell them anything."

"You won't die, Sylvia. You'll get better."

"I won't." She clutched the bed-sheet again, gasping. Her eyes shut. "Terrible pain. Almost sweet pain, though. I can bear it." Her voice was barely audible. "The last pains. You know, I wish – I wish I could have seen pneumonia bacilli under the microscope."

"Take a sip of this. Quick."

"You're very good, Naomi. Milton likes you."

"Sylvia, please try. Fight."

"Naomi."

"Yes?"

"I never loved him."

"Who?"

"Benny. I tried to delude myself. For the past two years I've been forcing myself to believe I loved him. That made… that made the defeat more… more disastrous. Complete. I was so ashamed of myself. I felt so empty. Futile. I'm not even capable of loving."

"Forget it, man. Buck up. You haven't met the right man yet, that's all."

"I can hear a kiskadee. The sun is shining. What time is it?"

"It's getting on for five."

"Greg isn't home yet from work?"

"No."

"I can hear a kiskadee." She was gasping again. After the spasm had passed, she smiled. "A lovely piece, that. Can you hear it? The Militia Band is playing it… on the Sea Wall… I can hear a kiskadee…"

She was quiet after that. The sun came in and touched her hand.

"Sylvia."

A car rushed past in the street.

"Sylvia."

But she continued to be quiet.

Profoundly quiet.

ABOUT THE AUTHOR

Edgar Mittelholzer was born in New Amsterdam in what was still British Guiana in 1909. He began writing in 1929 and despite constant rejection letters persisted with his writing. In 1937 he self-published a collection of skits, *Creole Chips*, and sold it from door to door. By 1938 he had completed *Corentyne Thunder*, though it was not published until 1941 because of the intervention of the war. In 1941 he left Guyana for Trinidad where he served in the Trinidad Royal Volunteer Naval Reserve. In 1948 he left for England with the manuscript of *A Morning at the Office*, set in Trinidad, which was published in 1950. Between 1951 and 1965 he published a further twenty-one novels and two works of non-fiction, including his autobiographical *A Swarthy Boy*. Apart from three years in Barbados, he lived for the rest of his life in England. His first marriage ended in 1959 and he remarried in 1960. He died by his own hand in 1965, a suicide by fire predicted in several of his novels.

Edgar Mittelholzer was the first Caribbean author to establish himself as a professional writer.

CARIBBEAN MODERN CLASSICS

2009/10 titles

Jan R. Carew
Black Midas
Introduction: Kwame Dawes
ISBN: 9781845230951; pp. 272; 23 May 2009; £9.99

This is the bawdy, Eldoradean epic of the legendary 'Ocean Shark' who makes and loses fortunes as a pork-knocker in the gold and diamond fields of Guyana, discovering that there are sharks with far sharper teeth in the city. *Black Midas* was first published in 1958.

Jan R. Carew
The Wild Coast
Introduction: Jeremy Poynting
ISBN: 9781845231101; pp. 240; 23 May 2009; £8.99

First published in 1958, this is the coming-of-age story of a sickly city child, sent away to the remote Berbice village of Tarlogie. Here he must find himself, make sense of Guyana's diverse cultural inheritances and come to terms with a wild nature disturbingly red in tooth and claw.

Neville Dawes
The Last Enchantment
Introduction: Kwame Dawes
ISBN: 9781845231170; pp. 332; 27 April 2009; £9.99

This penetrating and often satirical exploration of the search for self in a world divided by colour and class is set in the context of the radical hopes of Jamaican nationalist politics in the early 1950s. First published in 1960, the novel asks many pertinent questions about the Jamaica of today.

Wilson Harris
Heartland
Introduction: Michael Mitchell
ISBN: 9781845230968; pp. 104; 23 May 2009; £7.99

First published in 1964, this visionary narrative tracks one man's psychic disintegration in the aloneness of the forests of the Guyanese interior, making a powerful ecological statement about man's place in the 'invisible chain of being', in which nature is a no less active presence.

Edgar Mittelholzer
Corentyne Thunder
Introduction: Juanita Cox
ISBN: 9781845231118; pp. 242; 27 April 2009; £8.99

This pioneering work of West Indian fiction, first published in 1941, is not merely an acute portrayal of the rural Indo-Guyanese world, but a work of literary ambition that creates a symphonic relationship between its characters and the vast openness of the Corentyne coast.

Andrew Salkey
Escape to an Autumn Pavement
Introduction: Thomas Glave
ISBN: 9781845230982; pp. 220; 23 May 2009; £8.99

This brave and remarkable novel, set in London at the end of the 1950s, and published in 1960, catches its 'brown' Jamaican narrator on the cusp between black and white, between exiled Jamaican and an incipient black Londoner, and between heterosexual and homosexual desires.

Denis Williams
Other Leopards
Introduction: Victor Ramraj
ISBN: 9781845230678; pp. 216; 23 May 2009; £8.99

Lionel Froad is a Guyanese working on an archeological survey in the mythical Jokhara in the horn of Africa. There he hopes to rediscover the self he calls 'Lobo', his alter ego from 'ancestral times', which he thinks slumbers behind his cultivated mask. First published in 1963, this is one of the most important Caribbean novels of the past fifty years.

Denis Williams
The Third Temptation
Introduction: Victor Ramraj
ISBN: 9781845231163; pp. 108; May 2010; £8.99

A young man is killed in a traffic accident at a Welsh seaside resort. Around this incident, Williams, drawing inspiration from the *Nouveau Roman*, creates a reality that is both rich and problematic. Whilst he brings to the novel a Caribbean eye, Williams makes an important statement about refusing any restrictive boundaries for Caribbean fiction. The novel was first published in 1968.

Roger Mais
The Hills Were Joyful Together
Introduction: Norval Edwards
ISBN: 9781845231002; pp. 272; August 2010; £10.99

Unflinchingly realistic in its portrayal of the wretched lives of Kingston's urban poor, this is a novel of prophetic rage. First published in 1953, it is both a work of tragic vision and a major contribution to the evolution of an autonomous Caribbean literary aesthetic.

Edgar Mittelholzer
A Morning at the Office
Introduction: Raymond Ramcharitar
ISBN: 978184523; pp. 215; May 2010; £9.99

First published in 1950, this is one of the Caribbean's foundational novels in its bold attempt to portray a whole society in miniature. A genial satire on human follies and the pretensions of colour and class, this novel brings several ingenious touches to its mode of narration.

Edgar Mittelholzer
Shadows Move Among Them
Introduction: Rupert Roopnaraine
ISBN: 9781845230913; pp. 352; May 2010; £12.99

In part a satire on the Eldoradean dream, in part an exploration of the possibilities of escape from the discontents of civilisation, Mittelholzer's 1951 novel of the Reverend Harmston's attempt to set up a utopian commune dedicated to 'Hard work, frank love and wholesome play' has some eerie 'pre-echoes' of the fate of Jonestown in 1979.

Edgar Mittelholzer
The Life and Death of Sylvia
Introduction: Juanita Cox
ISBN: 9781845231200; pp. 362; May 2010, £12.99

In 1930s' Georgetown, a young woman on her own is vulnerable prey, and when Sylvia Russell finds she cannot square her struggle for economic survival and her integrity, she hurtles towards a wilfully early death. Mittelholzer's novel of 1953 is a richly inward portrayal of a woman who finds inner salvation through the act of writing.

Elma Napier
A Flying Fish Whispered
Introduction: Evelyn O'Callaghan
ISBN: 9781845231026; pp. 248; July 2010; £9.99

With one of the most delightfully feisty women characters in Caribbean fiction and prose that sings, Elma Napier's 1938 Dominican novel is a major rediscovery, not least for its imaginative exploration of different kinds of Caribbeans, in particular the polarity between plot and plantation that Napier sees in a distinctly gendered way.

Orlando Patterson
The Children of Sisyphus
Introduction: Kwame Dawes
ISBN: 9781845230944; pp. 288; August 2010; £10.99

This is a brutally poetic book that brings to the characters who live on Kingston's 'dungle' an intensity that invests them with tragic depth. In Patterson's existentialist novel, first published in 1964, dignity comes with a stoic awareness of the absurdity of life and the shedding of false illusions, whether of salvation or of a mythical African return.

V.S. Reid
New Day
Introduction: Norval Edwards
ISBN: 9781845230906, pp. 360; August 2010, £12.99

First published in 1949, this historical novel focuses on defining moments of Jamaica's nationhood, from the Morant Bay rebellion of 1865, to the dawn of self-government in 1944. *New Day* pioneers the creation of a distinctively Jamaican literary language of narration.

Garth St. Omer
A Room on the Hill
Introduction: John Robert Lee
ISBN: 9781845230937; pp. 210; September 2010; £9.99

A friend's suicide and his profound alienation in a St Lucia still slumbering in colonial mimicry and the straitjacket of a reactionary Catholic church drive John Lestrade into a state of internal exile. First published in 1968, St. Omer's meticulously crafted novel is a pioneering exploration of the inner Caribbean man.

Titles thereafter include...

Wayne Brown, *On the Coast*
George Campbell, *First Poems*
Austin C. Clarke, *The Survivors of the Crossing*
Austin C. Clarke, *Amongst Thistles and Thorns*
O.R. Dathorne, *The Scholar Man*
O.R. Dathorne, *Dumplings in the Soup*
Neville Dawes, *Interim*
Wilson Harris, *The Eye of the Scarecrow*
Wilson Harris, *The Sleepers of Roraima*
Wilson Harris, *Tumatumari*
Wilson Harris, *Ascent to Omai*
Wilson Harris, *The Age of the Rainmakers*
Marion Patrick Jones, *Panbeat*
Marion Patrick Jones, *Jouvert Morning*
Earl Lovelace, *Whilst Gods Are Falling*
Roger Mais, *Black Lightning*
Una Marson, *Selected Poems*
Edgar Mittelholzer, *Children of Kaywana*
Edgar Mittelholzer, *The Harrowing of Hubertus*
Edgar Mittelholzer, *Kaywana Blood*
Edgar Mittelholzer, *My Bones and My Flute*
Edgar Mittelholzer, *A Swarthy Boy*
Orlando Patterson, *An Absence of Ruins*
V.S. Reid, *The Leopard* (North America only)
Garth St. Omer, *Shades of Grey*
Andrew Salkey, *The Late Emancipation of Jerry Stover*
and more...